D0231929

PAYBACK

James Barrington is a trained military pilot who has worked in covert operations and espionage. He now lives in Andorra and this is his fifth novel. His previous novels, *Overkill*, *Pandemic*, *Foxbat* and *Timebomb*, also featured Paul Richter.

Also by James Barrington

OVERKILL
PANDEMIC
FOXBAT
TIMEBOMB

JAMES
BARRINGTON

PAYBACK

PAN BOOKS

First published 2010 by Pan Books
an imprint of Pan Macmillan, a division of Macmillan Publishers Limited
Pan Macmillan, 20 New Wharf Road, London N1 9RR
Basingstoke and Oxford
Associated companies throughout the world
www.panmacmillan.com

ISBN 978-0-330-46269-3

Copyright © James Barrington 2010

The right of James Barrington to be identified as the
author of this work has been asserted by him in accordance
with the Copyright, Designs and Patents Act 1988.

All rights reserved. No part of this publication may be
reproduced, stored in or introduced into a retrieval system, or
transmitted, in any form, or by any means (electronic, mechanical,
photocopying, recording or otherwise) without the prior written
permission of the publisher. Any person who does any unauthorized
act in relation to this publication may be liable to criminal
prosecution and civil claims for damages.

1 3 5 7 9 8 6 4 2

A CIP catalogue record for this book is available from
the British Library.

Typeset by SetSystems Limited, Saffron Walden, Essex
Printed in the UK by CPI Mackays, Chatham ME5 8TD

This book is sold subject to the condition that it shall not,
by way of trade or otherwise, be lent, re-sold, hired out,
or otherwise circulated without the publisher's prior consent
in any form of binding or cover other than that in which
it is published and without a similar condition including this
condition being imposed on the subsequent purchaser.

Visit **www.panmacmillan.com** to read more about all our books
and to buy them. You will also find features, author interviews and
news of author events, and you can sign up for e-newsletters
so that you're always first to hear about our new releases.

To Sally – thanks for always being there

Acknowledgements

Thanks are due to a number of people for their specialist knowledge and assistance that I drew on during the writing of this book.

To Doctor John, who would rather remain anonymous, and his family, friends and acquaintances in America, the Middle East and Israel – who must remain completely unidentified because of their current or past employment and also to avoid compromising their personal security – sincere thanks for their invaluable assistance with linguistic and other, darker, matters.

Thanks also to Peter N, who would prefer his last name to remain undisclosed for operational reasons, for his expert guidance on the operations, tactics and dialogue of the Metropolitan Police, and especially of SO15, the Counter Terrorism Command.

To Eric Davies, former British Airways 747 Training Captain for his prodigious knowledge of long-haul commercial flying operations, and to Leslie McCormick – a lady I knew in a former life – for her guidance on the intricacies of US flight-planning procedures and the operations of the Potomac Consolidated TRACON.

As ever, I must thank my agent Luigi Bonomi for his unflinching support, guidance and belief. To my new editor, Jeremy Trevathan, at Macmillan, my thanks for lunches and quick decisions, and to Peter Lavery for his assistance.

As usual, any errors of fact in this novel are mine and mine alone.

James Barrington
Principality of Andorra, 2009

Prologue

It was a little after ten-thirty in the morning of the last day of Saadallah Assad's life.

A white Toyota Land Cruiser with three men inside, each wearing a *gellabbiya* and a *kaffiyeh*, turned off Mu'awia. The driver had no option but to proceed slowly – the streets bustled with people, a colourful throng moving with noisy and cheerful purpose – but even if the roads had been empty he would still have been driving with great care.

Most of the pedestrians were women wearing all-enveloping black *chadors* and *burkas*, or at the very least a *hijab*, and carrying shopping bags already bulging with purchases.

About seventy yards before the Al-Hamidieh inter-section, the driver spotted a gap in the ragged line of parked vehicles and steered the Toyota to the kerb. It was already hot, so he kept the engine and the air-conditioning running. This was as close as he could get to the *souk* that runs from the Omayyad Mosque to Bab Al-Nasr, but it was near enough. It would only be a short walk for the *shahid*, and as far as the driver was concerned the further away he was parked the better.

For a few moments nobody inside the vehicle moved

1

or spoke. Then the driver and front-seat passenger turned to look at the man sitting behind them.

He was young – no more than twenty – and handsome in the classic Arab mould: deep brown eyes, shaded by impossibly long lashes, a straight nose and full lips. It was the kind of face that – without the embryonic black beard, so sparse and straggly that it appeared to have been applied to his cheeks hair by individual hair – might almost have graced the wall of a Hollywood film studio or some teenage girl's bedroom.

Almost. What would have prevented it was the expression in his eyes. They glowed with excitement and gave the young man's face a sense of purpose that was frightening in its intensity. He favoured each man with a brief, almost dismissive, glance, then looked ahead, through the windscreen of the Land Cruiser towards the *souk*, his gaze distant and unfocused.

'Are you prepared?' the passenger asked in fluent Arabic. Like the youth in the rear seat, his features were pure Arab, and his voice still carried faint echoes of Oman, where he had learned the language.

Saadallah Assad looked at him. 'I'm ready,' he replied.

'The *Jamiat* will be celebrated through your courage, my friend. We'll send out the video this afternoon,' the passenger added, 'while you are becoming acquainted with the *chouriyat*.' It was a weak attempt at a joke. 'Remember to avoid the mosque. It would be better to keep to the main thoroughfare, at the western end.'

'I know,' Assad agreed, with a touch of impatience. He glanced down at his watch. 'It's time, I think.'

The two men nodded silently. As the young man reached for the door handle, the driver – whose appearance was anything but Arabic, with fair skin and blue-green eyes – spoke for the first time.

'*Jazaka Allahu khayran*, Abdullah.'

The youth looked slightly taken aback at this remark, but he responded formally: '*La hawla wa la kuwata illa b'Illah*'.

Any Arabic-speaker might have been puzzled by this reply, since it is normally used by a Muslim only when he has suffered some major misfortune, or his life has been overtaken by events beyond his control, but neither of the other two men looked at all surprised.

Assad stared for a moment at each of them, his expression still confident and almost arrogant, then stepped out of the car. Just before he pushed the door closed, he murmured two words to the passenger, then moved away from the vehicle and headed towards the entrance to the market.

'What did he say to you?' the driver demanded, in English.

'*Abdu-baha*,' the passenger replied.

'Which means what?'

'It means he won't let us down.'

As Assad vanished into the crowd, the white *gellab-biya* flowing smoothly around his slight figure, the driver steered the Toyota away from the kerb and set off for the international terminal. They had confirmed reservations on a flight to Bahrain, with plenty of time in hand, but they wanted to get to the airport as quickly as possible.

The passenger didn't say another word until they

were almost a mile away from the *souk*. 'His name was Saadallah,' O'Hagan remarked.

'What?'

'Saadallah. His name was Saadallah Assad. But you called him "Abdullah". That's why he looked surprised.'

Petrucci shrugged. 'Whatever. He didn't say anything about it.'

'Of course not. He's an Arab, and that means he's polite, especially when he's dealing with stupid white foreigners. He wouldn't have dreamt of correcting you.'

'Will it make any difference to the *shahid*?'

'No,' O'Hagan replied firmly, 'it won't make any difference.'

Damascus is the oldest inhabited city in the world, dating back five millennia, but the Al-Hamidieh *souk* is comparatively new, having existed for only about one hundred and fifty years. It is noted for stalls selling clothes and fabrics as well as merchants offering spices, nuts, fruit and other foodstuffs, which are sold from shallow earthenware bowls or open sacks, and often still weighed on small hand-held brass scales, in a routine familiar to any visitor to a traditional Arab country.

The main entrance to the market is wide and flanked by a pair of lamp-posts, while a high vaulted semi-circular metal roof, pierced by tens of thousands of tiny holes, covers and protects the long, straight, central walkway.

Saadallah Assad ignored the approaches of the traders hawking their wares outside the entrance and joined a steady stream of people heading into the cool and wel-

coming interior. Immediately he was assailed by a con-
flict of sights and sounds – the babble of Arabic as
merchants and shoppers haggled with each other; the
intoxicating smell of herbs and spices, and the bustle of
shoppers in constant and restless motion. Disregarding
all these, Assad threaded his way deliberately through
the *souk*.

He walked as far as the Omayyad Mosque without
finding what he wanted, then retraced his steps. At
eleven-ten exactly he heard, rather than saw, what
he was seeking, and turned round to make sure of
it. Several American tourists – he counted at least six
of them – were heading towards him in a loose group,
ambling uncertainly through the crowded market while
commenting loudly to each other, blissfully confident
that although their remarks might be overheard, they
certainly would not be understood.

Like most of the Syrians in the *souk*, Assad did not
speak or understand English, but he easily recognized
the language, and the garish check shorts worn by two
of the men provided additional confirmation of their
nationality.

For the first time since he'd stepped out of the
Toyota, a slight smile crossed the young Arab's face. He
stopped and waited for the Americans to get closer to
him, as he had been instructed, and reached into the
right-hand pocket of his *gellabbiya* to clutch a small
cylindrical object nestling there.

The man leading the American group noticed the slim
young Arab standing in his path and muttered something *sotto voce* to his male companion, who grinned

broadly. Assad had no doubt that whatever had been said was uncomplimentary, but that thought didn't matter to him in the slightest. Nothing mattered now – or ever would again.

The American tourist stepped around the human obstruction, and the young Syrian smiled pleasantly at him as he passed by, waiting until he was surrounded by this slow-moving group of noisy – and, to Assad, vulgar and uncouth – strangers.

He glanced down at the object in his right hand, quickly checked the wires were still in place, then took a deep breath, looking up at the thin shafts of light lancing through the myriad holes that dotted the roof high above him, closed his eyes and began murmuring softly.

One of the American women thought the young man must be praying, and for the final few moments of her life she wondered why.

She was almost right, for the last words Saadallah Assad uttered were 'B'ism-Illah-ir-Rachmani-ir-Rachim' – 'In the name of Allah, the Most Compassionate, the Most Merciful'. These familiar words are found at the beginning of every *surah* of the *Qur'án* except for the ninth, and are routinely uttered by devout Muslims when starting a meal, or donning new clothes or beginning some new undertaking.

Assad lowered his head and paused for a brief moment while he focused on mental images of the faces of his parents and siblings, images that would be the last things he ever visualized, that he would take with him on this, his final journey. Then he looked up and met the eyes of the female American tourist, who smiled shyly at him. Assad smiled back at her and simultaneously squeezed his right fist tightly shut.

His *gellabbiya* puffed suddenly outwards, and a microscopic fraction of a second later he simply ceased to exist, as the blast of nearly three kilos – not one kilo, as he had been told – of detonating C4 plastic explosive instantly reduced his body to a spray of blood and unrecognizable fragments.

The two Americans had lied to Assad about this aspect of his martyrdom, as they had lied to him about almost everything else, but in this, they had had little option. Assad was a devout Muslim, and the only way they could persuade him to carry out his mission in the crowded *souk* had been to convince him that the explosive charge was small with a very limited lethal radius. He was anxious that there should be only a few Syrian casualties, so they'd assured him that if he picked his spot with care, he would kill only a bunch of infidel Westerners.

The effects of the explosion were truly devastating. All of the Americans died at the same instant, as did everybody else close to where Assad had been standing. The blast wave generated by three blocks of C4 slammed outwards from the point of detonation, its horrific power cutting down everyone and everything in its path. Men and women were themselves turned into missiles, ripped apart and blown away to smash with pulverizing force into the bodies of their fellow citizens.

The products on display – brass and silver trinkets,

lamps, mirrors, jugs, plates, bowls, boxes, sacks and their multitudinous contents, even carpets and bales of material – scattered and flew everywhere. Even the smallest, most innocuous and apparently harmless objects that weren't instantly disintegrated by the blast became deadly missiles, whistling like bullets in all directions. Glass shattered, the resulting fusillade of needle-sharp spears adding further to the carnage. Doors and window frames shattered, sending lethal splinters of wood ripping through the air to seek out soft and yielding human flesh.

High above the spot where Saadallah Assad's body had existed only a split second before, the arched metal roof covering the *souk* split apart, buckled upwards briefly and then crashed back, its panels tearing free and tumbling down to smash into what was left of the bodies beneath.

It was additionally unfortunate that Assad had been standing close to one side of the *souk* when he detonated the explosive, for the colossal blast tore an almost circular hole through the crumbling masonry, and the weight of the structure above then caused the whole wall to give way, shattered stonework and wooden beams crashing heavily to the ground. A choking cloud of dust billowed upwards into the air, obscuring everything from sight.

As the two Americans had anticipated – and was the reason they had selected the *souk* as their target – its shape acted almost like the barrel of a gun, funnelling the blast in both directions at once, and causing serious injuries to people standing dozens of yards from the point of detonation. Even those far enough away from the epicentre not to be seriously injured by flying debris still suffered agonies as their skin was burnt by the heat of the explosion, their eardrums ruptured and their flesh ripped apart by splinters of glass and wood.

The *souk* filled in an instant with the shattering blast, grotesquely magnified by the enclosed space it occupied. The detonation was followed immediately by a continuing cacophony as timber, masonry, glass and stone tumbled to the ground. An explosion of dust and debris erupted out of the Bab Al-Nasr entrance, scattering the traders and shoppers gathered outside.

When the last sliver of glass had smashed on to the ground and the final pieces of wood and stone had bounced to a standstill, a blessed moment of silence fell. For the briefest of instants the city seemed to hold its breath. Then the screams and wails began, the howls of agony from those who had survived the detonation but were lying, stunned and torn and bleeding, inside what was left of the market.

And, as a counterpoint to the escalating volume of vocal agony from within the *souk*, the yelling and shouting of people outside rose steadily to a crescendo and, moments later, the first of the sirens could be heard in the distance.

Standing in the airport car park, John Petrucci spun round when he heard the thump of the explosion and the atonic wailing of sirens a matter of seconds afterwards. He and O'Hagan had furtively removed their *gellabbiyas* to reveal ordinary Western business suits, and were now hauling their carry-on bags from the back of the Toyota.

'That sounded like our boy,' Petrucci said, slamming the boot closed.

'Sure did,' Alex O'Hagan nodded. 'Welcome to the world of the *shuhada*.'

Chapter One

Sunday
Northern slopes of Mynydd Eppynt, Powys

Paul Richter peered cautiously over the barrel of the Heckler & Koch MP5, and realized that this time they were going to find him.

In front of him the hillside sloped gently away from his observation point, but the target – a small white-washed farmhouse on the far side of the field – was now virtually invisible through grey curtains of drizzle. The same drizzle that had, Richter reflected with no undue sense of surprise, been falling without notice-able pause for the previous four days. And he knew that for a fact because he had been lying in the same OP throughout the entire period.

He was cold, wet, stiff, aching, hungry, thirsty, tired and moderately pissed-off, and not for the first time he wondered just what the hell had possessed him to agree to Simpson's suggestion that he get out of London for a few days. Actually, leaving London itself hadn't been that bad an idea, but going to Hereford to play war games with the SAS probably wasn't one of Richter's better decisions.

The only good thing so far, from a professional point of view, was that his OP had remained undetected. The briefing had been vague enough to allow him considerable latitude in choosing its location, so he'd avoided the obvious and picked a spot almost in the centre of the meadow itself, situated well away from the target. That had required a lot of extra spade-work, done entirely under cover of darkness during the first night, to ensure that his OP remained as invisible as possible.

And it had succeeded, because eight times he'd seen patrols cover the ground in front of him, concentrating on areas closer to the farmhouse, and each time they'd failed to get within fifty yards of where he lay hidden. On the last two occasions there'd been a clear sense of urgency in their searching, and he'd even heard shouting from the NCO in charge, the words whipped away by the constant wind.

But finally it looked like his luck had changed, and only six hours before ENDEX – the end of the exercise. A team of eight SAS troopers had now begun a slow and thorough sweep of the entire field, starting from the farmhouse itself and working their way, in line abreast, up the hill towards him. At least, he reflected, tucking the binoculars into a pocket on his DPM camouflage jacket, colloquially known as a 'you-can't-see-me-suit', he'd be able to get some hot food and drink inside him once he got back to Hereford, and take a crap somewhere other than into a sheet of cling-film.

These troopers were shouting to each other, or at least that's what it sounded like, which puzzled Richter, as it had done previously. Usually any group of soldiers, whether regular army or special forces, will take extreme care to make as little sound as possible. Noise attracts attention, and that is the last thing any patrol wants.

It was only when the first of them got to within twenty yards of his OP that he finally realized what they were calling. It was a single four-word sentence, repeated over and over again – 'Safeguard. Commander Richter. Safeguard.'

The moment he could hear the words clearly, Richter stood up, tossing aside the cam-netting and the greenery he'd painstakingly woven into it so that it would merge seamlessly with the scrubby grass and stunted bushes dotted around him. 'Safeguard' is the over-ride code-word signalling the termination of any exercise or activity, for external or safety reasons or when directed by a higher authority.

The moment he stood up, the approaching men stopped, swinging their weapons to cover him as they looked across the rutted ground. The corporal reached him first, glanced down at the hollow that Richter had called home for the previous ninety-odd hours, and nodded a grudging approval. Officers – or 'Ruperts' as they were known within the Regiment – were generally held in very low regard by the other ranks, and scruffy, insubordinate ex-Royal Navy officers like Richter didn't rate at all. To have received any kind of an acknowledgement from the NCO was high praise indeed.

'Thank fuck for that,' the corporal said, grinning at him. 'We've been looking for you for two days, and you're in deep shit. Your section called. They want you back in London immediately, and that's "immediately" as in just over forty-eight hours ago.'

Manama, Bahrain

He was neither the best nor most reliable of witnesses, because of the money, but the story the middle-aged Filipino told was so intriguing that Tariq Mazen immediately decided to investigate it further.

His new informant worked as a cleaner in the hospital on Al-Sulmaniya Avenue. He'd introduced himself as 'Karim', though it was an obvious alias. Mazen understood his caution: if word of what he was doing reached the wrong ears, his informant could find his life expectancy reduced to a matter of days or even hours. And there was no point in checking him out, anyway – his value was the information he was offering, not his real identity.

The story he told was simple enough. Three days earlier a patient had arrived at Al-Sulmaniya, which was hardly news in itself, but this man had received somewhat unusual treatment. Karim happened to be cleaning the corridor behind the admissions unit when this man and his entourage had appeared. The doctor leading the group had seen the Filipino as soon as he turned the corner and had hurried forward, ordering Karim into a side room.

The storeroom door had a narrow vertical window, and most of his view was blocked by the doctor's white coat but, as the surgeon finally stepped away from the door, for a bare second or two Karim had an unobstructed view of the patient walking slowly past.

'Are you sure it was him?' Tariq Mazen asked, for the fourth time.

'No, I'm not. I told you – I saw him for just a moment, and he was walking away from me.'

'So you saw only his profile? Only the side of his face?'

'Yes.' The Filipino nodded. 'And it was grey, like in all the pictures. And his beard has streaks, too. It's very distinctive, and his face is well known.'

That was something of an understatement. Hardly a week went by without that man's picture appearing somewhere, particularly in the Middle Eastern newspapers.

Karim had come to Mazen's attention by a somewhat circuitous route. Mazen himself was a member of the Special Intelligence Service – equivalent to Bahrain's secret police force – and ran a string of informants in and around Manama. Two of them had heard whispers about a reclusive sheikh arriving in Bahrain for medical treatment. This interested Mazen because, like all policemen, secret or otherwise, he was always keen to discover what was happening on his 'patch', and particularly the identity of any significant new arrival.

His open-source check showed that a certain 'Sheikh Rashid' and his advisers had recently flown to Bahrain in an executive jet. Having dealt with this air-charter company before, Mazen knew that its management would never divulge the real identity of any of its clients without a court order, and possibly not even then. Predictably, his carefully phrased and recorded telephone conversation with the Al-Sulmaniya Hospital administrator had proved fruitless.

But then one of his informants had overheard a Filipino talking in a restaurant in the Al-Adliya district about the man he'd seen, and had approached him. As a result, the following day Karim had been waiting nervously outside the Al-Hilal bookshop on Tujjaar when Mazen drove up.

'Remind me – how was he dressed?' He'd asked this question before, but he would cover the same ground as often as he thought useful, until he was certain that he'd extracted everything the witness could recall.

'I already told you,' Karim sighed, looking at the stocky Arab in the driving seat and wondering how many more times he would have to repeat himself. 'A *gellabbiya* and *kaffiyeh*.'

'Do you know where he is in the hospital now?'

Karim smiled with a kind of weary triumph. 'Yes. One of the nurses told me. He's on the third floor, where they send people with kidney trouble.'

The significance of the treatment the mysterious 'sheikh' might be receiving was not lost on Mazen, though he was still unconvinced. He would have to confirm the patient's identity, and maybe talk to one of the Western embassies – preferably the British. Despite the significant American influence in Bahrain – the US Navy has a major base at Al-Jufayr – Mazen was not over-fond of the Yanks. The British, he thought, might handle things rather more discreetly.

'And if it *is* him?' Karim asked. 'There's a big reward?'

Mazen looked at the shabbily dressed Filipino and smiled. 'If you *are* right, my friend,' he replied, 'then you'd better think about getting out of Bahrain and finding yourself a new name and somewhere else to live, because people you *really* don't want to meet will certainly come looking for you. But at least,' he added, 'you'll have enough money to do so in comfort.'

Hammersmith, London

Paul Richter walked into Richard Simpson's office and sat down, uninvited, in front of the desk. His boss – short, slim, pinkish, balding, generally bad-tempered and fastidious in all things – was reading a red file.

Richter himself wasn't in the best of tempers. Although the experience of lying in a damp hole for four days, clutching a sub-machine-gun loaded with blanks and watching a ramshackle Welsh farm cottage that appeared to have been sensibly deserted by its owner, was hardly the stuff of dreams, he had been seriously looking forward to ENDEX. Though a lifelong teetotaller, Richter had always enjoyed the camaraderie of a wardroom or officers' mess, and Hereford was something special.

But instead of enjoying a long soak in a hot bath, a decent meal and then a pleasant evening in the mess, he'd been forced to dump all his gear, grab a quick shower, and drive straight back to London.

The only redeeming feature of the day had been the drive, and only because it had finally stopped raining and Richter had gone up to Hereford in his favourite toy. His first love had always been motorcycles, and he hadn't even owned a car for three or four years, simply because it was so much easier to get around London on two wheels rather than four. So it was hardly surprising that when he'd finally decided to buy a car, what he'd chosen was more or less a four-wheeled motorbike.

It was a jet-black Westfield Sport 2000, a spiritual descendant of the original Lotus 7. Two seats, four wheels, a long bonnet covering a two-litre engine, rudimentary weather-proofing and a very basic interior, but with about the same power-to-weight ratio as a Saturn Five rocket. Or at least that was what it felt like to Richter. It was an animal. It could out-drag just about any alleged 'supercar' on the road, irrespective of make, model and price, and it had cost him about the same as a cheap family box on wheels. He simply adored it.

The journey back to London had been quick – very quick, as the traffic police officer indignantly pointed out to Richter when he finally caught up with him at a set of road works on the A5, south of Weedon Bec. Richter had listened politely, waited until the man had finished, then produced a small leather folder containing a laminated exemption card that he flipped open in front of the officer's face. It was basically a 'get-out-of-jail-free' permit issued to SIS – and by extension Foreign Operations Executive – operatives and agents.

Once he was certain the traffic officer had fully read and understood it, Richter closed the wallet, slipped it back into his pocket, waved a brisk two fingers under the officer's nose, then engaged first gear on the Westfield and dropped the clutch. The rear wheels spun for almost seventy yards, leaving two parallel black scars on the road surface. He hit sixty in a whisker under four and a half seconds, and he didn't see the policeman again.

'I wanted you back here two days ago.' Simpson closed the file and fired his opening salvo. 'I called your mobile, but it was switched off.'

'I was on an exercise. I was supposed to be carrying out covert surveillance, watching a target. I'd have looked a right prat if my bloody phone had started ringing in a hole in the middle of some field. Of course it was switched off. In fact, I didn't even have it with me.'

'Well, your little holiday playing war games with the SAS has severely inconvenienced us.'

'I'm very sorry to hear that,' Richter replied smoothly.

'Keep your sarcasm to yourself. And another thing. Next time you use your exemption card to avoid a prosecution for speeding, don't wave two fingers at the Black Rat who's stopped you.'

Richter glanced at his watch. By his calculation, the incident at the road works had happened less than two hours ago. 'How do you know about that?'

'I know almost everything, Richter, almost all of the time. In this case, he ran your registration plate through the PNC. The plate was blocked, of course, and that raised a flag which stopped his enquiry. The system forwarded the time, date and place of the incident to Vauxhall Cross, because Six issued the card. The duty officer contacted the patrolman who'd stopped you, and then he told me all about it. QED. Anyway, don't do it again.'

'So why did you want me back here in such a hurry? And why are you in the office on a Sunday afternoon? Isn't there any cricket on television?'

'You're here because the woodentops reckon they've discovered a terrorist cell lurking in an apartment pretty close to where we're sitting right now.'

'I presume you're referring to the Metropolitan Police?' Simpson's dislike of all police officers was legendary. Richter assumed he'd been nicked as a spotty youth by the local bobby – probably for something embarrassing. 'And what has that got to do with us, exactly? Just to remind you, the "F" in "FOE" stands for "foreign". That means we're not supposed to operate in Britain.'

'I do know that, Richter. I run this outfit – remember? The reason we're involved in this is quite simple. It's also classified Top Secret and SCI, code word "Jason".'

'I'm not cleared for "Jason".'

'You are now, with effect from fifteen twenty-two this afternoon.'

'Wonderful, thanks. So what's the story?'

'One of our people is on the inside,' Simpson said. 'We have someone in the terrorists' flat. He's supposedly a part of the cell.'

'Who is he, and what's he doing there?'

'You know him. In fact, you're one of the very few people working here who has ever met him, but that was a while ago. To everyone outside this room, his codename is Argonaut. Remember Salah Khatid?'

'Christ, I thought he was dead.'

'Not yet he isn't,' Simpson replied, somewhat enigmatically. 'He's been deep-cover ever since 9/11. We originally sent him out to Afghanistan to join the Taliban as a sympathizer. He gradually worked his way down through Pakistan and into Iran, then crossed the

Gulf into Saudi Arabia, sending us information the whole time. Good quality, real-time HUMINT. We've been filtering his information to Five and Six, and selected bits to the Company.'

Simpson frowned. 'About eight months ago he arrived in Germany, told us he'd made contact with a small group of Arabs, and then vanished. We assumed he'd been burnt, but six weeks ago we heard from him again. The group was on the move, heading for London, and we guessed the next thing we'd hear would be target details. Instead, on Friday morning we were advised by Six that a Met Police Legion Patrol had managed to locate Khatid's terrorist cell. Five was planning to send in CO19, mob-handed, early on Saturday morning. I had to spend some time convincing Six this was a really bad idea, and I've managed to get the assault delayed until tomorrow. Just as well, considering how long it took you to get back from Hereford. And I need you there because you know Khatid.'

'So what do you want me to do – go in and get him out before the plods kick down the doors?'

'Not exactly,' Simpson said. 'I want you to go into the flat with the cops, positively identify Salah Khatid and then kill him.'

21

Chapter Two

A somewhat battered three-ton truck with two men in the cab stopped in a small car park on the outskirts of Kondal. The driver, Alexei Nabov, turned the vehicle round so that it faced the road, then switched off the engine. Moments later, an elderly saloon car of Russian manufacture drove in and parked a few yards away, a middle-aged man behind the wheel.

Two men emerged from the hotel next to the car park. The names listed in their American passports were Richard Wilson and Edward Dawson, and they told anyone who asked that they were writers collaborating on a book about the transfiguration of the Union of Soviet Socialist Republics into the Confederation of Independent States and studying the effects this national trauma had caused to the former citizens of the USSR. It sounded reasonable enough, and accounted for their laptop computers and conversations in Russian – both men spoke the language fluently – with local workers and officials.

The single incongruous note was the fact that they didn't look like writers. Both men were tall, just over six feet, and broad with the solid bulk that comes from hard exercise. Their moustaches and comparatively long hair softened the image, but despite that, the impression they created was unmistakably military, or at least ex-military.

They both walked round to the back of the vehicle. Nabov and his companion, Boris Devenko, climbed down from the cab and followed them. Devenko released the padlock and pulled one of the rear doors open. The atmosphere was tense, the two pairs of men watching each other very carefully.

Dawson and Nabov climbed inside and Devenko pushed the door closed behind them. Without saying a word they removed the screws that secured the wooden lid of a large crate, and began emptying it. Some of the tools and equipment it contained were light enough to be lifted by hand, but for others they had to use straps and the roof-mounted chain hoist.

The last thing they removed was a battered wooden box, inside which was a bulky aluminium case, similar to those used to hold photographic equipment. Nabov unsnapped the two catches holding its lid closed.

The device inside was exactly what Dawson had been expecting, but he still checked it carefully, ensuring that all its components were properly attached. On the inside of the lid were instructions in multiple languages, including English, explaining precisely how the weapon was to be armed.

Dawson read these carefully, and even powered up the timing circuit – his actions observed with increasing alarm by the Russian – just to check that the battery was charged and the logic circuits intact, then he used the master switch to shut everything down. Fifteen minutes later they'd repacked the crate and refitted the lid.

The moment the Russian turned away, heading for the rear doors, Edward Dawson acted in a blur of lethally targeted aggression.

Manama, Bahrain

During his previous employment with the CIA, Alex O'Hagan had spent two years in Bahrain so he knew the country well and, more importantly, he still had his contacts there.

He and Petrucci were sitting in the back of a Mercedes cab driving down Sheikh Isa Avenue. An observer might have wondered at the route the vehicle was following, the driver making seemingly random turns, but the Americans had no interest in where they were going. The driver was one of O'Hagan's contacts and a member of an Arab terrorist group called Sharaf, and their whole attention was concentrated on what he was saying.

'The car's no problem,' he said, in fluent English. 'But the other things will take a little more time.'

'But you *can* get them?' Petrucci insisted.

The driver, whose work name was 'Ahmed', glanced round. 'Yes, I can get them, but I need something else from you.'

'More money?'

'No, I'm happy with what we agreed. What's important is the positioning of the device.'

'We thought maybe Government Avenue or Al-Khalifa,' O'Hagan suggested.

The driver turned into Al-Sulmaniya. 'We would

prefer one of the smaller roads,' he said. 'In fact, we've already selected the best street – the best for us, that is.'

'Which is where?' Petrucci demanded.

'Al-Mutanabi Avenue,' Ahmed replied, 'between Al-Khalifa and Tujjaar.'

'You have some particular reason for choosing that location?' O'Hagan asked.

'Yes, but it's not necessary for you to know what it is.'

Petrucci stirred uncomfortably. 'I don't like the sound of this. We need to be sure about what's going on here. Why that road?'

Ahmed glanced back at the American. 'You don't need to know, Mr Petrucci,' he said firmly. 'You've come to us for help with your plan, about which we know nothing, and we're prepared to assist you. In exchange, all we're requesting is that the device be positioned in a particular location and we feel that's not too much to ask. If you're unhappy with this arrangement, you're perfectly free to obtain what you need elsewhere.'

'That won't be necessary,' O'Hagan said, raising his hand in a calming gesture. 'We'll take what you're offering, no questions asked. Cool it, John. Remember, Ahmed and I go back a long way, and we understand each other real well. Right, Ahmed?'

'Right,' the driver agreed.

'When can we collect the stuff?' O'Hagan asked, after a pause.

The Arab considered for a moment. 'This afternoon,' he said. 'Come to Municipality Square at three-fifteen. I'll pick you up in this same cab again.'

'And then where do we go?' Petrucci asked, his tone still slightly belligerent.

'We'll go to the place where the car you need will be parked. That's all you have to know. Do not,' Ahmed added, 'forget to bring the money.'

Kondal, Russia

During and after the Second World War, an amazing variety of assassination devices were manufactured by the intelligence services of both East and West. These included single-shot pistols concealed in cigars, pens and even belt-buckles; poison-gas weapons hidden inside cigarette packets or wallets – a favourite with the KGB – and delayed-action devices like the microscopic ricin-filled pellet fired from a modified umbrella that was used by the Bulgarian *Darzhavna Sigurnost* to kill the dissident Georgi Markov in London in 1978.

For this operation, Wilson and Dawson had decided to adopt the 'KISS Principle' – keep it simple, stupid – and had chosen the most basic possible method.

Dawson shook his right hand and then dropped his arm straight down, allowing the ten-inch lead-filled cosh concealed up his sleeve to fall into his hand, its descent stopped by the security loop. As his fingers closed about its leather-covered fibre shaft, he swung the weapon with all his strength at the back of Nabov's head.

But the Russian must have heard or sensed something, and half-turned back, reaching inside his jacket for his pistol. It didn't help. The end of the cosh smashed

into the left side of his skull and knocked him unconscious. It wasn't a lethal blow, because he'd moved further and faster than Dawson had expected. Nabov fell
heavily to the steel floor, landing with a crash that the
American knew would have been heard clearly outside
the three-tonner.

Beside the truck, Boris Devenko immediately tensed
and reached for his Makarov. Wilson eyed him carefully, his own weapon within easy reach, wondering if
he should react. Then he relaxed as Dawson's voice
echoed from inside the vehicle.

'Be careful with that, you fool. Use the hoist.'

Devenko dropped his hand from his weapon, and
glanced at Wilson and the man who'd arrived in the car
– Yuri Borisov, a senior PO Start administrator. 'Alexei
is strong but he's always been clumsy,' he said, as a
kind of explanation.

Inside the van, Dawson straddled the unconscious
technician, grasped both sides of his jacket collar firmly
and pressed inwards with his knuckles, closing off the
blood flow through the carotid artery to the Russian's
brain.

'That's better,' he called out, maintaining the pressure
on the man's neck, his voice pitched lower but still
audible, he hoped, outside the truck. Then he relaxed
his grip, checked for a pulse, found nothing and stood
up.

'Screw the lid back on,' he said, tucking the cosh
back up his sleeve and now talking to a corpse. 'Wait a
moment. I'll get Boris to help you.' He stepped across
to the rear door and rapped on it with his knuckles.

Wilson opened it and looked up at his partner.

'Could you just help Alexei with the lid?' Dawson asked Devenko. 'Then I think we're done here.'

The Russian nodded agreement, grasped the bar on the right-hand side of the door opening and hauled himself up. He was two paces inside the cargo bay before he spotted Nabov's body, but by then it was too late.

Wilson's cosh – virtually the twin of Dawson's, and modelled on those carried for self-defence by CIA officers operating in Europe in the 1960s – crushed the back of the Russian's skull.

New Scotland Yard, London

'And who are you, exactly?'

The inspector from CO19 didn't look particularly impressed as Richter ambled into the briefing room at New Scotland Yard. He'd been due there twenty minutes earlier, but the traffic had been particularly heavy.

The room was already crowded with people, none of them known to Richter. Most were wearing civilian clothes, though several carried pistols in shoulder or belt holsters.

'Smith,' Richter said. 'From Vauxhall Cross.' Two statements, both factually inaccurate, and confidently delivered to a roomful of armed police officers. It probably wasn't a good start to the day.

'Let's see some identification,' the inspector demanded.

'Another fucking spook,' someone muttered.

Richter walked forward and proffered the identity

document he'd collected from Hammersmith that morning.

The inspector looked at it and frowned. 'Is your name really Smith?' he demanded.

'It might be,' Richter replied, 'and that *is* what it says there.'

'And we all believe that, of course. So what's your role in this exercise?'

'I'm just an observer.'

'An armed observer, I note.'

'Well spotted.'

The inspector had seen the butt of the Glock 17 protruding from the holster under Richter's left arm. He always preferred to carry a revolver, but there was a very good reason why Simpson had told him to take the automatic pistol.

'Right, have a seat. All we've heard so far is the intelligence summary from the CTC briefer, and I've just outlined the assault plan.'

As Richter sat down, the inspector decided to have some fun with him. He took up a pointer and gestured towards a diagram pinned on a board behind him. 'For Mr Smith's benefit, we've got six players at Tango One. We've two gunships, one of them a flounder, waiting at the jump-off here, plus two horses, each four-up. The premises are covered by fifteen footies, that's eleven plods and four plonks. When we kit-up at the FUP, don't forget your QRVs and HVCs. All clear about that, Mr Smith?'

Several people in the room chuckled. Richter looked up at the CO19 officer. 'Ever thought of a career on the stage, Inspector? Or are you hoping for another tour as senior dinosaur at Jurassic Park?' The chuckling suddenly stopped. 'I know the jargon as well as you do, so you can dispense with the comedy routine. I think what you mean is that you've got two unmarked Armed Response Vehicles, one of them a black cab, in place and ready to proceed as soon as you give the order. The horses – that's Trojan Horses, derived from the "Trojan" callsign that CO19 uses – are unmarked vehicles each carrying four officers. The target premises – Tango One – are occupied by six suspects and watched by fifteen surveillance officers, eleven male and four female. And I'm quite sure all of us in the room will remember to put on our high visibility caps and quick-release vests when we assemble at the forming-up point.' He paused, then added, 'After all, we wouldn't want this turning into a clusterfuck, would we?'

For a few seconds the briefing room fell absolutely silent. The inspector smiled, then laughed out loud. 'Thank Christ for that,' he said, 'a professional at last. I was getting really pissed off with all these pimply-faced geeks Thames House keeps on sending us. Welcome aboard, Mr Smith, or whatever your real name is. I'm Jessup. You're right about everything. The only other thing you need to known is that SO15 – the CTC – is the lead agency on this excursion, because their patrol stumbled across the cell. So apart from the spooks, it's just them and CO19.'

Forty minutes later the inspector wound it up. 'To recap, we've got surveillance groups in place at street level to take off any of the players who decide to walk. There are CO19 sniper teams covering all building entrances. There are known to be six targets using the flat, and once we're certain that they're all inside we'll take them down.'

With a glance at Richter, Jessup added: 'We would have been able to carry out the raid a couple of days ago, when we knew for sure they were all in the flat, if we hadn't had pressure from a certain organization not far from Vauxhall Bridge. Right, the last report was that two of the players were mobile, with footies in attendance. As soon as we've confirmed they're heading back to Tango One, we'll get everything prepped and hit them five minutes after they get inside. We'll be making broadcast calls to your pagers from the Special Operations Room here, with the baseman using the callsign "Golf Tango". As usual, all CO19 units will employ the callsign "Trojan" followed by their designated number. Any comments or questions?'

'I'll need a pager,' Richter said.

'No problem. See me as soon as we've finished. Any other questions?'

Richter stood up with everybody else, and walked to the front of the briefing room.

'Sorry about that,' Jessup said. 'I've been a bit pissed off the way Thames House and Vauxhall Cross have been trying to run this operation.'

'And I happened to be in the firing line?'

'Exactly.' Jessup opened a briefcase and pulled out a pager. 'I'd like that back, please, once the show's over. You don't need to do anything with it except turn it on. It's already pre-set to receive all the messages GT sends. Now, one question. What are you really supposed to be doing in this op?'

'I've been tasked with observation, Inspector,' Richter

said, 'but I have to get inside the flat as soon as possible. I need to identify one of the targets, because he may have links to an operation we're currently running.'

What Richter didn't say was exactly *why* he needed to identify one of the suspects. But Jessup – and everyone else – would find out very soon after they kicked down the door.

Kondal, Russia

Four minutes later, both Americans climbed down from the truck. Wilson closed and locked the door. The device was now safely in their hands, and the remainder of the transaction could now be executed.

When they'd first conceived the plan, the Americans had intended to kill the three Russians as soon as they'd got their hands on the weapon, but caution prevailed. A third death would have saved the Americans having to raise two million dollars, but that wasn't the overriding factor, and Wilson had already worked out a way around the money.

But the unexplained death or disappearance of three PO Start personnel, on the same day, would be too much for any investigating officer to ignore, and that would lead to an in-depth investigation at Zarechnyy. Which, in turn, could result in the discovery of the theft before the Americans had even cleared the area, and would render their documentation useless – they'd be stopped and held at the first road-block.

Their second choice was to play it straight, shake hands with their co-conspirators, hand over the passbooks to the three Swiss bank accounts as promised, and then go their separate ways. But that went totally against the grain, not least because the two million dollars they'd agreed to pay wasn't actually theirs.

So they'd decided to go with what they'd taken to calling Option One Alpha, which had necessitated taking Borisov partially into their confidence almost from the start.

The two dead technicians would accompany the weapon – at least on the first stage of its journey from Kondal, until Wilson and Dawson could find a suitable spot to dispose of their bodies – and Borisov's documentation would specify that Nabov and Devenko were the driver and escort for a consignment of 'machine tools' in transit to Turkey. The two Americans would wear the technicians' jackets and carry their identification. There wasn't a marked similarity in their appearance, but the pictures on Russian identity cards were usually small, grainy and very poor quality and they were, in conjunction with the other documentation, probably adequate to allow them to pass through a routine checkpoint.

That way, the absence of the two men from the PO Start facility could be explained by reference to a copy of the transit documents, and they wouldn't be missed for a few days.

The Russian hadn't liked this idea at first, but when Wilson pointed out that, if he agreed, the two-million-dollar fee they'd promised to the two technicians would instead be paid to him, he'd quickly changed his mind.

They walked back to where Borisov was standing, visibly nervous and now holding a Tokarev 7.62-millimetre semi-automatic pistol firmly in his right hand. Despite his reluctant agreement with their actions in killing Nabov and Devenko, Borisov trusted the two Americans about as far as he could spit a rat, and he knew he was now outnumbered two to one by armed men with fresh blood on their hands.

Wilson glanced around, checking they were still unobserved. The Russian handed him the docket containing the transit and export documentation. The American glanced at it, then passed it to Dawson.

'It was a pleasure doing business with you, Yuri,' Wilson said, and reached into his jacket.

Immediately Borisov raised his pistol and aimed it straight at Wilson's stomach, his eyes flicking watchfully between the two men, now alert for the first sign of hostile intent.

'Your money, Yuri,' the American said calmly. 'I'm just getting your money.' He eased his jacket open with his left hand, revealing no shoulder or belt holster, and reached into the inside pocket with his thumb and forefinger. He pulled out a dark blue booklet bearing what looked like an eagle insignia on the cover, and passed it across.

Borisov took a couple of steps backwards, his eyes dancing between the passbook and the two Americans, while still covering them with his pistol. He opened the book awkwardly, using his left hand. He checked the name of the account holder printed inside the front cover, and the certified balance, before he nodded in satisfaction and slipped it into his jacket pocket.

Wilson extended his hand, but Borisov didn't take it. He was still holding the Tokarev and had absolutely no intention of putting the weapon away.

'Perhaps,' he ventured, 'I might be able to do business with you again.'

'Perhaps you might,' Wilson echoed, though he already knew there was no possibility of this ever occurring. This deal was essentially a one-shot operation that would generate more money than any of them could hope to spend in several lifetimes.

Borisov retreated cautiously towards his car, almost walking backwards, still fearful of a double-cross even at that late stage. The Americans watched silently until he drove away.

They checked that all the doors on the truck were firmly locked, then returned to the hotel. Fifteen minutes later they were back outside in the car park, their trousers, brogues and sports coats replaced by jeans, work boots and the heavy dark-blue jackets stripped from the bodies of the two dead technicians – their transformation into a pair of truck drivers now complete.

Dawson stashed their two large suitcases and the laptop bags behind the seats, and drove off, taking the road towards Saratov.

The problem they still had was one of trust, or more accurately the complete lack of it. Borisov now had his Swiss bank-account passbook holding a balance of two million dollars – not a bad week's work for anyone – and they had the weapon they needed.

But the Americans knew there was no reason why Borisov shouldn't decide to make an anonymous call to the SVR or the FSB. And if their truck were to be stopped, the Russian would be more or less fireproof. There was nothing, apart from his signature at the bottom of the correctly completed transit and export documentation, that could possibly link him to the theft of the device. There was no record even of the opening of the secure storeroom which held the weapons, because he'd simply taken the keys from the office late one afternoon, met Nabov and Devenko at the storage building concerned and inside twenty minutes they'd completed the substitution. Just fifteen minutes after that, Borisov had been sitting at his desk, the keys back in the safe, and the two technicians were elsewhere on the site, filling the crate with the other items on the manifest he'd previously given them.

Every week, the administrator signed dozens of similar documents, and everybody in the office had ready access to the secure-storage keys, because the key safe remained unlocked during the working day. Any investigation might initially focus on Borisov, but there would be no way to connect him directly to the theft.

The Americans hoped he would be satisfied with the money and keep silent, but hoping didn't cut it.

Wilson had told the Russian that they'd be heading for the Turkish border at Leninakan in Azerbaijan, but they doubted he really believed them. And that, of course, was not the way they were going to leave the country. Their route out would be fast, and far from obvious. The first leg, from Kondal to Saratov, was the shortest, just a few miles, and Dawson calculated they'd get there late that afternoon, even after finding somewhere to dump the two bodies.

But first they had three small jobs to do. They had to repack the weapon, though that could wait until they found a secluded stretch of road. Dawson needed to make an international call to confirm they'd got the device, but that, too, could wait. The fund transfer couldn't, just in case Borisov decided to try accessing his Swiss bank account immediately.

The passbook that was tucked inside the Russian's jacket pocket was not all it appeared to be. It *was* a genuine passbook, issued by a real Swiss bank, and the account actually did contain two million American dollars. What Borisov didn't know was that the account was in joint names, the other signatory being Richard Wilson – or rather an alias chosen by him.

Dawson stopped the truck in a lay-by just as Wilson pulled out his mobile phone and his diary. He checked the bank's telephone number and called it. While he waited to be connected, he opened another passbook that was almost identical to the one they'd given Borisov.

When a bank official picked up the call, Wilson gave him the account number and the name he had used to set it up, and answered three security questions before being allowed access. Then he instructed that the entire balance, including accrued interest, be transferred at once to a bank in the Cayman Islands. There was no need for him to do anything else, because that finance house had standing instructions to immediately send any such receipts directly to another bank in Gibraltar.

Within twenty-four hours, the money would have been bounced around the world half a dozen times, and would be effectively untraceable. Bizarrely, its resting place for the next few days would be in Switzerland, at a bank two streets away from the first one in the chain, but in an account with a completely different name.

Wilson's only regret was that he wouldn't be able to see the expression on the Russian's face when he tried to draw on his 'investment'.

Chapter Three

'Here he is, at last. Fucking A-rabs got no sense of time,' O'Hagan muttered.

'You're late,' Petrucci snapped, as the two Americans climbed into the Mercedes.

The Arab shrugged as he pulled away. 'We've plenty of time.'

O'Hagan slouched sideways in the back seat, looking out of the rear window of the taxi to check for any following vehicles. 'I think we're clean,' he said, after a few minutes.

'I ran checks before I got to the Square. And even if we are being followed, you're just two American tourists out seeing the sights. This afternoon we're going to the Qal'at Al-Bahrain, the Bahrain Fort.'

'And are we?' Petrucci asked.

'No, but we're certainly heading that way.'

After passing the Pearl Monument, the King Faisal Highway turns south, and Ahmed continued along it, swinging right at the next junction on to the west-bound highway that runs to Al-Budayyi, over on the west coast of the island.

Just short of Jidd Hafa, he swung the taxi off the highway and down an unmarked and almost invisible

39

unmade road towards a cluster of whitewashed buildings. Although he slowed down, the car bounced and rattled, suspension creaking, as it lurched along the track, a plume of dust billowing out behind it.

He stopped the car outside a tiny stone building, its façade pierced by just two small and glass-less windows and a single door. Beside it was a ramshackle wooden framework roofed with sheets of corrugated iron acting as a rudimentary sunshade, and under that was a ten-year-old American Chevrolet. The car wasn't covered in dust, which O'Hagan assumed meant it had arrived there only recently.

The mid-afternoon heat was brutal after the air-conditioned cool of the taxi, a blanket of air so hot it almost hurt to breathe. Ahmed walked across to the door, rapped twice and stepped back.

The man inside had obviously heard them arrive, for the door opened almost immediately, and a shrivelled, burnt-brown face peered out at them. Ahmed dispensed with the customary Arab greetings and stepped inside.

If it had seemed hot outside, the interior of the house was almost literally baking, despite the gentle breeze blowing through the four small windows, the two at the front mirrored by a pair in the rear wall. The occupant gestured to cushions piled on the floor – they were the only things resembling furniture in the room – then walked across to a small refrigerator standing in one corner.

Petrucci puzzled at that for an instant, noticing that there were no electric lights or sockets visible, then he identified the faint hum of a generator running somewhere nearby. The man returned with four ice-cold

Cokes – they'd been hoping for beer, but that would have been too much to expect. The Americans opened their cans and drank.

The room was small and white-painted, and somehow conveyed an indefinable impression of transience, as if the current occupant had arrived there for the first time that morning – which, O'Hagan reflected, he quite possibly had – scattering the cushions on the floor and starting up the generator to power the fridge. He'd probably brought a couple of six-packs of Coke with him as well.

Ahmed sat down gracefully on a cushion, took a long swallow of his soft drink, then put down the can and looked across at the Americans. 'This,' he said, 'is Omar, and he's obtained the equipment you need.'

'The Chevrolet outside?' O'Hagan asked.

'Yes. Everything's already inside it.'

The two Americans remained seated. They knew Arabs, and they knew it would be some time before they would get to drive the car away. First, they would have to talk about the Chevrolet itself, and what was locked inside it, and then the route they were going to take back to Manama, and how difficult it had been to obtain all the equipment, and where they were going to park the car, and how they would set the timer, and anything else that either Ahmed or Omar decided was relevant. Only then would they be able to hand over the money – the bulky bundle of American dollars locked in Petrucci's briefcase – and finally get the hell out of there.

It was going to be a long, hot afternoon.

Between Kondal and Zarechnyy, Russia

It was one of those stupid, mundane annoyances that drivers face daily in every country in the world. The truck driver should have had somebody standing in the road behind his vehicle, stopping the oncoming traffic as he backed out. But he hadn't bothered because the road had seemed fairly quiet. All he'd done was wait until everything looked clear, then switch on his hazard warning lights, and begun to ease out slowly.

Three southbound cars approaching the entrance to the industrial area braked in time, but the driver of the fourth vehicle apparently didn't notice the looming obstruction until too late. He swerved out of his lane, moving around the rapidly slowing third car directly in front of him.

As he drove back towards Zarechnyy, Yuri Borisov was unaware of anything untoward until the overtaking vehicle suddenly lurched across the road in front of him. In an instant it filled his windscreen, and less than a second later slammed almost head-on into his car.

It wasn't the first time the Russian administrator had been involved in an accident. His elderly saloon car bore permanent and rusting testimony to a number of minor collisions, and the dents and scars resulting from bouts of acoustic parking.

But this collision was far from minor. The oncoming vehicle was braking hard, but Borisov – who for perhaps the first time in his driving career was entirely blameless – was travelling at around thirty miles per hour, giving a combined impact speed of almost fifty.

The sound of the crash was sudden and shocking, the bang echoing loudly off the walls of adjacent buildings. Both cars lifted and spun in opposite directions, their momentum dissipating rapidly as wings and bonnets crumpled under the impact. Tyres screamed as the cars lurched sideways, black rubber streaking the worn tarmac surface of the road, while a glittering cascade of safety glass tumbled from shattered door windows.

Both drivers were bounced violently from side to side as their cars gyrated and lurched. Borisov was arguably the lucky one because he was wearing his seat belt. The other driver wasn't, and at the first impact was thrown forward, crashing through the windscreen to end up lying unconscious, bleeding profusely from deep cuts in his head and neck, across what was left of his car's bonnet.

Borisov habitually drove with both hands holding the steering-wheel – which was good – but with his thumbs hooked around the wheel's rim – which was bad. When the two cars hit, the steering wheel spun hard to the left, instantly dislocating both his thumbs. The seat belt stopped his body hitting the wheel, but he smashed into the driver's door with such force that his left arm broke just above the elbow, and his head crashed through the side window, giving him a mild concussion. When the noise and the motion finally stopped he was both alive and conscious, but at that moment it's doubtful if he would have agreed that he'd been 'lucky'.

A police car, which had been less than two miles away when the accident happened, arrived on the scene within minutes, a fire appliance and ambulance arriving shortly afterwards. The unconscious driver was lifted as gently as possible from the remains of his car and driven straight to hospital. Borisov's vehicle needed more work because the doors had jammed, and there was less urgency because the Russian was visibly conscious and responsive.

In fact, as the police report stated later, he was *highly* responsive, trying as best he could with his mangled and useless hands to extract something from his jacket pocket. When the police officers realized that what he was trying to pull out was a pistol, their attitude changed immediately, and Borisov became less of a victim than a suspect. They promptly disarmed him and searched him thoroughly.

The Swiss bank passbook immediately attracted and held their attention. Once Borisov's arm was set and his injured hands treated at the hospital, he was given a pain-killing injection and taken straight to the police station in Kondal for questioning about the weapon and the huge quantity of American dollars lodged in a Swiss bank account in his name.

Bahrain

Omar finally stood up, nodded to the two Americans and walked to the door. He stepped out into the sunlight, leading the way around the house towards the parked Chevrolet. Taking a key from the pocket of his *gellabbiya*, he opened the boot and stepped back a couple of paces.

In an open cardboard box were four packets wrapped in clear plastic, along with a small toolkit. There were also several smaller items: a battery, a cable, six detonators, a soldering iron, a roll of black insulating tape and a battery-powered seven-day timer.

'And the other stuff?' O'Hagan asked.

'In the bag on the back seat,' Ahmed said, lowering the boot lid slightly and pointing through the car's rear window.

'Good. What is it – Semtex?'

'Yes. It's the easiest to get hold of, and it's very reliable.'

He was right on both counts. Semtex was invented in the village of Semtín – which inspired its name – in East Bohemia by a chemist named Stanislav Brebera in 1966. It was stable, odourless and had an indefinite shelf life. Unfortunately, terrorists immediately realized that Semtex was an ideal weapon for their purposes, as it passed with consummate ease through airport metal detectors, and could not be identified by sniffer dogs. Brebera recognized the danger, and later incorporated metallic compounds and chemicals within the explosive, but these measures were too little and too late.

Pan American flight 103 was brought down over Lockerbie in Scotland by twelve ounces of Semtex hidden inside a Toshiba cassette recorder, killing 270 people, and it was also the weapon used in the 1998 attack on the American Embassy in Nairobi, Kenya.

The manufacturing company, Explosia, has exported over 900 tons of Semtex to Libya, and about the same quantity to a handful of other hostile or unstable nations, including Iran, Iraq, North Korea and Syria. Altogether, it has been estimated that the world stockpile of Semtex is in excess of 40,000 tons.

'What's the total weight of the charge?' O'Hagan asked.

'Four kilos,' Ahmed said.

The American reached down to pick up one of the detonators, a slim aluminium tube about two inches long with a pair of silver-coloured wires emerging from one end. The wires, he noted with satisfaction, were twisted together. If they're left separate there's a possibility that they can act as antennae and, if a mobile phone or other radio device is used in the vicinity, they can spontaneously detonate.

Ahmed noticed O'Hagan's almost imperceptible nod of approval. 'We know our business here,' he added.

'I know you do, Ahmed, but it never hurts to check, particularly where this kind of stuff is concerned.'

'You're satisfied?'

O'Hagan replaced the detonator in the box. 'Thank you, yes.'

Petrucci spun the wheels of the combination locks on the briefcase, aligned the numbers and snapped the catches open. He lifted the lid, pulled out a bundle of banknotes and handed them over to Ahmed.

'As we agreed,' O'Hagan said. 'Please check the amount's correct.'

The Arab passed the money to Omar, who immediately began counting it. '*I* trust you, my friend, and I'm sure it's right. Omar, on the other hand, does *not* trust you, and he'll no doubt let us know if there's any discrepancy.'

As Petrucci slammed the boot lid shut, Omar nodded towards Ahmed and tucked the bundle of notes into his pocket. The Arab handed the car keys to O'Hagan.

'Remember our arrangement. Leave the car on Al-Mutanabi Avenue, between Al-Khalifa and Tujjaar, at the location we requested.' Ahmed extended his hand, and O'Hagan shook it. 'It was good to do business with you again.'

British Embassy, Government Avenue, Manama, Bahrain

William Ewart Evans – whose initials, emblazoned in gold leaf on his cases, had been the cause of prolonged merriment on his arrival as a spotty schoolboy at Harrow – was thirty-nine years old, tall, thin, fair-haired and a third secretary in the consular section at the British Embassy. His appointment was recorded in the Diplomatic List, and anybody enquiring by telephone for that particular third secretary would eventually find themselves talking to Evans. Despite this, he actually worked elsewhere in the large building on Government Avenue, and any callers genuinely seeking the help of the consular section would be politely passed on to someone else.

In reality, Evans was a career officer in the Secret Intelligence Service, responsible for local liaison and cooperation and, when he wasn't out operating on the streets of Bahrain, he could be found in the 'Holy of Holies', the name given to that section of the Embassy reserved for use by SIS officers.

The telephone call he received just after four-thirty that afternoon was both short and unremarkable.

'Bill?' The voice had a pronounced accent, and Evans recognized it immediately. He checked the caller-identification display on his desk phone and wasn't surprised that it reported a 'private number'. The clarity of the line suggested it was either a mobile or a car phone.

'Yes, Tariq?'

'I've found that album you were looking for. Could we meet this evening for a drink so that I can give it to you?' The man's English was precise but somewhat stilted.

Evans glanced down at the filing trays on his desk, all of which, with the notable exception of the 'out' tray, seemed to be depressingly full, but knew he had no choice, because the caller, Tariq Mazen, clearly had very urgent information for him.

The telephone code the two men used was simple, innocuous and very easy to remember, and relied on a handful of key words inserted into the kind of conversation any two male friends might have. 'Album' meant immediate, right now. The other options were 'book', which meant an urgent meeting within twenty-four hours; 'CD' within forty-eight hours, and 'DVD' within seventy-two hours. Simple enough: 'A', 'B', 'C' and 'D' in descending order of priority.

The second sentence contained the word 'drink', which meant that Mazen was already in his car waiting for him. For less urgent meetings he would have said 'meal', and also suggested a date, time and place and, as the two men were openly friendly with each other, they would meet in a restaurant as agreed. There Mazen would hand over an entirely normal book, CD or DVD, and Evans would pay him for it.

The information Mazen needed to convey would be

passed to Evans during the meal itself, if circumstances allowed, or afterwards as they walked back to their vehicles. Nothing in writing had been their rule from the first. If Mazen had to supply photographs or documents, he would simply seal them in an unmarked envelope and leave it at one of a dozen dead-letter drops scattered around Manama, and tell Evans using a simple number code which one he was going to use, and when the drop could be serviced.

'I'm sorry, Tariq,' Evans replied. 'I can't tonight. I'm up to my ears in work here, and I've just had another ten files dumped on my desk. If I can manage tomorrow, I'll give you a call.' That 'ten' meant he would be outside the Embassy building within ten minutes.

Evans glanced at the wall clock and stood up. He walked down a short corridor, knocked on a door and opened it without waiting for a response. Inside, a pretty, dark-haired woman of about thirty looked up from her laptop and smiled at him.

'Carole-Anne,' Evans began, 'I've just had a call from Tariq Mazen. He wants an urgent meeting so I'll be out for a while. Could you please record that I'm meeting him, subject and duration unknown, and I'll write up my work diary when I get back. But if I don't make it here by close of business, can you stick all my stuff in the safe and lock it?'

Carole-Anne Jackson – officially an American expatriate employed at the embassy as a typist, but in fact a CIA officer on exchange – nodded.

Evans made a drinking gesture, but she shook her head.

'No, not tonight, Bill. Prior engagement and all that.'

Evans's face darkened in mock anger. 'Who with?' he demanded.

'You find out,' Carole-Anne replied, her smile turning into an impish grin. 'After all,' she added, 'you are *supposed* to be a spy, aren't you?'

Saratov, Russia

Dawson stopped the truck on the dockside just after five. The transit documents supplied by Borisov had been scrutinized at the gate, and no eyebrows had been raised. The cargo-carrying motorized barge they'd booked space on was already waiting alongside the dock. It was scheduled to sail at six-fifteen, so their timing was just about perfect.

Wilson walked up the gangway and onto the barge, while Dawson opened the rear doors of the lorry. A waiting forklift truck lifted out the crate and deposited it next to a crane, and minutes later it was swung into the cargo hold and the barge's hatches then closed.

Wilson came back down the gangway, having concluded his arrangements with the barge master. The crate was an unscheduled addition to the vessel's cargo that the Americans had booked only two days earlier, so payment in cash had been agreed, half in advance and the rest on delivery to Volgograd. The barge master wasn't interested in paperwork, only in the money, and the operating company would know nothing about the unscheduled load, which suited everyone just fine.

The vessel would take about four days to cover the two hundred and fifty miles down the river. While the barge was heading south, Dawson and Wilson would ditch the truck. They'd already located a commercial vehicle park on the outskirts of Atkarsk that would do nicely. It would be bad luck if anybody took any notice of one extra truck, but even if it did get spotted and questions were asked, the pursuit would at least be stalled for some time in the town. From Atkarsk, the two Americans would take a train back to Saratov, and from there on to Volgograd.

'OK,' Wilson said, hauling himself up into the passenger seat, 'let's get out of here.'

Dawson fired up the diesel, engaged first gear and drove back towards the dockyard entrance. Unless they met any unforeseen problems, they calculated that they should be in Volgograd by mid-evening.

Manama, Bahrain

Evans strode out of the embassy and paused for a moment, looking round. He spotted Mazen's dusty Mercedes parked about seventy yards away, but gave no sign of recognition. He turned in the opposite direction and began walking slowly along the pavement. Two minutes later Mazen pulled up beside him. Evans quickly opened the door and climbed in.

'Tariq,' Evans acknowledged. 'I gather you've got something for me?'

Evans spoke fluent Arabic – a requirement in his

posting – but he knew Mazen was proud of his linguistic abilities and preferred to conduct their meetings in English.

'It's just a story, Bill,' Mazen said, accelerating gently down the road, 'and it may all prove to be a false alarm, but I believe it's worth looking into.'

Forty minutes later, having discussed everything from the strength of the Bahraini dinar to the latest problems in Israel, Mazen finally broached the actual subject of their meeting with a somewhat dramatic announcement.

'We could, my friend,' he said, 'be sitting about two kilometres away from where Osama bin Laden is lying helpless in a hospital bed, plugged into a kidney-dialysis machine.'

Stratford, East London

The sports centre lay at the end of Gibbins Road. It wasn't an ideal location, because Tango One was a full half mile away, but it had a car park where the unmarked white Transit vans – the 'horses' Jessup had referred to – and the ARVs could park without attracting undue attention.

There were also two saloon cars there, in one of which Richter had hitched a ride from New Scotland Yard, sharing the back seat with a slim young man with reddish hair and an embryo moustache that didn't look as if it was going anywhere. The other passenger had ignored him for the entire journey, and Richter guessed he was probably one of the 'pimply-faced geeks' from the Security Service that Jessup had complained about earlier.

There are few activities more tedious than waiting for something to happen, especially when creature comforts are somewhat limited. There was nowhere to sit except inside the cars, and nowhere to go apart from a handful of cafés in the nearby streets.

They'd already been waiting for over four hours before the first message arrived:

'Standby all units. Players Five and Six returning direction Tango One.'

The mood changed now that it looked as if the endgame was near. There were few cars and fewer pedestrians around as the armed officers – which was most of them – checked their weapons.

Richter pulled out the Glock, extracted the magazine and inspected it carefully. Then he reloaded the pistol and pulled back the slide to chamber a round.

Fifteen minutes later, GT sent a further message:

'Players Five and Six now inside Tango One. All units move to FUP and report readiness.'

Immediately the car park was filled with the sound of engines starting, and within seconds all six vehicles were mobile. Minutes later, they pulled to a halt in Bridge Road, their designated forming-up point.

Now speed was important. Vehicle doors opened and officers piled out, donning Kevlar quick-release vests and equipment belts. As they checked their weapons again, a group of teenage boys standing on a nearby street corner stared at them wide-eyed, then retreated a cautious fifty yards, several of them pulling out mobile phones and taking pictures. Shoppers and pedestrians paused to look at the increasingly familiar sight of armed police on the streets of London, then philosophically continued about their business.

Once all the final inspections were complete, the group leaders used their standard-issue 75 radios to check in with the baseman at GT. Then it was just a matter of waiting.

'All units stand by Go signal. Estimate minutes zero four.'

And three minutes later they were mobile. No sirens, screeching tyres or flashing lights, just a gentle and steady drive for the two hundred yards that still separated them from their destination.

The target flat – Tango One – was situated on the third floor. Four CO19 officers took the lift, the rest climbed the stairs. Three armed police stayed in the lobby to cover the building's main entrance. On the landing, one burly officer produced an enforcer – the steel battering ram that has become a trademark of CO19 operations – and waited beside the apartment door. The rest made a final check of their weapons, because professionals check everything repeatedly, and waited.

Up to that point, they'd tried to keep as quiet as possible, but when the enforcer smashed into the apartment door, just above the lock, everything changed. The door crashed open, and suddenly the building resounded with bellowed shouts of 'Armed police, armed police!' as the CO19 officers surged inside the apartment.

Richter was right behind the first group, making him the sixth man to enter. The hallway was long and narrow, three bedrooms and a bathroom opening off it, with a combined lounge and dining room at the far end, next to a tiny kitchen.

Two men were in one of the bedrooms – they'd apparently been using a laptop computer that sat on a wooden desk against one wall – and they stared in shocked bewilderment as a couple of officers raced into the room, weapons aimed straight at them. A third was taking a shower, the bathroom door closed but not locked, his terrified face peering at the arresting officer from behind the shower curtain.

The other three were in the lounge, with a television set blaring. The CO19 men ran down the corridor so fast that two of them were still sitting down when the lounge door burst open.

The Glock ready in his hand, Richter ran into the lounge directly behind two of the police officers. More shouts of 'Armed police! Don't move,' echoed around the apartment. Richter had already checked the suspects in the bedroom and bathroom as he stormed down the corridor. None of those had been Salah Khatid, but as he looked across the lounge he immediately recognized the slim dark-haired figure standing beside the window, despite not having set eyes on him for several years.

Richter stepped slightly to one side, ensuring that both the CO19 officers were clear of his line of fire, and brought his Glock up to the aim. 'Remember Abu Sabaawi,' he shouted – the precise but incomprehensible message Simpson had given him.

Khatid stared across the room at him, and almost visibly flinched. Then he tried to run, but it was too late for that.

Richter aimed carefully and squeezed the trigger.

His first shot missed, the sound appallingly loud in the small room, the nine-millimetre bullet screaming past the young Arab's head and smashing through the window, but his second found its mark. The left side of Khatid's chest bloomed red, and his body slammed back against the wall before crumpling to the floor.

'What the fuck are you doing?' one of the CO19 officers yelled, swinging his Heckler & Koch round to cover Richter. 'He was unarmed, no threat to anyone. That was just a cold-blooded fucking execution, you stupid bastard spook.'

Richter ignored him and walked across the room to kneel beside Khatid's broken body. He checked for a pulse, then nodded in satisfaction, stood up and looked at the CO19 officers, now joined by three others. Pointing at the two young Arabs who were staring at Richter and the body of their fallen comrade with a kind of sick fascination, he ordered: 'Get them out of here. I'm taking over this scene as of now.'

'I'll see you in court, you bastard,' one of the CO19 officers shouted. 'I don't care who you are – you're not above the law.'

'Just do it,' Richter snapped, 'and get Jessup in here.'

At that moment the inspector himself walked into the lounge. 'What the hell's happened?'

'This fucking spook just slotted an unarmed man, that's what happened. And now he's trying to take over.'

Jessup stared across at Richter, and then at the two frightened Arabs. 'Get them out of here,' he instructed. 'I'll sort this out.'

He stepped across to Richter and held out his hand. 'Give me your weapon.'

'No,' Richter said simply.

'Don't be stupid,' Jessup said. 'You've just shot an unarmed man in front of two police officers. It doesn't matter who you are or what your orders were, you're under arrest for murder. Now hand over your weapon.'

'No,' Richter repeated. 'Get these officers out of here, and then I'll tell you why I had to do what I did.'

For a moment Jessup just stared at him, then turned round and pointed at the remaining two Arabs. 'Take those two outside, caution them and arrest them, and the other three, on suspicion of CPIA under TACT – you know the form. Then just wait outside.'

Once the other police officers had left the room with their captives, Jessup turned back to Richter. 'This had better be fucking good,' he snarled.

'Oh, it is,' Richter said. 'I can guarantee that.'

And, directly behind him, Salah Khatid stood upright again, with a broad smile on his face.

Chapter Four

Monday
Manama, Bahrain

They left the Chevrolet in a car park lot abutting the King Faisal Highway and walked from there to the Al-Jazira Hotel, which they'd chosen primarily because of its constantly changing clientele. The car was parked far enough away that, unless somebody was already following them, which O'Hagan was pretty sure was not the case, nobody could connect it with them. And even if someone – some section of the Bahrain security apparatus – did seize or search the vehicle, there was nothing inside it to incriminate anyone. The weapon components, the discovery of which would certainly have resulted in the immediate arrest of the two Americans, were now in the large briefcase Petrucci was carrying.

Stratford, East London

Jessup pushed open the door of the café and they walked inside. Richter sat down in a booth at the back. 'Just coffee?' the inspector asked, received two answering nods, and walked across to the counter to place the order.

'It's been a long time,' Richter said, looking across the table at Khatid.

'I couldn't believe it when I saw you pointing that pistol at me. And then the code-phrase. It was lucky I still remembered it. Simpson gave it to me before I went to Afghanistan after 9/11.'

'Presumably it meant you were about to be extracted?' Jessup asked, sitting down beside Richter.

Khatid nodded. 'I think he had a less dramatic exit in mind, but that was the general idea.' He opened his jacket to reveal the huge red stain on his shirt. 'What is this stuff?'

'Something the boffins at Vauxhall Cross cooked up, I believe. It's a mixture of dye, some kind of powder and a binding resin. The resin holds the round together when it's fired, the powder provides the knock-down effect when it hits, and the dye itself looks remarkably like blood. You'll have a bad bruise on your chest for a couple of weeks.'

'But the first round was live?' Jessup asked.

'Yes. My boss wanted this execution to be as realistic as possible, so I deliberately missed with the first shot to prove that my weapon *was* firing live ammunition. Only the second bullet was a dummy.'

'I don't understand why our friend here had to be "killed". Why couldn't we just have arrested him and then handed him over to your lot?'

'Three reasons,' Richter explained. 'First, we've got another job waiting for Argonaut here – and that has to be one of the silliest code-names yet devised – which is apparently somewhat urgent. Second, getting our asset back would have taken days or maybe weeks, once he'd been arrested, but taking possession of a corpse takes no time at all. Finally, Simpson thought that you'd have an easier time getting the other members of the cell to cooperate if they've just seen one of their own shot dead right in front of them.'

'Why didn't you confide in me before the operation?'

'If you'd known what I intended to do, you'd have insisted on briefing your entry team. And unless they're trained actors, which I doubt, they'd have reacted in exactly the wrong way. But by doing it for real, with no pre-briefing, they responded precisely the way a couple of good coppers should have done.

'Now, as far as the world is concerned, one of these six terrorists was shot dead when armed police attempted to arrest him. The five remaining know he was in fact executed, which might mean they'll be easier to handle, and Argonaut can start his new undercover operation as soon as he's ready. All in all, an excellent result.'

Manama, Bahrain

Assembling an IED isn't difficult as long as you know what you're doing, as has been proved by the IRA and other terrorist groups on many occasions.

The most difficult weapons to fabricate are those using improvised explosives, usually based on ammonium nitrate fertilizer mixed with fuel oil. Such devices are bulky and unstable, but can be devastating. The Oklahoma City truck bomb that killed over 160 people in 1995 contained about two tons of ammonium nitrate fertilizer, and the IRA used the same substance to construct the half-ton bomb that caused such massive damage to London's Canary Wharf in 1996.

The problem with these types of IED is the bulk and weight of the components, and mixing the fertilizer and fuel oil requires both care and a large container. Delivery of such bigger devices also presents problems, normally requiring a substantial vehicle. John Petrucci's task was a lot easier, because everything he needed was inside the briefcase.

'You want a hand with anything?' O'Hagan asked, but Petrucci shook his head.

'No. I'll just grab a coffee in the bar, and then I'll start.'

'OK, we'll aim to position it this afternoon at six, so work out your timing based on that. I'll check the flights and book us a hotel in Cairo.'

Petrucci returned to his hotel room and locked the door. He pulled on a pair of surgical gloves – fingerprints on bomb components unaccountably seem to survive even the most powerful explosions – opened the briefcase and placed all the components in front of him on the writing desk.

He was methodical and experienced, and had plenty of time. He proceeded with small, simple steps, checking each component carefully before he attached it, and then each function as he completed it.

Fifty minutes later he made a final check of the connections and timer settings, then stepped out into the corridor and headed for the lifts, briefcase in hand.

Kondal, Russia

'You're obviously a member of the Mafia,' the interrogating officer snapped, as Borisov lowered his aching body onto a seat in the interview room.

The officer was dressed in civilian clothes and had introduced himself simply as 'Investigator Litvinoff', so Borisov had no idea what rank he actually held or even which branch of the police force he represented. The administrator's worry was that Litvinoff might not be a police officer at all, but instead a member of the FSB – the *Federal'naya Sluzhba Bezopasnost* – responsible for domestic counter-espionage, anti-subversion and counter-terrorism. The pistol and the bank passbook were both red flags that would immediately suggest either criminal activity or some form of treachery.

'How else can you explain these?' Litvinoff demanded, confirming Borisov's unspoken thought as he gestured at the unloaded Tokarev, and then the passbook, sitting on the table between them.

The room was small and square, with stained and grubby white-painted walls, a low ceiling, and a very solid door. The only furniture was a metal table, its legs bolted to the floor, and three hard wooden chairs.

For a few moments Borisov said nothing, wondering desperately what he could do to retrieve the situation. He'd been trying to work out what he should say ever since he'd stared at the unavoidable sight of the oncoming car on the road outside Kondal, but he still had almost no idea. His best option, he decided, was to play dumb and innocent, as far as he could.

'The pistol is for my own protection,' he ventured.

Litvinoff snorted. 'Protection, Borisov? You work at the PO Start manufacturing plant in Zarechnyy. What enemies can a mere administrator' – he sneered the word – 'expect to make? Tell me that.'

'I sometimes have to carry important documents outside the plant. These papers carry a high security classification, and I must be able to protect both them and myself.'

'We found no such documents in your car,' the investigator pointed out. 'In fact, we found nothing of interest there apart from this bank book. Why do you have a foreign bank account?'

Borisov knew he was fighting a losing battle, but he wasn't prepared to give in without a fight. 'I work as a consultant,' he replied, a hint of desperation in his voice. 'The companies that employ me often pay in dollars, so that means I must have a bank account outside Russia.'

Litvinoff opened the bank passbook and studied the entry on the first page with exaggerated care. 'It looks to me as if there has only ever been one deposit made into this account,' he said. 'One deposit only, of two million American dollars. Two *million* dollars. What sort of consultancy work pays you that well, Borisov? What skills do you have that can command that kind of remuneration?'

'The work I do is confidential, so I can't discuss it. That passbook is for a new account. I've only just opened it, and the money was transferred there from another bank.' That, at least, was true.

The investigator looked at Borisov and shook his head. 'Your story makes no sense,' he snapped, 'but let's assume for the moment that this money, this two *million* dollars, which is more than most workers in this country could earn in several lifetimes, has indeed been paid to you for some work you've done. But look at you. Your car is at least fifteen years old and your clothes are shabby and worn. If you had been acting as a consultant and getting paid these sums of money, you would be well able to afford a decent car and good clothes. And you certainly wouldn't still be working at Zarechnyy as an administrator.'

Litvinoff leant forward across the table, and Borisov moved back slightly.

'There are only two ways you could have acquired this money,' Litvinoff hissed. 'You're either involved in some kind of criminal activity or you've sold something to a foreign power. You're already in deep trouble for carrying a concealed and unlicensed firearm. What I have to decide is whether you're a traitor, or just a criminal, and whether you're going to prison for the rest of your life or if we should just take you outside and shoot you now.'

Borisov stared back across the table, wondering whether to try to buy his way out of the situation. He had adequate funds – that was abundantly clear to both him and the investigating officer – and he could afford to be generous, even split the balance down the middle. What worried him was that any attempt to offer a bribe might backfire.

There could be surveillance devices hidden in the interview room, though he could see no indication of a microphone or camera lens. If he tried to persuade Litvinoff to let him walk out, he might find that his troubles were only just starting. But he had to try, because the alternative simply didn't bear thinking about. What encouraged him was that he was talking to only one investigator, and he knew that usually two officers conducted such interrogations, often playing 'good cop, bad cop' roles. The fact that Litvinoff was questioning him alone might mean he was hoping for an offer.

'You're wrong,' Borisov insisted. 'I do work as a consultant, and it pays very well. I could even employ an assistant for some jobs.' That should be enough to bait the line.

For a moment or two Litvinoff stared at him, then dropped his eyes to the passbook. 'Two million dollars is a *lot* of money,' he said. 'If you were to employ some-one, what sort of payment would you expect to offer him for his services?'

Borisov felt he could breathe again, knowing he'd set the hook. All he had to do was negotiate a figure. He'd start as low as he dared, and hope Litvinoff wasn't too greedy.

'Probably about twenty-five per cent of the gross remuneration,' he said casually. 'For this job I've just done, that would mean half a million American dollars. A very substantial payment for very little work.'

'That's true, but you must appreciate the nature of what's involved here. A more reasonable payment would be half the total – one million dollars each for you and your assistant.' Before Borisov could reply, the investigator continued. 'Think of the problems you face. If you can't walk away from here, you'll never see any of this money. You'll spend the rest of your life behind bars, or even face a firing squad. Now, if somebody could arrange for all charges to be dropped, I think you'd agree that service was worth rather more than five hundred thousand dollars. But, of course,' Litvinoff finished, 'it's entirely up to you.'

Borisov didn't hesitate. 'What you say makes sense. If I could be assured that no charges would be filed, I'd be happy to pay the sum you suggest.'

'Right,' Litvinoff said. He picked up the pistol and the passbook and smiled for the first time. 'I'll see if I can find somebody who can assist you. Meanwhile, I'll have some refreshments sent in.'

Manama, Bahrain

Alex O'Hagan walked out of the Al-Jazira Hotel, John Petrucci following, briefcase in hand. They'd already checked out, and their bags were waiting in the lobby. O'Hagan had explained to the desk clerk that they had a meeting to attend in Manama, and they'd be returning to collect their luggage before going to the airport.

The car park lay north of the hotel, but they headed south and stopped at the end of Al-Mutanabi. While O'Hagan conducted an entirely imaginary conversation on his mobile phone, Petrucci stood beside him, apparently idly waiting, but in reality checking the road for any cameras that could record them when they eventually parked the car.

He spotted two. One was fixed, covering the Al-Khalifa junction, and was presumably a traffic camera.

The second was located on a nearby building and was mobile, pointing up the street for about two minutes at a time, before rotating to point in the opposite direction.

Three times Petrucci lifted his left arm, apparently checking his watch. In fact, he was holding a digital camera, scarcely bigger than a credit card, and each time he raised his arm he took a picture.

When they reached the car park, they didn't immediately approach the Chevrolet. O'Hagan again made a 'call' on his mobile while they scanned the surrounding area, checking that nobody was watching.

O'Hagan unlocked the doors and slid behind the wheel, immediately starting the engine to get the air-conditioning working. Petrucci sat in the passenger seat, the briefcase on his lap. As the air inside the car cooled, he opened the case to make a final inspection of the weapon. O'Hagan glanced down at the deadly contents and nodded. Petrucci closed the briefcase and scrambled the combination locks.

On the back seat of the car was a holdall containing a *gellabbiya* and *kaffiyeh* for each man, a basic disguise that instantly changed their appearance from that of Western businessmen to just a couple of locals. The outfits would help to muddy the waters slightly if any cameras did manage to record their images when they positioned the vehicle. Once they'd both pulled the Arab clothing on over their suits, O'Hagan put the car into gear and drove slowly away.

On Al-Mutanabi, he manoeuvred the car into the only parking space he could find, but left the engine running. The vehicle wasn't positioned precisely where Ahmed had requested, but it was close enough, and O'Hagan wasn't prepared to wait for one of the spaces right outside the building to become vacant.

'OK to arm it now?'

O'Hagan nodded. 'I hope to Christ you've set the timer right.'

'Trust me,' Petrucci replied, but he still held his breath as he removed insulating tape from two wires that protruded from holes drilled in the side of the briefcase. He twisted the exposed strands of copper together, then pushed the briefcase under the seat until it was invisible.

O'Hagan adjusted the exterior mirror until it was pointing well above the horizontal, and carefully angled it so that he could see the motorized camera on the side of the building behind them. The camera was facing towards the Chevrolet but, as he watched, it swung round to point in the opposite direction.

He switched off the engine, climbed out and locked the car, then both men started walking away, towards Tujjaar. Directly underneath the camera mount they stopped and appeared to engage in conversation, before walking on again the instant the camera turned back to point at the Chevrolet. When they reached the end of the road, Petrucci looked back down Al-Mutanabi, just as the camera swung towards them. He couldn't help himself. He waved, then walked on.

The Americans continued along Tujjaar until they reached the Capital Hotel, where both men headed for the toilets. When they emerged, the Arab clothing had gone, now stuffed deep into the used paper-towel basket in the lavatory. Stepping outside, they flagged down the first taxi they saw. Just a few minutes later they'd collected their luggage from the Al-Jazira and were heading towards Muharraq Island and Bahrain International Airport.

Buraydah, Saudi Arabia

They'd travelled to the country from all over the Middle East, and the car park on the outskirts of Buraydah was their penultimate rendezvous. The town had been chosen because it was a long way from the site of the operation, and distance was important. More practically, there weren't that many places in the area that could supply the equipment they needed, but they'd found a source on the outskirts of town, and had already made the booking.

Once they'd finished their brief discussion, the men dispersed, climbing into their dusty four-by-fours – two Mitsubishis, a Toyota Land Cruiser and a Nissan Patrol. Three of these vehicles were carrying goods in their luggage compartments. The Nissan held two bulky fabric bags, each about three feet long, which clanked metallically as the vehicle moved off. The two Mitsubishis each carried four bales of hay. These appeared normal in every respect except one – they were too heavy, and the extra weight was entirely due to the oblong package that lay concealed in the centre of each bale. The packages had been inserted very carefully, one end of each bale being cut out so as to retain its shape, and some of the hay then repacked into the cavity. Without a detailed inspection, the bales would appear completely normal.

The two Mitsubishis headed out into the desert, while the Toyota and Nissan drove towards the centre of Buraydah. All the vehicles were ultimately heading for the same destination, some two hundred kilometres to the north-east, but these two had a stop to make first.

Protected by a high chain-link fence, interrupted only by a set of wide double gates, the construction equipment yard was predominantly open space. More or less in the centre stood a single-storey office building surrounded by a couple of acres of concreted surface, upon which stood a wild profusion of machinery: diggers, bulldozers, concrete mixers, cherry-pickers and other equipment.

The driver of the Land Cruiser – the name he was using was 'Saadi' – stepped out of the vehicle and walked across to the office.

Inside it, three men were sitting at a long desk, a variety of maps, documents and calculators scattered in front of them, with a couple of computer terminals at one end. Saadi produced a sheet of paper which he offered to the Arab who stood up to greet him.

'Is it ready?' he asked.

'Yes.' The man scanned the paper and nodded. 'We just have to load it on the trailer. You have brought a tow vehicle?'

Saadi nodded assent and proffered a gold credit card.

A couple of minutes later he walked outside again and backed the Toyota up to a four-wheel trailer, while a company employee drove a small digger around the building, manoeuvred it onto the trailer and secured it with chains.

Less than twenty minutes after they'd arrived at the yard, the two jeeps drove back out through the open gates, Saadi's vehicle now hauling the trailer. They were running altogether over an hour behind the two Mitsubishis, but that didn't matter because the others wouldn't start until they got there.

Hammersmith, London

'This is a joke, right?' Richter said.

'I don't tell jokes and I don't make jokes, as you well know,' Simpson snapped, turning slightly pinker. 'You can think whatever you like about this, but the tasking came straight from our Cousins across the pond.'

'Via Vauxhall Cross,' Richter pointed out.

'As you say, via Vauxhall Cross, but it's still a CIA request and we've been instructed by Six to implement it. And I've chosen you.'

'Why? Am I at the top of your shit list again?'

'Not quite, as it happens. You got Khatid out of that flat in Stratford very competently, so this is by way of being a reward.'

'A reward? This tasking is complete bollocks. It's just a stupid waste of time and effort, and you know that as well as I do.'

'You're wrong,' Simpson said. 'The report from Dubai was very specific. Holden definitely predicted Friday's suicide bombing in Damascus. There's absolutely no discrepancy about the dates. His statement was filed over a week beforehand, and they've got that in writing. And don't forget that he's been back to the embassy since, and that's what the Americans are really interested in.'

'The first report could have been a coincidence.'

'The Americans don't think so, and they've got something of a track record in this field. Haven't you ever heard of Sun Streak? Or Grill Flame? Or even Star Gate?'

'Like the TV series?' Richter asked. He'd recently had Sky television installed at his flat, and was already beginning to regret it.

Simpson shook his head. 'No, not like the bloody TV series. They were US government-funded projects, and they all dealt with this kind of thing. Get the relevant files out of the Registry and read them, and anything else we've got – and do that today.'

'And then?'

'And then you can pack your swimming trunks and bucket and spade and get yourself out to Dubai and find out exactly who this Holden character is, and just what the hell else he knows. And Richter,' Simpson warned, 'this is a simple, straightforward investigation of an event that has no immediately obvious logical explanation, so not even you should be able to make a Horlicks of it. But remember this when you're lying about and soaking up the rays out there in the Gulf – fuck this one up and I'll drop you deeper than whale shit. Got it?'

'Got it,' Richter agreed. The briefing appeared to be at an end, but he just sat there.

'Well? What are you waiting for?'

Richter looked across at Simpson appraisingly. 'There's more to this, isn't there? Why would you waste your time sending me all the way out to Dubai just to talk to this guy, when any of the Six officers at the local embassy could do it? What else do you know?'

Simpson nodded slowly. 'Very perspicacious, Richter,' he muttered grudgingly. 'You're quite right. If we'd just been given the tasking by itself, I'd have told Vauxhall Cross to stuff it, but there's more, and I suppose you might as well hear about it now. Between you and me, that Legion Patrol didn't just stumble across Khatid's cell in Stratford – we leaked the location to them, through a low-level informer.'

'That makes more sense,' Richter said. 'I suppose Khatid asked for an emergency exfil?'

'Exactly. I do have a new tasking for him, but it's not that urgent. Khatid wanted out because of what he heard in Berlin, and there was no other way to debrief him.'

'So what did he hear?'

Simpson shrugged. 'He thinks Osama and his merry men have another plan afoot, but this one's a bit different.' He leant forward and depressed a button on his desk intercom unit. 'Is Khatid still in the building?'

There was an answering squawk that made no sense to Richter, but Simpson nodded briskly. 'Good. Tell him to get his arse up here right now.'

A couple of minutes later there was a knock on the door and Khatid walked in, smartly but casually dressed in designer jeans, shirt and leather jacket, and walked across to the other seat in front of Simpson's desk.

The only incongruous note was his personal grooming: his hair was unwashed, long and unkempt, the black beard straggly and untrimmed, his nails cracked and dirty. He also wasn't wearing deodorant. It completely ruined the effect created by the clothes, but Richter knew exactly why it was important. When Khatid went back to Afghanistan or Pakistan under deep cover, any trace of contact with Western civilization – such as the smell of deodorant or even washed hair – could spell his death warrant.

'You're going back that soon?' Richter asked, as Khatid sat down.

'You think I'd want to smell like this if I wasn't? I'm still waiting to hear exactly which godforsaken country I'm being sent to but, yes, apparently it's imminent.'

'And then it's back to camels and donkeys instead of black cabs and limos?'

'Only if I'm lucky,' Khatid said. 'I think I walked most of the way across Afghanistan last time.'

'If you two want to chat, do it in your own time,' Simpson snapped. 'Khatid, tell Richter what you heard in Germany.'

'Right, Paul. It isn't much, and it's fairly non-specific. While we were in Berlin, I drove Hussein – he was the leader of our cell – to a meet with an Al-Qaeda planner. The two of them talked in private, in a small safe house. I was told to guard the door, which meant I was very close to them, and I could hear some of their conversation. Mostly, the planner discussed tactics and techniques, and I've already passed that data on to Five and Six.'

'It was much better information than we've had for a while,' Simpson interjected.

Khatid looked pleased, and continued. 'Anyway, right at the end of their conversation the planner told Hussein

74

that a new attack was imminent, and that although there would only be a small number of people involved, the results would be spectacular.'

'There weren't many terrorists on the front line in 9/11, and I think you could say the results of that attack were pretty spectacular,' Richter pointed out.

Khatid shook his head. 'Hussein said something like that, but the Al-Qaeda planner told him it would be completely different, not a direct attack on the West at all. It wouldn't be a big bang, he said, but the effects would be felt all around the world.'

'You mean they're not aiming to blow up a building or hit an embassy, nothing like that?'

'That's the impression I got. Based on what I over-heard, my best guess is that this time Al-Qaeda's chosen an economic target, and probably one located some-where in the Middle East.'

'Like what?' Richter asked. 'An oilfield?'

'That's an obvious possibility,' Simpson said. 'We don't know any more at the moment, though Six has put some feelers out. Anything else, Khatid?'

'No, that's it. That was all they said.'

Richter stood up and shook hands with him. 'Take care of yourself, Salah. Send me a postcard from Kabul.'

When the door closed behind Khatid, Simpson fin-ished his briefing. 'Right, so although I'm expecting you to check on this Holden character, you're really going out to Dubai for two different reasons. First, because that Damascus suicide bombing might have something to do with whatever foul little scheme the Al-Qaeda planners have come up with – it's in the right area, at any rate. And the second reason is that I want somebody out there, one of my people rather than a Legoland paper-pusher, just in case the shit does hit the fan.'

Kondal, Russia

Borisov had hoped to be out of the police station soon after Litvinoff left the interview room, but so far that hadn't happened. The promised refreshments – tea and a selection of small cakes that appeared to have been retained well beyond their sell-by date – duly arrived, but of Litvinoff there had been no further sign.

By ten-thirty Borisov was getting worried, though he tried to remain as calm as possible, just in case there were hidden cameras watching him. At eleven the door opened, and a uniformed officer appeared to escort him to the detention area, but Borisov noted that he was being treated with a little more respect. Perhaps Litvinoff had instructed the officers that he was not just some common criminal.

But they still locked him up for the night. The cell contained almost nothing – a tiny and inadequate radiator, barely warm; two bunk beds, each with a thin mattress, a pillow, a blanket and a discoloured single sheet; a steel toilet bowl and sink bolted to the wall in one corner, and a small hand-towel. The only illumination was a bright bulb inside an armoured wall light, mounted well out of his reach above the door.

Borisov guessed it was going to be a cold and uncomfortable night, and in that he was right. He dragged all of the bedding to the lower bunk, tucked the cleaner of the two sheets around the mattress and put the other sheet and both blankets on top. Then he slid into bed, still fully clothed apart from his jacket and shoes, closed his eyes and tried to sleep. In this endeavour he wasn't helped by the light, which remained on all night, or by the stabbing pain from his broken arm and swollen hands as the effect of the painkillers wore off. It was well past midnight before his body finally succumbed to fatigue and he finally dozed off.

Chapter Five

Volgograd was the rock that broke the back of the German advance in the Second World War. Then known as Stalingrad, its strategic location on the Volga ensured that the Germans had to take it if they were to conquer Russia. The assault began in August 1942 and ended six months later, with the city virtually flattened, almost half a million German soldiers lying dead, and an ignominious surrender for what was left of Hitler's Sixth Army.

Of course, neither Dawson nor Wilson knew any of this, and wouldn't have cared if they had. Their sole concern was to get themselves and the weapon out of the CIS as quickly as possible. And now they were running late.

It had taken them longer than they'd anticipated to dump the truck and get back to Saratov, and the train on which they'd booked tickets was long gone by the time they reached the station. The next available train to Volgograd was running late – very late – and didn't reach its destination until after midnight. Not surprisingly, they found they'd missed the Astrakhan connection they'd planned to catch by over two hours.

Despite the lateness of the hour, all the waiting rooms

were packed with people, presumably waiting for something other than a train, as the last scheduled departure of the evening – a Moscow express – had already left. Wilson opened the door to one waiting room, peered inside, then swiftly withdrew. The combined odours of stale tobacco, alcohol, unwashed bodies and the inevitable boiled cabbage were more than he could take.

'So what do we do now?' Dawson asked. 'Find a hotel?'

'At this time of night? No way – the last thing we want is to attract attention, and two foreigners checking into a hotel in Russia at one in the morning would definitely ring alarm bells. We'll go find ourselves a train. Any train. It's too cold to sit on the platform, and we can't go tramping round Volgograd lugging this lot.' Wilson gestured to the two large suitcases and computer bags lying on the platform beside them.

'And if somebody finds us camping in a deserted carriage?'

'We're stupid Americans. We'll just say we thought it was the Kiev express.'

Ten minutes later, they closed the compartment door of a carriage standing at a deserted platform on the far side of the station, stretched themselves out on the lumpy bench seats and closed their eyes.

Al-Shahrood Stables, Ad Dahnā, Saudi Arabia

The two Mitsubishi Jeeps drove down the tarmac road that ran past the stud farm. Beyond the entrance, both drivers slowed their vehicles, turned round and drove back, stopping about five miles from the farm, on a wide parking area just off the highway. And then there was nothing the six men could do but wait for the other two jeeps to arrive, with the digger and the four remaining members of the team.

A little over two hours later, one of the drivers spotted approaching headlights, and stepped out of his vehicle. By the time the other two four-by-fours had stopped, dust and sand swirling in their headlight beams, all six Arabs were standing ready, waiting.

Massood and Saadi – both randomly chosen names, a very basic security precaution for all the team members – climbed out of their vehicles.

'Any problems?' Saadi asked.

'No, none.'

'Good. Then we'll run through the operation one last time.'

Saadi opened the glove-box of his vehicle and removed a plan of the nearby stud farm. Massood flicked on the parking lights of the Toyota to provide some illumination as Saadi squatted down and unfolded the diagram, the others all clustering around him.

For fifteen minutes Saadi sat there with the men who had been placed under his command, ensuring that each knew exactly when to act and what to do. Then he stood up and opened the boot of the Nissan. Unzipping the first fabric bag, he reached inside it and pulled out a Kalashnikov AK47 assault rifle, its magazine already attached. He passed this to Massood, then seized another. Within minutes, each man was holding a Kalashnikov and two spare magazines.

Saadi glanced at his watch. It was just before dawn,

ideal timing. 'Is everybody ready? Good. We'll start now.'

The four jeeps pulled back onto the road and headed for the entrance to the stud farm. The gates were wide open and Saadi guessed that they were probably cosmetic, intended to create the right impression as owners and trainers drove in, and not designed with any security considerations in mind.

Lights now switched off, they drove slowly towards the house and farm buildings. Both sides of the drive were lined with white-painted three-bar fences, beyond which they could occasionally see the dark bulk of horses.

The ground plan of the farmhouse that Saadi had been given was based on the architect's original drawings, and was extremely accurate. In fact, calling it a 'farmhouse' hardly did it justice, for the elaborate building boasted six bedroom suites, a formal dining room, an indoor swimming pool and games room, plus servants' quarters. It was the kind of house that Saadi – who had never set foot in America – thought was far more suited to California than to Saudi Arabia. He wondered briefly if this particular farm had been selected because of its obvious opulence, or just because of the horse.

The vehicles parked quietly in front of the house. Saadi and Massood walked over to the main door while the other men dispersed to their pre-briefed positions. Two remained close to Massood, while the other six slipped away, vanishing like wraiths into the lightening dawn, heading for the rear of the farmhouse and the stable block beyond.

Saadi silently motioned for Massood to stand aside,

then pressed the buzzer. Immediately bright security lights, positioned on either side of the door, flared on, and Saadi looked up into the dispassionate gaze of a security camera right above him. He ignored it and waited. Even if the camera was attached to a video recorder, it didn't matter. They would check the house security system and remove any tapes before they left.

After a couple of minutes the two lights switched off. Saadi pressed the buzzer again, and this time kept his finger on it. If they couldn't get the owner or a staff member to open the door, they would just have to break in.

Through a glass panel in the door Saadi saw the hall lights come on, and a vague shape approaching. A key turned in the lock and the door swung partially open: framed in the gap stood a young Filipino man, obviously roused from sleep. For a brief second he stared at Saadi, his expression puzzled, then the Arab stepped forward and kicked out, knocking him violently backwards into the wide entrance hall.

Seconds later, all four men were inside the house, and the Filipino manservant lay sprawled on his back, staring up into the muzzles of three assault rifles.

Kondal, Russia

Breakfast was some barely edible *kasha* porridge, served in a steel bowl, and a cup of weak tea. Borisov tried a couple of spoonfuls of the porridge, then gave up and just drank the tea.

He emptied the remains of the meal down the toilet, swilled out the bowl and mug in the sink, and attempted to wash himself in the icy water. The tiny piece of soap produced barely any lather, and his hands were still really painful, but he did his best. He had neither toothbrush nor toothpaste, so he rubbed his teeth with the end of the towel. His rudimentary ablutions finished, he put his jacket and shoes back on, lay down on the bunk and waited.

An hour or so later the cell door opened, and another police officer appeared. He gestured, and Borisov stood up and preceded him down the corridor. The policeman gave him a shove in the back as he passed, and Borisov made a mental note to complain to Litvinoff when he saw him again. In fact, that turned out to be almost immediately.

The policeman opened the door of the interview room and gave Borisov another hefty push. As the prisoner stumbled inside, he saw Litvinoff sitting at the table. The investigator didn't look pleased, and Borisov guessed that something unforeseen had happened. He said nothing then, just walked to the other chair and sat down.

Litvinoff was studying the bank passbook, turning it this way and that in his hands, and ignored Borisov. Finally he tossed it across the table.

'You must think I'm a fool,' he snapped.

Borisov had no idea what the other man was talking about. 'What?' he asked, in surprise.

'That.' Litvinoff pointed at the passbook. 'Very funny indeed. It must have amused you, sending me off with that. Perhaps it won't seem quite so hilarious when you're being sentenced to twenty years' hard labour or you find yourself looking at a firing squad.'

Borisov still had no idea what Litvinoff meant, but whatever had irritated the investigator was clearly serious, and might have disastrous consequences.

'I'm sorry,' he said, 'I really don't know what you mean.'

Litvinoff stared at him blankly for a moment, then reached across the table and retrieved up the passbook. 'This,' he shouted. 'This is what I'm talking about. This *two million dollars*.' He gave a hollow laugh. 'You must have known, even before I left here yesterday.'

'I must have known what?'

'You must have known the account was already empty.'

It seemed to Borisov as if the floor of the interview room had suddenly vanished, and he was falling backwards down a long dark tunnel. For a few moments he just shook his head, his mouth working soundlessly as his brain struggled to accommodate what he had just been told.

Watching him closely, Litvinoff realized that either Borisov was one of the finest actors he had ever encountered in his long career with the FSB, or the man genuinely hadn't known the account balance was zero.

'I checked it very carefully through our foreign banking section. The outstanding balance was transferred yesterday to a bank in the Cayman Islands. From there they think it was sent back to Europe, but they couldn't trace it any further.'

Borisov just gaped at him, shaking his head helplessly,

his mind still refusing to accept what the other man was saying.

'I assume your partner-in-crime found a better home for those funds than Switzerland.'

'Partner? What partner?' Borisov asked, his mouth dry and his voice quavering.

Litvinoff picked up the passbook again and pointed to a single word inside it. 'Do you know what "*Gemeinschaftskonto*" means? It's German,' he added helpfully.

Borisov shook his head.

'Pity. If you'd looked a bit more carefully, you might have noticed it. The word means "joint account". You had a joint account, and either party had authority to access all the funds. Your partner – the man you claim you didn't know about – removed everything yesterday. The whole balance. And this is the best bit. Would you like to know your partner's name?'

Litvinoff glared across the table at Borisov, who nodded desperately.

'His name was rather unusual. He was a Mr M. Mouse. We managed to find out from the Swiss bank that his first name was Mickey. Mr Mickey Mouse. He's probably the richest rodent you're ever likely to meet. And now, Borisov, I think it's time we had a *serious* talk.'

Al-Shahrood Stables, Ad Dahnā, Saudi Arabia

Saadi stood in the centre of the spacious hall and held up his hand for silence. The house seemed totally still, no noise anywhere, but that didn't mean that nobody else was awake. He gestured to Massood, pointing down the hall towards the back of the house, and his colleague moved away, heading for the rear door.

Saadi looked round. The hall was long and wide, the floor marble, the walls decorated with English hunting prints and paintings – probably expensive, Saadi thought, his lip curling in disdain. At one end a winding staircase led to the upper level, and on either side of that corridors ran off to the left and right, leading to the various ground-floor reception rooms.

He gave the manservant a brief, dismissive glance, then looked back down the hall, where Massood had just reappeared, followed by two other members of the group. The other four would be securing the stable block and detaining the staff who lived there. He looked again at the Filipino, then nodded to one of the men standing beside him.

'No blood,' he ordered, his voice a whisper.

Bashar nodded, slung the Kalashnikov over his shoulder, and stepped behind the recumbent figure. He pulled out a roll of wide gaffer tape, a loop of stout cord and finally a short length of wood from the pocket of his *gellabbiya*, and beckoned. Two of the men stepped forward and seized the manservant, pulling him to his knees and holding him firmly in position.

Bashar tore off a six–inch strip of tape and swiftly stuck it over the Filipino's mouth to silence him. Then, with a single unhurried movement, he dropped the loop of cord over the young man's head, where it settled around his neck. The manservant finally realized what was about to happen, and began to struggle violently, trying desperately to pull his arms free from the Arabs who were holding him.

It did him no good. Bashar slipped the length of wood into the back of the loop and began turning it, holding the twisted cord in his left hand while rotating the wood with his right. When the garrotte began tightening on the Filipino's neck, Bashar changed position and seized the wood with both hands, so as to exert maximum force.

Saadi and Massood watched impassively as the young manservant's face bloated, the skin flushing red. His strug-gles grew more and more desperate, then suddenly weaker. Finally the light went out of his eyes and he slumped forward. But Bashar maintained the pressure on the garrotte for another minute, just to make sure, before he removed the cord.

'Leave him there,' Saadi hissed, turning away and heading towards the staircase.

Volgograd, Russia

The two Americans woke early, stiff and cold. They'd barely slept and both were feeling the strain. They climbed out of their uncomfortable and unauthorized overnight accommodation back on to the platform, pulling their cases behind them. They could hear the sounds of the station coming to life, and the last thing they wanted was to find their carriage shunted onto a siding or, worse, hitched to a locomotive and taken off to Moscow or Kiev or somewhere.

They were determined to linger in Volgograd no

longer than was necessary but, as Wilson checked the departure boards, he realized they were not going anywhere soon, because almost all the trains were heading the wrong way. The first three were destined for Saratov, Perm and Brest respectively, which meant they were heading north, back into the heart of Russia.

'OK,' Wilson muttered, craning his neck to check the boards again, 'there's no point in waiting for the Astrakhan train because it doesn't leave for nearly twelve hours, and I don't want to hang around here that long. We could take the Groznyy train at four, but I think we'll head the other way. We'll take the five o'clock to Adler.'

'Where the hell's that?' Dawson asked.

'On the eastern shore of the Black Sea, just south of Sochi,' Wilson replied. 'It's closer to the Turkish border than either Astrakhan or Groznyy.'

'That still leaves us with eight or nine hours to kill.'

Wilson looked around him before replying. 'What we don't do is hang about this damned station all day. We'll go find a coffee shop, or whatever this place has to keep passengers from starving to death. We'll grab a quick breakfast and use their bathroom to wash up. Then we'll check into a hotel real close to the station and try to get some sleep. And this afternoon we'll come back here and catch that train.'

Kondal, Russia

Yuri Borisov seemed to have fallen apart. The money the Americans had paid him was gone, with no hope of its ever being recovered. He had colluded in the theft of a highly classified weapon and was, by implication if not in fact, an accessory to two murders. He'd been caught by the police carrying an unlicensed firearm. He had a broken arm and two hands that were almost useless. Finally, and of no importance whatsoever, his car was a total write-off. To say he was vulnerable was a grotesque understatement, and Litvinoff planned to get as much as he could out of the plant administrator before he recovered his senses.

'We might be able to do a deal,' the investigator suggested, though he had no intention of keeping his word. That one million dollars had seemed so close he had almost been able to smell it. All his career he'd been hoping for a score that big, one he could use to get himself and his wife out of Russia for good, with enough money to live comfortably for the rest of their lives. When he'd opened the passbook he'd realized that he finally held the key to their new life in his hands. His disappointment had been even greater than Borisov's – but Litvinoff was angry as well.

'Tell me exactly what happened,' he urged, his voice soft and persuasive, 'and we'll try to work something out.'

Borisov was slumped in the chair, his head in his hands, trying desperately to think of some way – any way – that he could talk his way out of this mess. He had, he now realized, only two options: he could tell the unvarnished truth, which at best would virtually guarantee he'd never leave prison for the rest of his life, or he could give Litvinoff a version of it that incriminated him as little as possible. He knew there would be a full-scale inquiry at Zarechnyy, so whatever he said now had to cover the facts. It wasn't a difficult choice.

'As you know,' he began, 'I'm an administrator at PO Start. A few weeks ago I became suspicious about the conduct of two of our technicians.'

'Their names, and how did they arouse your suspicions?'

'Boris Devenko and Alexei Nabov. They were asking questions about the secure-storage facilities, obviously trying to find which building held certain pieces of equipment.'

'What equipment?' For a moment Borisov didn't answer, and Litvinoff looked up from his notebook. 'What equipment?' he repeated.

'I have a problem here,' Borisov said, something of an understatement in the circumstances. 'I can't be specific without knowing your security clearance, and seeing your identification.'

'You're in no position to start making demands, Borisov,' Litvinoff snarled.

'I don't have a choice. This information is highly classified, and I could get into very serious trouble if I reveal it to anyone without the proper clearance.'

'You're *already* in very serious trouble,' Litvinoff pointed out.

'I know, but still I can say nothing.'

'Very well.' The investigator pulled out a small leather wallet and flipped it open on the table between them. Borisov recognized the distinctive shield immediately – FSB officers were not infrequent visitors to Zarechnyy – and for the first time he learned that he was talking to Vaslav Litvinoff, a senior field investigator. He nodded, closed the wallet and pushed it back across the table.

'I'll ask you again. What equipment were they looking for?'

'Portable nuclear weapons,' Borisov replied, and Litvinoff dropped his pen.

Al-Shahrood Stables, Ad Dahnā, Saudi Arabia

Saadi's men had cleared the house. They'd found another seven servants – two Filipinos and the rest Pakistanis – plus four members of the wealthy Arab family that owned the stables. None had resisted, because when each was kicked awake they found themselves facing at least one Kalashnikov assault rifle.

And any faint stirrings of resistance evaporated the moment they were all assembled in the hall, hands bound behind their backs and adhesive tape stuck over their mouths, and saw the body of the young manservant dumped face-down on the floor, a small pool of urine discolouring the marble tiles by his groin.

Saadi stepped off the bottom tread of the staircase – he'd been making a final check upstairs – and walked across to join Massood in front of their terrified prisoners.

'Get the digger,' he ordered, 'and take that with you.' He pointed at the corpse.

Saadi nodded to Bashar, and the tall Arab led the way towards the rear door of the farmhouse, the other men herding the captives behind him. Outside, he could hear the diesel engine of the Bobcat starting, the sound fading as Massood drove it past the house towards the open desert lying to the north of the stables.

The Bobcat was a single-seat digger, smaller than an average car, its steel bucket supported by two hydraulic arms on either side of the driver's compartment. Though he had never handled one before, Massood had no difficulty in controlling the small vehicle. He drove on past the stable block, found the track that had been marked on their maps, and turned the digger to follow it. Some hundred yards further on, the grassed fields gave way to open desert, but he continued for yet another hundred yards before turning off the track, the Bobcat bouncing roughly as it hit the uneven dunes.

He stopped the machine and checked the terrain in front of him by the light of the Bobcat's headlamps, now supplemented by the rising sun. The sand was fairly level and relatively firm, so the digger's fat tyres hardly sank in at all. It was good enough, Massood thought. He raised the bucket, the Filipino's body tumbling out. Then he turned the machine, dropped the bucket and dug the lower edge into the sand, powering the Bobcat forward to move as much as possible. He lifted the hydraulic arms, drove the digger a few feet to one side and emptied the contents of the bucket. Then he backed up and repeated the operation, the hole already beginning to take shape.

Saadi stood by the edge of the track and watched. Behind him, Bashar and the other men had formed a loose ring around their fifteen prisoners – they had found four staff asleep in the stable block – and were watching the thirteen bound men and two women carefully.

After twenty minutes Massood had excavated a pit

about fifteen feet long, ten feet wide and eight feet deep. He decided it was adequate, then manoeuvred the digger around the hole until the vehicle was positioned on the uphill side, behind the heap of sand he'd dug out.

Saadi walked forward and looked down. The width and length were fine. He would have preferred it a little deeper, but time was passing and they still had a lot to do. He turned and issued a crisp order to the men guarding the prisoners. Intimidated by the threat of the Kalashnikovs, the captives walked over to the hole in single file and lined up along the longest edge of the pit.

It was only then – in that long moment of silence before the shooting started – that the appalling reality of their situation finally dawned on them. Their captors moved to stand in two groups, one at either end of the hole, their assault rifles trained on the prisoners.

The quickest way to finish the job would have been to use the Kalashnikovs, but over the years Saadi had developed a taste for a more personal kind of execution.

He stepped behind the first of the bound men and without haste drew a Browning Hi-Power semi-automatic pistol from a holster under his *gellabbiya*. He extracted a suppressor from his pocket and attached it to the end of the barrel. Then he racked back the slide and released it to chamber a round, the sound of the mechanism loud and unmistakable in the silence.

'Kneel down,' Saadi ordered, not the faintest trace of emotion in his voice. As the Pakistani servant obeyed him, he aimed the pistol at the back of the man's head and without hesitation pulled the trigger. The weapon coughed once. The nine-millimetre copper-jacketed bullet smashed into the man's skull, bored straight through his brain, and emerged in a fountain of blood through his left eye. His instantly lifeless body flopped forward, tumbling into the pit.

Saadi glanced down at the corpse, then stepped across to the next man. 'Kneel down,' he instructed, but the man shook his head in a pathetic display of defiance. Saadi shrugged indifferently, took a half-step back, raised the pistol and shot his victim where he stood.

As the second body fell forward, a man at the other end of the line broke ranks and began running away, heading straight out into the desert. He made less than twenty feet before two of the Kalashnikovs fired, four bullets ripping through his torso and sending him screaming to the ground, his body arching and twisting in agony.

Saadi made no move to administer a *coup de grâce*, and neither did anyone else. Instead, he raised his voice slightly. 'If you try to run, you'll die slowly and very painfully. If you stand still, it will be quick and it won't hurt. But you *are* all going to die.'

The stable's owner was the tenth man Saadi reached, and he turned to face his executioner as the body of the man beside him fell into the open grave. He had managed to work loose part of the tape covering his mouth, and as Saadi raised the pistol he looked straight into his eyes and uttered a single word: 'Why?'

'You don't need to know,' Saadi replied, and squeezed the trigger.

The man who'd run was still alive by the time Saadi reached the end of the line. He walked over and watched his agonized writhing for a few moments, then aimed

the Browning and shot him through the head. At a nodded instruction, two of his men picked up the body and
tossed it on top of the others. Another couple of his men
swung the corpse of the Filipino manservant into the hole
as well. Saadi approached the edge of the grave and
looked down in satisfaction, even as Massood started the
Bobcat to begin filling the hole.

Fifteen minutes after the last execution, Massood swung
the digger onto the track and headed back towards the
farmhouse. Before he left the site, Saadi carefully checked
that no traces were visible. The terrain looked virtually
the same as when they'd arrived and the bodies, he hoped,
were buried deep enough not to attract scavengers.

In the stables, a dozen or so jittery horses looked out
of their stalls as the men walked through the central yard.
Saadi stopped and looked round. 'Find it,' he called, and
moments later Bashar gestured to him.

From a stall in one corner, the head of a large chest-
nut horse was peering out inquisitively, showing no fear
of the new arrivals. Bashar pointed to the wall beside the
split stable door, where an ornamental plaque had been
screwed. It bore a single word: 'Shaf'.

Chapter Six

Their hotel was located on the outskirts of Old Cairo. It offered them a view of the Sphinx and the pyramids of the Giza Plateau lying on the other side of the Nile – at least from one of the corridor windows on the top floor, if you leant out far enough – though that was pretty much its only redeeming feature. But the two Americans weren't bothered. They were used to accommodation of almost every type and standard, and they were only staying in Cairo until Dawson and Wilson arrived with the weapon. Then they'd head for the United Arab Emirates, but this time travelling in style.

O'Hagan picked a cyber café right in the centre of Cairo, and sat down at the keyboard while Petrucci ordered coffee. The system unit was on the table beside the monitor, and had a couple of USB sockets below the DVD drive. That was exactly what O'Hagan had been hoping for.

He logged on to the Internet and accessed mail2web. com, typed his email address and password, and pressed 'Enter'. The connection was broadband, and the first messages appeared in seconds. There were only half a dozen in all, four of which he deleted immediately. He then opened the first of the remaining two, and noted its contents with satisfaction.

He looked up to ensure that Petrucci was still distracting the waiter's attention, then reached into the breast pocket of his shirt. He pulled out a memory stick and swiftly slotted it into one of the USB sockets.

He first copied the open email message onto the memory stick, then clicked 'Reply' and rapidly typed an answer. Again checking he was unobserved, he attached three image files from the USB stick to the email and clicked 'Send'. The images were small and the message only took a few moments to be transmitted. Then he opened the second message, and also copied that onto the memory stick.

O'Hagan extracted the USB device and nodded to his companion. Petrucci finally chose a couple of cakes, and let the waiter carry them over to the workstation. By that time, the flash drive was back in O'Hagan's pocket, and he was busily reading the headlines on CNN.

British Embassy, Government Avenue, Manama, Bahrain

'Fuck a duck,' Julian Caxton muttered, as Evans finished explaining why Tariq Mazen had requested their meeting.

The expletive was hardly characteristic, for Caxton was a devout Christian who rarely raised his eyebrows, let alone his voice. To Evans and his fellow SIS officers in Bahrain he appeared an anachronism, a throwback to the older, more genteel days of the service. An old-fashioned gentleman in a world that had largely forgotten what the very word was supposed to mean.

'How certain is Mazen about this?' Carole-Anne Jackson asked, frowning.

'He's not,' Evans said. 'That's the trouble. His only witness is a Filipino hospital cleaner, and Mazen doesn't even know his real name.'

'I don't believe it,' Caxton said firmly. 'I know bin Laden has sympathizers in Bahrain and, let's face it, he's got support all over the Middle East, but I simply don't think he'd have the unmitigated gall' – that was more like Caxton; Evans would have said 'sheer balls', or worse – 'to come here for medical treatment.'

'I agree it's not likely, but perhaps he had no alternative,' Evans replied. 'If it *is* bin Laden, his kidney complaint might now be so serious that, without dialysis or a transplant, he'll die within just days or weeks. If that's the case, he might be prepared to take the risk because he literally has nothing left to lose.'

'And kidney dialysis isn't something he could arrange in the Hindu Kush or the mountains of Pakistan,' Jackson added. 'He'd need a very well-equipped clinic.'

'It's still difficult to believe.' Caxton shook his head. 'Despite being *persona non grata* in Saudi, I would have expected him to go there, rather than Bahrain.'

'That,' Evans said, 'may be exactly why he chose to come here, because he may have predicted that nobody would ever expect him to turn up in a place like this. Let's face it, bin Laden has enough money to convince almost any doctor that it's worth bending the rules to give him the treatment he needs, and then persuade him to keep his mouth shut afterwards.'

Carole-Anne Jackson was nodding, and even Caxton now looked less incredulous.

'Perhaps you're right. The question, I suppose, is what we should do about it. What do you suggest, Bill?'

'We have to check out this Sheikh Rashid, and that's not going to be easy. Mazen has already tried through the hospital administration and got nowhere. He has no other sources he can tap and he's reluctant to involve the police in case it's all a big mistake. Bursting into the hospital with a SWAT team, if the target really *is* an important Arab sheikh, would be a very good way to lose goodwill and attract some extremely unwelcome attention. Mazen thinks, and I agree with him, that the only way to be certain about this man's identity is to get somebody onto the ward with a camera.

'The problem, I suppose, is who gets to carry the Kodak. We're not supposed to be active here, and Vaux-hall Cross wouldn't be too impressed if one of us got arrested for crashing Sheikh Rashid's party. I suggest we tell London what we know and let them decide what to do. That way, if we're ordered to investigate and the shit hits the fan, at least we've got ourselves top cover.'

Caxton looked somewhat pained at Evans's turn of phrase. 'Carole?' he asked.

'I agree with Bill. I think you should tell London and wait for a direct instruction. If it was my problem, I'd let Langley make the decision for me.'

'Right,' Caxton said. 'I'll talk to Vauxhall Cross. Bill, keep Mazen in the loop, and if you hear anything else about this Sheikh Rashid make sure I'm the first to know about it.'

Al-Shahrood Stables, Ad Dahnā, Saudi Arabia

Saadi started one of the farm Range Rovers and drove it into the courtyard. Massood had already loaded the Bobcat on the trailer and was inside the stable office, sorting out the documentation for the journey to Dubai. Bashar was waiting by Shaf's stall, ready to open the door once the horsebox was safely in position. The stables owned half a dozen specialized trailers, and Saadi's men were now manhandling the biggest one they'd found into the courtyard. Saadi carefully man-oeuvred the big four-wheel-drive vehicle, and moments later the horsebox was attached to the towing hitch.

The Al-Shahrood horsebox would more properly be called a horse transporter. It was a large vehicle, sup-ported by three pairs of wheels, with a separate storage compartment at the front for saddles, boots, helmets, whips and everything else that might be needed during a race meeting. Behind was the equine passenger's accommodation – though in fact it could carry two horses, side-by-side, with a central partition separating them – and also included a storage area for hay and a large water tank supplying a steel drinking trough.

Saadi supervised the loading of the bales, each requir-ing two men to carry it, and they were careful to ensure that the opened ends were placed against the sides of the trailer, just in case anyone did inspect their cargo. When they'd finished that, Saadi dropped the steel shut-ter that screened off the storage area – the last thing he wanted was for the horse to eat its way through the hay and expose the packages concealed inside.

He ordered one of his men to fill the water-supply tank and bring in more hay to ensure that Shaf would become neither thirsty nor hungry on the journey. Personally, he cared not one jot for the horse's comfort, health or welfare, but he didn't want a ton or so of angry thoroughbred to try kicking its way out of the trailer when they got a few hours down the road.

And, besides, the water tank was the ideal place to secrete the three Kalashnikov AK47 assault rifles and three pistols they would be taking with them. Saadi had a watertight black rubber bag that he would stash them in well before they reached the airport.

He ordered portable fencing to be erected between the stable and the transporter but needn't have bothered: without fuss Shaf walked up into the trailer and immediately began eating the hay. Bashar carefully secured the animal's bridle, stepped out of the transporter and closed the rear door.

'You found everything?' Saadi asked Massood, more a statement than a question.

'Yes. All the documentation was ready, including the tickets and passports. Four people were scheduled to accompany the horse.'

'We'll have to explain that one was taken ill. Did you reschedule the flight?'

'Yes, exactly as you instructed.'

'Excellent. Then we're ready to go.'

Massood climbed into the passenger seat of the Range Rover while Bashar made himself comfortable in the back. Saadi took a final look around the vehicle, checking the coupling and the rear door, then climbed in and drove out of the courtyard, heading towards the house. When he reached the driveway he stopped and all three got out.

The other seven men were standing beside their own vehicles. Saadi walked across and, as if by common consent, they clustered around him. He solemnly embraced each of them – for he knew they would never see him alive again – then stood back and bowed his head.

'Ma'assalama, my friends,' Saadi murmured solemnly. 'Go in peace.'

For a moment nobody responded, then one man took a step forward, as if acting as a spokesman for his comrades. *'Assalamu alaikum wa rahmatulahi wa barakatuhu.'*

'Walaikum assalam,' Saadi replied formally. And then, louder: *'Abdu-baha.'*

His seven companions then walked back to their vehicles, and within minutes all four jeeps had departed. Saadi's instructions had been most specific: the Bobcat and trailer were to be returned to the hire company; the weapons, magazines and ammunition would be buried in a location specified by the mission planners, being far too valuable to simply discard; and they were to return the four-by-fours to the various companies from which they'd been hired.

Saadi, Massood and Bashar were faced with the longest journey, but it was still early morning and he hoped they'd complete the first leg, two hundred kilometres back to Buraydah, by noon and the second leg, to Riyadh Airport – which meant another four hundred kilometres – by late afternoon. They were booked on a flight to Dubai that same evening, and Saadi had every intention of catching it.

Kondal, Russia

Litvinoff's attitude had changed completely. He'd suspected that the administrator was involved in some kind of treachery – serious enough in itself to warrant a full investigation – but Borisov's revelation that a suitcase nuclear bomb had been spirited out of Zarechnyy had changed everything. The investigation of the plant administrator could wait. Litvinoff's first priority was to track down the missing weapon.

'These two Americans,' he demanded, 'where did you meet them?'

'I saw them only once, when I followed Devenko and Nabov to their meeting. It was there one of the Americans gave me the bank passbook. They'd already agreed, through Nabov, to pay me the money to buy my silence.'

That simply didn't ring true, and Litvinoff guessed that Borisov had been much more deeply involved than he was admitting. If he had literally stumbled upon the plot to steal the weapon, the Americans would probably have just killed him out of hand – a far more effective way of ensuring his silence than buying him off. And, anyway, the Swiss account would have taken time to set up. Borisov had to have been an integral part of the conspiracy from the beginning. Once the immediate situation had been resolved, Litvinoff would dig deeper, until he found the truth.

'How were these Americans going to get out of Russia?'

'They told me they would be driving the truck straight down to the Turkish border at Leninakan, in

Azerbaijan, but I don't know if that's what they really intended to do.'

'If that's what they told you,' Litvinoff snorted, 'you can be quite certain that's the only route we needn't bother checking. They're definitely going to take another way out. Did they say anything else to you?'

When Borisov shook his head, Litvinoff pressed a buzzer on the wall. The door opened and a police officer escorted the prisoner back to his cell. Once he again had the room to himself. The investigator opened up a map of south-western Russia, and began studying it closely.

Central Intelligence Agency Headquarters, Langley, Virginia

'Just before noon last Friday,' David Stevenson began, 'an eighteen-year-old Arab boy named Saadallah Assad walked into the Al-Hamidieh *souk* in the centre of Damascus and blew himself up.' Stevenson was a short, slightly overweight – he normally described himself as 'undertall' – fair-haired desk jockey, and was one of the case officers on the Operations staff, with particular responsibility for the Middle East.

Five men looked back at him with varying degrees of interest, though only four of them were being tasked. The fifth man, sitting at the far end of the table, was John Westwood, the Company Head of Espionage, who was present purely as an observer.

'Initial reports from the local news media, and from our own people in Syria, suggest that he used around three kilos of plastic, probably C4, triggered by a hand-held detonator. This estimate has been confirmed by the

Syrian intelligence service, the *Idarat al-Mukhabarat al-Jawiyya*, following its own analysis.

'Nineteen people died immediately, eight of whom were American tourists. The rest were Syrian nationals, three of whom have yet to be formally identified simply because there's virtually nothing left of them *to* identify. Seven others suffered such severe wounds that they died later, and there are nearly ninety victims still hospitalized in Damascus, receiving treatment for everything from burns to head injuries caused by flying debris. It's likely that some of these will also die, so the death toll could rise to around thirty. That makes it one of the most destructive solo suicide bomber attacks ever.'

He paused to observe their reactions, then continued. 'The damage to the *souk* was considerable. The blast blew out part of a wall on one side, causing a major collapse. Half the *souk*'s been closed while repairs are carried out, and it will take at least a month before it reopens.'

He glanced at his notes. 'A videotape was received at the Al-Jazeera television station in Qatar. On it was a fairly typical pre-attack speech delivered by the suicide bomber. He was sitting in front of a defaced Syrian flag, holding a copy of the *Qur'án* and claimed that he was carrying out the attack in support of the *Jamiat Al-Ikhwan Al-Muslimun* – the Society of Muslim Brothers or Muslim Brotherhood.

'To remind you, that's an old organization and an ideological forerunner of Al-Qaeda. It reached the height of its power at the end of the seventies, but it was virtually destroyed on the instructions of President Hafez Assad. In 1982 he ordered the Syrian army to shell the Brotherhood's stronghold at Hama, roughly halfway between Aleppo and Damascus. The organization was outnumbered and outgunned and by the end of the action, at least ten thousand – some estimates suggest twenty thousand – members of the Brotherhood, as well as a lot of camp-followers and innocent civilians, lay dead, and virtually all those that survived finished up rotting in jail. That purged the Brotherhood within Syria, but the appalling brutality of the government's response virtually ensured that the organization would endure, albeit in a shadowy form.'

By now he had their full attention.

'Once the tape was broadcast, the Syrian authorities investigated Assad immediately. Like a lot of the *shuhada* – the Muslims refer to suicide bombers as "martyrs", the singular being *shahid* – he came from a good family, and was apparently well liked and respected, with no strong political leanings. His family insisted that they had no prior knowledge of his intentions. It's worth explaining a little about suicide bombers. First of all, they're volunteers. As far as I'm aware, nobody has ever been coerced into acting as a *shahid*. For some it's a quick route to instant immortality. As you know, according to a verse in the *Qur'án*, a martyr never dies—'

'If I'm not mistaken, the *Qur'án* also says that you should not take life,' John Baxter interjected. He was a short, slim, dark-haired junior agent, sitting immediately on Westwood's right.

'That's quite true, but irrelevant. The *Qur'án*, like all religious tracts, can be "interpreted" to suit whatever purpose some fanatic requires. For a *shahid*, the usual interpretation is that he will immediately enter paradise, meet the Prophet Muhammad, be in the presence of Allah, and spend the rest of eternity with the *chouriyat*, the seventy-two heavenly virgins. As a bonus, the *shahid*'s immediate family can look forward to enjoying the same fringe benefits in the future.'

'Not so much life insurance as a kind of a death insurance policy?' Baxter suggested.

'That's one way of looking at it, I guess. The *shahid*'s families are usually proud of them, and of what they've done, and their standing in their local community is greatly enhanced. It's considered a religious obligation to admire and honour the family of a *shahid*. They even get paid for it.'

'Jesus,' Baxter muttered. 'You mean they do it for money?'

'Absolutely not.' Stevenson shook his head. 'One of the most important elements in becoming a *shahid* is *niyya* – purity of motive – the concept of imposing the will of Allah. No true *shahid* would ever act out of any kind of self-interest or personal glory. The payments their families receive are just intended to provide support for the loss of a breadwinner, not as a reward for what he has done.'

'Who pays them?' asked Grant Hutchings. He was tall, blond, with a face just the wrong side of being handsome and was the senior agent being briefed. He had a reputation within the Company for clear thinking, direct action and a very low bullshit-tolerance threshold. This latter characteristic was the reason why, at the age of forty-three, his career was generally considered to be over. Everyone knew that to reach the higher echelons at Langley, you didn't merely have to tolerate bullshit:

you had to be adept at shovelling large quantities of it around.

'For the Palestinian bombers who attack Israeli targets – and they're the most common – the funds come mainly from the Gulf States, particularly Saudi Arabia. Saddam Hussein created a fund as well, but obviously he's no longer making payments.'

'But why do they – the *shuhada* I mean – do it?' Baxter asked.

'That's a simple question with a complex answer,' Stevenson replied. 'Most of the analytical work has been done in Israel, so doesn't apply here, but there the *shahid* is acting, as he sees it, to rid his legitimate homeland of its Jewish invaders. That's the general reason for the attack, but most *shuhada* also have a second, more specific, reason for carrying out their mission, usually involving something like a desire to exact revenge for the death of a close friend. In the case of the Palestinians, there's also the feeling that the suicide bomb is the only viable weapon they possess. And this is a weapon that's extremely difficult to detect or counter. There's also fear and the moral element.'

'And that means what, exactly?' Hutchings demanded.

'Fear, because almost anyone, anywhere, at any time, could turn out to be a *shahid*. Fear that the man standing next to you at the railway station, or at the bus stop or in the elevator or in the queue at the shop, could have a belt of TNT wrapped around his waist, and might choose this very moment to pull the trigger. Can you imagine the constant strain of living like that, day after day? For the planners in Hamas and Hezbollah, striking fear into the hearts of the Jewish population is just as important as the deaths caused by the attacks.'

Stevenson took a sip of water, then continued. 'And in a sense the *shuhada* manage to seize the moral high ground as well. Their victims are to some extent of secondary importance, what you might almost call collateral damage, but the *shuhada* themselves are making the ultimate sacrifice, being forced to take their own lives because of the immoral acts of their perceived enemies. A suicide bomber achieves a kind of nobility simply because of his own sacrifice.'

'We don't need to get too deep into this aspect, David,' John Westwood interrupted.

'Agreed, sir. Well,' Stevenson went on, 'this kind of attack is very common in the present political climate, though Damascus is a somewhat unusual target. The Syrians are still puzzled by Assad's claim to be acting on behalf of the Muslim Brotherhood, because in that country the organization is virtually extinct. But they found reading material in Assad's rooms that had clearly been inspired by the Brotherhood, so they've concluded that the motive he claimed was probably genuine.'

Again he paused to ensure he had their full attention. 'You're here because of two unique aspects of this particular attack. To go back a step, the Palestinian suicide bombers are normally sent out by dispatchers who brief them carefully on their target, the route they must take, and how to initiate the detonation. The dispatchers will also make a videotape featuring the *shahid*, to release after the bombing. Frequently they can be heard acting as prompters, or asking questions to produce the answers they want the rest of the world to hear. Sometimes they themselves will even feature on the video, masked and anonymous of course, and interview the *shahid*. On Assad's tape, there are no such prompts, no questions, no hint of an interview. He just reads out a short speech, obviously memorized.'

'So?' Hutchings asked.

'We got a first-generation copy of the tape from Al-Jazeera, and our techies here have been analysing it. They were looking for the usual stuff – clues to identify where it was made, extraneous sounds and so on – but nothing showed up until right at the very end of the tape, in the last second and a half, to be exact, and I'll come to that in a moment.

'The technicians also deduced that Assad wasn't wearing a microphone, or speaking into one somewhere out of shot. They believe that the mike being used was the one built into the video camera itself, which is important for two reasons. First, it suggests this was an amateur or at least a low-budget operation, because the professional dispatchers usually supply either a clip-on mike or one on a stand in front of the *shahid*. They want the bomber's message to be clearly heard and understood.

'The second point is an extraneous sound they detected. Just before the video ends there's a very faint noise on the soundtrack. Before enhancement, it sounds like a cough. Once the techies had cleaned the tape and amplified it, they realized it was actually a single word, spoken very quietly. The word is "good", and the voice that's speaking it is an adult male – most likely American, but just possibly Canadian.'

British Airways Flight BA107

Paul Richter sat in only moderate discomfort in the economy section of the Boeing 777, contemplating the remainder of the seven-hour direct flight to Dubai without any particular degree of enthusiasm.

He didn't know quite what to make of Salah Khatid's information. He had no doubt that the Arab was accurately reporting what he'd heard, but there was frankly too little data to go on for him to do anything about it. He would just have to keep his eyes open. But there had been something he could do about Holden's alleged premonitions. Richter had spent the previous afternoon reading through half a dozen files he'd requested from the Registry. And what he'd read in them had, frankly, surprised him.

Three of the files were unclassified, and had originated from the American Defense Intelligence Agency. They dated from the seventies and weren't directly relevant to his tasking, but still provided some useful background information. The first was DST-1810S-387–75 entitled 'Soviet and Czechoslovakian Parapsychology Research'; the second was ST-CS-01–169–72, 'Controlled Offensive Behavior'; and the third DST-1810S-074–76, 'Biological Effects of Electromagnetic Radiation (Radiowaves and Microwaves) – Eurasian Communist Countries'.

He'd also read three files classified 'Secret' that had originated at Vauxhall Cross. All dealt with an American remote-viewing project primarily based at Fort Meade in Maryland, at first called Star Gate, then Center Lane and finally Sun Streak, before being shut down. The author of the file suggested that the 'shutdown' had been more cosmetic than real, designed to divert government and media attention away from the programme while its research continued in a covert environment, supported by 'black' funding. The project had possessed an operational wing, known as Grill Flame, which had been used by American intelligence for active espionage against the then Soviet Union.

Richter had read it all thoroughly, and it had sounded like science fiction – and bad science fiction at that. What surprised him most was how much money the Americans had poured into the project over the years. They'd actually *admitted* to spending in excess of twenty million dollars, which suggested that the actual budget had probably been a hell of a lot higher.

After that, he'd read a fourth pink file, classified Top Secret and bearing a WNINTEL caveat, and that one had surprised him even more. Like the other three, it had been prepared by analysts at SIS, and it detailed what little was known about 'Black Box', the Western codename for a top-secret Russian psychic research unit located a few miles from St Petersburg.

The details were sketchy, to say the least, and it looked to Richter as if the data contained in the file had been acquired from somebody who had visited or worked at the target establishment only occasionally. HUMINT was usually the most accurate and reliable information source, but obviously more or less constant access was needed to produce comprehensive results. But even the incomplete picture obtained by SIS showed that the Russians had been spending prodigious sums of money – the file suggested an *annual* budget greater than the total the Americans had spent over a ten-year period – in wide-ranging investigations and experimentation in various fields of paranormal activity.

The other obvious difference was that the US effort had been primarily directed towards remote viewing – what might be termed psychic spying – while the Russian research seemed to have been offensive. They had experimented with influencing at a distance, trying to get inside the minds of their enemies, studied various types of radiation to manipulate entire populations, and ultimately investigated psychic assassinations. They'd tried methods intended to stop the hearts of their targets; to create blood clots to cause strokes; to rupture capillary vessels inside the brain, and so induce severe depression that might lead to suicide.

Their most ambitious project had been nicknamed 'Woodpecker' by American intelligence analysts. Starting in 1976 and continuing until the collapse of the Soviet Union, seven huge radio transmitters based near Kiev, and initially powered by the ill-fated Chernobyl nuclear reactor in the Ukraine, emitted a ten-Hertz pulse at frequencies of between 3.26MHz and 17.54MHz and with an estimated peak power of around fourteen *million* watts. These signals were beamed directly at the populations of Western Europe, North America, Australia and the Middle East, and were capable of penetrating virtually anything from reinforced concrete bunkers to the huge depth of water above a submerged submarine.

It was the world's largest ever experiment in psychotronics, using ELF-modulated signals. The Russians had discovered that exposure to certain radiated frequencies could produce effects ranging from depression to aggression. They'd also found that prolonged exposure to such signals could cause permanent changes in the brain, by physically altering the neural connections. An American medical expert later estimated that 'Woodpecker' could have caused neurological changes in up to thirty per cent of the target populations.

If the American studies had sounded like science fiction, the Russian experimentation bordered on fantasy. But Richter couldn't dismiss the money. Between them, the world's only two superpowers had spent an absolute *minimum* of a quarter of a billion dollars, over a ten-year period, on investigations into the kind of thing that even the most hysterical and irresponsible elements of the British tabloid press routinely dismissed as nonsense.

Saratov, Russia

The police reached the dockside that afternoon and began questioning the workers.

Once he'd finished interrogating Borisov, Litvinoff had ordered checkpoints to be set up on all the roads between Kondal and Rostov, and telephone enquiries had been made to all trucking companies in the area. The latter course of action produced results almost immediately, when a small transport company in Atkarsk reported that a truck they'd rented to someone called Nabov had been found empty and apparently abandoned in a lorry park just a day later, with the keys still in the ignition.

The company manager assumed Nabov must have changed his mind, and simply had the lorry brought back to his yard. The vehicle was now being pored over by police and forensic scientists.

Luckily for Litvinoff, the company had taken mileage readings both before the truck was driven away, and again after it had been found. This at least told the FSB man exactly how far the vehicle had travelled while still in Nabov's custody. That provided him with the dimensions of a search area, which included Saratov, while the police and other FSB investigators, hastily called in by Litvinoff to assist in what now amounted to a full-scale inquiry, tried to find whatever alternative form of transport the Americans had decided to use.

The river Volga was an obvious choice, particularly as Borisov claimed that the weapon was hidden inside a large and heavy crate. That meant either another truck or something else big enough to handle it, like a barge or aircraft, for example.

Litvinoff knew that getting the crate onto an aircraft, or even a train, would have meant filling in a whole sheaf of forms, so he guessed that they'd either obtained another lorry, or transferred the cargo to a barge.

It didn't take the police long to discover that two men, non-Russians but speaking the language fluently, had driven to the port in a lorry. A large wooden crate had been transferred from the back of the vehicle to the cargo hold of a barge waiting to depart for Volgograd.

'Two men? You're sure?' Litvinoff asked the dock worker who had operated the forklift truck.

The man nodded. 'I didn't see inside the cab of the truck, but only two men got out,' he insisted.

Litvinoff made a note to search the main road, and

every side road too, between Kondal and Saratov. If only two men had been in the lorry when it arrived, it seemed likely that the pair of Russian technicians had outlived their usefulness. They'd probably been killed by the Americans and their bodies dumped.

He would set the wheels in motion for a search, using the local police force, but for the moment finding the two technicians, whether dead or alive, was of secondary importance. Finding the barge, and the crate it was carrying, was very much his first priority.

Central Intelligence Agency Headquarters, Langley, Virginia

Stevenson looked at the five men, stares of disbelief imprinted firmly on their faces.

'American?' Westwood echoed.

'That's what the techies reported, sir. They're ninety per cent certain that when Assad made his videotape, there was an American behind the camera. They further deduced that the American speaks, or at least understands, Arabic, because he says "good" immediately after Assad has finished speaking. The logical conclusion is that he was pleased with the boy's performance, and muttered "good" without thinking. His comment wouldn't have been audible to anyone else, but the camera's mike just managed to pick it up. A camcorder's microphone points forward to record whatever the camera is filming, so it's not particularly sensitive to noises from behind, unless those sounds are loud or in the very near vicinity. That suggests the American was probably the man filming Assad's statement.'

Hutchings opened his mouth to speak, but Westwood beat him to it.

'Why the hell would some American be filming the last words of a Syrian suicide bomber who's just about to kill himself in support of a political group that's been effectively non-existent for a quarter of a century?'

'Sir, I have not the slightest idea, and neither has anyone else. That's one reason for organizing this operation. The second noteworthy thing about this attack,' he went on, 'is that just a week before, a middle-aged Englishman named James Holden walked into the British Embassy in Dubai and described it in considerable detail.

'He painted a fairly accurate word-picture of Saadallah Assad, and even got his name pretty much right. The only thing he didn't know was exactly where and when the attack was going to take place. And he said that the reason he didn't know these two crucial pieces of information was that he had actually dreamt the whole thing.'

British Embassy, Government Avenue, Manama, Bahrain

'Bill,' said Caxton as he strode into Evans's office, 'I've just heard from Vauxhall Cross. They're convinced this is a case of mistaken identity, no matter what Mazen's source claims. The latest intelligence suggests that bin Laden is still holed up somewhere in northern Pakistan, and London simply doesn't believe he could have got all the way to Bahrain without somebody seeing or hearing something.'

'So what do they want us to do now? Sit on our arses and pretend that nobody saw anything? We can't just ignore a report like this, no matter what some geek analyst sitting thousands of miles away at a workstation in London might think.'

'If you'd just let me finish, Bill,' Caxton said mildly. 'Vauxhall Cross don't want *us* to investigate – their view is that nobody from this embassy should get involved overtly – but they do want the report followed up.'

'So how—'

'Bill, just be quiet and listen. There's somebody on his way out to Dubai right now, to investigate some other unrelated matter. He's going to be retasked to come to Bahrain instead, and should be arriving here sometime tomorrow morning. I'd like you to act as his liaison officer, so go and meet him at the airport. Give him a full briefing and any help he needs, and with luck we should be able to finish this thing no later than Thursday.'

'That's more like it. What's his name, this SIS man?'

Caxton glanced down at the sheet of paper he was holding. 'He's called Richter,' he said. 'Paul Richter. Do you know him?'

Evans shook his head. 'Nope, never heard of him.'

Central Intelligence Agency Headquarters, Langley, Virginia

'Sounds like bullshit to me,' Grant Hutchings muttered, and John Baxter's nod suggested that he wasn't alone in this view.

To his surprise, Stevenson nodded as well. 'I agree,'

he said. 'It does sound like bullshit. Every time anything like this happens, a bunch of crazies crawl out from under their stones, and almost always they're just that – crazies. But everything we have on file about Holden suggests he's a normal, regular guy. According to the Brits in Dubai, he seemed really disturbed by his premonition. Initially they assumed he was just some crackpot and tried to get rid of him, but he wouldn't leave until they agreed to write down everything he could recall. He insisted the attack would occur within a short time, probably inside a month. The embassy staff said he seemed so upset they suggested he go see a shrink.'

Stevenson checked his notes again. 'What Holden claimed was *really* accurate, far too exact to be dismissed as mere guesswork. He said the bomber would be a Syrian national, aged under twenty, first name beginning with the letter "S" – he thought it might be "Sayeed" – and his last name was "Abbas" or "Assad". He gave a physical description that wasn't quite detailed enough for you to pick him out of a line-up, but was real close all the same.

'When he claimed the attack would be carried out on behalf of "the brothers", everyone assumed this referred to his fellow Muslims. Nobody at that stage made the connection with the *Jamiat*, of course, but even if they had, it probably wouldn't have helped. But it does show how accurate Holden's premonition was.'

'So what exactly did the British Embassy do about this report from their eyewitness-in-advance?' Hutchings demanded, in a tone edged with sarcasm.

'They filed it,' Stevenson said. 'What else could they

do? All they had was a physical description, and the possible name, of a possible suicide bomber, who might be intending to carry out an attack at an unspecified location, in an unknown country, within an indeterminate period of time. They ran a basic "anything known" check on Holden, which came back negative, so they just filed the report.'

'What about the location?' Westwood asked. 'Did Holden's dream give any hints?'

'With hindsight, sir, that was accurate too. He said the bombing would take place in a dark passage, with lots of people walking about. Not a bad description of a typical Arab *souk*.'

'Or an underpass or a railroad station or a bus terminus or pretty much anywhere else,' Hutchings added dismissively.

'Agreed, but he also described the roof as metallic and curved with lots of small holes in it. That didn't mean anything to anyone at the time, but one of the distinctive features of the Al-Hamidieh *souk* is its roof. It's metallic, semi-circular in cross-section, and the metal is pierced by thousands of small holes. And that is almost a word-for-word match with what Holden described.'

There was a short silence, before Hutchings spoke again. 'OK, maybe it's not pure eighteen-carat bullshit, but it sure sounds to me like we're getting into *X-Files* territory here. You briefed Mulder and Scully yet?'

Westwood chuckled and the other agents smiled. Stevenson shook his head. 'No, but the Fibbies are taking a keen interest in all this.'

'And what exactly is the Company planning on doing now?' Hutchings asked.

'We've been in discussion with the authorities in the UAE and the other Gulf States. You have to bear in mind that Dubai, in particular, is a very sensitive area. There's been a huge level of investment in the Emirates over the last few years. The rulers know the oil revenues are finite, and they've been spending enormous sums in diversification, building up Dubai as a financial capital, a real estate investor's paradise and a holiday destination. Even the slightest possibility that the city could be hit by a terrorist bomb frankly terrifies them. The four of you are going out there for two reasons. The first is obvious: we want you to talk to this James Holden and find out whatever you can about him.'

'Bit of a stable-door reaction, isn't it?'

'Not really,' Stevenson said. 'The Damascus bombing is history as far as we're concerned, and how Holden managed to predict it isn't what's important. What we're really interested in is what happens next, and that's the second reason for this mission. The Dubai authorities want our assistance because they've so little experience of suicide bombers and terrorist activity. You've been chosen to go precisely because you *do* have the relevant expertise. They want you to work closely with the Dubai police, to make absolutely certain that the city hasn't been targeted—'

Westwood interrupted. 'David, you still haven't explained why they're suddenly so worried. I'm not aware of any credible threat.'

'A lot depends on how you define the word "credible", sir. What's concerning them is that Holden has been back to the British Embassy again to tell them about another dream he's had. This time he says he can see a major hotel in one of the northern Gulf States getting hit by a biggie, maybe even a tactical nuke. That really *does* interest us, and it's already scared the shit out of the people in Dubai.'

Chapter Seven

The Speedbird had landed at Dubai at ten-fifteen local time the previous evening, but as far as Richter was concerned it was only quarter past six, so he knew he was going to have a bad night. He had never been very good at long-haul flying, in either direction. He some-times said, half-joking, that the only time he hadn't got jetlag on reaching America was when he travelled there by ship.

The International Airport is close to the city centre, and it was only a short ride in the beige Dubai Transport taxi to the hotel. Along Shaikh Zayed Road, Richter experienced a brief feeling of déjà vu: the area is con-sidered the commercial centre of Dubai, and the road is lined with modern skyscrapers, very reminiscent of parts of New York. Then the taxi had pulled up outside the Crowne Plaza.

The hotel was a surprise. Simpson didn't normally approve costly accommodation for his operatives and Richter had been expecting a budget or at best a middle-range hotel, but the Crowne Plaza was neither. Unfor-tunately, the air-conditioned room and comfortable bed hadn't helped. He turned off his mobile and slid between the sheets at twelve-thirty local, eight-thirty UK time, and lay there, eyes closed but with his brain still enthusiastically keeping him wide awake for over two hours. Then he'd finally dropped off, to be awoken what seemed like fifteen minutes later – but eight-thirty local time according to his alarm clock.

He'd just found himself a seat in Cappuccino's coffee shop, on the second floor, when one of the girls from the reception desk appeared beside his table. On showing her his passport, he received a white A4-size envelope in exchange. It was marked 'URGENT. Strictly Private and Confidential'. He didn't think was a good sign at all, so he waited until he'd finished his coffee before opening it.

The envelope contained a single sheet of paper with a brief message printed on one side only. Like all communications that might be intercepted or read by third parties, the text was innocuous and capable of more than one interpretation.

RICHTER, CROWNE PLAZA, DUBAI. PROCEED MANAMA, BAHRAIN, SOONEST. NEW PROCESS DEVELOPED BY PARENT COMPANY. ASSESS VIABILITY AND REPORT CONCLUSIONS. EVANS, LONDON.

It was the kind of communication that any ordinary businessman might receive, but for Richter the hidden meaning was perfectly clear. 'Parent company' meant SIS, and 'Evans' was the name of the officer who would contact him when he reached Bahrain. The rest of the message was essentially padding, but by implication the local Six office had discovered something they needed help to resolve. Or, even more likely, there was some kind of a dirty job that needed doing, and Richter had been volunteered by Vauxhall Cross, via Hammersmith, to do it.

'Bugger,' he muttered. His investigation of James Holden would just have to wait.

Al-Ramool district, Dubai

As Richter was heading for his room in the Crowne Plaza, James Holden walked into the tiny space he called his study – actually the third bedroom – sat down at the desk and turned on his computer. Until his wife left him a couple of weeks earlier, he'd invariably locked the door before switching on the power. Now there was no point in turning the key because there was nobody else in their small apartment to see what he was doing.

Holden was a long-time resident of the Middle East, and for most of his career he'd been employed as an accountant in the oil industry, but that job had ended abruptly five years earlier. He'd been reduced to working part-time as a waiter – the only job he'd been able to find. He hadn't been entitled to a pension due to the circumstances of his dismissal from the oil company – in fact, he'd been lucky to escape prosecution when details of his attempted theft of almost half a million dollars had been revealed.

So when he'd been approached just over a year earlier and invited to participate in a scheme likely to make him a great deal of money, he'd jumped at it.

Holden first opened Outlook Express and checked his inbox. He'd been expecting at least one email, and he grunted in satisfaction when he recognized the sender's name. He read through the short text, then copied the message itself and the three jpeg files attached to it into a hidden directory on his hard drive, before he looked at the pictures.

The quality wasn't as good as he'd been hoping, but they were clear enough. Holden studied each picture for a couple of minutes, then he closed the directory, deleted the original message from his inbox, and purged the 'deleted items' folder as well.

Once he'd shut down the computer, Holden sat in thought for a few minutes, then took a pen and a slightly crumpled sheet of paper and began scribbling notes, just single words and disjointed phrases, scrawled apparently at random across the page. Then he reread what he'd written, folded the paper and stuffed it into his shirt pocket.

Ten minutes later he walked away from the apartment building. He hadn't arranged an appointment, but he was sure his new friends at Al-Seef Road would be pleased enough to see him, bearing in mind what he'd told them before.

Kamyshin, Russia

Vaslav Litvinoff stood on the quayside and watched the scene unfolding in front of him. The motorized barge was almost alongside, its crew out on deck ready to throw mooring lines to the waiting stevedores. Some twenty police and FSB officers were standing in position around the berth, their Kalashnikov AK47 assault rifles trained on the approaching vessel. Beyond the barge, and in a low hover over the dark waters of the Volga, was the reason the barge's captain had been persuaded to deviate from his planned itinerary.

When Litvinoff had deduced that the stolen nuclear weapon was probably stowed in the cargo hold of the barge, he'd contacted the closest military base – Volgograd – and requested an armed helicopter. He'd explained to the base commander that he believed the barge was carrying stolen weapons – he'd not mentioned the nuclear bomb – and emphasized the vital importance of stopping it.

The officer had believed him, and had dispatched what amounted to a one-aircraft army, and every tank commander's worst nightmare; a Ka-50 Black Shark or Werewolf. The helicopter wasn't normally based at Volgograd, which is primarily a MiG-29 repair facility, and was simply passing through, but it was undeniably the ideal tool for the job.

Many helicopters look ungainly, some look sleek and luxurious, but the Black Shark is probably the only one that manages to look implacably evil. From its fifteen-metre-diameter twin main rotors to the pair of stubby wings carrying an awesome array of weapons, it looks more like something dreamt up by a Hollywood special-effects studio than a real aircraft.

This highly classified combat helicopter, designed by the Kamov Company and built by Sazykin Aviation, entered service with the Russian army back in 1995. Powered by a pair of two-thousand horsepower turboshaft engines that gave it a top speed of nearly four hundred kilometres an hour, the helicopter was designed as a tank-buster, but its two-ton combat weapon load meant it could tackle virtually anything.

Stopping – or even sinking – the barge would have been easy using the armour-piercing and explosive incendiary rounds fired by the standard thirty-millimetre cannon, but the pilot had taken no chances. The aircraft was also armed with a dozen Vichr supersonic anti-tank missiles, each capable of destroying a main battle tank at five miles, and with a laser-beam guidance and control system that virtually guaranteed a hit probability of one.

The barge captain had taken one look at the jet-black helicopter, bristling with ordnance and hovering a mere ten feet above the forward deck of his vessel, and had immediately decided to follow the instructions that issued from the aircraft's loudspeaker.

As soon as the mooring ropes were secured, a gang-plank was lowered into position by a waiting crane, and Litvinoff quickly led his men on board. The captain was waiting on deck, and the FSB man wasted no time. As his men fanned out to search the vessel, he stepped forward and showed his identification.

'Captain, are you carrying any unauthorized passengers?'

'No, of course not.' The man shook his head in bewilderment. 'This is a working cargo vessel, not a pleasure cruiser.'

'Good. At least I know you're telling the truth about that. So what about your cargo?'

'What about it?'

'Are you carrying anything that doesn't appear on your manifest? And, before you answer that question, let me tell you that I have come here direct from Saratov.'

The barge captain stared at Litvinoff for a long moment, then dropped his eyes.

'We collected a single crate there, yes. It was an unscheduled addition, but why are you interested? Why all this?' The captain spread his arms to encompass just about everything from the armed men on the quayside to the hovering Black Shark.

Litvinoff ignored his questions and watched as one of his own men approached. 'We've searched the vessel, sir, and there is no one on board except for the crew members.'

'Good. Now contact the helicopter and thank the pilot for his help. We won't be needing the aircraft any longer.'

As his subordinate moved towards the gangway, Litvinoff turned back to the captain. 'Who delivered this crate?'

'Two men in a lorry.'

'How did they pay you?'

Again the captain looked uncomfortable. 'We agreed payment in cash. It seemed easier because that saved having to generate all the usual paperwork. And it was only one crate.'

'Where are you supposed to be taking it?'

'Volgograd. They said they would arrange a vehicle to collect the crate there.'

'Right. Wait here.'

Litvinoff walked back across the gangway to where one of his subordinates was standing ready. Above him, the noise of the Black Shark's engines increased markedly, as the aircraft accelerated and began a climbing turn away from the barge.

'Contact FSB headquarters at Volgograd. It seems the Americans will be waiting there to collect the weapon. Initiate a check of all vehicle-hire firms and hotels, and have local units pick them up.'

Litvinoff turned on his heel and remounted the gangway. 'Captain, you and your men are guilty of numerous offences, but I'm frankly not very interested in pursuing the matter. My sole concern is that crate you loaded at Saratov. Instruct your crew to prepare it for immediate unloading.'

'Yes. At once.' The barge master hurried off and began barking orders.

Ten minutes later, the dockside crane lifted the crate from the hold and deposited it on the quay. Two stevedores stepped forward and unhitched the fabric straps.

For a few moments, Litvinoff just stared at the crate, then waved one of his men forward. The man approached cautiously, his right hand extended in front of him, holding what looked like a small microphone. His entire attention was fixed not on the crate but on the Geiger counter gripped in his left hand. The instrument had begun to make a ticking sound that was audible all over the quay. The FSB man stopped right next to the crate, then walked slowly around it.

He made two complete circuits, moving the sensor methodically up and down the wooden sides, then walked across to where Litvinoff was standing. 'Nothing significant, sir. Normal background radiation only.'

'Does that mean the weapon isn't inside the crate?'

'No, sir.' The officer shook his head. 'The fissile material should be properly shielded and no radiation should escape. If I'd detected a significantly higher reading than normal, it could mean that the casing had fractured.' The man shrugged. 'As to whether the device is actually in the crate, I've no idea.'

'Right,' Litvinoff nodded. 'Open it.'

Two other FSB men walked forward carrying battery-powered screwdrivers, and within a couple of minutes the lid lay on the ground to one side. One of his men placed a short step-ladder beside the crate and Litvinoff climbed up to peer inside. He saw a jumble of tools and equipment, but he knew that the weapon itself would be hidden at the very bottom.

'Empty it,' he ordered.

Al-Shahrood Stables, Ad Dahnā, Saudi Arabia

Sheikh Tala Qabandi had two passions in life – Rolls-Royce motor cars and thoroughbred racehorses – and it was difficult to say which inspired him the most. He was well on his way to owning one example of every single model that Rolls-Royce had produced, though not even his enormous wealth would allow him to complete his collection. That was because many of the early models were incredibly rare, and most of them were now housed in museums or private collections and were never offered for sale anywhere or at any price.

Horses were in many ways a lot easier. In the world of bloodstock, money talked, and with the funds the sheikh had at his disposal, his was a voice that couldn't be ignored. What he wanted, he usually got, simply because he could outbid almost anyone else. The result was a stable of first-class horses accommodated at the best training establishments throughout the world. He had five in England, three of them at Newmarket; four in the States, in Kentucky; another four stabled just outside Paris, and a couple in Spain. In the Middle East he kept three horses, all of them at Al-Shahrood, and of these his favourite was Shaf.

This year, he'd entered the horse for the Godolphin Mile thoroughbred event, part of the annual Dubai World Cup race meeting, with total prize money amounting to one million dollars. The money was almost an incidental as far as Qabandi was concerned. For him, the thrill was watching his horse run – preferably at the head of the field – and the annual meet-and-greet with other owners during the event.

As was his invariable custom, Qabandi was visiting the Al-Shahrood stables to check on his horse before its departure. Despite his love of Rolls-Royces, the sheikh had long ago decided that the stables were too remote for access by road, and he travelled there, as today, in his private Bell Jet Ranger. There was no designated helicopter landing spot at the stables, but the wide parking area at the end of the drive in front of the farmhouse was entirely adequate.

The helicopter arrived overhead Al-Shahrood just before noon. The pilot swung the Jet Ranger around in a tight circle, checking that the parking area was unobstructed before he landed. Then he turned the aircraft into wind – the small windsock attached to a pole near the farmhouse was barely moving – and set the aircraft down in a cloud of dust and light debris, almost in the centre of the tarmac.

Qabandi stepped out of the Jet Ranger, in his flowing white *gellabbiya*, followed by his personal secretary, William Alexander. The sheikh had decided to employ the young Englishman after a succession of Arab assistants had failed to measure up to his exacting standards. The trouble with his fellow nationals, Qabandi had found, was that they didn't regard punctuality as a virtue, and he expressed this sentiment as an Arab himself. Like many scions of the wealthiest of the Gulf families, Qabandi had been educated in England, where the concept of always being on time had been instilled in him. He found he simply couldn't cope with the 'any time this week will do' attitude of his previous assistants. Alexander had proved himself quiet, competent and highly efficient, and now Qabandi almost literally couldn't manage without him.

As usual, Alexander was carrying a large briefcase which contained two phones – a GSM mobile and a satellite unit – plus a Sony Vaio laptop computer which basically contained Qabandi's entire life. It held copies of almost every business document he had ever generated or received, all his letters, his agenda and his address book. All those documents were contained within a directory protected by a twelve-digit password known only to Alexander and Qabandi himself. The Vaio's documents were duplicated on two desktop computers kept in separate locked rooms in the sheikh's palace outside Riyadh, each protected by a different password. There was nothing, Alexander believed, quite so important as duplication and back-up.

'This is unusual,' Qabandi frowned, as the two men walked towards the farmhouse. 'Normally Osman comes out to meet us.'

But Osman bin Mahmoud didn't appear from the stable block, or from anywhere else. Alexander rang the bell and knocked on the farmhouse door without eliciting the slightest response.

'Surely somebody must have heard the helicopter,' Qabandi said, his irritation clear.

'They must all be up at the stables,' Alexander suggested. 'Perhaps there's a problem with a horse.'

But when they reached the stable block, they found that was deserted as well. What was more worrying was the noise of the animals housed there. Almost all were whinnying or snorting, some kicking at their doors, and a glance into the nearest stall immediately explained why. The water trough was completely empty, and there was barely a scrap of hay left.

'Nobody's been here for at least twenty-four hours. What's going on?'

Alexander supposed this was a rhetorical question, and ignored it. Instead, he stared around the courtyard, looking at the individual stalls. All but a handful were clearly occupied but, when he looked at the far corner, he suddenly realized that he couldn't see Shaf's head sticking out. In fact, it looked almost as if the thoroughbred's stall door was ajar. He started walking across the courtyard, then ran.

He reached the stable, pulled the door open and looked inside. One glance was all it took. Shaf was gone.

Manama, Bahrain

Richter retrieved his passport, walked into the Arrivals hall and looked round. He spotted an attractive, dark-haired woman standing at the edge of the crowd, holding up a sheet of A4 paper bearing the name 'EVANS'. He strode forward and stopped directly in front of her.

'Are you waiting for me? Paul Richter?'

'Yes.' She smiled. 'I'm Carole-Anne Jackson.'

'Not Evans, then? I take it you're American?'

'Well spotted. You're right, I'm not Evans. Something came up at the office and he got delayed. Come on, I've got a car outside.'

The heat outside the building hit Richter like a punch in the face – he'd never been terribly comfortable in hot climates. Jackson led the way to a white BMW saloon. Richter opened the boot and put his case and computer bag inside, then sat down in the passenger seat. The heat from the black leather upholstery seared instantly through his light jacket, and he jerked forward involuntarily.

'Christ, that's hot.'

Carole-Anne Jackson gave a chuckle. 'You don't need to tell me. Next time I buy a vehicle I'll tell them to stuff the executive leather interior and give me some good old-fashioned cloth.'

'I hope this heap of German tin is air-conditioned.'

'You don't like Beemers, then?'

'Not much, no. In Britain they always seem to be driven around by arrogant pricks who think owning one gives them the absolute right to cut everyone up. It could be worse, though.'

'Really?' Carole-Anne Jackson gave a slight smile as she started the engine, and a welcome rush of ice-cold air blasted out of the dashboard vents. 'How?'

'It could be a Mercedes.'

Jackson had her hand on the gear lever, but removed it to look straight at Richter. Most people didn't criticize her choice of car the moment they met her, and she found his outspoken comments rather irritating. Irritating, but also somehow intriguing. 'What's wrong with Mercedes?' she asked. 'They're beautifully engineered cars.'

'So I'm told. Personally I think they're over-engineered, overweight, underpowered, *really* expensive to maintain, vulgar, ugly, unreliable and grotesquely overpriced. And I've never found one yet with comfortable seats. Apart from that, I'm sure they're really good.'

Jackson stared at him for a few moments, then slid the gear lever into first and eased the car forward. 'You're what I think my mother would have called contrary. Is there anything else you don't like, so I can try to avoid the subject?'

'Sorry,' Richter muttered, 'I'm not in the best of tempers today. I'm still jetlagged, so my body clock is running about four hours behind – or maybe ahead of, I'm never really sure – what my watch is telling me. Added to that, I'm permanently at the top of my boss's shit list, and he's just sent me out to Dubai on what I absolutely *know* is a wild goose chase.'

'Ah.'

'And what does that mean?'

Jackson glanced at him. 'You could find yourself

chasing rather more than one wild goose out here, I'm afraid.'

'You want to explain that?'

'This car's clean, so I suppose it's as good a place as any to give you an initial briefing. First, I take my orders from Langley, not from Vauxhall Cross, and I've been working here as an exchange officer with the local SIS people for about eighteen months. Somebody, somewhere, obviously must have thought it was a good idea.'

'And you don't?'

'It's a job, I guess, but I'm not too wild about the Middle East, and Arabs aren't my favourite people.'

'Nor mine, but don't tell anyone that.'

'OK, that's me. Now, one of our contacts in the Special Intelligence Service – that's more or less Bahrain's secret police force – has an informer who believes Osama bin Laden is currently a patient in a local hospital.'

It was a few moments before Richter managed to reply. 'Is this somebody's idea of a bad joke?'

Jackson shook her head. 'Not as far as I'm aware. To the best of our knowledge, the sighting was genuine. We passed the information back to Vauxhall Cross, and they presumably decided you were the ideal man to investigate it.'

'I'll bloody kill Simpson,' Richter muttered. 'Every credible report that's crossed my desk for the last six months has suggested that bin Laden is either dead or still skulking around the Pakistani–Afghan border region. How the hell is he supposed to have checked himself into a hospital here?'

Jackson explained what they knew about 'Sheikh Rashid' and his arrival in Bahrain by private jet.

When she'd finished, Richter shook his head. 'I don't doubt this Filipino cleaner is genuine in what he thought he saw, but it must be a misidentification. He saw this man for a matter of a few seconds, and not even full-face.'

'You're probably right,' she sighed. 'So what do you intend to do?'

'I'll talk to my section, not that it'll do any good. Then I'll check it out, I guess. I mean, there probably *is* about a one in a million chance bin Laden might have slipped through the net.'

Jackson eyed him curiously before returning her attention to the road. 'OK, now *I've* got a question. You just said "your section", but I assumed you were from Vauxhall Cross?'

Richter shook his head. 'No, I don't work at Lego-land, I'm pleased to say. My employer is a short, bald-ing, bad-tempered ex-mandarin who heads a small unit tucked away in the backstreets of Hammersmith. Offi-cially, it's a research and investigation section affiliated to the SIS. In reality, we get given the dirty little jobs that the people at Six don't want to risk soiling their aristocratic hands with.'

'Like this one, you mean?'

'Exactly like this one.'

'OK, I see. Well, the first step is for you to meet Evans, as this is his operation, not mine. We've checked you into the Sheraton Hotel. I presume that'll be OK?'

Richter had a sudden mental picture of the expres-sion he was likely to see on the cashier's face when he presented his credit card vouchers for this particular excursion, and smiled at her.

'Yes, that's fine. Right, Evans – when can I meet him?'

Jackson glanced at the dashboard clock. 'He should be at the hotel by now.'

A couple of minutes later she stopped the car outside the Sheraton, expertly manoeuvring it into a parking space. Richter picked up his cases and followed her into the lobby, a large open space adorned with ornate columns, chandeliers and a wild profusion of plants. She headed straight for the reception desk, then turned and saw Evans sitting in an easy chair, reading a two-day-old copy of *The Times*.

'Bill,' she said, 'this is Paul Richter from London. Paul, Bill Evans.'

Evans stood up, shook hands and then subsided back into his seat.

'Paul thinks this is a complete waste of time,' Carole-Anne Jackson began.

'And I agree.' Evans grinned boyishly at him. 'I still don't think our Saudi friend would have a chance of getting here without somebody spotting him.'

'Even if he's still alive.'

'Exactly. My guess is that his corpse is rotting in a cave somewhere, and his camp followers aren't going to tell the world until they think the time is right. But London wants us to check, just in case.'

'Right,' Richter said. 'I'd like to speak to your local contact, if you've no objection.'

'None at all,' Evans replied. 'I can set up a meeting tonight, over dinner.'

'Fine. Now, I gather from what Carole has told me that the suspect is in a local hospital, in a ward that's under surveillance, and he's surrounded by personal body-guards. How, exactly, am I supposed to get inside and check him out?'

Cairo, Egypt

The taxi stopped near the city centre, and O'Hagan and Petrucci climbed out. They stood together on the pavement for a few moments as the vehicle shot back into the traffic amid a sudden angry blaring of horns, the driver – like most Egyptians – not bothering to look behind him or check his mirror.

'Take your life in your hands every time you step into the street here,' Petrucci grumbled.

'You said it,' O'Hagan replied. 'Right, see you in ninety minutes.'

The two men headed off in opposite directions. O'Hagan knew exactly where he was going, because he'd checked the local directory and identified three vehicle-hire companies within walking distance. The first one he tried had nothing suitable, but the second offered a choice of two white Mercedes vans. Picking the one with the fewest dents, he signed a hire agreement for three days, paying with a credit card bearing a name that was not his own, and backed it up with an international driving licence in the same name. He spent a few minutes studying a street map of Cairo, then drove off.

There was about a twenty-minute wait before Petrucci appeared, clutching two bulky bags.

'Get everything?' O'Hagan asked.

'Yup. Had to dig around a bit for the letters, is all.'

O'Hagan stopped the van outside a company offering storage solutions and they went inside. They emerged a few minutes later carrying lengths of racking and shelving, a cardboard box containing plastic storage boxes, and four small green tarpaulins.

Next, they stopped outside an electrical wholesaler and bought a selection of plugs, sockets, cable ties, junctions, chock-block connectors, insulating tape and a few other bits and pieces. They also purchased various tools: circuit testers, soldering irons, screwdrivers, pliers and so on. An electrician might have puzzled at their selection – they had soldering irons but neither solder nor flux, for example – but what they'd just purchased was never going to be used. It was simply camouflage to provide support for their cover story.

'When do you want to do the van?' Petrucci asked.

'Now, I guess. Then we'll be ready to move as soon as we get the call.'

O'Hagan steered the van down a narrow street near their hotel. At the far end was a block of six large garages, each secured by a padlocked metal up-and-over door, and owned by the hotel they were staying at.

They'd hired the biggest garage for a week, though they'd need it for no more than two days, but it had been essential to find somewhere they could do their work away from prying eyes.

As Petrucci released the padlock and lifted the door,

a blast of heat rolled out to greet him. O'Hagan drove the van inside, keeping close to the right-hand wall, leaving the maximum possible space on the other side of the vehicle.

Petrucci took four sets of white overalls from one of the bags and tossed them to O'Hagan, then extracted a plastic sheet, some spray paint, masking tape, self-adhesive letters and a bunch of other stuff. At the rear end of the garage was a collapsible table. He took everything over to it, unrolled the plastic and secured it to the table top. Then he shook the adhesive letters out of the bag and started arranging them on the sheet.

Behind him, O'Hagan laid out the overalls face-down on the floor of the van. He took a stencil, a felt-tip pen and tape measure, and began marking the back of the first set.

Just under an hour later, Petrucci had finished at the table, and O'Hagan had completed his work. The two men then began securing the sheet of plastic in line with marks O'Hagan had already made on the side of the Mercedes. This took quite some time because it was important for the template to be stuck as firmly and accurately as possible to the metal before they started painting. For what they were planning, the finished job needed to be really sharp and professional-looking.

Once O'Hagan was finally satisfied, he pulled on one of the face masks, climbed onto an empty wooden box they'd found at the back of the garage, and began spraying the side of the vehicle through the template. Spray-painting wasn't a skill either man possessed to any great degree, but O'Hagan knew enough to make a reasonably good job of it.

While they waited for each coat to dry, they busied themselves with erecting the racking. Inside the van, they built a line of shelves secured with horizontal braces, then arranged the plastic storage boxes on them and finally put the tools and electrical components inside them. By the time they'd finished, the rear of the van looked like any vehicle used by a technical tradesman.

After removing the stencil from the side of the vehicle, they opened the garage door, which did almost nothing to reduce the temperature inside. O'Hagan backed out the Mercedes and then reversed it into the garage so they could repeat the process on the other side.

'We're done,' O'Hagan announced, some ninety minutes later. 'Let's go get a shower and a beer. My throat feels like the fucking Mojave Desert.'

'Amen to that,' Petrucci replied, stuffing all the tools and other things they'd used into one of the bags. He tossed it in the van, reopened the garage door and padlocked it behind them, safely locking away the Mercedes with its brand-new 'Cairo Specialist Aviation Services' decals affixed to each side.

Dubai

They'd left the Range Rover at Riyadh Airport, but Massood had pre-booked a Land Cruiser to tow the horse trailer while in Dubai. After delivering Shaf to the stables the previous evening, Saadi had explained to the staff that there was a problem with the brakes on the transporter, and he promised it would be delivered the following day.

That morning, Massood and Saadi left the hotel after checking out. Massood climbed into a taxi while Saadi carried his own bag and Massood's across to the transporter, which was backed up against a wall, with the Land Cruiser already attached to the towing arm.

Saadi knocked twice, and twice more, then inserted the key and swung open the side door of the transporter. Inside, Bashar was sitting on the pile of blankets that had formed his bed, a Kalashnikov for company.

'You're ready?' Saadi asked, and Bashar nodded. 'Do you need anything before we start?'

'No, I'll eat something when we return.'

'Good. Massood's collecting the hire car. It's time to open the bales.'

They lifted all the bales from their storage. Saadi opened a clasp knife, sliced through the binding cords on the first one and pulled out the packet which had been concealed inside it. They stuffed the loose hay into the storage area and then opened the second bale.

Half an hour later, Saadi stopped the Toyota alongside a Renault Clio parked just off the Oud Metha Road, a little way beyond the Camel Racetrack. He walked back to the transporter and opened the door on the side facing away from the road. Massood opened the Renault's boot and Bashar began handing the packages to Saadi.

Once the transfer was complete, they closed the boot of the Renault, which now contained three Kalashnikovs, two boxes of 7.62-millimetre ammunition and one box of fifty 9-millimetre Parabellum rounds, along with the eight sealed packages. Bashar started the Land Cruiser just as Massood and Saadi drove away in the Clio. All three men were now armed with loaded pistols.

PAYBACK

Kamyshin, Russia

Litvinoff stared at the scatter of tools and boxes on the dockside in front of him. He'd been convinced that they'd find the suitcase nuclear device inside that crate, but it was now perfectly clear that the weapon simply wasn't there.

That was the bad news – and in fact there was no good news as far as the FSB officer could see. Despite his earlier threats, he now couldn't even charge the barge master with anything more than a misdemeanour, because every single piece of equipment found inside the crate was correctly listed on the paperwork the captain possessed.

The conclusion was inevitable, and highly uncomfortable to contemplate: the Americans had just been using the barge as a decoy. Litvinoff had wasted vital hours on this fruitless pursuit, and he was still no nearer finding them or, more important, the weapon. They must have planned a completely different escape route out of Russia. But as he stood silently on the quayside, eyeing the jumble of broken and rusted equipment around him, Litvinoff hadn't the slightest idea what that other route might be, or how he was ever going to find it.

Chapter Eight

Wednesday
Al-Shahrood Stables, Ad Dahnā, Saudi Arabia

The local police dutifully arrived at Al-Shahrood less than two hours after Sheikh Qabandi's peremptory summons.

In the meantime, the sheikh and his men had been busy. Qabandi had summoned his two pilots to help him and Alexander fill the water troughs and sort out feed for the horses, so that by the time the police cars arrived the animals were again quiet and settled.

'How many people should there be here?' the inspector asked, as his men began searching the stable-block accommodation.

'Usually a minimum of twelve,' Qabandi replied. 'That includes at least two members of the bin Mahmoud family, their household staff of about six and roughly the same number of people living at the stables.'

'What do you think has happened to them?'

'I've no idea, but something is definitely wrong. I've dealt with Osman bin Mahmoud for six years now, and I've never known him go off and leave the horses unattended. There's *always* somebody here at the stables, day and night.'

'Perhaps there was an emergency, something that meant everyone had to leave. You told us that your horse' – the inspector referred to his notes – 'yes, your horse Shaf is missing. Suppose the horse bolted,' he waved his arm in a vague gesture, 'and they've all gone off to fetch it back.'

Sheikh Qabandi frowned impatiently. 'That's a most unlikely scenario. The horses here may be thoroughbreds, all highly strung animals, but they seldom bolt, as you put it. Whenever they are outside their stalls, they always wear a bridle, and are attended by one of the staff.'

'But supposing an insect bit one, or something like that—'

'Inspector' – Qabandi was starting to get annoyed – 'let's assume your scenario might be correct, and that the staff here failed to obey the simplest and most basic procedures they follow every single day, and that my horse did manage to run off. At most, it might need half a dozen people to recapture it. Where's everyone else? Or are you suggesting that literally everybody, even Osman bin Mahmoud's *wife*, went rushing off into the desert to search for it? And that they're still out there now, at least twenty-four hours later?'

'How do you know there's been no one here for twenty-four hours?'

'By deduction, Inspector. When we arrived, none of the stalls had water and most had no fodder. I know the routine here. The water troughs are filled every morning and evening as a matter of course, and checked during the day. If they had been filled this morning, they would all be over half-full. And if they'd been filled last night, most of them would still have some water left. So the last time they could possibly have been filled was yesterday morning.'

'Right,' the inspector said, closing his notebook. He didn't like the arrogant tone of the sheikh standing in front of him, but he had to concede that the man seemed to know what he was talking about. 'We'll search the farmhouse next.'

'And then what will you do?'

'I don't know. Let's see what we find in the house first.'

Adler, Russia

'Are you feeling unwell, sir?' the waiter asked.

The question was ridiculous. It was perfectly obvious to even the most untrained observer that Edward Dawson was sick. He was lying on a couch in the hotel lounge, his tie loosened and his shirt unbuttoned at the neck. His skin had an unhealthy pallor, almost grey, and he was breathing in short, painful gasps. His companion had opened a small black bag and was now extracting a stethoscope and blood-pressure cuff.

'Stand back, please,' Wilson ordered in Russian. He listened to Dawson's heartbeat for half a minute or so, checked his blood pressure, tested the reaction of his pupils with a small pocket torch, and gently felt his forehead with the back of his hand. 'This man needs immediate specialist hospital treatment,' he said. 'That means he'll have to be flown to Moscow or Kiev. Do you have an air ambulance here?'

'I've no idea.'

'We need to find out, and quickly. Fetch the manager, please.'

As the waiter hurried away, Dawson sat upright and vomited copiously onto the patterned carpet. The waiter looked back in alarm at the sound, then left the lounge at a run.

Less than a minute later a middle-aged man wearing a dark suit walked over to the couch. He looked with distaste at the splatter of vomit, then at Wilson.

'I'm the hotel manager, so how—' he began, but Wilson cut him off almost immediately.

'My colleague requires urgent medical attention,' Wilson repeated. 'I'm a doctor, and I suspect he may be suffering from encephalitis or meningitis. We need an air ambulance immediately.'

'We have doctors and a hospital here in Adler. I'm not sure we need to—'

'Listen,' Wilson interrupted, 'if my diagnosis is correct, we have to get this man into a specialist hospital as soon as possible. We'll need complex laboratory tests to determine whether he's suffering from a viral or a bacterial infection, and then use specific antiviral or antibacterial drugs to cope with it. We'll also need sedatives and anticonvulsants, and probably corticosteroids to reduce the inflammation of his brain. I know that this scale of treatment is completely beyond the facilities likely to be available in any local hospital. The nearest major centres are Kiev and Moscow, so that's where he's got to be taken. If he doesn't get emergency treatment very soon he could die, possibly within hours. Now, I'll ask you again. Is there an air ambulance available here in Adler?'

The manager stared down at the sick man, then looked up. 'I'll see what I can do,' he said abruptly, then turned to leave. 'You' – he gestured to a waiter – 'find one of the cleaners and get that mess cleared up.'

Volgograd, Russia

Litvinoff had at least received one piece of good news. He'd ordered a check of all hotels and vehicle-hire firms in Volgograd, but had assumed that the search would be fruitless because his quarry would have gone somewhere else. But it turned out that luck was on his side, and Litvinoff and two of his men had immediately driven south to follow up the new lead.

A hotel located near the main railway station had reported that two men carrying American passports had checked in that morning. That was unremarkable in itself, but what had caused the staff to remember them was the short duration of their stay. They'd arrived early in the morning, taken a twin-bedded room, but left the hotel that same afternoon. That meant they'd had to pay for two nights' accommodation, despite having spent only six hours in the hotel – none of them during the night – because the hotel's 'day' started at twelve noon.

'What were their names?' Litvinoff demanded, standing in the lobby.

The hotel manager opened the register. 'Johnson and Hughes.'

'I assume you made a note of their passport numbers?'

'No. It's far simpler to just photocopy the documents.'

Litvinoff couldn't believe his luck, as the manager

retrieved a loose-leaf folder from a slot below the reception desk and extracted two sheets of paper.

The passports would certainly be fake, Litvinoff knew, because only idiots would use their real identity documents in Russia if they were engaged in criminal activity, but he now had two things he hadn't possessed three minutes earlier – a pair of poor-quality photographs and two of the false names the Americans had been using. All he had to do now was find out where 'Johnson' and 'Hughes' had gone when they walked out of the hotel.

And the main railway station, just down the road, seemed the obvious place to start.

Al-Shahrood Stables, Ad Dahnā, Saudi Arabia

'The house is deserted,' the inspector announced, stepping out of the rear doorway of the large property.

'Any signs of a struggle?'

'No, nothing at all. Several of the beds are still unmade, as if everyone just got up and walked out of the house at the same time.'

'Shades of the *Marie Celeste*,' Qabandi murmured bitterly. 'So what now?'

'We can issue a missing-persons report, but that won't be easy because we don't know *who* is missing, or even how many people. Obviously you'll be able to help, at least with the names and descriptions of the owner and his immediate family.'

Qabandi nodded. 'Of course, Inspector, but there's

something else. While you were checking the house, my associates and I took another look around the stable block.'

'We specifically told you not to go inside the accommodation,' the police officer snapped, his voice growing decidedly angry.

'I know you did – and we didn't. We looked only in the outbuildings.'

'We searched those already.'

'Yes, but *we* knew what we were looking for.'

'Which was what, exactly?'

'In the garage, each car has an allocated parking space, clearly marked with its registration number and the type of vehicle. A Range Rover is missing.'

'Perhaps it's being serviced.'

'I don't think so, because a horse transporter is also missing. It's an easy deduction that my horse could have been taken away in that transporter, towed behind the Range Rover.'

'That might explain the missing horse, but not the missing staff. That many people couldn't all have been crammed into a horsebox, especially not if there was a horse already in it. Something else must have happened to them.'

'Exactly.' Qabandi nodded. 'It seems to me that there are only two possibilities. Everybody could have been kidnapped and taken away from here in whatever vehicles the attackers arrived in. It could hardly be for a ransom demand, otherwise there would have been some contact already. And the horses stabled here are far more valuable than the people employed to look after them.

That means any reasonably intelligent kidnapper would have taken the horses instead of the staff.'

That thought had not occurred to the inspector. 'How much are these horses worth?'

Qabandi thought for a few moments. 'Altogether, I don't know for sure. Maybe forty to fifty million dollars. Shaf alone is worth over three million, and there are at least another fifteen thoroughbreds stabled here at the moment.'

'That does suggest other possibilities,' the inspector agreed, glancing thoughtfully towards the stable block. 'How many horses should be here?'

'I've no idea, but most of the stalls seem to be occupied, so my guess is they took only Shaf and maybe one or two others. And there's only one transporter missing, so if they took more than two horses they must also have used a horsebox of their own. The other possibility is that bin Mahmoud and his staff have been taken away somewhere and killed just to eliminate any witnesses. Inspector, I think you should stop treating this as simply a missing-persons case, and start seriously considering the possibility everyone here was murdered.'

Volgograd, Russia

None of the station staff remembered seeing the Americans, but it still made sense to Litvinoff that they would have left Volgograd by rail.

It was also most likely that they would have caught a train shortly after leaving the hotel. Litvinoff was certain they'd head south for the nearest Russian border, and that limited their possible destinations. The FSB man quickly came up with a shortlist of three possibilities – Astrakhan, Groznyy and Adler – and he ordered checks on every hotel, restaurant, taxi firm and vehicle-hire company both in and around these three locations.

He also reinforced the watch order he'd issued to the Border Guards, responsible for the physical security of the frontiers of the CIS. Following his interviews with Borisov, his first instruction had been rather vague, simply because the administrator had been too traumatized to provide him with accurate descriptions. Now he knew that the device was no longer in the crate but was probably, he guessed, inside a large suitcase – that was, after all, the concept behind the design of the weapon – the watch order could be much more specific. Both the Border Guards and the police now had the names and photographs of the Americans, so all Litvinoff could do was wait for somebody to provide him with the sighting he needed.

Adler, Russia

Dawson looked even worse than before. His skin was ashen and he'd vomited several times, though a relay of basins provided by the hotel staff had saved further damage to the carpet.

Wilson had told the manager that Dawson was running a high fever, and that he increasingly feared for his life. His obvious concern had finally produced the result he was hoping for.

'I've made some calls, Mr Johnson,' the manager said, entering the closed-off lounge – Wilson had refused to let the hotel staff move his colleague. 'An air ambulance is on its way to the airport at Sochi and should arrive here in about thirty minutes. There's no medical attendant on board, just the pilot, but that shouldn't be a problem as you're a doctor.'

The manager paused, looking almost embarrassed, as if troubled by some new concern.

'Yes?' Wilson asked.

'The ambulance company will require a cash payment in advance, specifically in US dollars, before they will embark your friend.'

'That's not a problem. What's the total cost of the flight?'

'Three thousand five hundred dollars.'

Wilson nodded agreement. 'Can you arrange an ambulance to take us to Sochi Airport? Obviously I'll pay for your time as well as the appropriate fee.'

'Thank you.' The manager's face cleared instantly. 'Shall we say five hundred dollars in cash for everything? Payment for your room is already covered by your credit card.'

'That's fine,' Wilson said. 'Please stay here with Mr Hughes while I fetch down our cases.'

Ten minutes later, the manager was back in his office, carefully counting the dollar bills Wilson had just given him. Dawson was lying on a stretcher in the back of an elderly but perfectly serviceable ambulance, with Wilson and a Russian paramedic sitting beside him, as the vehicle headed north out of Adler, headlights on and siren wailing, a police car in front.

Cessna 340 air ambulance, callsign Romeo Charlie Three Six

The aircraft was already waiting. Because they were flying to a destination within the CIS, there were no passport or customs checks, and the only concern of the airport staff was to get the sick man airborne and on his way to hospital as quickly as they could manage.

With Dawson safely strapped on the narrow cot in the rear compartment of the twin-engine aircraft, Wilson walked forward to the cockpit and handed over the fee agreed for the flight. 'Three thousand five hundred dollars. Is that correct?' he asked in Russian.

'Yes,' the man replied. 'I understand you want to go to either Moscow or Kiev. I suggest we wait until we're airborne before checking which hospital is best prepared to take care of him.'

Wilson nodded. 'That's just what I was going to suggest.'

The pilot slid the envelope into his jacket pocket, glanced back into the Cessna's cabin to check that everything was properly secured, then turned again to Wilson. 'If you'd like to take your seat back there, Mr Johnson, we'll get moving now. My name, by the way, is Vassily.'

Just ten minutes later the Cessna was heading northwest, away from Sochi, and climbing smoothly through ten thousand feet.

Wilson waited until Vassily had switched on the autopilot before he went back to the cockpit. 'There's been a change of plan,' he said firmly. 'We're not going to either

Moscow or Kiev. Turn this aircraft round immediately and take up a heading of one nine zero.'

For a moment Vassily seemed to think Wilson was joking, but his smile faded rapidly when the American produced a semi-automatic pistol. The weapon surprised and shocked the Russian, but he was completely stunned by the sight of Dawson standing behind Wilson in the cockpit doorway, complexion ashen and looking ghastly, but smiling and clearly *compos mentis*.

Wilson smiled too. 'It's amazing how bad a couple of pieces of cordite can make you look and feel.' Chewing cordite produces a grey complexion, nausea and vomiting, and was a dodge used by nineteenth-century British soldiers and sailors as a way of getting undeserved sick leave, or even a discharge. The effect starts within about thirty minutes of ingestion, and can last for some hours, depending on how much is swallowed.

'Right,' Wilson continued, 'it's facts-of-life time. Don't even think about making a radio broadcast or altering your transponder settings. I promise you I'll notice – and then I'll kill you. Our new destination is Cairo.'

Vassily shook his head desperately. 'It doesn't have the range—' he began, but Wilson interrupted.

'Don't try and take me for a fool. A Cessna three four zero has a range of just over two thousand six hundred kilometres cruising at one hundred and seventy knots. Your tanks were full on take-off. I checked. From Sochi to Cairo is about sixteen hundred kilometres. That means you can get there and about halfway back with what you've got in your tanks right now.

'And before you come out with any other stupid

remarks, my friend and I are both qualified pilots and could fly this aircraft to Cairo without the slightest difficulty. Whether you live or die is now up to you, but I would prefer your cooperation. If I get it you'll live to walk away from this. OK?'

Vassily stared at the gun in Wilson's hand. 'OK,' he said hoarsely. 'What do you want me to do?'

'First, start the turn. Inform Sochi that the patient's condition has worsened, and we're diverting to the Ain Shams University Specialized Hospital at Abbassia. Tell them that you're altering course for Cairo, and request that they advise the Turkish and Egyptian authorities.'

'What about a flight plan?'

'There's nothing to stop you filing an en-route plan if either the Turks or the Egyptians insist, but they probably won't. After you've talked with Sochi, contact Turkish Air Traffic Control. You'll be entering their airspace between Samsun and Trabzon, so you should call Ruzgar for clearance. Their initial contact frequency is one two three decimal one. They'll hand you on to Yayla and Gazi as we transit across the mainland.'

Vassily stared at Wilson. 'You've worked all this out, haven't you?'

Wilson grinned at him. 'You'd better believe it. OK, it's your choice. Make the calls and play it straight, and you'll get to land this aircraft at Cairo, and keep the money we've paid you, and live. If you don't, you'll be taking a long dive into the Black Sea.'

Volgograd, Russia

The first responses Litvinoff received were negative. As far as the police could ascertain, no two Americans had stayed in any of the hotels in Astrakhan or Groznyy. The reports from Adler and Sochi took longer to arrive, but proved worth the wait. As soon as he read the response from a hotel manager in Adler, Litvinoff knew he had the Americans cornered.

The town lies close to the Turkish border, but not that close – the frontier is actually four hundred kilo-metres away – and Litvinoff was confident he could end the pursuit long before his quarry could escape in that direction. His first call was to the Adler police station.

'You have two Americans named Johnson and Hughes staying in your town. They're using false passports and are wanted for the theft of military equipment from a base near Moscow. They should be considered armed and dangerous. Put a squad together immediately and arrest them. Under no circumstances are they to be allowed to leave Adler.'

When the inspector replied his tone was apologetic. 'I'm afraid that won't be possible, Investigator Litvinoff.'

'Why not? I have the necessary authority to order this operation.'

'No, it's not that, sir. About half an hour ago we were advised that an ambulance would be collecting a critically ill guest named Hughes from his hotel. He was suffering from meningitis or encephalitis, and an air ambulance had already been arranged. In fact, we provided a police escort for part of the ambulance's journey.'

In that instant, Litvinoff realized exactly how the Americans had planned to get themselves and the stolen nuclear weapon out of Russia, and he swore under his breath.

'Where did the aircraft depart from? Which airport?'

'Sochi. It's about twenty kilometres from here.'

'Has the flight already taken off? If not, hold it on the ground.'

'Stand by and I'll check.' Litvinoff heard background noises, raised voices, and then the inspector came back on the line. 'It got airborne ten minutes ago. It seems the pilot didn't file a flight plan because it was a medical emergency, but he told Sochi that he would be landing at either Kiev or Moscow.'

'Right,' Litvinoff snarled, and slammed down the phone.

For a few moments he just sat there. One thing was certain: the two places he could guarantee the air ambulance would not be landing were Moscow or Kiev. By now, the Americans would have pulled a gun on the pilot, and the hijacked aircraft would be heading south for Turkey.

He'd been cleverly outmanoeuvred, but there was, he hoped, still time to stop them. What he needed now was an aircraft – an armed fighter aircraft, to be exact – and he thought he knew where he could get one.

Within the North Caucasus MD there are numerous military airfields. Litvinoff's immediate problem was that he didn't have the authority to contact one directly to request the launching of an interceptor. In fact, he wasn't sure he had sufficient authority even to approach the Military District headquarters in Rostov. But if he hadn't, the FSB headquarters in Moscow at *Lubyanskaya ploshchad* certainly would have, and fortunately he'd already briefed a succession of duty officers there on his progress – or lack of it – in apprehending these Americans.

Before contacting Moscow, he called the Sochi Airport control tower. The information he gleaned was unwelcome, but not unexpected. Litvinoff briefly thanked the controller, then called Moscow.

'You want a what?'

'A fighter interceptor,' Litvinoff insisted. 'The Americans have managed to organize an air ambulance to fly them out of Russia. The only way to stop them is to shoot it down.'

'How do you know they're leaving the country? Perhaps this American is genuinely sick and they are heading for a hospital.'

'I very much doubt that. I've just talked to one of the controllers at Sochi Airport, and the aircraft is now heading south, towards Turkey. The pilot advised the controllers that the American's condition had worsened, and they'd decided to fly him to a hospital in Egypt.'

'And how do you know that isn't true?'

'Three reasons,' the investigator replied, with as much patience as he could muster. 'First, Egyptian medical care is no better than you can find in our Russian hospitals, and it will take them even longer to reach Cairo than get to Moscow. Second, the pilot wouldn't risk his licence by flying outside Russian airspace without first filing an international flight plan.'

'And the other reason?'

'The third reason,' Litvinoff almost shouted, 'is that the fucking aircraft has a stolen nuclear weapon on board. Now, do I get a fighter or not?'

'Very well. I'll make the call.'

Chapter Nine

Wednesday
Cessna 340 air ambulance, callsign Romeo Charlie
Three Six

Wilson was pleased: Vassily was doing exactly what he was told but, despite his own earlier assurances, the biggest problem they now had was fuel. The Cessna was flying at around twenty-two thousand feet, but they'd increased speed to just over two hundred knots, and that would have reduced the Cessna's range significantly.

The other worry was that the Sochi controller – who hadn't approved their change of route, but merely acknowledged the pilot's transmission – might have alerted a Russian fighter base, and a couple of MiGs could be heading towards them right at that moment. If that happened, neither American was under any illusions about the outcome. Even at the Cessna's maximum speed, it stood no chance of out-running a Mach 2 interceptor.

Sheraton Hotel, Manama, Bahrain

Before leaving London, Richter had drawn an Enigma T-301 mobile phone, a unit that offers military-level encryption as long as both parties are using compatible equipment.

He first checked into his room, then took the Enigma outside the building. He had absolutely no reason to believe that the hotel might contain surveillance devices, but Richter never trusted anyone, and he certainly didn't want his conversation with Simpson to be overheard. It took only a few seconds before he heard the less than amiable tones of his superior.

'Yes, Richter, what is it? Have you seen this man Holden?'

'No. I'm in Bahrain, not Dubai.'

'I know that. I sent you there, remember? I thought you might have seen him before you left the Emirates.'

'There wasn't time. Do you actually know why Six wanted me out here?'

'They needed someone to run an identity check.'

'Did they tell you who they think the subject is?'

'No.'

'Osama bin Laden.'

For a few moments there was silence. When Simpson spoke again, there was an angry edge to his voice. 'No, they didn't tell me that. The fucking idiots just requested one of our operatives, and stated that a briefing would be given on-site.'

Richter explained why they thought the hospital patient might be the Saudi renegade.

'That's rubbish, and you and I both know it. There's no way bin Laden could have got to Bahrain without somebody tipping off the intelligence services. There's just too much reward money involved.'

'So what do you want me to do?'

'Well, since you're there, you might as well do what

Six want. Go run the check, then get back to Dubai and see Holden. Meanwhile, I'll have a quiet word with Vauxhall Cross.'

Richter smiled as he ended the call. Simpson's 'quiet word' would be the kind of debriefing that could end a man's career.

960 IAP (Fighter Aviation Regiment), Primorsko-Akhtarsk, Krasnodar, Russia

The call from FSB headquarters didn't produce the rapid results Litvinoff had hoped for. The colonel commanding the 960 IAP at Primorsko-Akhtarsk – the closest airfield to Sochi that had fighters immediately available – hadn't accepted the identity of the FSB officer, and had insisted on calling him back through the military telephone system just to verify his location and authority to issue intercept instructions.

That had taken precious minutes. And, when the colonel had finally realized the genuine urgency of the matter, it had taken a further sixteen minutes before a MiG-29 aircraft and pilot had been assigned and four R-60M air-to-air missiles loaded. Known in the West as the AA-8 (NATO reporting name Aphid), this weapon is a short-range Mach 2 missile designed for tactical air combat.

The colonel delivered the mission briefing personally over the telephone to the pilot, Lieutenant Viktor Beleshayov.

'The target's a Cessna three four zero air ambulance.

It left Sochi and is now heading for Turkey. Once you're airborne, we'll pass you an accurate fix from the air-defence system.'

'And you want me to shoot it down? An air ambulance?' Beleshayov was incredulous.

'Yes,' the colonel confirmed. 'The orders from Moscow are absolutely specific. The target is to be intercepted and shot down. The aircraft has been hijacked by American spies who have stolen an item of highly classified military equipment.'

'What kind of equipment?'

For a few moments the colonel didn't reply, wondering whether to divulge what the FSB officer had told him. Finally he decided it might be a good idea if his subordinate knew exactly how serious the situation was.

'Is there anyone near you? Anyone who can overhear?'

Beleshayov glanced round. 'No, nobody.'

'Right, this is for your ears only. The Americans have stolen a tactical-yield nuclear weapon. Now you know why it's vital you stop that aircraft getting away.'

MiG-29 interceptor, callsign Zero Six Eight

Beleshayov held the Mikoyan-Gurevich MiG-29C (NATO reporting name Fulcrum) on the toe brakes, pushed the throttles forward to run the Kilmov/Sarkisov RD-33 turbojets up to full cold military power, then released the brakes and engaged the burners as the aircraft started its take-off roll. Ninety seconds later the interceptor was flying level at thirty-five thousand feet, heading south and approaching twice the speed of sound.

'Zero Six Eight, Primorsko. Vector one seven zero. Frequency change approved.'

'Zero Six Eight chopping to operational.'

Moments later, Beleshayov had established contact with the air-defence radar unit. 'Zero Six Eight, vector one seven five. Target bears one six zero, range four hundred.'

Beleshayov quickly did the calculations. His aircraft was now travelling at twice the speed of sound, still in afterburner, and on an intercept course with the Cessna four hundred kilometres ahead of him. He should get a radar lock on it within about seven minutes, and reach the missile release point just four minutes after that – the R-60M is a very short-range weapon. But he was going to have to come out of burner well before that, because his aircraft was travelling far too rapidly to engage such a slow-moving target.

And, despite his briefing, Beleshayov was planning to carry out one unauthorized action. He was going to do a visual fly-by, a final personal check that the target had been correctly identified. There were numerous aircraft flying around the area, and Beleshayov had no intention of releasing his missiles until he was absolutely certain that he was targeting the right one.

Riyadh, Saudi Arabia

Sheikh Tala Qabandi climbed out of the Jet Ranger in the courtyard of his palace and walked over to the building's imposing entrance. Alexander followed dutifully a few paces behind. They'd left Al-Shahrood following further inconclusive investigation. Despite widening the search to cover the desert immediately surrounding the stables, not the slightest trace of anyone had been found.

The police inspector had already initiated a missing-persons report on Osman bin Mahmoud and his wife – the only people Qabandi was *certain* would have been at the farmhouse – and placed a watch order, effective throughout Saudi Arabia and all the adjoining states, for the missing Range Rover and the horse transporter. And that, as the inspector said, was about all they could do, since there was still no proof that any crime had been committed.

Inside the palace's cool interior, William Alexander headed straight for his office. He had a few lines of inquiry he wanted to check himself, the first of which was the most obvious. To his surprise it produced immediate results.

The transport itinerary for the racehorse Shaf had been supplied by bin Mahmoud a few weeks earlier, and it specified the flight to Dubai, the stables booked there and the staff accommodation. All these arrangements had been charged to the sheikh's account and, as the horse had now vanished, they could be cancelled and refunds obtained. Alexander was used to paying close attention to such minor details, which was one of the reasons Qabandi employed him.

But when he got through to the airline office at Riyadh to cancel the tickets, the response was not what he had anticipated.

'I'm sorry, sir, but no refund is possible.'

'Why not?' Alexander demanded.

'Because the tickets have already been used.'

'What?'

'According to our computer records, Osman bin Mahmoud rescheduled the flight so that the horse and stable personnel flew out to Dubai twenty-four hours earlier. Would you like the revised flight details?'

Alexander grabbed a pen and paper. 'Yes, please.'

Six minutes later he put down the phone and leant back in his seat. As soon as he'd finished the call to the airline he'd contacted the Dubai stables where Shaf had been booked for the duration of the World Cup. It had turned out to be a very confused call, and difficult to say which party was the more perplexed: the stable manager who knew perfectly well that Shaf was alive and well and eating hay in his stall, or William Alexander who was trying to work out what the hell was going on. Why would someone kidnap or maybe even kill about a dozen people, steal a three-million-dollar horse, only to deliver it safely to the place it was supposed to go, and then walk away? It made no sense at all unless, he reflected with a slight smile, the kidnappers happened to be Irish.

But it was progress of a sort, and he was certain that Qabandi would want to fly immediately to the UAE to check on his treasured thoroughbred. So before he told the sheikh what he had discovered, he booked seats on the first available flight to Dubai, organized a limousine to collect them at the airport there, and confirmed their pre-booked hotel suites.

Merzifon Air Force Base, Turkey

The Turkish Air Force is one of the best-equipped units in the eastern Mediterranean, operating a wide variety of aircraft, principally of American manufacture. Because of the country's proximity to the old Soviet Bloc, Turkey also possesses an extensive radar network to provide early warning of aircraft or missiles approaching from the north and north-east.

The long-range radar had detected the Cessna long before its pilot called Ruzgar and identified himself, but the slow-moving target was not assessed as a threat. Once the Turkish controllers had established the aircraft's identity, allocated a squawk and given the pilot permission to transit Turkish airspace, they basically forgot about it.

The Fulcrum was a different matter. The air-defence radars located at Sinop, almost the most northerly point on the Turkish mainland, detected it as Beleshayov was approaching Novorossiysk on the Black Sea coast, and an 'unknown' track identifier was allocated to it. Sinop is jointly operated by the Turks and the Americans, who refer to the facility as 'Diogenes Station' after the ancient Greek philosopher, who was born close by.

When the unidentified aircraft continued heading south, directly towards Turkey, and accelerated to Mach 2, the 'unknown' label was replaced by 'hostile', and scramble orders were sent to Merzifon.

151 Filo, the on-alert squadron, operates General Dynamics F-16C 'Fighting Falcon' air-superiority fighters and, within eight minutes of the scramble call, two

interceptors, equipped with full tanks and live weapons, turned on to the end of the duty runway, paused for just seconds as they waited for take-off clearance, then accelerated hard as the burners cut in.

Once airborne, the two aircraft moved into battle-pair formation, the number two positioned behind and to the right of his leader, and then turned north-east, directly towards the incoming MiG-29. And approaching a point some five miles above the Black Sea, where the Turkish fighter control computers had already calculated that their interceptors would meet the unknown Russian aircraft, the Cessna 340 continued its relatively slow but steady progress towards Turkey.

Cessna 340 air ambulance, callsign Romeo Charlie Three Six

'Romeo Charlie Three Six, Ruzgar, traffic information. You have very fast-moving traffic, five o'clock at range eighty-five, heading towards. Single contact. No height information.'

Wilson was in the co-pilot's seat, headset draped around his neck. When he heard the start of this message over the loudspeaker he pulled up the earphone and listened intently. 'Just acknowledge it,' he instructed.

'Three Six, Roger.' Vassily glanced at Wilson. 'What is it? A Russian fighter?'

'That's what I was expecting, but it changes nothing. Just keep going.'

'I can increase speed – another thirty or forty knots.'

'Don't bother. It wouldn't make any difference if they are going to intercept us, and it would reduce our range too much. We must have enough fuel to make Cairo.'

'How long before we cross the border?' Dawson asked from the cockpit doorway.

Vassily studied the GPS display in front of him, then the navigation chart. 'Ten, maybe fifteen minutes.' He turned to Wilson. 'Listen, if we increase speed we can—'

'It wouldn't help, and we don't need to. There's another factor here.'

The pilot looked sceptical. 'What other factor? That interceptor could blow us out of the sky before we even see it.'

Wilson nodded. 'I know it could, but it won't happen. Just wait.'

'For what?'

The noise from the speaker broke the sudden silence in the cockpit. 'Romeo Charlie Three Six, Ruzgar, with additional traffic for you. Two identified high-speed contacts in your one o'clock position range fifty-two, heading towards, level at Flight Level two eight zero. Maintain your present level and heading.'

'For that,' Wilson announced. 'That's a pair of Turkish fighters going to intercept the Russian. *That* was what I was waiting for, and that's why there's no need for us to increase speed.'

MiG-29 interceptor, callsign Zero Six Eight

'Zero Six Eight, target bears one seven five at forty-five.'

Beleshayov stared at his radar screen. The return he believed to be the Cessna was painting clearly, forty kilometres directly ahead. He pulled the MiG-29 out of afterburner. He had to start reducing height and speed, otherwise he'd overshoot it by miles.

'Zero Six Eight, caution, caution. Two fast-moving contacts twelve o'clock range seventy-three. Possibly Turkish interceptors, high-speed and heading towards.'

Beleshayov cursed under his breath. This was a common problem whenever Russian aircraft were conducting manoeuvres over southern Georgia or the Black Sea. Occasionally the dogfights strayed a little too far south, and as soon as they approached close to Turkish airspace, a pair of fighters would be scrambled to intercept them.

Normally these incidents fizzled out well before the opposing aircraft got near each other, the Russian fighters retreating to the north-east, and the Turkish interceptors holding position close to their own territorial boundary until it was obvious that the other aircraft were heading home. That, Beleshayov knew, would not happen in this case. The colonel had made it perfectly clear that the air ambulance was to be destroyed, even if the MiG-29 was forced to tangle with Turkish fighters to achieve its objective.

The only let-out Beleshayov had was the colonel's final, very specific instruction: if the Cessna managed to reach the coast, or even a point over the Black Sea from which the debris from its destruction could land on Turkish soil, he was to abandon the intercept. This caveat had been explicitly included in the orders issued by FSB headquarters in Moscow.

The colonel had been emphatic. 'If that happens, just let it go. It won't be our problem any more.'

Cessna 340 air ambulance, callsign Romeo Charlie Three Six

'There they are,' Wilson pointed through the windscreen.

Dawson and Vassily stared in the direction he was indicating, and then both men nodded as they spotted the two fast-moving aircraft heading towards them, six thousand feet above.

Vassily pulled on his headset and depressed the transmit key. 'Ruzgar, Romeo Charlie Three Six. Contact with the traffic in our one o'clock position.'

'Roger.' The controller sounded somewhat harassed, and Wilson guessed he was monitoring, perhaps even controlling, the two fighters simultaneously.

'They're F-16s,' Dawson muttered, as the two aircraft passed over the Cessna.

'Now what?' Vassily asked.

'Not our problem,' Wilson said. 'Keep heading for the border and maintain your present heading and speed. Don't forget, we're just an air ambulance on a mission of mercy. Whatever your lot sent up after us, I'm quite sure those two Falcons can handle it.'

MiG-29 interceptor, callsign Zero Six Eight

Beleshayov's Fulcrum was now twenty kilometres behind the Cessna, and he'd reached a similar conclusion to Wilson. If he tangled with those two F-16s, he knew that he'd probably come off worst.

The MiG-29 is a highly capable aircraft, and in one-to-one combat could certainly hold its own against most American air-superiority fighters – in fact, the Fulcrum was in part designed to match the performance envelope of both the F-15 and the F-16 – but up against two Falcons it would be a very different matter. And the Turkish coastline was clearly visible below and in front of him. It was going to be very tight.

He ran through a handful of scenarios in his mind, trying to work out the actions most likely to enable him to achieve his objective. Eventually, he settled on what seemed to offer the best chance of success, and that might also allow him to complete the intercept without the F-16s getting involved.

'Zero Six Eight, request situation report.'

'Stand by.'

Beleshayov could imagine the scene back at the air-defence centre as the controllers struggled to make sense of the contacts on their radar screens. There would now be four returns, all within about ten miles of each other, and with the very slow data-update rate – air-defence radar heads turn much more slowly than those used by Air Traffic Control units because of the need for the maximum possible range – it would be very difficult to keep track of what was going on, even using the intercept

computers. But right then he had other things on his mind. He would give the controller an update only when he felt able to.

The MiG-29 was now subsonic, but still travelling at more than twice the speed of the Cessna, and heading directly towards the north Turkish coast. Beleshayov scanned ahead, checking the position of his target before confirming its identity with the data-linked symbol on his radar display. Then he turned his attention to the two Falcons.

They were about two thousand feet above, heading towards him and inside five miles, and they too had reduced to subsonic. He knew they would be carrying live weapons, but he also knew that the Turkish pilots would be very reluctant to engage him.

As the F-16s passed over his MiG-29, and began descending to follow him, Beleshayov started a gentle turn to starboard, a manoeuvre that would take him away from his target, and also away from the coast. That might convince the Turkish pilots that he was just on some kind of training exercise, and had simply strayed a little too far south. But the turn would also allow him to get close to the Cessna.

Beleshayov divided his attention equally between the radar display and the view from the cockpit, picking his precise moment. As he closed to less than a mile from the target, he tightened the turn, rolling the MiG-29 further to the right until its wings were almost vertical.

He'd timed it to perfection. As the fighter banked hard, turning starboard through west so as to head away from the coast, Beleshayov looked straight down towards the Black Sea and there, three thousand feet below him, he saw the Cessna. It was only in view for a couple of seconds before the MiG-29 accelerated away, but that was long enough.

Beleshayov, like most professional pilots, was an expert in aircraft recognition, and that brief glance was enough to identify the 340. But even if he hadn't recognized the model, the prominent red crosses on the wings told him all he needed to know.

Riyadh, Saudi Arabia

'Have you informed that police inspector yet?' Qabandi demanded.

'Not yet,' William Alexander replied, with a slight smile. 'I thought you might prefer to talk to him yourself.'

'You have his mobile number?' Alexander passed him a slip of paper. 'You've booked our flights to Dubai? And confirmed the hotel and the car?'

The inspector answered on the second ring. 'This is Sheikh Qabandi and I have some slightly confusing information for you. I confess I don't know what's going on, but we've discovered that somebody rescheduled the flight for my horse's journey. The air tickets have already been used, and Shaf is currently in Dubai, at the same stables we booked weeks ago. We're going there immediately, and I suspect you might find the missing Range Rover in the Riyadh Airport car park.'

'This isn't just some misunderstanding? Bin Mahmoud didn't simply decide to travel to Dubai earlier than originally planned?'

'No. He would never have changed the reservations without telling me, and there's still the fact that the stables were left completely unattended. I'm still convinced that bin Mahmoud has been kidnapped or more likely murdered. You may find forensic evidence in the Range Rover which could help identify the perpetrators.'

'Very well, Sheikh Qabandi,' the inspector sounded somewhat resigned, 'I'll initiate a search at the airport for the vehicle, and I'll keep you informed.'

Cessna 340 air ambulance, callsign Romeo Charlie Three Six

The three men heard the roar of the MiG-29's turbojets as the interceptor turned directly above them. Wilson peered up in time to catch a brief glimpse of the Russian fighter.

'What is it?' Dawson asked.

'A Fulcrum, and loaded for bear.'

Vassily stared upwards, his face pale, as the echo of the powerful jet's engines faded away. Then he looked round nervously, his hand stretching involuntarily towards the throttles.

Wilson stopped his movement with a gesture. 'Don't worry.'

The pilot didn't look convinced, and even Dawson, crouching down at the rear of the cockpit, appeared somewhat nervous.

MiG-29 interceptor, callsign Zero Six Eight

Beleshayov continued his turn, rolling out on north. For the moment he ignored the Cessna and instead checked the F-16s. They were still in battle pair, about three thousand feet above him and turning right, clearly following him as he moved away from the Turkish coastline.

Beleshayov eased the throttles forward slightly, and the MiG-29 began accelerating. He wanted to convince the two Turkish pilots he was returning to base. Then he could execute a quick turn, take out the Cessna and head for home.

He checked his radar. As he'd hoped, the F-16s hadn't accelerated to keep pace with him, but had continued turning, hopefully to head back to their base inside Turkey. The worst scenario would be for them to remain in their present location, flying a holding pattern, until he'd cleared the area completely.

He checked his radar again: the Cessna was some ten miles south, the F-16s six miles south-east. Beleshayov had just one chance to get it right. He throttled back the MiG-29 to an indicated airspeed of just over two hundred and fifty knots, and held the aircraft on a north-easterly heading while he began his combat preparations. it

The tactic he'd devised was a simple, one-shot option. He'd decided not to use his R-60M missiles against the Cessna, since the Aphid is a Mach 2 missile using an all-aspect infrared guidance system and with active laser proximity fusing, and Beleshayov doubted if the comparatively low heat emissions from the Cessna's engines would be enough to guarantee a lock. But they would certainly come in handy if the Falcons did decide to join the party.

Instead, he was going to haul the MiG-29 round in a tight starboard turn, and then kick in the afterburners to close the distance to the Cessna in the shortest possible time. Once the target was within range of his cannon, he'd engage it and then head north, hopefully before the Turkish pilots could do anything to stop him.

'Zero Six Eight. From command, situation report.' The controller sounded irritated.

Beleshayov made a quick check of his navigation computer, then thumbed the transmit button. 'Zero Six Eight is position north forty-two ten, east thirty-eight zero five, heading north-east at Flight Level two five zero and preparing to engage the target. Target bears one nine zero range fifteen, three thousand below. Two number Turkish foxtrot one six interceptors bearing one five zero range nine, three thousand above.'

As he finished this report, Beleshayov pulled the MiG-29 into a tight right-hand turn and eased the throttles forward. As the Fulcrum steadied on its new heading, the intercept controller responded. 'Zero Six Eight. Roger. Stand by.'

What exactly was that supposed to mean? Beleshayov wondered as he checked the range of the Cessna. He didn't want to be travelling too fast when he fired, because he had to be able to change direction quickly, before the pilots of the F-16s could react. The faster an aircraft is flying, the wider the radius of any turn. Beleshayov was planning on engaging full military power and getting the hell away from the area the moment he'd shot down the air ambulance, and that meant the tightest possible turn to the north-east.

His finger was actually resting on the firing button when the voice of the intercept controller sounded in his earphones.

'Zero Six Eight. From command. Abort, abort, abort.'

Beleshayov instantly moved his finger, but he didn't immediately alter course. 'Confirm abort?' he demanded.

'Zero Six Eight. Abort confirmed. Break off and return to base immediately.'

'Roger. Zero Six Eight is aborting.'

Beleshayov deselected the Master Arm switch and hauled the MiG-29 round to starboard, away from the two F-16s which had already left their holding pattern and were heading towards him. The moment the Fulcrum was established in the turn, he engaged the afterburners and waited for the kick as they cut in.

Seconds later, the MiG-29 punched through the sound barrier and began opening to the north at almost one thousand miles an hour. The F-16s followed him for nearly two hundred kilometres – Beleshayov watching them carefully on his radar – but the pilots made no move to intercept him. No doubt the Turks would file a protest with Moscow during the next few days, but that wouldn't be his problem, since he had just been following orders.

As he headed back towards Primorsko, now sub-sonic to conserve fuel, Beleshayov reviewed his actions, and those of the intercept controller, and came to the conclusion that the Cessna must have been just too close to the Turkish coast. And, in truth, he was pleased. The idea of shooting down an unarmed aircraft was repugnant to him, no matter who or what the air ambulance had been carrying, and he was also keenly aware that, if he had completed the intercept, he would likely have been attacked in his turn by the two Turkish fighters, and might not have survived. All in all, it was a pretty satisfactory outcome.

A long way south, the three occupants of the Cessna looked down at the town of Tirebolu, on the Black Sea coast of Turkey, and experienced a similar sense of relief.

Chapter Ten

Paul Richter walked into the Al-Safir restaurant in the Sheraton and paused to look round. The huge picture windows offered a stunning view of the Arabian Gulf, and several tables were already occupied. He spotted Carole-Anne Jackson in the far corner, and walked over to join her.

'Hullo again,' he greeted her. 'Where's Bill?'

'He's gone to pick up Tariq.' She smiled. 'Is your room OK?'

Richter nodded. 'Fine, thanks. I'm trying hard not to get used to this five-star living. I've got the reality of my normal life back in London to look forward to when this lot's over.'

'And that, I suppose, is not exactly fine dining at the Dorchester? That,' she added, 'is about the only hotel in London I've ever heard of.'

'On my salary, I can't afford to even buy a coffee in the Dorchester, far less eat there.'

'It sounds like your salary scales are remarkably similar to ours. Where do you actually live?'

'I've got a top-floor alleged mansion flat – really just a converted attic – in a pretty scruffy area called Stepney. Have you ever been to London?'

183

'No ... Well, yes, I did visit, but back when I was about sixteen. It was a typical American school-kids' "do Britain in five days" trip. A day and a half in London – Westminster and the Tower of London, if I remember right. Then Stratford-upon-Avon and Edinburgh' – Richter smiled slightly at her pronunciation – 'and a bunch of other places. But I'm sure I've never been to Stepney.'

Richter glanced up to see Bill Evans approaching, accompanied by a short and stocky man with dark skin and a thick mop of black hair.

'Hi, Paul,' Evans began. 'This is Tariq Mazen, one of our local colleagues. Tariq, this is Paul Richter, from London.'

The new arrivals sat down as a waiter approached, menus in hand. After they'd ordered, Evans leant forward confidentially. 'Tariq is the man who brought us the report about the mystery patient in the hospital. I've already explained to him why you don't think the sighting can be genuine.'

'It might be,' Richter conceded, 'but it's far more likely just a case of mistaken identity.'

Mazen nodded. 'I agree,' he said, 'but we still had to check it out.'

'One question,' Richter asked. 'Why did you come to us instead of the Americans? They're the people most anxious to find this man, and they're the ones offering the reward.'

Mazen nodded again. 'That's true, but here we've always had much closer ties with Britain than with the United States, and I was worried about how the Americans would react. They so often seem to have a somewhat arrogant and macho attitude to senstive situations.

I don't include you, of course, Carole: I regard you as an honorary Englishwoman.' Jackson inclined her head but didn't respond. 'I guessed the Americans would probably want to surround the entire hospital with tanks and troops, and maybe even send in a SWAT team. On balance, I thought the British would react in a more discreet manner.'

'Yes, we're big on discreet,' Richter agreed, 'and the reality is that, after the latest defence cuts, we probably don't have enough tanks and troops left to surround anything quite as big as a hospital.'

'Yes,' Mazen smiled. 'There's that, too.'

Once they'd been served their meals, Richter again asked the question he'd posed earlier. 'As we have to confirm this man's identity, how do I get to see him if his ward is securely guarded?'

'Perhaps "guarded" is the wrong word,' Mazen suggested. 'Entry to his ward is controlled, certainly, but my informant tells me that medical personnel are able to enter and leave quite freely. I believe that the measures are mainly intended to protect this man's privacy.'

'That's another reason why your informant's probably mistaken.'

'Exactly.' Mazen shrugged. 'We can probably get you inside fairly easily, just by giving you a white coat and a stethoscope.' As a plan, Richter thought, that left something to be desired. 'What might prove more difficult is actually taking a photograph of the target. Will London insist on a picture, or would your eyewitness testimony be enough?'

All three of them looked at Richter. 'We'll definitely need a picture,' he decided.

'And you can't just wander on to the ward waving an Instamatic, in case it really *is* our Saudi friend,' Jackson suggested.

'Absolutely right. Do you have a technical intelligence section here? Or just a Minox or something I could use?'

'I think we can get you a buttonhole camera with a remote shutter release, something like that,' Evans said.

'That should work.' Richter turned back to Mazen. 'As well as the white coat I'll need to be carrying some kind of identification. I won't be able to march straight in – I presume the bodyguards will be checking names at the very least.'

'That shouldn't be a problem. My informant has already obtained the identification card of a doctor who won't be back at the hospital for a week. He's currently at a medical conference in Kuwait.'

'Your hospital cleaner knows that for a fact?' Richter's voice was openly sceptical.

Mazen smiled patiently. 'No, Paul. He's a simple man who just obtained what I asked him to find. I have a separate contact on the hospital's administration staff who made the travel arrangements for the doctor. Unfortunately he doesn't have access to medical records or admissions information, otherwise all this might not be necessary.'

'Right,' Richter said, 'that sounds like it should work. Let's meet here again for breakfast tomorrow morning, to finalize details for the entry.'

Volgograd, Russia

Vaslav Litvinoff had endured a somewhat fraught evening because he was now effectively out of the loop. He'd abdicated his responsibility to the staff at the FSB headquarters in Moscow, and they in turn were relying on the Air Army of North Caucasus to stop the Cessna.

He called Moscow three times, but on each occasion he was told there was no news. Finally, he went out to eat a solitary meal in a restaurant close to the FSB office, his mobile phone on the table beside him, while he anxiously waited for the call that would signal the conclusion of the incident. But when FSB headquarters finally contacted him, the news wasn't what he'd expected.

'We've let it go.'

'You've done *what*?' Litvinoff could hardly believe what he was hearing.

'We had no option. The Cessna had almost reached the Turkish border before the fighter got to it, and by then the Turks had launched two interceptors of their own. The air-defence staff decided it was safest to order the pilot not to engage the Cessna. If he had done, the Turks would probably have shot him down.'

'But the nuclear weapon. That—'

'That,' the FSB officer interrupted firmly, 'is no longer our problem. Whatever those Americans are planning, we're reasonably certain it won't involve any of our own territories. We'll advise the SVR and the GRU, so they can take appropriate steps, but our initial analysis suggests that these Americans may have been working for the CIA, so they may have stolen the weapon simply to study its design and construction.'

'I am not feeling so confident,' Litvinoff growled.

'Your views are noted. I must also inform you that an internal inquiry has been ordered. The loss of this weapon is a very serious matter and the investigation will be reviewed at the highest level. You are instructed to travel to Moscow forthwith, under escort.'

Litvinoff ended the call without another word, and for a few moments sat with his head in his hands. The delay in the FSB headquarters calling him suddenly made perfect sense. He crumpled his napkin and threw it on the table, stood up and turned towards the door of the restaurant, where two men in heavy overcoats already stood waiting for him.

Cairo, Egypt

'Romeo Charlie Three Six is clear to land runway two three right. Wind light and variable. Altimeter one zero one seven. After landing, call Ground on one two zero decimal one.'

The pilot acknowledged, then glanced over at Wilson, sitting in the right-hand seat. 'Your colleague?'

Wilson turned and called out. 'Strap yourself in back there. We're long final.'

'OK.' Dawson reached down to tighten the straps that he'd already positioned in readiness over his legs, then attached another over his chest.

After landing, the Cessna taxied across to a hardstanding where a white Mercedes was parked, the rear section grossly enlarged to permit people to stand up in it, and with red crosses painted prominently on the side.

Vassily applied the parking brake and switched off the engines. Then he turned to look nervously at Wilson. The American grinned at him. 'Don't worry, my friend, we've no quarrel with you. Keep your mouth shut, and we'll never meet again. But breathe a word of this to anyone at all and be assured one of us will come back to Russia and find you, and you *really* don't want that to happen.'

Studying the expression on the American's face, Vassily believed him – absolutely.

'OK, our ride's moving this way, so let's get the patient ready.'

Just under two hours later the Mercedes ambulance arrived at Ain Shams Hospital where Dawson, still apparently semi-conscious, was admitted for overnight observation. Wilson booked himself a room in a nearby hotel, and went to bed almost immediately. He would have a lot to do the next day, and a very early start, and now he needed his sleep.

Potomac Consolidated TRACON, Vint Hill, Fauquier County, Virginia

The Potomac Consolidated TRACON was created to rationalize the Air Traffic Control procedures that had previously applied in the twenty-three thousand square miles surrounding Washington D.C. This is one of the busiest aviation sectors in the world with around two million movements annually, and is arguably the most sensitive piece of airspace in America because of the buildings that stand on the ground beneath it.

Before the Potomac facility opened, five separate TRACONs had controlled traffic within the area. The controllers were based in different locations, using separate radar systems and communications which had necessitated continuous coordination between the various units. The Potomac facility had resolved the problems by consolidating the airspace into a single entity, controlled from the new building at Vint Hill in Virginia.

Gillian Thorpe had worked as an Operations Supervisor for a little over ten years, and at the Potomac TRACON ever since it became operational. Four weeks earlier a tall, well-built, dark-haired man named Charles Rogers had walked into her office, without an appointment, and showed her his FBI identification.

He'd sat in the chair in front of her desk and for about thirty minutes explained the measures the Bureau had taken in the aftermath of the events of 9/11 to check the legitimacy of both commercial and non-commercial aviation. Most of what he'd said Gillian already knew, either professionally or through reports in the media, but some of it was news to her. These measures, Rogers told her, had proved successful, but it was now felt that a further independent check should be instituted regarding certain types of flight plan.

The majority of flight plans are those filed by airlines themselves for their scheduled movements, and although they are submitted individually, the basic information remains the same. For instance, every morning a British Airways 747 flies from London Heathrow to John F.

Kennedy Airport at New York and then, with a fresh crew on board, does the same journey in reverse, departing JFK in the early evening and arriving at Heathrow early the following morning. The scheduled departure times are always the same, as are the aircraft callsigns – British Airways use 'Speedbird' followed by a number – but what changes each day is the route the aircraft will follow, because of the Atlantic weather systems.

These commercial flights were not a problem, Rogers had said, because of the stringent security measures now imposed at all American and major international airports, but the FBI was growing concerned about charter flights, cargo carriers, private aviation and even government-operated aircraft. These categories, he explained, posed different kinds of dangers. There was always the possibility that a group hostile to America could hire, steal or commandeer an aircraft and, after evading security at some small airfield, turn it into a flying bomb.

To counter this possibility, the FBI had increased its surveillance measures across the country. Most of the new procedures had already been applied at the points of origin – airfields, flying clubs, maintenance facilities and the like – but the Bureau believed that significant additional data could be extracted from analysing flight plans. Initially, this was being done on a random basis, choosing areas of the country likely to be particularly targeted by terrorist organizations. Selecting Washington D.C. and the Potomac Consolidated TRACON had been a no-brainer and that, Rogers had added, was where Gillian Thorpe could help the Bureau.

And so, for just under a month, Thorpe and her fellow

supervisors had been analysing all non-commercial flight plans processed by the TRACON, selecting those which met the FBI's criteria, and sending the data they extracted to the email address Rogers had provided. Twice the TRACON had received acknowledgements from him, and three times requests for additional information about some particular flight.

That morning, Thorpe scanned the overnight plans, identified those that she would need to extract data from, and began working on them. The thirty-seventh flight plan she opened had been filed the previous evening by the State Department. It was for a Gulfstream G450 out of Andrews Air Force Base, destination Dubai, with a single refuelling stop planned in Barcelona, Spain, and departing the following afternoon.

This flight plan had been filed with the Andrews Airport Traffic Control Tower and forwarded to the Potomac TRACON and, Thorpe noted, well ahead of the required minimum time, which was ninety minutes before take-off. Most such plans are filed as late as possible, after the aircraft's operating authority has finalized all the details, because it's much easier to file late than to submit early and then have to make changes. State, Gillian Thorpe presumed, had no intention of altering any aspect of that flight.

After extracting the data, she would send it on to Washington Center. From there it would be routed to Boston Center, to the Canadian authorities and thence to Eurocontrol, thus ensuring that all controlling agencies that would handle any portion of the flight were aware of the programmed movement.

She wasn't to know it, but this particular flight plan

was the only one that Charles Rogers had the slightest interest in. Rogers – his real name was Roy Sutter, and the closest he'd ever got to the Federal Bureau of Investigation was when he drove past the J. Edgar Hoover Building in Washington D.C. – had been waiting for two particular pieces of information extracted from that plan for the whole of the last week. Minutes after he opened the email in a cyber café in Paris, he made copies of the relevant sections, pasted them into a new message and sent it on to another email address.

He would monitor the messages sent by the TRACON supervisors for another twelve hours, just in case there were any changes to the Gulfstream's details, and then he'd send Thorpe the email he'd already prepared. This would tell her the Bureau no longer considered the arrangement necessary, and thank her and her colleagues for their efforts and cooperation in assisting the FBI to combat international terrorism.

But before he did any of that, he'd catch the first available flight down to Barcelona, because the next phase of the operation was starting about twenty-four hours sooner than he'd expected.

Sheraton Hotel, Manama, Bahrain

Richter was lying in bed, reading a bad novel that he hoped would eventually send him off to sleep, when he heard a brief double knock on the door. He pulled on his dressing gown and padded over to open it.

Carole-Anne Jackson was standing outside in the corridor. Richter said nothing, just opened the door wide.

Jackson walked in, stopped in the middle of the room and glanced round.

'Very nice,' she said. 'I'm glad I'm not paying for it.'

'So am I. Is there a problem?'

Jackson sat down in one of the easy chairs and looked at him thoughtfully. 'Not really. It's been called off.'

'Why? Does that mean the geniuses at Vauxhall Cross have finally come to their senses?'

'That would be a bit too much to expect. No, it's something simpler and more obvious than that. Twenty minutes ago Tariq Mazen rang me. He'd just come from an emergency meeting called by his informant, the cleaner at the hospital. The sheikh's private ward is now empty.'

'He's gone? Does he know where?'

Jackson grinned. 'Nobody knows *exactly* where he's gone, but it really doesn't matter. The sheikh died early this afternoon, and now we know precisely who he was.'

'Brilliant,' Richter muttered. 'So who was he?'

'His name wasn't Rashid, but he *was* a sheikh and a minor member of the Saudi royal family. He'd come to Bahrain for dialysis, as we guessed, but then he died of liver failure following some kind of complication.'

'Well, that bears out what we all thought. It's a pity he didn't die a couple of days earlier – then I wouldn't have had a completely pointless journey.'

'Oh, I don't know. Your visit here might not have been a total waste of time.'

For a long moment Richter said nothing, just looked at her. 'Well,' he said slowly, 'I can't deny it's been a pleasant interlude being here. A good meal this evening, very pleasant company, not to mention the five-star accommodation.' Jackson still said nothing, just smiled. 'You do realize,' Richter added, 'that the pointy-heads at Legoland have strict rules about their employees fraternizing?'

'Point one: fraternizing was not what I had in mind. Point two: they're never going to find out unless one of us tells them. Point three: you don't work there, and nor do I, so they can stuff their rules. Now stop dithering about and pour me a drink.'

Chapter Eleven

Thursday
Sheraton Hotel, Manama, Bahrain

Richter woke early. He glanced to his left, expecting to see Carole-Anne Jackson lying there, but the bed was empty. In fact, the sheets were pulled up neatly, and her clothes had gone from the back of the chair where she'd left them the night before.

'So much for breakfast in bed,' he muttered, though in truth he wasn't bothered. He'd always found 'morning after' conversations difficult, especially when he hardly knew the woman who'd shared his bed. Most of his infrequent sexual encounters tended to be of the one-night stand variety and, on the one occasion when he had become deeply involved, it had ended in disaster.

He was usually happy to follow the pithy advice of a wealthy but alimony-weary American friend many years earlier: 'If it flies, fucks or floats, rent it.' Cynical maybe, sexist certainly, but not having a wife or a permanent girlfriend meant Richter had one less thing to worry about.

But as he relaxed on the pillows, the bathroom door opened suddenly and Jackson appeared, fully dressed. She smiled at him. 'Sorry to rush off now, but I've got an early start. I've had a call from Caxton.'

'I didn't hear the phone.'

'I left my mobile set to silent and I found I'd missed a call from the office, so I've just rung in. Julian Caxton, our Head of Station, wants to meet you here at the hotel before you leave for the UAE.'

'No problem. What about?'

'He didn't say. Probably just to apologize for your wasted journey.'

'As you said last night,' Richter pointed out, 'it wasn't *entirely* wasted.'

'No,' Jackson agreed, 'not entirely. Anyway, Caxton will be here around ten, and he'll see you down in the lobby. Something urgent's come up at the office that I have to deal with, so I'd better go now.' She walked round to Richter's side of the bed, bent down and kissed him. 'I guess I'll see you around,' she added.

'I don't think I'm likely to get back out here. Once I've finished in Dubai my boss will expect to see me hunched over my desk in Hammersmith, pushing piles of paper around.'

Jackson smiled down at him. 'I don't know why,' she said slowly, 'but I have the distinct feeling that we're going to run into each other again.'

Nad Al-Sheba Racecourse, Dubai

Saadi lowered the miniature binoculars and looked thoughtfully towards the Nad Al-Sheba racecourse. When the operation had been formulated in Afghanistan, the planners had realized that without detailed knowledge of the racecourse's layout and security systems, the question of obtaining access could not be addressed. So they'd left Saadi to work it out for himself.

But getting inside wasn't going to be as easy as he'd hoped. With a full programme of racing already in progress, the racecourse was constantly active, with groundsmen, caterers, bar staff and other tradesmen milling around, not to mention thousands of spectators.

'My friends,' he turned to Massood and Bashar, 'I would welcome your suggestions. How are we going to breach their security?'

'I think we've only two options,' Massood said at once. 'We must enter either openly by day, or by stealth without being detected. By openly I mean that we would have to assume the identity of regular tradesmen you might expect to see at the racecourse, as electricians or caterers, perhaps, or we attend as spectators. Otherwise we'll have to go in at night, avoiding the guards.'

'Which do you think offers the best chance of success?'

'Impersonating tradesmen might be risky, since we don't yet know the layout of the racecourse, or what sort of identification is required. And we would need to steal or hire a suitable vehicle, with sufficient tools and equipment to convince the guards that we were legitimate.'

'We could steal a vehicle from a company that's already working here,' Bashar suggested.

'That's true,' Massood agreed, 'but we would probably have to kill the workers themselves, and that would leave a trace. A husband who doesn't return home, a son who goes missing – questions would soon be asked. Entering as race-goers wouldn't work because of what we have to take with us. The gate guards would not allow us inside the racecourse without inspecting our bags, so it looks like we'll have to slip in at night.'

Saadi turned to Bashar. 'Do you agree?'

'Yes. Massood is right. We'll only succeed if our intentions remain unknown.'

'This evening we can work out exactly what extra equipment we'll need, but now we have to decide where to cross the fence. That means surveying as much of the perimeter as we can.'

As Saadi put the Renault into gear and drove it down the road closer to the racecourse, Massood picked up the piece of paper on which he'd already made copious notes.

Sheraton Hotel, Manama, Bahrain

Richter was waiting in the lobby when Caxton and Evans walked in. Evans made the necessary introductions, then ordered drinks.

'I'm sorry your trip out here has been to no purpose,' Caxton began, 'but we had to check the report, however unlikely it might seem.'

'It wasn't a problem,' Richter replied, 'though the timing could have been better. If I'd got the call a day later I might have finished in Dubai and then flown back to the UK from here.'

'What were you up to in the UAE, assuming that isn't classified information?'

Richter smiled at that, but didn't respond until the waiter was out of earshot. 'You're the SIS Head of

Station here, so I think I *ought* to be able to trust you. But it wasn't classified, and I think I'm going to be wasting my time there as well. It involves checking out an expatriate Englishman who claims he experiences dreams about terrorist bombings before they actually happen. You've probably seen something about him in the traffic coming from Vauxhall Cross.'

'Oh, yes, James Holden.' Caxton stirred his coffee thoughtfully. 'I gathered some kind of investigation was in progress, but I was surprised they'd sent someone all the way from London. I would have thought a local officer could have been tasked.'

'So would I, but I don't think SIS really believed there was any substance in what Holden was claiming, so they decided to pass the investigation over to my outfit. We tend to get given the jobs that Vauxhall Cross doesn't like the look of.'

'And how is Richard Simpson these days?'

'You know him?' Richter was surprised, knowing that his boss tended to keep a low profile.

'I've run into him a couple of times, and I also know a bit about your organization at Hammersmith. He's still keeping cacti, I suppose?'

'Yes, whole flocks of them. You can barely get near his desk for the prickly little green bastards.'

'So what do you think about Holden?'

'I don't know. If he'd just pitched up after the event, we'd have dismissed him as one of the usual loonies, but his statement in advance of the Damascus suicide bombing was very detailed. Maybe he's a genuine psychic, able to tune in to certain future events. If he is, then at least we have to look seriously at his claim that a Gulf

State hotel is about to be hit. That's the logical conclusion, but my personal opinion is that it's all rubbish, and there's actually something else going on that we know nothing about.'

Evans glanced at Caxton. 'Perhaps our friend Holden can help find out what happened to Shaf,' he suggested with a smile.

'Shaf? Who's Shaf?' Richter asked, puzzled.

'It's not a "who", more a "what",' Caxton explained. 'Just a little local happening that doesn't seem to make much sense. Shaf's a prize racehorse, entered for the Godolphin Mile event and ... do you know anything about horse racing?'

'The square root of sod-all,' Richter replied. 'I've got no interest whatsoever in any form of organized sport.'

'Not even cricket?'

'Especially not cricket,' he said firmly.

'Right, then. The World Cup was first run in '96 at the Nad Al-Sheba track in Dubai. It's now the world's richest horse race, with prize money totalling six million US dollars. The Godolphin Mile is itself worth a million. The money's one thing, of course, but the World Cup's as much a social event as sport. The locals are mad about horse racing, and most of the nobility of the Arab world turn up there.'

'And Shaf?' Richter demanded. Caxton seemed to have drifted somewhat from the point.

The SIS officer explained what the police had found at the Al-Shahrood stables.

'There doesn't seem to be much of a mystery,' Richter said finally. 'It sounds to me like a straightforward theft. OK, the missing item's a bit unusual, but my guess is that there'll be a ransom demand in the post any time now.'

The smile hadn't left Evans's face yet. '*That* isn't the mystery. What nobody can work out is why Shaf is at this very moment scoffing hay in his pre-booked stables over in Dubai.'

'Say again?'

'The mystery is why Shaf was apparently kidnapped – or whatever the correct term is for a stolen horse – and then delivered to his stable in Dubai about twenty-four hours earlier than originally planned. Vets there have checked the horse for drugs, but found nothing, and there've been no unusually large bets placed on him for the race.'

'You're right,' Richter said. 'That doesn't make any sense at all. What about the missing people from the stables in Saudi – have any of them turned up so far?'

'Not one,' Caxton replied, 'and yet there were no signs of violence. The men who delivered Shaf to Dubai never checked in to their pre-booked hotel in the city, and nobody has any clue where they are, or even who they are. Sheikh Qabandi, the horse's owner, is a powerful man, and he hasn't been reticent in driving the police investigation. I think they would have been happy enough to file it as a missing persons report, and just wait until one of the stable staff eventually turned up. As the police see it, there's no evidence that a crime has been committed, but Qabandi won't let them drop it. He's insisted on area-wide coverage, which is why we know about it here in Bahrain.'

'Forensic scientists have been all over the stables back in Saudi,' Evans explained, 'and the only thing to raise a question mark was a small patch of dried fluid in the entrance hall of the main house. When they analysed it, they found it was urine, human in origin. Anyway, perhaps Holden can sleep on it and then let us know what really happened.'

Nad Al-Sheba Racecourse, Dubai

After two hours of checking, Saadi and his colleagues had identified three points along the boundary fence where they believed they could effect an entry without being detected.

'You've seen enough?'

Massood glanced down at his pages of notes and nodded. Saadi eased the Renault away from the kerb, heading back towards Dubai city.

'We must plan this final phase with great care,' Massood remarked. 'I don't think we'll have time to make all our preparations today. We've a lot to do, so we'll have to position the device tomorrow night. But that will still leave enough time.'

Manama, Bahrain

'I told you I'd see you again,' Carole-Anne Jackson said cheerfully, as Richter climbed into her BMW outside the Sheraton.

'I don't think you driving me to the airport counts as a date.'

His cases were already in the boot, and he had a

reservation on the next flight to Dubai, scheduled to depart in about three hours.

Jackson smiled at him. 'What's your plan now?' she asked.

'I'm going to talk to this Holden guy, and tell my boss what I think. Then I'll book a flight back to Heathrow and try to get through Dubai International without getting sucked in to any of the duty-free shops. My credit card can't take too much of a pounding right now.'

Jackson smiled at him again as she started the engine. 'And would you be interested in having a personal guide to the sights of Dubai before you head back to London – where it's raining at the moment? That's according to Bill Evans, who monitors the World Service for coded messages all the time.'

'You have someone in mind?'

'Yes, me, obviously. I've got a couple of days' leave due, so I could nip over tomorrow afternoon, say, which would give you time to sort out Holden during the morning. If you booked your flight back on Monday, that would give us most of Saturday together and all day Sunday. No strings, just a bit of sightseeing, some decent food and anything else you fancy.'

'Anything?'

Carole-Anne glanced across at him. 'Almost anything. I don't do whips and chains, latex or leather, but I'll consider pretty much anything else.'

'You know something?' Richter said, settling back in the seat. 'This might turn out to be the most entertaining trip I've been on for a long time. You've got my number. Give me a call when you're on your way, and I'll come and meet you at the airport.'

They were crossing the Sheikh Hamad Causeway when Jackson's mobile rang. She pulled the BMW over to the side of the road as soon as she could, and answered it. Her face clouded immediately and she spoke mostly in monosyllables, then ended the call abruptly.

She put the mobile back in its cradle, slipped the BMW into gear and accelerated hard. 'We'll have to scratch the Dubai interlude,' she said, 'and you'll have to change your flight.'

'Why?'

'Holden's been back to the embassy there, and now he claims he can see a car bomb exploding imminently – maybe today, tomorrow at the latest. He gave a lot of precise details and the Six people in Dubai believe the location is probably Bahrain itself. Right here in Manama, in fact.'

'And?'

'And Julian Caxton has talked to your Mr Simpson and you've been reassigned. The Six office will keep tabs on Holden until you eventually get back to Dubai, but in the meantime you're temporarily attached to us here in Bahrain, to help us find this bomb before it goes off.'

'Stuff a stoat,' Richter muttered.

'I couldn't have put it better myself,' Jackson replied, turning the BMW to head back towards Manama.

British Embassy, Government Avenue, Manama, Bahrain

'What exactly did he say this time?' Richter asked.

Bill Evans consulted the printout of an encrypted email sent from SIS Dubai less than an hour earlier.

'It's a car bomb that's already been positioned by two men wearing traditional Arab clothing. The vehicle's a big saloon, possibly American, and it's been left on a long straight road that either points towards the sea, or runs parallel with the seafront. That description, of course, could include most of the cars in Bahrain, and almost every street in Manama.'

'Or just about any other Gulf State town or city,' Richter pointed out. 'So why is SIS Dubai convinced the device is here?'

'Holden claims that when he dreams these events he sees them from above, so they asked him if he'd noticed anything else distinctive. The only thing he came up with was a civilian aircraft – or, at least, a big white jet which doesn't sound too military – landing on a nearby island.'

'Muharraq,' Carole-Anne Jackson breathed.

'Exactly,' Evans said. 'Bahrain is the only Gulf State where the airport is located on an offshore island. That's precisely why they think we're in the firing line.'

'Still sounds like bullshit to me,' Richter muttered, 'but I suppose we'll have to go through the motions. Do you have procedures for this? Like a street-clearance plan that the local police implement?'

Evans shook his head. 'As far as we know, they don't have any contingency plans like that, simply because there's never been any need for one before. All we can do – in fact what we've done already – is tell them what we think we know.'

'You didn't say where you got the information from, I hope?'

'No way,' said Evans with a grin. 'We don't want

our friends to think we spend our time here reading fucking tea leaves and decoding cats' entrails. We just told them the tip-off came from an anonymous source, and left it at that.'

'And what are they going to do?'

'Probably not a lot. They'll put more police on the streets, I suppose, and they'll check out any cars that fit the profile we've supplied, but realistically it's needle-in-a-haystack time. There are cars parked all over Manama on roads that fit Holden's description and any one of them could be the bomb vehicle. That's always assuming this guy isn't just yanking our chain for reasons of his own.'

'Amen to that,' Richter said. 'So what do you want me to do?'

'The same as the local plods. Caxton wants us out there on the streets, keeping our eyes open. We'll operate in pairs – one driving, the other watching, mobile phones switched on. The local SIS – the Bahraini outfit – is involved as well, and Tariq Mazen will be here any minute to pick me up. Are you happy to partner Carole?'

'Of course. And if we spot something?'

'Retreat to a safe distance and call it in. There's a bomb squad here, but I don't know how good their people are. I suppose this is one way of finding out.'

Manama, Bahrain

Carole-Anne Jackson swung the BMW out of Government Avenue, heading for King Faisal Highway.

'I've said it before,' Richter remarked, 'but I still think we're wasting our time.'

'So how's Holden doing it?' she asked. 'From the reports I read, he definitely predicted the Syrian suicide bombing.'

'He predicted *a* suicide bombing, without a doubt,' Richter conceded, 'but whether his prediction actually involved Damascus is another matter.'

'Well, most of the details were pretty much on the money, and he even got the bomber's name almost right.'

'Yes, but Assad isn't exactly an uncommon Arab name. I'd have been a lot more impressed if the *shahid* had been named Winston Churchill or something really unusual, and Holden had known that. Where are we going now, by the way?'

'If there is a genuine car bomb, I doubt if we'll find it in this area, but Caxton wanted all the roads covered. So we're going to drive out to the west side of Manama, and then start working our way down through the more likely locations – meaning the streets where a car could be parked in the same spot for a couple of days without attracting too much attention.'

'Do you have any favourite locations?'

'You mean where would I choose to leave a car bomb if I was a nasty Arab terrorist instead of a career officer in the internationally renowned Central Intelligence Agency?'

'You could have given me the short version but, yes, that's exactly what I mean.'

'Probably somewhere in the Kanoo, Fadhel or Ras Rummaan areas.'

Jackson's mobile phone rang, and Richter answered it. Julian Caxton's voice was perfectly clear, and there was no mistaking the urgency in his tone. 'The Bahraini police have located a possible suspect vehicle. A large American saloon parked in Qassim Al-Mehze, near the Al-Jazira Hotel. Please investigate it and report back.'

'Right.' Richter said, ending the call. 'The Al-Jazira Hotel,' he instructed, and Jackson immediately increased speed. 'That was Caxton,' he explained. 'The local plods have found a possible device in the vicinity. We've drawn the short straw, but at least he said "please".'

'He always does. He may be a bit of an old woman, but at least he's a polite old woman.'

The suspect vehicle was in fact some distance from the Al-Jazira, near the junction of Qassim Al-Mehze with Tujjaar, but that didn't matter because there were two Bahraini police cars parked to bracket the target, and in the process they were also blocking the road.

Jackson eased to a stop and they climbed out. She identified herself to the police officers, then beckoned Richter forward. He followed her and they stopped a few feet short of two other officers, who were peering through the windows of a cream-coloured Buick saloon.

'That's not the smartest move if there *is* an IED in that car,' Richter observed.

'True, but irrelevant. If it blows now, none of us would survive. Let's just see what they've found and then get the hell away from here.'

Richter looked into the car. It was immediately apparent what had made the police suspicious. On the rear seat lay two closed, square cardboard boxes, and between them a coil of wire and assorted tools. Below the wire he could just make out one corner of a dry-cell battery. He looked carefully for a few seconds more, then turned to Jackson.

'This isn't it,' he said.

'What?'

'There's no bomb in this car. My guess is it's owned by a part-time electrician. Those two boxes are probably full of switches or sockets or bulbs or something. What they're absolutely not full of is explosive.'

'How do you know? Are you sure?'

'I know something about IEDs. I also know something about the mentality of your typical terrorist,' Richter said. 'If there is a car bomb here somewhere, you probably won't be able to see it through the car window because it'll be hidden in the boot or under a seat. And if it is in plain view it'll be inside a box or a suitcase, something like that. You definitely won't be able to see a battery and coils of wire.'

Jackson studied him for a few moments. 'You're positive?' she asked.

'Absolutely,' Richter nodded. 'I still don't think there's a bomb here at all, but if there is one, *this* thing definitely isn't it.'

As he spoke the last word, there was a thunderous, echoing bang that seemed to shake the very ground they were standing on, and a billowing plume of dust rose from a nearby street.

'Told you so,' Richter said, already running back towards the BMW. 'At least I was half right.'

PAYBACK

Al-Qusais district, Dubai

On the eastern outskirts of Dubai, the three Arabs sat inside the Renault. Massood was running through the list of equipment they would need to assemble the following day.

'We need three or four bags to carry everything. We'll also need dark clothing – Western-style would be best. Everything black – trousers, shirts, even sports shoes. And then two rope ladders for the fence.'

'Wouldn't it be easier simply to cut through it?' Bashar asked.

'It would be easier, yes, but we dare not leave any trace of our presence there. That means we must go *over* the fence,' Saadi said. 'Now, do we have enough wire?'

'I believe so,' Massood replied, 'because all the packages will be positioned so close together. We should assemble a small toolkit, though. We'll need things like tape, sharp knives, pliers and wire-strippers.'

'Will you need to buy them individually?' Saadi asked.

'No. It should be possible to purchase a basic kit, and then add any extras we require.'

'Is there anything we've forgotten?'

Massood studied the list he'd prepared, then shook his head. 'I think that's everything, but I'll go through it again this evening to make absolutely sure.'

Saadi looked at his two comrades and smiled. 'We'll make our purchases in the morning. Tomorrow night we'll enter Nad Al-Sheba and complete the final preparations for our *jihad*. And the day after tomorrow will see a new dawn, and a new beginning, in Saudi Arabia. *In'shallah.'*

'*In'shallah,*' echoed Bashar and Massood.

Manama, Bahrain

Jackson swung the BMW round and accelerated hard. 'I think it's in Al-Mutanabi,' she announced.

Moments later she braked hard, spun the wheel and accelerated, but then almost immediately stopped. They stepped out of the vehicle and were greeted, predictably enough, by a scene of total chaos.

Above Al-Mutanabi, a huge cloud of dust was hanging, grey and brown and almost stationary in the still air, an ugly assault on the cobalt-blue sky. But Jackson and Richter barely gave it a second glance. Their eyes were instantly drawn to the carnage in front of them.

The road was covered with debris, mostly of a mechanical origin – bits of a car or several cars – but some clearly derived from a different source. Tattered scraps of cloth, stained deep red; unrecognizable fragments of tissue; body parts – a hand and arm, a foot in a ripped sandal – and, most upsetting of all, a severed head that had rolled across the road to come to rest against the front wheel of a parked car.

Small fires burned on the road surface, the smoke adding to the pall that already hung over the whole area. Further away, the blackened and twisted remains of the floor pan of a car sat next to the kerb, tortured metal shapes surrounding it. Richter had seen the effect of high-explosive detonations often enough to recognize immediately that this had been the bomb vehicle itself. When the device exploded, the force of the blast had ripped off the doors, roof and panels, twisting the thin steel into surreal shapes, blown the engine and transmission out of the chassis, and shredded pretty much everything else. But the floor pan had nowhere to go – the detonation had simply slammed it down onto the unyielding surface of the road beneath.

The cars that had been parked close to the IED had been blown away from the epicentre of the explosion, but at least they were still recognizable as cars. All the windows and doors in the closest buildings had vanished, the glass and wood offering almost no resistance to the blast wave. Right beside the twisted floor pan, the adjacent building had lost most of its façade, and it looked as if the whole front section could collapse at any moment.

What they could see was bad enough, but what they were hearing was worse. From somewhere beyond the wrecked cars they could hear a high and almost continuous wailing, a sound that seemed barely human in origin, but there was no mistaking the agony it conveyed. Almost drowning that out were the shouts and screams of Bahraini pedestrians and drivers and people who'd been inside the buildings when the bomb detonated, now running to and fro without clear purpose, wringing their hands and in deep shock.

Even worse than the noise was the smell: the acrid and unmistakable stench generated by the detonation itself, overlaid by an unholy amalgam of petrol, oil, burnt rubber, smoke, dust and charred human flesh.

'Get the rescue services mobile, if they aren't already,

and tell Caxton,' Richter instructed, conscious that Carole-Anne Jackson was looking somewhat green. 'I'll check out the rest of the street.'

As Jackson began dialling, Richter reached the epicentre of the explosion and stopped to look around. The source of the wailing – now markedly weaker and more intermittent – was immediately obvious, for some thirty yards beyond the remains of the bomb vehicle a middle-aged Bahraini businessman lay sprawled on the pavement, clutching at his right thigh. There was nothing left of his leg below the knee, just a shattered bone poking out of a sodden mess of flayed and bloody flesh.

Richter's medical expertise was virtually non-existent, but he immediately did what he could. He pulled off his tie, stepped across to the victim, and fashioned a makeshift tourniquet around his thigh. Richter wasn't even sure if the injured man realized what he was doing, the incredible pain and massive shock probably rendering him incapable of coherent thought or any real awareness of his immediate surroundings. He patted him on the shoulder and stepped away, hoping that an ambulance would arrive before the loss of blood killed him.

There were four other people sprawled on the pavement, but it took Richter only seconds to confirm that they were beyond anyone's help. Further away from the site of the explosion, men and women sat or lay on the pavement and the street, some leaning against the sides of parked cars or adjacent buildings, all in shock and most of them injured, but none too seriously, as far as he could see. It looked as if the death toll was going to be fairly modest relative to the size of the IED, which had obviously been substantial.

There was nothing else he could do to assist the victims, and he could now hear the sound of approaching sirens, so he knew the ambulances and paramedics were almost there. Richter's training had prepared him for this kind of situation. His two highest priorities now were security – was there another device in the area? – followed by observation and surveillance.

He doubted there was a second IED. The first blast had been so devastating that its detonation could have disrupted the firing mechanism of another nearby device. When terrorists doubled-up explosive charges, they usually detonated a fairly small IED first, designed to cause only limited damage. Once the rescue and medical services were on the scene, they would trigger a second and much more powerful weapon, so as to maximize the loss of life. It was a cowardly – and fortunately not very common – technique, and Richter wasn't aware of any Middle Eastern terrorist groups known to employ it.

That left surveillance. He was still checking the street when Jackson stopped beside him.

'Caxton's on his way: he should be leaving the embassy right now. Tariq and Bill will be here any minute,' she said briskly, then looked around. 'Christ, what a mess.'

Richter nodded. 'There's one guy seriously injured over there behind that car – he's lost most of one leg – and there are at least four dead.'

At that moment the first ambulance swung into Al-Mutanabi, the noise of its siren fading to silence as

the driver stopped the vehicle. Doors opened and paramedics clambered out, bags in hand, and ran across the
street.

Jackson noticed that Richter was no longer looking at
the destruction that surrounded them, but was staring
down the street, his eyes focused on something about
halfway up the side of one of the buildings.

'What is it?' she demanded.

'There,' Richter replied. 'That's a surveillance camera,
and it's pointing this way. We need to get access to the
tapes – assuming the camera isn't on the wall just for
show.'

'We can't request it ourselves, but the police can get
it. Tariq shouldn't have any trouble.'

'I won't have any trouble doing what?' Mazen asked,
jogging up beside them, Bill Evans a few feet behind
him. 'May Allah forgive them,' Mazen muttered, eyes
widening as he took in the scene in front of him.

'Paul's spotted a video camera up there,' Jackson
said, pointing down the street. 'It may have recorded
whoever planted the car.'

'And we'll need the tapes quickly,' Richter added.

Mazen peered at the building. 'I see it,' he said.
'Leave it to me.'

As he strode away, heading directly for two uniformed police officers, Bill Evans, who'd so far been
staring in silence at the destruction, shook his head.
'Bastards,' he muttered, almost to himself. 'Murdering
fucking bastards. And for what?'

'Good question,' Richter said. 'Unless I'm missing
something, there's nothing special about this street, so
why would anyone position the bomb here?'

'I've no idea,' Jackson said. 'Do you know anything about this area, Bill?'

'Not much. There was just a shop on the ground floor and several apartments above it, I think.'

'But nothing government or political?' Richter pressed.

'Nothing that I know of.'

'So why the bomb, then? Terrorists don't plant IEDs just on a whim. They have a reason for what they do, maybe using twisted logic that doesn't make much sense to anyone else, but there's *always* a reason.'

'I don't know,' Evans said, 'but Tariq can make some inquiries.'

'Couldn't it just be simple terrorism? I mean,' Jackson suggested, 'a bomb positioned just to cause damage and loss of life? Something like the Canary Wharf or Bali bombings?'

'I doubt it,' Richter shook his head. 'And even those two bombs certainly weren't random. There was a reason for detonating this device here, and if we can work out what it was, we'll be a lot closer to discovering who was responsible.'

At that moment Tariq Mazen emerged from a building further down the road, a plastic bag in his left hand, and headed over to where they were standing. Evans pointed at the bag.

'The tapes,' Mazen explained. 'I've obtained all the videos from the surveillance-camera system for the last week. We should at least be able to find out when the vehicle was positioned, and with luck see whoever drove it here.'

'What's the resolution like?' Evans asked.

'Reasonable, according to the owner of the property, but it's only intended for short-range work. How clear the images will be at longer distances I don't know.'

'Tariq,' Evans said, 'have you any idea why this particular building might have been targeted?'

Mazen glanced up and down Al-Mutanabi Avenue. 'I'm not aware of anything significant here,' he said, 'but obviously I'll check.'

Barcelona, Spain

Tall, slim and dark-haired, Josep Matero was thirty-eight years old and was completely unaware that he was being followed as he left work that afternoon. He also had no idea that he'd been followed home the previous day as well.

The first surveillance operation, carried out by a man called Jeffrey Haig, had been intended solely to check the Spaniard's domestic arrangements – if it turned out he had a wife and children one of the other three technicians on Haig's shortlist would have been chosen instead, because they wanted as few complications in Spain as possible.

But Matero's wife had left him two years earlier, and he lived alone at the edge of the university area on the southern outskirts of Barcelona. Though the apartment was small it was convenient for his job. The airport lies to the south of the city, and Matero could get there on his small motorcycle in about fifteen minutes.

He was working a split shift that day, which meant he had to get back on site the same evening. He arrived home just after three, after stopping off at a local bar for a light meal of *tapas* and a half-bottle of *rioja*. The prospect of a lazy afternoon stretched pleasantly ahead of him: there might even be some football on TV.

He'd already changed out of his working clothes and was on his way to the kitchen to make coffee when he heard the unexpected knock, and stepped back into the hallway to answer the door.

He didn't recognize the man standing in front of him. Matero opened his mouth to ask what he wanted but, before the words could form, the stranger stepped forward and punched him violently in the chest.

The pain was incredible, like nothing Matero had ever experienced, and he stumbled backwards, falling to the tiled floor. As he tried to get up, there was no strength in his limbs, and the pain in his chest was even worse. For a few seconds Matero wondered how the stranger had done it. And in the last agonizing moments of his life he wondered *why*.

Roy Sutter closed the door behind him and watched without emotion as his victim died on the tiles right in front of him. Then he went looking for the bathroom. When he found it, he wiped the blood off the five-inch blade of the push-dagger, threw the toilet paper down the loo and flushed it. He folded the knife and replaced it in a leather belt sheath.

It was an unusual but extremely effective assassination weapon, T-shaped with a slim stiletto blade hinged in the centre of a shaped metal handle. The attacker held the handle firmly in his palm, the blade projecting between his third and fourth fingers, and simply punched the victim in the chest or back. If the blow was delivered strongly and accurately enough, the blade would penetrate for its full length, and easily rupture the heart.

Sutter checked that the apartment was empty before he returned to the hall. He seized Matero's feet and dragged the body into the lounge, dumping it in the centre of the room. He toyed briefly with the idea of trying to make the scene look like a burglary gone wrong, but then decided he couldn't be bothered. The body would likely be found soon enough, but within hours he would be on a different continent.

He only needed two items from the apartment. He found the first in the fitted wardrobe in the bedroom, and the second lying on a small desk in the living room.

Less than ten minutes after he'd entered the building, Sutter walked away from it with a bulging plastic carrier bag in one hand, the gloves he'd worn the entire time already dumped in a nearby rubbish bin.

Twenty-five minutes later, and half a mile closer to the city centre, Jeffrey Haig emerged from another apartment building, where his actions had almost exactly replicated those of Roy Sutter.

Andrews Air Force Base, Maryland

Richard Watts waited patiently for a break in the stream of calls, and finally depressed the transmit button. 'Andrews Ground, Gulfstream November Two Six, requesting engine start and taxi clearance.'

'Two Six, engine start approved. Call ready to taxi for runway zero one right.'

'Roger. Engine start approved, runway zero one right.'

The APU was already running, and Watts had both the Rolls-Royce Tay turbofans started within minutes. The cockpit of the G450 is fully computerized, the four flat-panel LCD screens of the Gulfstream/Honeywell PlaneView integrated avionics system facing the two pilots providing all the information required. Each pilot sees one screen displaying flight instrumentation – air-speed indicator, compass heading, horizontal situation indicator and so on – while the two central screens show navigation data and engine status.

Eleven minutes after engine start, the Gulfstream turned on to the end of zero one right, and waited a few moments for another jet to clear the active runway.

'November Two Six, Andrews Tower. Clear take-off. Wind zero two five at fifteen. When airborne, contact Potomac Departure on one two five six five.'

'Roger, Tower. Clear take-off and to Potomac on one two five six five when airborne. Good day, sir.' Watts pushed the throttles smoothly forward, and the G450 began accelerating rapidly down the runway.

In the beautifully equipped cabin of the Gulfstream, Grant Hutchings and John Baxter sat facing each other in two of the sumptuous leather armchairs. The other members of the investigation team – Andy Franks and Roger Middleton – sat in matching seats on the other side of the aisle.

As the Gulfstream lifted into the air, Franks looked across at Hutchings and smiled. 'Sure as hell beats flying commercial, sir.'

'Just don't get too used to it,' Hutchings growled.

'I've been in the Company for over twenty years, and this is exactly the third time I've ever flown private.'

British Embassy, Government Avenue, Manama, Bahrain

Desperate times call for desperate measures, and Tariq Mazen decided to break the rules and visit the British Embassy.

Evans met him in the foyer and escorted him to the 'Holy of Holies', where Richter and Jackson sat in the small conference room, studying the initial reports about the bombing. Six people had died in total, five in the road close to the car, and another one in the adjacent building, while about another dozen were seriously injured. The man Richter had tried to help was still alive, following emergency surgery – one small piece of good news.

'We've had some luck,' Mazen reported, 'but we aren't much closer to finding out who planted the device.' He passed each of them a set of three photographs. 'The vehicle appeared on the street just before six o'clock on Monday afternoon, and it was parked there by people who either knew exactly what they were doing or were unbelievably lucky.

'The first of those pictures shows Al-Mutanabi at five-fifty on Monday. The second shows the same scene, but now you can see the bomb vehicle parked by the roadside. It was an American Chevrolet, about ten years old. Now, this surveillance camera sits on a swivel mount and swings through a half-circle once every two minutes, so it only records activity in that section of Al-Mutanabi for half the time.'

'Brilliant,' Jackson hissed. 'What genius thought that one up?'

'I asked the owner of the building, and he has no idea either. Now, if you look closely at the second picture you'll see two figures sitting inside the car. Our analysts think they were both wearing *gellabbiyas*, but they can't be certain. In the third photograph, the vehicle is still there, but you can see that the occupants have vanished.

'Now,' Mazen glanced round the table, 'it could just be luck that these two bombers managed to get out of the car while the surveillance camera was pointing in the opposite direction, but we really don't think so. We believe they were using the exterior mirrors to watch the camera, then walked away quickly before it swung back in their direction. We think they crossed over to the building on which the camera is mounted, waited there until it swung back, then continued down to Tujjaar and turned left.'

'Why left?' Jackson asked.

'Because of this.' Mazen now handed out a fourth photograph. It showed the south-east section of Al-Mutanabi, and at the end of the street two figures in white *gellabbiyas* were visible – one turning left into Tujjaar, the other immediately behind him but staring down Al-Mutanabi.

'Now this is somewhat tenuous, but because these two men are so close together we believe they must be the perpetrators. The surveillance camera showed no other pair of men together anywhere in Al-Mutanabi, in either direction. The rest were either in groups of three or more, or individuals.'

'"Tenuous" is right, Tariq,' Richter interrupted. 'There were two men in the car – the photograph makes that clear – but they could have separated as soon as they got out of the vehicle, and headed in different directions.'

'I would agree with you,' Mazen replied, extracting another set of photographs from his briefcase, 'except for this.'

Richter studied the image carefully. In this one, the first of the two men had already disappeared into Tujjaar, but the second was still staring down Al-Mutanabi and, even though the image was too low-resolution to show much detail, he appeared to be smiling and waving his arm.

'We think the bastard was waving at the camera, knowing he couldn't be identified at that distance.'

'You may be right, Tariq,' Evans said, 'but it doesn't get us any further forward. You certainly can't identify the man from this photograph. In fact, you can barely make out his features.'

'I agree with Bill,' Richter remarked. 'I don't think we're going anywhere with this. All it tells us is that the vehicle containing the bomb was delivered to Al-Mutanabi by two men, who then probably walked into Tujjaar and vanished. I'm more interested in why they decided to position the Chevy just there. Have you found out anything significant about the location?'

'We've one possible lead,' Mazen replied, 'but first

there are some things I need to explain to you. The
political situation here is fragile, with numerous pressure groups demanding radical changes. Not including
the political parties, we have at least seven active organizations. They all have different agendas, but are united
in their opposition to the present system. They're also
opposed to each other, and we suspect that this car bomb
may have been an attack by one group upon another.
Investigation shows that three rooms in a building about
seventy yards from the explosion were occupied by a
small but aggressive group called Bahraini Jihad. This
building was only slightly damaged.'

'Perhaps they couldn't park right outside the target,'
Evans suggested, 'so they got as close as they could, just
to send a message.'

'A hell of a message,' Richter said sourly, 'to kill half
a dozen people but leave the target virtually unscathed.
If hitting Bahraini Jihad was the objective, Tariq, who
do you think was responsible?'

'It might have been another small militant group here
known as Sharaf. That word means honour, Paul, and to
an Arab male the most important thing, even more
important than his own life, is his honour. But such honour has to be earned through deeds that will bring him
praise and renown.'

'What do you know about them?'

'Not a great deal,' Mazen replied, 'and a lot of the
evidence is circumstantial. Two months ago a terrorist
plot was discovered, aimed against the American base
at Al-Jufayr. The plotters had assembled over fifty kilos
of high-yield explosive, automatic weapons and plenty

of ammunition. We had no idea at all that an assault was being planned, but then we received an extremely accurate tip-off, purportedly sent by Bahraini Jihad. By working with the local police, and the base's security force, we succeeded in arresting all those named. Under interrogation, one of the conspirators admitted to being a member of Sharaf, and that was the first time we'd heard of the group. He further claimed that Sharaf was dedicated to the complete removal of all American interests from the Gulf.'

'I would have thought most local terrorist groups would have that on their agendas,' Richter observed.

'Not all of them, actually. One peculiarity of Bahraini Jihad is that its principal objective is the permanent removal of the ruling Hamad family, not the Americans; they even believe that the base could prove a useful bargaining counter in future negotiations with the West.'

'So,' Evans interjected, 'that is presumably why they blew the whistle on Sharaf.'

'It makes sense,' Richter admitted.

Carole-Anne Jackson, who'd been sitting silently throughout this discussion, now looked up. 'There's something else,' she said, 'something we haven't yet considered, which is Holden's premonition. Assuming Tariq's right about the two men wearing *gellabbiyas*, Holden was correct in every important detail, including the type of car used. So how the hell could he possibly have known?'

'I've no idea,' Richter said, 'but I'm going to find out. Look, there's not a lot more I can do here now the bomb's gone off. I'll probably be better employed finding out whatever else Holden has up his sleeve, so I think I'll go back to Dubai.'

'Not tonight you won't,' Evans said, 'because the last flight's already left, but we'll get you a seat on the first available aircraft tomorrow morning.'

Chapter Twelve

'Barcelona Ground, November Two Six requesting taxi instructions.'

The Gulfstream G450 had just landed at Barcelona after the transatlantic flight for its single scheduled refuelling stop.

'Two Six, Barcelona Ground. Take the first taxiway to the left and continue straight ahead. You'll be parked at Terminal C for refuel.'

Three minutes later, Richard Watts applied the parking brake and shut down the engines. As the turbofans spooled down, his co-pilot, Frank Pertwee, selected the passenger-address system.

'This is Barcelona, and we'll be on the ground for about forty-five minutes while we refuel. You can take this opportunity to stretch your legs, but remember we're parked at an active terminal so watch out for vehicles and aircraft. Directly in front of us is Terminal C, where there are restrooms and a cafeteria, if you really want a change from the delicious coffee and sandwiches you've enjoyed up to now. But make sure you're back on board in forty minutes.'

The passenger door on the left-hand side of the aircraft opened and a set of integrated steps slid down smoothly. A few moments later Grant Hutchings walked down them, followed by Baxter, Franks and Middleton.

'I know that's a real comfortable aircraft, but I'm not sorry to be on the ground again,' Baxter muttered, taking a deep breath and then wishing he hadn't as his nostrils filled with the stench of burnt kerosene. Beyond the hardstanding, a Boeing 737 in the livery of a cut-price airline touched down on the runway, and moments later the air was filled with a sudden roar as the pilot engaged reverse thrust to slow down the aircraft. All around them was the constant sound of engines and the movement of vehicles, because despite the time the airfield was working at full pace.

'OK,' Hutchings raised his voice against the background noise. 'Let's go get ourselves something to eat.'

As the four men walked across the hardstanding, a bowser arrived to refuel their aircraft. This took about twenty minutes and, once it had been completed, the bowser driver went into the Gulfstream to process the paperwork, emerging a few minutes later.

Once the bowser had moved away, two men in white overalls approached the G450 and stood looking at something beneath the fuselage. None of the ground engineers nearby noticed anything unusual about them, and no one paid any attention when one of them climbed the steps to enter the aircraft.

Roy Sutter was wearing a set of white overalls, and a visual identification card showed his name as 'Josep Matero'. Entering the cabin of the Gulfstream, he knocked on the cockpit door. Inside, Watts was reading notes attached to a clipboard, while Pertwee checked the route for their onward journey to Dubai.

'Yes?' Watts turned round and looked up. 'What is it?'

Sutter smiled slightly nervously and gestured back over his shoulder. 'It is probably nothing, *señor*,' he replied, in heavily accented English, 'but there is fluid leaking from underneath the aircraft. Perhaps you should take a look?'

Watts muttered something under his breath, and turned to his co-pilot. 'Go check it out, will you, Frank? It's probably just a spillage after the refuelling.' On the Gulfstream, the refuelling point is more or less in the centre of the underside of the fuselage.

Pertwee stood up and walked into the passenger compartment. Just before they reached the exit door, Sutter swung a lead-filled cosh hard, smashing it into the back of the co-pilot's head. Instantly knocked unconscious, he collapsed without a sound. Sutter grabbed him, lowering his limp body to the floor.

He glanced back towards the cockpit, making sure the pilot wasn't coming out, then took a thin garrotte from his pocket. Looping it over the co-pilot's head, he pulled it tight around his neck. Then, after a couple of minutes, he released it and checked for a pulse.

Satisfied, Sutter retraced his steps to the cockpit door. 'The other pilot, *señor*,' he said, 'he would like you to look. It may be a problem with the hydraulics.'

Watts nodded wearily and stepped out of the cockpit. He stopped in his tracks the instant he saw Pertwee's lifeless body in front of him, but by then it was already too late. The cosh crashed into the back of his head, cracking his skull and starting internal bleeding. Watts toppled forward, already dying. Sutter completed the process with his garrotte, then stood back.

Two down, another four to go.

Sheraton Hotel, Manama, Bahrain

Carole-Anne Jackson lay comfortably beside Richter in his double bed. The lights were out, the curtains pulled open. Through the picture windows, the yellowish glow of the lights of Manama provided enough illumination to distinguish objects in the darkened room.

'Another drink?' Richter asked. 'The champagne's all gone, but I think there's still some white wine left.'

'If there *is* another microscopic bottle, I might just be able to force it down.'

Richter climbed out of bed and padded across to the minibar.

'Thanks.' She took the glass. 'You haven't forgotten my offer to act as your guide in Dubai, I hope?'

'Certainly not.'

Carole-Anne Jackson took a sip, then gazed across at Richter, who was now lying back and staring at the ceiling.

'You seem a bit preoccupied, Paul. What is it?'

Richter turned to her and grinned. 'Sorry. You're right – one thing *has* been puzzling me. Something Caxton told me about this horse, Shaf. What happened at those stables makes no sense.'

'To be ruthlessly accurate,' Jackson said, 'we still have no idea *what* happened there. So far, nobody who

231

worked or lived there has turned up, dead or alive. It's as if they all just vanished into thin air.'

'People don't vanish, Carole, and especially not leaving several million dollars' worth of equine assets behind. Not unless they want to, and I can't think of any reason that makes sense. Somebody else made them disappear.'

'You mean coercion – blackmail or something?'

Richter shook his head. 'Nothing so mundane. Not with that many people. That sheikh . . .'

'Qabandi,' Jackson supplied.

'Right, Sheikh Qabandi. He said there should be at least a dozen people permanently at the stables. There's only one way you can get that many to vanish and have absolutely no trace of them turning up. My gut feeling is that they're still somewhere nearby, but dead and buried. And there's another piece of evidence that everybody seems to have ignored.'

'The trace of urine?'

'Exactly,' Richter agreed, 'the urine. Human urine in a bathroom makes sense, but in the entrance hall of a really expensive property it doesn't, except in one context, of course.'

'You mean someone was killed there?'

'When somebody dies violently, they often lose control of their bladder.'

'There wasn't any blood found in the hall,' Jackson pointed out.

'That just means the victim was killed using a method that didn't involve a puncture wound. He wasn't shot or stabbed, but he could have been strangled or suffocated. The killers obviously wanted to avoid leaving traces of their crime. Bloodstains immediately suggest foul play, but urine is more of a puzzle.'

'I suppose that makes sense. So what are you going to do about it?'

'Not a lot. I've no authority here, and my only task is to investigate Holden in Dubai. Getting involved in the disappearance of a dozen people in Saudi lies well outside my remit. But I think it would be worth your while suggesting that the Saudi police take a close look at the entire area surrounding the stables, using sniffer dogs if they've got them. I think they'll find the bodies if they look hard enough.'

Barcelona Airport, Spain

The cabin door was still open and Sutter peered out, looking for the four CIA officers. There was no sign of them, but he knew there was no time to waste.

He seized Watts' body around the chest and pulled the dead man to the rear of the passenger cabin, then opened the toilet door, dragged him inside and sat him on the bowl. Two minutes later, he jammed Pertwee on top of Watts and forced the door closed.

He walked back to the cockpit, quickly peeling off his white overall. Underneath, he was wearing the universal uniform of corporate pilots – a short-sleeved white shirt, very dark blue slacks and black shoes. He glanced out of the door. The other 'ground engineer' – Jeffrey Haig – looked up from his position near the foot of the steps, and Sutter nodded.

Moments later, Haig joined him, carrying a toolbox.

It contained two special items they'd purchased that afternoon in Barcelona: a forged-currency detector and a set of assay tools designed to check the purity of precious metals.

'You got the capsules?' Sutter asked. Haig nodded silently and pulled a small plastic bottle from his pocket. 'OK. I'll drop the rubber jungle. Be quick.'

Haig walked back into the passenger compartment, where overhead panels had now opened and from which oxygen masks were dangling. He pulled on a bio-filter mask, opened the plastic bottle and, with a pair of tweezers, inserted one capsule into the oxygen tube feeding each mask. The capsules were a simple but clever design, with a central hole to allow free flow of oxygen, but containing a powerful and virtually odourless narcotic.

On his way back to the cockpit, Haig glanced out of the door and saw the four Americans leaving the terminal building. He re-entered the cockpit and dropped into the co-pilot's seat. 'They're all on their way back now,' he announced.

Sutter pulled on the blue jacket Watts had hung up in the crew wardrobe – it wasn't a bad fit. He then stood at the cockpit door, his back towards the passenger cabin, as the CIA men resumed their seats. Then he walked across, scratching an imaginary itch on his forehead to partially shield his face, and closed the cabin door. But none of the passengers took the slightest notice of him.

Locking the cockpit door behind him, Sutter sat down in the captain's seat. Haig was still working his way through the last couple of items on the checklist.

'Strictly speaking,' he remarked, 'we should be doing these checks together.'

'I trust you.' Sutter grinned at him. 'Finished?' Haig nodded. 'Good. Switch on the "seat belt" sign and let's get going. But make sure you keep the toilet door locked. We don't want one of our passengers going to take a leak and finding the john's full of stiffs.'

The G450 taxied smoothly off the hardstanding towards the threshold of the active runway. Sutter held a commercial pilot's licence and instrument rating in his real name and, though he'd never flown this model before, he had no doubt that he would be able to handle it.

Ten minutes after engine start, Sutter eased back on the control column, listened to the rumble as the landing gear retracted, and turned the aircraft gently onto an easterly heading for the transit across the Mediterranean and its next, and unscheduled, landing at Cairo.

Gulfstream G450, callsign November Two Six

Well under an hour later, the Gulfstream was already two hundred miles from Barcelona, cruising at 0.78 Mach, and holding level at forty-one thousand feet on upper air route UM601 heading east. The aircraft had just passed beacon Balen, about midway between Barcelona and the island of Sardinia.

'Time we sent our passengers to sleep,' Sutter decided. 'You ready?'

Haig nodded, and pulled his seat belt a little tighter.

Sutter checked the navigation radar to ensure no other aircraft were in their vicinity, then disengaged the auto-pilot, throttled back, and pushed the control column forward. The Gulfstream reacted immediately, pitching sharply nose-down, and the two men felt the increasing tension as their bodies pushed against their belts. Sutter eased the column back gently, still keeping the G450 in a fairly steep dive, and adjusted the throttles.

'Drop the rubber jungle,' he ordered and, as Haig released the cabin's oxygen masks, Sutter selected passenger address.

'We've a slight problem. A possible cabin pressurization failure, and we've just started a rapid descent as a precaution. Place an oxygen mask over your face, pull the tube to start the flow of gas, and then just breathe normally. There's no immediate cause for alarm.' Sutter left the P.A. enabled as he called across to Haig: 'Make a Pan call and tell them we're in an emergency descent requesting fifteen thousand or lower.' Then he de-selected the switch. 'That should make sure our passengers do what they're told.'

Haig was already talking to the en-route controlling authority.

The reply came swiftly. 'November Two Six is cleared initial descent to Flight Level two zero zero against opposite direction traffic range twenty-eight level one eight zero. Call approaching two four zero. Expect further descent clearance shortly. Squawk emergency.'

Haig keyed in 7700 on the SSR transponder. 'Roger, Marseille. November Two Six is squawking emergency, in descent to two zero zero to call approaching two four zero.'

In the cabin, the four CIA officers adjusted the oxygen masks over their faces and pulled on the hoses, as they'd been instructed. Grant Hutchings was slower to react than the other three and, just a few moments after he'd tugged on the hose, he pulled the mask off his face and sniffed suspiciously. He'd breathed pure oxygen before, and knew it was effectively odourless, but the gas coming out of the mask had a definite smell. Very faint, but unmistakably there.

Hutchings took a deep breath and looked round with a puzzled expression. He was having no trouble at all in breathing but, if there *had* been a depressurization, that should be impossible because the aircraft was still far too high. Normal breathing would not be possible until the Gulfstream had descended to about twelve thousand feet. And the cabin should be getting colder – a lot colder – which it wasn't. Then there was the strange odour. Something wasn't right.

Hutchings released his seat belt and stood up. John Baxter was sitting directly opposite him and, as Hutchings looked across the cabin, he suddenly fell forward limply against the restraint of the belt. Hutchings spun round to look at the other two men. Roger Middleton was already slumped sideways across his seat and, even as he watched, Andy Franks also suddenly collapsed.

Hutchings stepped over to Baxter and ripped off the oxygen mask, then did the same for Middleton and Franks. What the hell was going on here? Realizing the oxygen supply had to be contaminated, he bent over Franks and pressed his hand to the side of the man's neck. He found a pulse, weak and irregular, but it was there. He then checked Middleton with the same result.

Something in the emergency oxygen tanks had knocked the other three men unconscious. But at least they were alive, and now they were breathing normal cabin air, so they'd presumably soon come round.

But how had this happened? Clearly the aircraft had been sabotaged. Somebody on the ground at Andrews or somewhere had tampered with the emergency systems. What about the flight crew? Did they breathe from the same oxygen supply as the passengers? Hutchings was suddenly aware that the Gulfstream was still in a rapid descent, but were the pilots lying unconscious over their controls as the aircraft headed straight down towards the Mediterranean?

He crossed to the cockpit door and turned the handle. The door was locked. That was now mandatory on commercial flights, but it struck him as being unusual procedure in a State Department executive jet engaged on official government business. He rapped sharply on the door and called out.

Sutter and Haig turned and eyed the locked door. 'Sounds like someone didn't do what he was told,' Haig murmured.

Sutter nodded and undid his seat belt. 'I'll go sort it out. Level us at fifteen.' They'd received further descent clearance less than a minute earlier. He removed the push-dagger from his jacket pocket, locked the blade in place and slid it into the rear waistband of his trousers. Then he released the bolt and opened the door.

Grant Hutchings was almost blocking the doorway. 'There's something wrong with the oxygen supply,' he said. 'Maybe the plane's been sabotaged.' He turned to indicate his three companions.

You got that right, Sutter thought, pulling out the dagger and stabbing it hard towards the CIA officer's back, just as he moved away. But at that moment Hutchings turned back towards him, as if wanting to say something else.

Hutchings reacted instinctively when he saw the weapon, his basic unarmed-combat training taking over. He continued turning, swinging his left arm across to block the blow. He punched hard with his right fist, aiming for Sutter's solar plexus, and if the blow had connected that would have been the end of it.

But while Hutchings had received basic training in self-defence, the other man was an expert. Sutter was skilled in karate and some half-dozen other forms of unarmed combat, so the punch got nowhere near him. He blocked it effortlessly, knocking Hutchings's arm to one side, and at the same time dropping the dagger. He folded his fingers at the second joint, wedging his thumb firmly against his index finger and stiffened his right hand into a blade. He smashed his hand into Hutchings's throat, delivering a short-arm jab that fatally crushed his windpipe.

The big CIA agent staggered backwards, lifting both hands to his neck, which just made Sutter's job easier. He punched Hutchings twice in the stomach and he fell to the floor. Then Sutter stepped back to pick up the dagger and bent over the injured man.

Over the flaring agony of his ruined throat, Hutchings sensed his life ebbing away. The last thing he heard was his killer's contemptuous remark, just before the dagger ripped through his rib-cage, its point slamming into his heart.

'Why didn't you just breathe through the fucking mask, you stupid bastard?'

For a few seconds, Sutter ignored the corpse in front of him and looked at the other three passengers. All appeared to be still unconscious, but unconscious wasn't what he needed.

He moved quickly from one to another, replacing the oxygen masks on their faces, then turned back to Hutchings. He checked for a pulse but predictably found nothing, and there was surprisingly little blood from the fatal wound, because the heart had ceased pumping almost immediately the dagger had entered the chest cavity.

Leaving Hutchings where he was lying, Sutter made a final check of the other three men, then returned to the cockpit. The narcotic would be seeping slowly into the air, and he wanted to spend as little time as possible in the cabin.

'OK now?' Haig asked, as Sutter closed the cockpit door and refastened the bolt.

'Should be. One of them didn't put his mask on quickly enough, or maybe he smelt something. Anyway, he's dead now. Another ten minutes should be enough for the others, then we can turn off the oxygen. We'll stay down here at fifteen for a while, then ask for clearance back to high level. When you talk to the controller again, tell him we think the problem was instrumentation rather than an actual depressurization, but we'll need to land at Cairo just to get it checked.'

Thirty minutes later the Gulfstream was back up at forty-one thousand feet on autopilot. Sutter and Haig were relaxing in the cockpit, sharing the sandwiches they'd found in one of the catering packs provided for the G450's passengers, and Cairo Air Traffic Control had already been alerted to expect the unscheduled arrival.

Cairo, Egypt

O'Hagan and Petrucci had set their alarm for three. The two men made coffee – one of the few amenities the hotel possessed was coffee-making facilities in each room – and then sat waiting for the phone call that would determine exactly when they'd have to leave.

O'Hagan's mobile rang just before three-thirty. He listened carefully for a few seconds. 'Right, see you then.' He turned to Petrucci. 'They'll arrive in about ninety minutes, so we need to be out of here soon. I'd better get Wilson moving.'

'We'll be mobile in fifteen,' he announced when his call was answered. 'Which hotel?' He scribbled down the name and address. 'We'll be in a white Mercedes van.'

'Right,' Petrucci said. 'I'll go grab my stuff and get the Merc. I'll see you outside in ten minutes.'

In his hotel room at Abbassia, Richard Wilson rang Dawson's mobile. 'It's me,' he said. 'Check yourself out right now.'

Twenty-five minutes later Petrucci pulled the Mercedes over to the kerb outside the hotel where Wilson was standing waiting with the cases beside him. O'Hagan opened the passenger door and stepped out, his face creasing into a smile as he extended his hand.

'Hi, Dick. Good to see you. Is that it?' He was pointing towards the larger of the suitcases sitting on the pavement.

'That's it.'

'And where's Ed?'

'Ain Shams Hospital. They held him overnight for observation, but I gave him a call just after you reached me, so he should be out by now.'

Wilson and O'Hagan heaved the cases into the rear of the van as Petrucci got back behind the wheel, and the Mercedes eased away from the kerb. The hospital was nearby and when the van turned into the access road running past the admissions unit, they all saw the lone figure standing outside.

'Everything OK?' Wilson asked.

'No problems,' Dawson replied. 'Once I told them I was feeling fine, they let me go as soon as I'd filled in a "you can't sue us if you walk out of here" form. Is the plane here?'

O'Hagan glanced at his watch. 'Not yet. They're about an hour from touchdown, so we're in good time. They're in a Gulfstream G450. We're technicians going to inspect the aircraft. We won't need passports or anything, because we're only going as far as the tech site. Once the G450 is down – and Roy will call me as soon as he's parked it – we'll talk our way in.'

'And then?' Wilson asked.

'And then we'll find out from them what the score is and what else we have to do before we can take off for Dubai.'

PAYBACK

Gulfstream G450, callsign November Two Six

'Cairo, November Two Six on handover and requesting airfield information.'

'November Two Six is identified. Active runway is two three right, wind light and variable, altimeter one zero one eight. You're number two in the pattern, no delays expected.'

Haig called out the pre-landing checks as Sutter disengaged the autopilot and lined up the Gulfstream with the extended-runway centreline. He progressively increased the angle of the flaps as Sutter reduced the throttle settings and brought the speed down, then he lowered the undercarriage. With final checks complete, he flared the aircraft as they passed over the piano keys, and waited for the main wheels to make contact with the runway.

'Cairo Ground, November Two Six is down and requesting taxi instructions. Be advised we're expecting a maintenance check because of a suspected depressurization problem en route. We don't require a refuel or customs clearance and we won't be leaving the aircraft.'

Fifteen minutes later Sutter shut down the engines on the assigned stand and peered out of the cockpit windows towards the approach road. Then he reached for his mobile phone and made a ten-second call.

Cairo Airport, Egypt

Petrucci was driving, simply because he spoke the best Arabic. He stopped the Mercedes at the gate leading to the airfield's technical site while the guards checked his identification and that of the other three men, who were now all wearing white overalls.

They weren't held up for long. The control tower already knew the Gulfstream had experienced a problem, and Sutter had told them he'd contacted a local maintenance facility on a company frequency, so the van's appearance at the airfield was expected.

The guard emerged from the building beside the tech site gate and handed back their 'Cairo Specialist Aviation Services' identification cards, printed two months earlier in the States. After giving them directions to the hardstanding where the G450 was parked, he recited a very brief list of tech-site driving rules, and finally raised the barrier.

'There it is,' O'Hagan said, pointing through the windscreen. Petrucci turned onto the hardstanding and parked.

'You didn't get rid of the bodies,' O'Hagan said, staring at four dead CIA officers, as Sutter emerged from the cockpit to greet them.

'We couldn't. We'd planned to dump them in the Med, but this aircraft has integral stairs on the door, so though we could have got it open, we would never have been able to close it again after dropping the stiffs. Shouldn't be a problem, though. We can get them into the van and bury them somewhere in the desert, right?'

244

'As long as we don't get stopped on our way out it should be OK,' Petrucci agreed. 'How many?'

'These four and another two – the original crew – locked in the john.'

'Six? Oh, Christ. We'd better make two trips. Maybe three, for safety. We'll go out once empty and I'll tell the gate guards we've got to go and pick up equipment or something – and if they don't check the back of the van we'll do two more trips immediately.'

Transferring the bags and suitcases from the van to the Gulfstream took under three minutes; moving the bodies, however, was clearly going to be more difficult and take longer. Petrucci climbed into the Mercedes and started the engine, O'Hagan joining him. Sutter watched from the door of the Gulfstream as the vehicle drove away.

Wilson and Dawson stripped the bodies of their weapons and holsters, and all identification documents, then removed their watches and rings, because they could be engraved, and even cut the labels from their clothing. They would need the pistols and CIA identification themselves, but it was just as important to ensure that there would be no easy way to identify the bodies once they'd been dumped. They wouldn't have time to bury them deeply, so the corpses might be discovered within weeks or even days. That didn't bother them, but it was essential that the bodies were not identified for at least four days.

And then there was nothing they could do but wait for O'Hagan and Petrucci to come back with the Mercedes.

Chapter Thirteen

As the van reappeared beside the Gulfstream ten minutes later, Petrucci opened the doors while O'Hagan climbed the aircraft steps to where the others were waiting.

'Everything go OK?' Wilson asked.

'No problems,' O'Hagan replied. 'They're much more interested in what comes into the tech site than what goes out, so I think we can risk shifting all the stiffs at once. And if they decide to search the van once we get to the gate, it's only a drop-down barrier so I think we can drive straight through it and then just dump the vehicle somewhere with the bodies inside. That has to be a last resort, of course.'

'Yeah, but if you do crash the barrier, what then? You have to get yourself back here.'

'This place isn't like a major US airport, and security's pretty lax. I reckon we could sneak over a fence somewhere. We'll be wearing overalls so we'll look like we belong.'

It was early morning, with little activity on the hardstanding, but still they took no chances. Petrucci brought up the four tarpaulins from the van and they wrapped them round the corpses. Sutter and O'Hagan left the aircraft and waited by the Mercedes, but almost immediately heard Petrucci call out a warning: 'Vehicle approaching.'

They watched as a small van drew up beside the Gulfstream, the lettering on the side proclaiming that it came from a ground handling company. Two smartly dressed Arabs stepped out and approached them.

'Good morning, gentlemen,' the first one said, in perfectly fluent English. 'I see the specialist assistance you requested has arrived. Do you require any services from airfield technical support?'

'No thanks,' Sutter replied. 'We think the problem was instrumentation, but the technicians here need to carry out a few more checks to be certain. If that's all it is, then we'll be leaving here later today.'

'Excellent,' the Arab said, 'but just contact us if you do need any further assistance. Do you require any food or drink?'

'Yes, that would be very welcome.'

'One of our catering vans will come over. Is there anything else?'

'Just one thing,' Sutter said. 'You have our flight plan details, I believe. Could you please send a message to Andrews Air Force Base, Maryland, information Dubai International, advising them that we've landed here and that our arrival in Dubai will be delayed by up to ten hours. You'll be advising both airfields once we get airborne?'

The Arab nodded. 'Of course. That just leaves your landing fees.' He pulled a sheet of folded paper from his inside pocket.

'You're happy with American dollars?' Sutter asked,

glancing at the sum due before opening his wallet and pulling out a wad of notes.

'Yes, naturally.'

Sutter returned the invoice and the cash to cover it. The Arab signed it with a flourish at the bottom, tore off the top sheet and handed it back, then they walked to their vehicle and drove away.

'That wasn't too bright an idea, was it?' O'Hagan said. 'Getting a catering van sent over here, I mean?'

Sutter nodded. 'Yes, it was, because it's what he would have expected. With this flight delayed for several hours, and then it's another three hours to Dubai, we're going to *need* food and drink before we get airborne. If we hadn't accepted his offer, it might have seemed odd, and the last thing we want to do is start them thinking.'

'I hope you're right,' O'Hagan muttered, watching the van drive off the hardstanding. 'Right, all clear,' he turned and shouted. 'Get those stiffs down here. Move it.'

Crowne Plaza Hotel, Dubai

Climbing out of the taxi, Paul Richter wondered how long he'd be spending in Dubai *this* time. He checked in again, took the elevator back down to the lobby and walked outside. There he pulled out his Enigma and punched in one of the secure numbers at Hammersmith.

'Where are you this time?' Simpson demanded.

'Back in Dubai,' Richter said. 'I've just got off the

flight from Bahrain. You heard about the bomb in Manama?'

'Yes. The Six duty officer briefed me last night. What's your take on it?'

Richter described what little evidence they'd found, and added Mazen's deductions.

'Terrorists terrorizing terrorists? I like it,' Simpson said. 'Have you seen Holden yet?'

'No, but I plan to interview him today.'

'Right. Check in with me once you've talked to him. Anything else to report?'

'Yes,' Richter said. 'Just a little local mystery that's bothering me.' He explained about the theft of the thoroughbred racehorse.

'Not really our scene, Richter, horses. What are you expecting me to do? Arrange for some hay to be delivered?'

'Not unless you really want to. I'm sure the stable staff are all dead, probably buried somewhere in the desert, and I think whoever's behind it is planning something here in Dubai. That just might tie up with what Khatid heard in Berlin, and it's the only thing that explains why they sent the horse here. Now, at the moment I'm just some guy from London sent out here to investigate an expatriate Englishman. I'd like you to let the local police know I'm here officially, and that I'm looking into both James Holden and the missing racehorse. I'd like Six credentials if possible, because that will give me more credibility with the locals, and I'd also like permission to carry a personal weapon.'

'That's not going to be easy in Dubai, Richter, even if

I can get a diplomatic passport issued to you. I'd need a really good reason to even suggest it, so you'd better come up with something I can use. Why do you want a pistol?'

'Right now I don't have a valid reason, but there's definitely *something* going on out here. I have a gut feeling that whatever it is could blow up really fast, and I'd like to be ready. You wanted someone on the spot, remember, and if I'm not armed I'm not going to be much use to anyone.'

'Gut instinct isn't good enough, Richter. To get you a carry permit I'll need something that will persuade the Dubai authorities that a weapon is justified, and even then they may not agree. Without something compelling, there's no way I'll even approach them. But I can at least get on to the embassy and ask them to brief the local plods about you.'

Cairo Airport, Egypt

Three hours later, Petrucci stopped the Mercedes beside the G450 while his passengers climbed out, and then drove off again. He'd spotted a group of vehicles parked about a hundred yards away, and was going to leave the van alongside them.

'Any problems?' Sutter asked, handing him a soft drink from the new supply recently delivered by the catering van.

'Not really,' Dawson replied, opening his Coke before slumping down in one of the seats. 'We drove way out of Cairo, but the roads were always full of people.'

'Not to mention cars and trucks and camels,' O'Hagan added.

'Eventually we got out into the desert and found what looked like a dried-up stream bed, about fifty yards off the road. We dumped the bodies there and shovelled sand on top of them. I don't think anyone could have seen us.'

'How long before somebody stumbles across them?' Haig wondered.

'The vultures will smell them pretty soon, I guess, but it might be a few days at least.'

'Long enough, then,' Sutter decided.

'Long enough,' O'Hagan echoed, as Petrucci climbed the stairs into the cabin. Wilson pulled the door closed, then sat down and they all strapped in.

In the cockpit, Haig fired up the engines, then waved away the power cart and the fire crew who'd been sent over to monitor the start.

Ten minutes later, the Gulfstream accelerated down the runway and lifted smoothly into the air. Sutter received an almost immediate clearance to turn to port on a south-easterly heading, and soon, as the G450 passed fifteen thousand feet in the climb, it crossed over the Suez Canal, heading towards the Red Sea.

They'd now completed the most difficult phase of the entire operation, though none of the men in the aircraft underestimated the magnitude of the task which still lay before them. But, as O'Hagan remarked once the Gulfstream reached top of climb, if everything went well in less than five days they'd be on their way home – or, to be more accurate, heading for the Cayman Islands, where the banking authorities had a relaxed attitude to total strangers making substantial cash deposits.

Glavnoye Razvedyvatelnoye Upravleniye Headquarters, the 'Aquarium', Khodinka Airfield, Moscow

Viktor Grigorevich Bykov surveyed the files piled on the desk in front of him with a certain amount of dissatisfaction. It's a regrettable truism, applicable to the armed forces of all nations, that the higher the rank attained, the less time the holder has to do anything other than sit at a desk and read things – files, reports, statements or whatever. Bykov shifted slightly in his chair, wondering once again if you really could develop haemorrhoids from prolonged sitting, and reached for the large, bright-red and heavily sealed envelope that had now surfaced at the top of his in-tray.

Bykov was tall – just over six feet two – and thin, with noticeably sharp features. His greatcoat hung from a rack in the corner of his spacious office on the top floor of the building, the large windows offering an excellent view over the huge and largely deserted airfield.

He sliced open the envelope and pulled out a file. The title was uninformative and, as he was about to find out, also highly misleading: 'Inventory errors at Zarechnyy, Penza Oblast'. He opened it more with curiosity than any particular enthusiasm. The document was classified above Top Secret, and its distribution was severely restricted: Bykov was one of only three GRU officers on the list.

By the time he'd reached the end of the first page, Bykov was beginning to see why the author of the file, a senior official at Zarechnyy, had given it such an innocuous title. He'd probably hoped nobody would bother to read a file purportedly dealing with some accounting discrepancies at an obscure plant in the middle of Russia. That ruse hadn't worked, because the FSB had been involved in the investigation from the start, and had insisted that the file be properly classified and circulated throughout all the higher echelons of the security apparatus of the CIS. That was why it was now sitting on Bykov's desk at the Aquarium.

When he finished reading, he leant back in his chair and deliberated for a few minutes. Following the arrest of the miserable administrator Yuri Borisov, currently languishing in Lefortovo Prison in Moscow awaiting trial and probable execution – ironically only three cells away from Investigator Litvinoff, who was facing charges of gross negligence – a check of the secure storage areas at Zarechnyy had revealed that one suitcase nuclear device was missing. All the other weapons had been removed immediately and sent to another location – a classic stable-door reaction, Bykov recognized – but the FSB investigators were still no further forward in finding the two American criminals who'd orchestrated the theft.

The decision not to shoot down the air ambulance so close to Turkey had probably been correct, Bykov decided, but that didn't mean Russia should wash her hands of the entire affair. Two potential terrorists were

now on the loose, armed with a nuclear device having a calculated yield of one thousand tons of TNT. That classified it as a tactical rather than a strategic weapon, but its detonation within a major city would be devastating. The official estimates included in the file suggested a likely death toll of around t
hirty-five thousand from the blast alone, and probably a further two hundred thousand fatalities resulting from the radiation and the subsequent fallout. Perhaps as many as a quarter of a million people in all, and the utter destruction of the urban environment.

What appalled him was the recommendation of a senior FSB investigator, who had suggested just forgetting about the whole business. What the idiot apparently didn't realize was that all nuclear explosions leave behind residue that can allow experts to determine the likely origin of the weapon involved. If the stolen bomb was detonated, Bykov could guarantee that it would be identified as being of Russian construction within a matter of weeks.

There was only one way to ensure this scenario never occurred. He picked up the direct line to his superior, then thought better of it. Sometimes the personal approach was more effective than using the telephone.

British Embassy, Dubai

The receptionist studied Richter's passport. 'Who did you wish to see, sir?'

'Michael Watkinson.'

'Please take a seat. I'll see if he's available.'

Richter nodded his thanks and retrieved his passport. All he'd been given by Hammersmith was the man's name, so he had no idea what Watkinson's official title was, but he presumed he was one of the handful of SIS officers based in Dubai.

A few minutes later a tall dark-haired man appeared in the reception area and approached him.

'Mr Richter? I'm Michael Watkinson. May I see your passport, please?' Richter handed it over for perusal. 'Do you have any other form of identification?'

'If you're asking if I've got a neat little leather folder issued at Legoland,' Richter said in a low voice, 'well I haven't, because I'm not actually employed at Vauxhall Cross.'

Watkinson looked somewhat taken aback. 'So where do you work then? We were expecting a Six officer.'

'Somewhere in the backstreets of Hammersmith. If you haven't heard of my section, it's because you haven't needed to know about it. We get lumbered with all the shitty little jobs nobody else wants. And this is one of them.'

'Right,' Watkinson said, returning the passport. 'You'd better follow me.' He led the way to a doorway in one corner, waved a card at a portal reader and pushed open the steel-lined door. Richter followed him down a corridor to a small office containing a desk, three chairs, six filing cabinets and an air-conditioner that sounded as if it was fighting a losing battle with the heat outside.

Watkinson slid behind his desk and gestured vaguely towards the other chairs. 'Take a seat,' he said. 'We were expecting you a couple of days ago.'

'I was retasked, which meant I got sent out to Bahrain

to run an identity check that never happened because the subject died, and then they held me in Manama because of the bomb threat. I only got back here this morning.'

Watkinson nodded. 'And how is George Caxton these days?'

'His name is Julian, as I think you know perfectly well. He seems fine. Bill Evans and Carole-Anne Jackson also send you their best wishes.'

'Thank you. I'm satisfied you are who you say you are.'

'Oh, good,' Richter murmured.

'You know we have to take precautions, especially with people who turn up without the normal documentation. Now, about Holden – you've been briefed, obviously?'

Watkinson stood up, opened the top drawer of one of the filing cabinets, removed a beige folder and passed it across his desk. File covers are colour-coded: Secret is red; Confidential is green, and Restricted and Unclassified are both beige. Richter glanced down at the title, 'HOLDEN, James', and confirmed the classification: 'Restricted'.

'He lives in a small apartment in the Al-Ramool district, just south of the International Airport. I've had a couple of my people keeping an eye on him, but we don't have the manpower for total surveillance, and it's difficult to justify spending too much time watching him.'

'The result?'

'Nothing.' Watkinson shook his head. 'Or at least nothing suspicious. His daily routine is depressingly predictable. He works part-time as a waiter, so he's out most evenings and rarely arrives home before midnight. He gets up quite late and always leaves his apartment during the morning to walk to the local shop where he buys a newspaper – he's a *Daily Express* man. Then he goes to a café where he has coffee and a couple of cigarettes while he reads it.

'He returns to his apartment before lunch. If he goes out at all in the afternoon, it's just to do some shopping. In the early evening he leaves home again to walk to the restaurant. He doesn't seem to have any close friends, and never goes to visit anyone. Even at the café he never spends any time talking to people. He just marches in, orders his coffee, takes it over to a table and sits down with his newspaper, always keeping to himself.'

'The newspaper?'

Watkinson nodded. 'We thought about that, too, but there's nothing there. The shop has a daily delivery of most British papers and Holden simply grabs the front one from the rack. We've had people there watching him, and we've three times taken the front copy of the *Express* immediately before he arrives. We've never found anything in the paper, no hidden messages, no enclosures, and Holden never seems bothered if somebody removes a copy just before him. That daily newspaper, we're quite sure, is just a newspaper.'

He smiled slightly. 'Thanks to the Dubai police, we've also had a tap placed on his phone. They gave us the tapes, but there was nothing interesting apart from his estranged wife calling him every couple of days to complain about something.'

'Any idea why she left?'

'If his routine is anything to go by, probably just terminal boredom.'

'There's not much left.' Richter shrugged. 'Did you do a mail intercept?'

'No. Mail intercepts out here need legal backing. The phone tap we managed quietly on the "old boy" basis.'

'Did you bug his apartment?'

'No, for the same reason as the mail intercept. An illegal bug isn't worth the risk. I'm a firm believer in the Special Theory of Cock-ups as it relates to Sod's Law. If we'd placed a bug and Holden had discovered it and gone to the authorities, we'd have been dumped in the shit up to our necks.'

Richter thought for a moment. 'Has he got a computer?'

'Yes. It's a fairly standard desktop running Windows and protected by a password. We sent a couple of people in to his apartment one evening. They were trained in burglary, not computer science, but they had a boot disk that enabled them to circumvent the password and a big external hard drive. They copied the contents of Holden's entire hard disk. My resident computer expert checked the copy but it looks as if there's nothing there.'

'Anything else in his apartment?'

'Not that we could find. My men took pictures of every room and they're in the file in front of you.'

'OK, I'll look at them later. You checked the restaurant, too?'

'Yes. We've had people there several times. Holden's a waiter. He takes orders, carries plates to the tables and delivers the bills. The clientele is mixed, and he never pays anyone any special attention. If he's receiving messages from customers, we don't know how he's doing it. And even if somebody *is* somehow passing information to him, then you have to ask the other obvious question.'

'Exactly,' Richter nodded. 'Where are *they* getting it from?'

'That's the real problem here. Maybe James Holden is a genuine seer, and all he's doing is telling us exactly what he's dreaming.'

Richter grunted. 'Do you really believe that?'

'No,' Watkinson replied, with a rueful smile. 'I'm a rational man, with a degree in physics. My personal belief is that time only flows one way, and I can't see how anyone can witness an event that hasn't happened yet. Another possible angle – which seems just about as unlikely – is that Holden is telepathic. He's somehow able to access the minds of the people who are placing these devices, and so what he's "seeing" is not the actual explosion itself but the way the perpetrators visualize it happening.'

'That's just replacing one unproven paranormal technique with another one that's equally unproven,' Richter objected.

'I agree. None of this makes sense. The only other way Holden could be getting his information is obvious, but then there's the problem of motive.'

'Yes. He could be in contact with the people who are planting the devices, so he knows about the bombs because they're telling him. But why would they do that? What possible motive could there be for a terrorist organization to leak details of its bombing campaign to someone who can then trot along and tell the authorities? And the other problem is that the Damascus *shahid* and the Manama car bombing were carried out by totally different groups. That makes the idea of Holden being used as a deliberate conduit even more unlikely, unless the activities of those different groups were being coordinated by somebody else. But even then, I *still* don't understand why.'

Al-Qusais district, Dubai

When Massood and Bashar returned to the hotel, they were laden with packages. They went straight to Saadi's room and placed all their purchases on the spare bed. Although both men seemed certain they'd found everything they needed, Saadi was too conscious of the importance of their mission to leave anything to chance, so he checked and inspected every single item before he declared himself satisfied.

'We'll leave everything in here until this evening,' he decided. 'Then we'll prepare the packages and transfer them to the car just before we leave for Nad Al-Sheba. You'd better try to get some sleep this afternoon, because we've got a very long night's work ahead of us.'

Dubai International Airport

Sutter applied the brakes and the Gulfstream came to rest on the hardstanding. Even as the whine of the jets died away, he saw two cars approaching, both white with dark green doors signwritten in Arabic, and preceded by a small Air Traffic Control van with a roof bar, the yellow lights flashing. Leaving Haig to finish the shutdown, Sutter went back into the passenger cabin.

'Two cars are heading this way,' he announced. 'These guys are probably your liaison officers, so good luck.'

'Right,' O'Hagan said, standing up and walking across to the cabin door. As he opened it, a blast of baking air rushed into the aircraft. 'Shit, that's hot,' he muttered. He peered out, saw the approaching cars brake to a halt at the edge of the hardstanding, and turned to face the other three men. 'All ready?'

None of them replied, but O'Hagan hadn't expected them to. They had no idea *what* the CIA had arranged with the Dubai security forces, so they were going to have to play everything by ear.

'Roy,' O'Hagan instructed. 'You and Jeff book into a hotel, once you've cleared customs and immigration. Then tell us where you're staying, and both keep your mobiles switched on. You'll get the aircraft turned round and refuelled, of course.'

Sutter nodded. 'We'll do that right away. This plane will be ready to leave as soon as we are.'

O'Hagan turned back towards the cabin door. 'One guy approaching. Western suit. Two others standing by the cars, dark green uniforms, green berets, so I guess they're police drivers. OK, Ed, over to you. You're the ranking agent.'

When they'd stripped the dead CIA officers, each of the four men had selected the identification card bearing the photograph that was closest to their own likeness. Grant Hutchings had been the ranking agent, and Edward Dawson just happened to look most like him.

The Arab reached the open door of the Gulfstream and peered inside. 'Agent Hutchings?' he asked, in virtually accentless English.

'That's me.' Dawson stepped forward, extending his hand to flash Hutchings's CIA identification.

'I'm delighted to meet you,' the Arab said, barely glancing at it. 'My name's Saeed Hussein and I'm a senior police inspector.'

Dawson introduced his fellow 'CIA agents'.

'One question, Inspector,' Dawson said. 'We're all carrying personal weapons, as we're required to do back in the States. Do you have any problem with us being armed here in Dubai?'

Hussein shook his head firmly. 'We expected that any officers sent here would be carrying weapons, so I've already arranged the correct documentation.'

Ten minutes later the convoy moved off.

'You've been booked into the Al-Khaleej Hotel in Deira,' Hussein explained, then turned to offer Dawson a card. 'Those are my office, home and mobile numbers, so if you have any problems, just call me. I'm based in the police station at the Old Fort on Naif Road. I'll send a car for you at three, and then we can discuss our strategy.'

'Thank you, Inspector. We'll need to check in at the American Consulate sometime soon. Is that anywhere nearby?'

Hussein smiled. 'Dubai isn't really very big, and

nowhere's too far away. Your consulate is located in the World Trade Centre on Shaikh Zayed Road, only about four kilometres south of your hotel. But must you go there in person? We have secure communications at the Old Fort you can use.'

Dawson appeared to consider this question, but in reality he had no intention of going anywhere near the American Consulate. Hussein had hardly looked at his identification, nor those carried by the other three. Clearly he'd been told to expect a CIA team to arrive at Dubai in a Gulfstream. Expectation has a way of dulling the critical faculties, and because the four men were exactly what he'd been expecting, he hadn't done a proper check.

Dawson knew the consulate guards would be more thorough. His vague resemblance to the deceased Grant Hutchings wouldn't be enough to satisfy them. But they had to check in because if they didn't it would ring alarm bells at Langley. So even if Hussein hadn't offered the use of the police station's communication facilities, Dawson would certainly have suggested it.

'Thank you, Inspector,' Dawson said. 'That'll save a trip to the consulate, and time is, I think, now of the essence.'

British Embassy, Dubai

'Have you seen Holden?' Richter asked, closing the file, and Watkinson nodded. 'What were your conclusions?'

'He appears genuine enough. He seems disturbed by what he's describing, and despite multi-questioning he always sticks to the same story.' Asking the same question several times using different forms of words is an old interrogator's trick, often known as multi-questioning. 'Ideally, I would have liked to strap him to a polygraph, but we've no power to make him submit to that kind of testing. I did ask him if he'd do it voluntarily, but he got quite upset.'

'A guilty reaction?' Richter suggested.

'Perhaps. Or perhaps not. You could look at it either way.'

'OK. Is there anything else you need to tell me about him?'

'No, I don't think so. Do you need to look at the file again?'

Richter shook his head and slid it across the table. 'No. Interesting but not helpful – that more or less sums it up.'

Just as Richter stood, his Enigma mobile rang. 'Yes, Carole.' He recognized her voice immediately.

'This line's secure,' she confirmed. 'There's been a development at the Saudi end. The police have had a presence at the Al-Shahrood stables ever since Qabandi blew the whistle, and the missing staff finally turned up this morning.'

'Dead, I assume?' Richter asked.

'Yes, all dead. A pack of wild dogs had congregated at the back of the stables, and when the inspector noticed they were scratching in the sand he organized a digging party. They'd got down four feet when they found the first corpse. There are about a dozen bodies in total. They're running a full forensic work-up now, but it looks like they were killed execution-style: one bullet each in the back of the head.'

'Well, that certainly makes the case of the missing horse look a hell of a lot different. Any leads yet?'

'No, but obviously this has now become the highest priority for the Saudi police force.'

'What was that about a missing horse?' Watkinson asked, as Richter ended the call.

'Shaf,' Richter said shortly, and explained about the grisly discovery at the stables.

Watkinson shook his head. 'We knew the horse had gone missing in odd circumstances, but this certainly puts a different complexion on things.'

At that moment there was a brief double-tap on the door and a junior officer appeared with a buff envelope in his hand. 'Secret Flash traffic from London, sir,' he said, glancing curiously at Richter. 'For your eyes only,' he added, passing the envelope across the desk.

Watkinson signed the classified-document register, ripped open the envelope and extracted a single sheet of paper. 'This more or less confirms what you've just told me,' he said. 'Vauxhall Cross has tasked us with assisting the Dubai authorities to find the men who flew here with Shaf. That isn't going to be easy, because apparently they were travelling on passports belonging to three of the stable staff, who were dead long before the horse was loaded aboard the aircraft at Riyadh. The only possible lead is that the Saudi police are examining a Range Rover from Al-Shahrood. The vehicle was abandoned at Riyadh Airport, and they think it was used to tow the horsebox. I suppose they might manage to lift some fingerprints from it.'

'That only helps if the bad guys are on record some-where,' Richter pointed out. 'They'd have needed another vehicle at this end, so the Dubai police should be checking hire firms here. My guess is that they'll have hired a big four-by-four to deliver the horse, then turned it in for a less conspicuous car from a different company. The other obvious lead is the transporter. These guys didn't kill a dozen people just for the pleasure of delivering a racehorse to a stable here. They must have brought something else in the horsebox, guessing security would be reasonably lax for a known horse entered in an event like the World Cup. By now they'll have removed whatever they concealed in the trailer, but there might still be traces left.'

Watkinson nodded. 'I'll suggest they use sniffer dogs, because I don't think they have electronic explosive detectors here. That *is* what you mean, isn't it?'

'Yes. They'll definitely have brought in explosives, and probably a lot of them. Nothing else makes any sense, as far as I can see.'

'Agreed. Right, what are you going to do now?'

Richter shrugged. 'I came out here to see James Holden, so that's what I'm going to do. This horse thing isn't my problem – at least, not until my boss tells me otherwise.'

Chapter Fourteen

Friday
Al-Khaleej Hotel, Dubai

The four men checked in, locked their bags in their rooms, then three of them met in the coffee shop. The missing man was John Petrucci, whose luggage consisted of a computer bag and overnight case, plus a large and heavy suitcase. Since the latter contained the nuclear weapon they'd obtained from Russia, there was no way they were going to leave that unguarded.

'Baxter won't be joining us,' Dawson explained, using Petrucci's assumed name. 'He's feeling a little jetlagged so he's taking a nap. Our car will arrive in about thirty minutes, but only two of us will be going to the Old Fort. Baxter isn't fit enough, so I want you' – he pointed at Wilson – 'to start checking out the gear. Get Baxter to help you, and ensure everything's taken care of this afternoon, because I don't know what timescale Hussein will be working to.'

The instruction didn't make any obvious sense, but Wilson nodded, stood up and left.

Bur Dubai

'Do you want me to come with you?' Michael Watkinson asked, as they sat over coffee after lunch.

Richter thought for a few moments. 'Yes, that would be helpful. If I just turn up out of the blue and start grilling him, Holden may not be particularly receptive. Since you've met him before, you can just introduce me as a colleague from London.'

Watkinson glanced at his watch. 'Now's probably as good a time as any. Holden will almost certainly be at home.'

Al-Khaleej Hotel, Dubai

Richard Wilson knocked twice on the hotel room door. 'It's Agent Franks. Open up.'

Petrucci swung the door wide. 'Hi, Andy,' he said. 'Where are the others?'

'Waiting for the car. You feeling OK?'

'Not too good, but definitely better.'

'Good. I'm going to check the gear we've brought out with us. Let me just wash my hands, and I'll get started.'

He motioned towards the en-suite bathroom and Petrucci nodded, walked in and turned on the cold water tap to confuse any listening devices. Wilson began speaking very quietly. 'Now we have to move quickly. They'll be going to see Holden this afternoon, so we've got very little time to sort things out.'

'You're sure O'Hagan wants it done now?'

'Yes. He'll try and delay heading off to Al-Ramool as long as he can, but realistically they could be leaving the Old Fort any time after three.'

'OK. You want to do it yourself?' Petrucci asked.

'No.' Wilson shook his head. 'Holden's building may be under surveillance, so it has to be you, wearing a *gellabbiya* and a *kaffiyeh*, because you've got the language and I haven't. And he knows you – I might have a problem getting inside.'

'Right,' Petrucci said. 'I'll get ready. You'll stay here, then?'

'Yes. If anyone knocks at the door, I'll just be a guy looking out for a sick friend who's busy throwing up in the bathroom.'

Wilson turned off the taps and they walked back into the bedroom. Petrucci opened a case, rummaged around until he found a white *gellabbiya*, and pulled it on over his shirt and trousers. A *kaffiyeh* followed, then he slid a cosh into his pocket.

'Don't take a taxi until you're well away from the hotel,' Wilson reminded him, his voice barely audible. 'And don't forget the computer.'

'Oh, yeah.' Petrucci went back to the case and pulled out a CD-ROM in a plastic sleeve. He checked his appearance in a mirror. 'That's it. I'd better go.'

Old Fort Police Station, Dubai

'Agent Hutchings,' Inspector Hussein said as the two Americans entered his office. For a moment he looked expectant, then puzzled. 'Agents Baxter and Franks aren't with you?'

Dawson shook his head. 'No. Baxter's suffering from mild food poisoning, and Franks is checking some of the equipment we brought with us.'

'Very well,' Hussein said. 'I'll order some refreshments. Then we can begin.'

Ten minutes later Dawson and O'Hagan were seated in a briefing room, a selection of soft drinks on the table in front of them.

'Right, gentlemen,' Saeed Hussein began, 'we all know why we're here. My government's very concerned that this man Holden might be genuine, and that a credible threat exists against us here in Dubai. I presume you were briefed at Langley on why we asked for assistance?'

'Yes, but in case we missed anything, could you run through it again, starting with Holden's first approach to the British Embassy.'

By hearing what the Dubai police had to say, they would find out what the real CIA agents had been told.

In anticipation of this request, the slide projector beside the lectern was already loaded with photographs of the devastation in Damascus. The three men studied these extremely graphic images in silence. The Manama bomb was still being analysed, but Holden's very accurate prediction about it, and his premonition of a bomb exploding in a waterfront hotel, had the Dubai authorities severely concerned.

'The problem,' Hussein finished, 'is that we have whole roads of hotels running along the coast, and any one of them could be the building Holden thinks he saw being attacked in his dream. Or, of course, the target might be in Abu Dhabi, Bahrain, northern Oman, Qatar, or even Kuwait or Saudi Arabia. If Holden's right, and one of these hotels *is* a terrorist target, the biggest problem will be finding out which one.'

'What about motive?' Dawson asked. 'The suicide bomber in Damascus claimed to have been acting for a political group that barely even exists.'

Hussein nodded. 'The *Jamiat Al-Ikhwan Al-Muslimun*. It doesn't make sense, but nobody can think of a valid reason why Assad should claim to be acting on their behalf if he wasn't doing so. He was a suicide bomber, so obviously no one was going to ask him questions *after* the event. And the bomb at Manama was different in almost every way.'

'Could the Manama weapon have been positioned by the Muslim Brotherhood?'

Hussein shook his head. 'Nobody has claimed responsibility, but the Bahrain authorities think the bomb was part of a local feud between two underground groups called Sharaf and Bahraini Jihad.'

This was news to Dawson, but O'Hagan glanced at him with a suppressed smile. That explained why Ahmed had been so insistent about the positioning of the weapon: he and Petrucci had unwittingly been drawn into an ongoing fight.

'As far as we can tell at the moment, these two bomb attacks were unconnected, the only common factor being that this man Holden was apparently able to foresee both of them. But,' Hussein added, 'it's early days yet, so we might well find that the conclusion the Bahrainis have drawn is incorrect.'

271

I wouldn't hold your breath waiting, O'Hagan thought.

'I myself have interviewed Holden,' Hussein added, 'and he seems genuinely disturbed by these dreams he claims to be having. He's been interviewed repeatedly, and his story remains the same. Even if he has a hidden agenda, there's still the problem of his uncanny accuracy.' He glanced round the room with a slightly apologetic smile. 'That's the crux of the matter. How could he be obtaining such accurate information about future events?'

'I don't think any of us really believe Holden's claims,' Dawson said, 'but we can't argue with the facts. We'd like to see him ourselves this afternoon, but no matter what he tells us, or what we think of him, we've been instructed to assist you as much as possible, and we're assuming that the threat is real. We have explosive detection equipment with us, and we intend to check all likely targets – which will be the biggest and most expensive hotels along the coast.'

This was actually true: part of the equipment the CIA agents had brought out with them included half a dozen sophisticated detectors presently stored in Wilson's hotel room.

'How do these detectors work?' Hussein asked.

'You could call them highly sensitive sniffers,' Dawson replied. 'They analyse the air, but they can also examine swabs taken from suspect packages or materials. All explosives emit tiny particles and vapour, and this equipment is really sensitive – it can detect traces into the low nanogram level. That means they're sensitive enough to detect one molecule of explosive in several million molecules of air. We'll need to test the air at different loca-

tions in each building we investigate. That's because
your hotels are air-conditioned, so the air moves around
constantly. Even so, it shouldn't take more than about
thirty minutes in each.'

Hussein smiled. 'Even at that rate, Agent Hutchings,
you have a considerable amount of work ahead of you.'

'That's why we want to interview Holden. We hope
he can help us narrow the search.'

Al-Ramool district, Dubai

James Holden had just opened a can of beer when he
heard a knock. He walked into the hall and peered
through the spy-hole viewer. For a few moments he
stared at the unfamiliar figure, then recognition dawned
and he opened the door.

'Hullo, John.'

'Hi, James.' Petrucci stepped inside and glanced
round, looking and listening for the sight or sound of
anyone else inside the property, and reminding himself
of the layout. He'd only been there once before, over a
year earlier. 'Your wife not around?'

Holden shook his head. 'No. Margaret and I have
parted company, permanently this time. Sad for her,
maybe, but good for me. Is everything on schedule?'

Petrucci nodded, again surprised at the arrogance
of the man. Holden had always been the weakest link
in the chain. After O'Hagan had originally devised the
plan, it had taken him six months to recruit the five other
members of the team who would carry out the operation,
and another three months to find Holden.

He'd needed someone living permanently in Dubai, but a resident with no affection for either the country or its people and, of course, for whom money was important. Holden had seemed ideal, though it wasn't until later that O'Hagan had realized exactly how ideal he was – the man was a very convincing actor. The big problem was his attitude: once he'd grasped the scope of their plan, he seemed to consider himself a full partner, demanding an equal share of the take. O'Hagan had agreed to this, but only to keep the Englishman in line. He'd told Petrucci immediately they'd left the apartment building thirteen months earlier that Holden was an expendable asset. And now this particular asset had just become a liability.

'Yes.' Petrucci pulled the CD-ROM out of his pocket. 'I've brought some more information for you, for the next phase. Where's your computer? I can't leave this disk here, so you'll have to copy the files.'

Holden led the way to his study and switched on the PC. When the password request appeared, he typed in an eight-digit code, then waited for the Windows desktop to appear.

The moment it did, Petrucci swung the lead-filled cosh down hard against the side of the Englishman's head. Holden toppled to the floor without a sound.

'Thanks very much for all your help,' Petrucci murmured, then ignored the unconscious man and sat down. He picked up the CD-ROM and inserted it in the DVD drive. When its contents were displayed, he chose one file and double-clicked it. The program was a file-destruction utility that would overwrite every byte on the hard drive with random characters five times over.

Fortunately, Holden's computer had a fast processor and lots of memory, but even so it was going to take some time for the operation to finish.

Only then did Petrucci turn his attention back to the Englishman. He bent over him, seized his throat in a choke-hold and squeezed hard for nearly two minutes. Then he relaxed his grip and checked Holden's neck for a pulse.

Petrucci checked his watch. Two fifty-five. If O'Hagan managed to delay his departure from the Old Fort until three, Petrucci would be gone long before anyone arrived at the flat. But if Hussein decided to leave earlier, it'd be a close-run thing.

He looked across at the computer screen. The program was approaching the end of its first over-writing operation. While it was running, he had other things to do.

He went to the kitchen, found a plastic carrier bag and returned to the study. He opened all the drawers on the computer table and rifled through their contents. He found a few floppy disks and CD-ROMs, two unmarked DVDs and a USB memory stick, and tossed them all into the bag. Beside the monitor were some CD cases, containing operating system and software-installation disks, and he took those as well. He checked all the other drawers and shelves in the study, but found no other types of storage media, then walked into the lounge and looked around. There were some DVD disks in cases next to the TV set, and he opened each to check that it contained a pre-recorded disk.

Petrucci wasn't really expecting to find anything else in the apartment: it looked to him as if Holden had kept everything to do with his computer in the study. They'd told him that nobody, not even his wife, should know what he was doing. They had also told him not to take backups, but even if he had, Petrucci was confident they were now in his carrier bag.

He returned to the study. The deletion program had finished so he ejected the disk and pulled the computer's power plug out of the socket. He took a last look round to ensure that he'd left nothing behind, then picked up the carrier bag and left the apartment.

Old Fort Police Station, Dubai

Inspector Hussein glanced at his watch. 'If there's nothing further, gentlemen, I suggest we drive over to see Mr Holden now. He's confirmed that he'll be at home this afternoon. Is there anything else before we leave?'

'Only the use of your communications equipment to talk to the American Consulate.'

The inspector led Dawson down some stairs and ushered him into a room protected by a steel door. The noise hit them immediately: a constant whistling, chattering hum generated by the sound of air-conditioners, fans running inside cabinets, relays opening and closing, all overlaid by the faint noise from speakers and headphones.

'I'll get you connected.' Hussein pointed to a chair in front of a desk, on which stood a red telephone. The inspector spoke to the communications officer, and ten seconds later the phone started to ring. Hussein nodded to Dawson, who picked up the receiver.

'American Consulate,' announced the voice in the earpiece.

Dawson pulled a small notebook out of his jacket pocket. The inspector left the room as the American spoke into the microphone. 'Richard Owens, please,' Dawson said, using the contact details Grant Hutchings had recorded in his neat script.

Five minutes later, Dawson emerged from the office to find Hussein and O'Hagan waiting outside. 'Any problems?' the inspector asked.

'None at all,' the American said truthfully. In fact, it had been a lot easier than he'd anticipated. Owens, the ranking CIA officer at the consulate, had been expecting Hutchings to contact him, and he'd been happy to provide an update over the phone.

Not that there was very much to update. Two further victims had died from injuries sustained in the Manama explosion, but there was still no further information about the perpetrators. According to Owens, the conclusion drawn by the Bahraini Special Intelligence Service was quite likely to be correct.

Al-Ramool district, Dubai

Hussein stepped out of the lift and strode down the corridor to a blue door. Dawson and O'Hagan stopped beside him as he knocked.

There was no answer. Hussein shrugged and knocked again, still without result. He flicked open his mobile phone and pressed a few keys. All three could hear a phone warbling inside. Hussein let it ring for a minute.

'I don't understand this,' he said. 'I rang Mr Holden at lunchtime and he said he'd be staying in all afternoon.'

'Maybe he went out to buy something,' Dawson suggested. 'Does he have a mobile you could try?'

Hussein rang again and they heard a distinctive trilling ringtone from within. Again nobody answered it.

'It's not a problem,' Dawson said. 'Let's go grab a drink somewhere and come back in half an hour.'

Ten minutes after they'd left the building, a light-coloured saloon car stopped on the opposite side of the road, about fifty yards from the apartment block. Paul Richter got out and followed Michael Watkinson into a nearby café.

Sitting near a window, with an uninterrupted view down the street, was a fair-haired middle-aged man dressed in casual clothes and apparently reading the *Daily Telegraph*.

'George Blakeney,' Watkinson introduced him. 'This is Paul Richter. Any movement since I called?'

Blakeney shook his head. 'Nothing since he came back from the café at about eleven. He read the *Express*, smoked three cigarettes, drank two cups of coffee, and went home.'

'Three cigarettes?' Watkinson observed. 'Usually he just has two.'

'His nicotine intake's increasing, but I doubt that's significant. He's had no visitors that I'm aware of. People go in and out of that building all the time, but they're mainly Arabs. Holden doesn't seem to have many Arab friends – or many friends at all, in fact.'

The two men left the café and crossed to the apartment building. Watkinson pressed the lift button for the third floor.

Five minutes later, he called a number on his mobile. 'George? We're outside Holden's apartment, but there's no answer. We've tried his landline and mobile and we can hear the phones ringing inside. Are you certain he never left the building?' Watkinson listened to Blakeney's reply. 'Right, I'll try again. But if I can't raise him, I'm going to blow the whistle.'

Watkinson looked at Richter. 'Blakeney's certain Holden didn't come out of the front door, and there's no exit at the back because there's another apartment building directly behind. There's a fire escape on one side, but it leads to the street, so Blakeney would still have seen him. I don't like this at all.'

He hammered on the door again, then pressed his ear to the faded paintwork and listened closely. 'Nothing,' he said, after a few seconds.

Richter examined the keyhole. 'This looks like a fairly standard Yale-type,' he said. 'I'm not that good with locks, but I think even I could get past this one.'

'The local police take a very dim view of breaking and entering,' Watkinson warned.

'I'm not breaking anything,' Richter replied, 'and I think any minute now you'll recall that this door was slightly ajar when we arrived here. If the flat's empty, we'll just walk away. If something's happened to Holden, whether the door was open or closed is going to be the last thing on anyone's mind.'

He pulled out his wallet and selected a yellow card. 'Now, let's just see how helpful the Automobile Association can really be.' He slid one corner between the door and the jamb, moved it down until he felt the catch of the lock, then jiggled the card until the corner eased under it. Then he pushed firmly, and with a sudden click the door opened.

'We haven't got gloves,' Richter reminded him, replacing the card in his wallet, 'so don't touch anything apart from the outside of the door.'

The hall was a tiny square space with two doors leading off it. Richter pushed the outside door closed, then wrapped a handkerchief around his hand and opened the door to their right. That revealed a small toilet, so he tried the other one.

Immediately the two men stepped into the lounge, it was obvious that the place had been ransacked, clothes, books and magazines scattered about the floor, furniture upturned or pushed aside to allow easier access to the drawers and cupboards.

'This doesn't look like a burglary to me,' Watkinson remarked, glancing round. 'A thief would have taken the DVD player at least, and probably the TV.'

Richter walked across the room to where the flat-screen television was positioned on a stand. 'That's odd,' he said, looking down. 'All these DVD cases have been opened but not closed again, and the discs are still inside them.'

Watkinson shrugged. 'Maybe Holden's the lazy kind and doesn't bother shutting them.'

'On one or two, maybe, but on all of them? I don't think so. And there's a digital camera and an iPod on that table over there. Whoever did this was searching for something in particular.'

'Makes sense to me. But where's Holden?'

Richter nudged open the door on the opposite side of the lounge. He took one look inside and immediately stepped back.

'Michael.' The SIS officer swung round to look at him. 'Time to call this one in,' Richter said. 'Somebody's popped your star witness.'

Chapter Fifteen

Friday
Al-Khaleej Hotel, Dubai

'Any problems?' Wilson asked quietly, as Petrucci stepped into the hotel room and began pulling off his Arab garments. Music was playing from the bedside radio to confuse any microphones.

'Nobody followed me, and no one seemed to take the slightest notice of me at the apartment building.'

'And Holden?'

'James Holden,' Petrucci replied, with a wolfish smile, 'is now a sleeping partner – sleeping peacefully, and permanently.'

'Good. What's in the bag?'

'A bunch of disks and stuff from his study. I don't think he made copies of anything we sent him, but if he did they'll be amongst this lot.' Petrucci lifted up the plastic carrier bag. 'I wiped the hard drive on his PC, so that's now been sanitized. I don't think we need worry any more about James Holden or his predictions.'

Al-Ramool district, Dubai

It didn't take Inspector Hussein long to respond to the call, because he was sitting with Dawson and O'Hagan in a nearby café.

As he reached the apartment door, Michael Watkinson stepped out to meet him.

'OK, Michael,' Hussein began. 'Tell me what happened here.'

'My colleague and I came to interview Holden. I checked that he was at home: one of my men is watching the building. The apartment door was ajar, but there was no reply, so we entered to investigate.'

Hussein looked at Watkinson. 'What time was this?' he asked.

'About twenty minutes ago.'

'That's very interesting,' said Hussein with a slight smile, 'because I was in this area on a very similar errand. These two gentlemen' – he gestured towards Dawson and O'Hagan – 'are Grant Hutchings and Roger Middleton from the CIA and this' – he changed hands – 'is Michael Watkinson of the British Secret Intelligence Service. We also wanted to talk to Holden, but when we were here about half an hour ago, the door was locked.'

The Arab eyed Watkinson appraisingly, just as Richter appeared behind him. 'Are you absolutely certain the door was open when you arrived?'

Watkinson glanced at Richter before replying. 'Let's just say the door was closed but, when we applied pressure, it opened.'

'Quite,' Hussein said, putting a wealth of meaning into the word. 'Don't give me any more details of the "pressure" you applied. And this would be your colleague?'

Richter stepped forward and held out his hand. 'Paul Richter. I was sent out from London to investigate this man Holden. But I guess I'm a little late for that now.'

'I have a forensic team on the way over,' the inspector said. 'Stay here, please, while I check the place myself.'

He pulled on a pair of latex gloves, and was back in under a minute. 'Have you disturbed anything in there?'

Richter shook his head. 'No. We realized it was a crime scene the moment we went in. Once we found the body we knew we were dealing with a murder, so we waited in the hallway for the police to get here. We didn't touch or move anything.' He glanced at the two Americans. 'I gather you're from Langley?'

'Yup.' Dawson nodded. 'I'm Grant Hutchings, the senior agent, and this is Roger Middleton. I got your name, but who do you work for – exactly?'

'An outfit that's attached to the British SIS. We act in what you might term a supporting role.'

Dawson didn't look entirely happy with this reply. 'You carrying some kind of ID?'

'Only a passport. Why?'

'I like to know who I'm dealing with,' Dawson snapped.

'So do I,' Richter replied, 'and if we were on your home turf in the States, I'd be happy to provide whatever you needed. Out here, we're all guests of the government of Dubai, and you've no authority to check my credentials, any more than I can check yours. So unless you want to get involved in a serious pissing contest, I suggest you just accept what I've told you and leave it at that.'

Dawson glared at Richter, but O'Hagan shook his head. 'Leave it, Grant. He's right – we're all here under sufferance.'

Watkinson and Hussein watched this exchange with bemused expressions.

Dawson still looked less than happy, but then shrugged. 'OK, so you've been inside. What the hell happened in there?'

'We don't know for sure,' Richter said, 'but I think Holden was strangled. Whoever did it was searching for something. Every drawer and cupboard has been emptied.'

'Could it have been a burglary?' Dawson suggested.

'I don't think so, because there are several attractive items still inside. Thieves usually grab whatever's going. This has all the hallmarks of a professional search operation. What I don't know is exactly what they were looking for.'

'Can we go inside?' Dawson asked Hussein.

The inspector shook his head. 'I'm afraid not. This is now a murder scene, so nobody – apart from the pathologist – can enter until the forensic people have finished their work.'

'OK,' Dawson said, 'so there's nothing else we can do here until tomorrow, I suppose.'

Hussein nodded. 'I should have the preliminary report by lunchtime. But there's nothing you can achieve here, so I suggest you take a taxi back to your hotel.'

'I'll need to tell Langley about this,' Dawson said. 'Can I use the communications at the Old Fort again to talk to the consulate?'

'Of course. Tell the taxi driver to take you there, and then get a police car to return you to the hotel.'

Dawson and O'Hagan nodded briefly to the other men, then walked back to the lift.

'I think the same applies to us, Saeed,' Watkinson said. 'Paul and I will let you have our statements tomorrow.'

Once outside the building, Watkinson turned to Richter. 'I've two questions for you. First, what the hell was that spat with the Americans about?'

'Some CIA officers have the knack of rubbing me up the wrong way,' Richter replied, 'and that Hutchings character had it in spades. They stomp in as if they own the place and expect everyone to jump just because they've come all the way from Langley waving the star-spangled banner. And usually they're only on a seagull mission anyway.'

'Seagull mission?' Watkinson asked.

'They fly in, shit all over everyone, and fly out again.'

'Oh, right.' He smiled. 'I'll remember that. The second question's more serious. I *was* waiting there in the hallway of the apartment, just as I told Hussein, but you weren't. What were you doing?'

'Nothing contentious, but I knew that once the plods arrived we'd be booted out, and have to wait days to be told what they managed to find. I don't think we've got days to spare, so I was trying to work out what the guy who killed Holden was looking for.'

'And did you?'

'I think so, though trying to see something that isn't there can be a difficult trick. The only room where anything struck me as unusual was the study. There were no computer disks anywhere. These days you don't often need CDs or floppies, but you always keep the master installation disks, just in case the whole thing crashes, and anyone with any sense makes regular backups. There were no disks anywhere in that room.'

'So you think Holden's killer took them?'

'Yes, and something else pretty much confirmed it.'

'What?'

'While you were waiting for the Thin Blue Line to arrive, I tried to boot up Holden's computer. Someone had pulled the plug out of the socket, which is unusual unless you're paranoid about power surges. When I finally switched on the PC it wouldn't start, and the error message reported no operating system could be found. That means the hard disk is faulty, missing, or it had been wiped. The disk was still in the machine, because I could hear it running, and hard drives are very reliable, so the most likely explanation is that somebody ran a wipe utility on it.'

'Just as well we've got a copy, then. But we couldn't find anything on it that was even slightly interesting, and certainly nothing worth killing for.'

'Which must mean,' Richter reflected, 'that whatever it is must be very well hidden. I'll talk to your computer man when we get back to the embassy, and see if we can come up with anything.'

'Lady,' Watkinson said.

'What?'

'My computer man is actually a computer lady. Her name's Christine Halls, but everyone calls her Chris.'

British Embassy, Dubai

'How did you check the contents of Holden's hard drive?' Richter asked.

'I analysed the overall directory structure and

looked at the program files and utilities,' Chris Halls replied, 'because you can gauge a user's ability by seeing what software they have in addition to the standard stuff.'

Halls was a slim and attractive woman of about thirty, long dark hair framing a pert and pretty face, square-lensed spectacles giving her a somewhat studious appearance. She had a degree in computer science, and had worked for the SIS ever since university.

'And Holden?'

'He was a user, but not an expert. Take a look.' She pointed at the nineteen-inch flat-panel monitor on which the cloned copy of Holden's hard drive was displayed. 'He's using Windows Vista Home Premium, and that's a clue straight away because it's still pretty buggy. Serious users tend to run XP Professional or Linux. For application software he's got a basic version of Office, and that came with the computer because it's an OEM edition.'

Richter nodded. 'Original Equipment Manufacturer,' he said. 'What else has he got?'

'What you'd expect, bearing in mind the spec of the machine. He's got a standard DVD player, and an oldish version of Nero for burning CD and DVD disks for backup. That probably came with the machine and he's never bothered updating it. His firewall, anti-virus and so forth are all perfectly good programs, but he's using the free editions. A serious user would either run the bought versions or more likely an integrated suite like Norton. This looks like a machine owned by somebody who either doesn't know too much about computers, or doesn't care. As long as the PC did the job, I don't think he was bothered.'

'What about data files?'

'There were a few hundred files in the "my documents" folder, divided up the way you'd expect – letters to the bank, that kind of thing. I scanned the whole disk, doing wildcard searches for likely filenames. I also looked for text strings within files, choosing words associated with the bombs Holden told us about, but found nothing.'

'And then?' Richter asked.

'And then nothing, really. We were never certain that there *was* anything to find on Holden's computer. The people we sent in only copied the hard drive because it seemed like a good place to look for information. The last thing I did was check his copy of Outlook Express. He had no files at all in his inbox, which was a surprise. Most inexperienced users end up with hundreds or thousands of messages there. But Holden seems to have been good at filing them, and he had a lot of folders. I scanned them all, but still nothing came up. No pictures, no mention of the words "Damascus", "Syria", "Assad", "suicide", "bomb" or "*shahid*". I also searched for "Bahrain" and got a few hits, but they were all to do with that new waterside development at Manama. The only slight oddity was that his "deleted items" folder was also empty. Most people delete messages they've read or they're not interested in, and then they sit there until they do a purge and empty the entire folder.'

'He might have just done that, so it could be a coincidence the folder was empty.'

Halls nodded. 'You could be right, but you could also argue it indicates a regimented use of the email client, with Holden eliminating every message that he didn't file. And I'm not a big fan of coincidence.'

'Neither am I,' Richter said, 'and now that we know somebody killed Holden and took the trouble to wipe his hard drive, we can be sure there was something on that machine the killer didn't want us to see. We also know that what Holden was telling you people was probably sent to him by email, and that he was no more psychic than I am.'

'So what do you want to do now?'

'That's your department, I think. There's something on that hard drive we need to find, and it's obviously very well hidden. How could Holden have managed that, if you're right and he wasn't a sophisticated user?'

'We can rule out techniques like steganography, so my guess is that he did one of two things. He could have used online storage, but I've checked his favourites in Internet Explorer and none of them links to a storage site. Most probably, somewhere on that drive,' Halls pointed at the external hard disk, 'is a security program Holden used to create a hidden folder, or even a hidden partition, that won't show up using normal search tools.'

'Are you sure it's still there? I mean, did the people who accessed Holden's computer copy *everything*?'

'Yes.' Halls nodded. 'They didn't copy the hard disk – they cloned it. That means they made an exact, byte-for-byte replica of it. This drive is identical to the hard disk in Holden's computer on the date our people entered his apartment. If there was a hidden directory or partition on his computer then, it'll be here on this drive.'

'Can you find it?'

'Yes, probably. As this investigation has moved from being merely about an anomaly nobody could explain to a murder hunt, my priorities have changed. Watkinson's told me I can spend as much time as I like playing with this.'

Al-Khaleej Hotel, Dubai

Dawson's update for Langley had inevitably proved to be somewhat protracted. The man they'd travelled to Dubai to interview had been murdered, and his apartment ransacked. With their witness – using the word in its loosest possible sense – dead, the primary reason for their presence in Dubai had vanished, and Owens had recommended that they return to the States immediately.

This had always been a potential problem, because local CIA officers usually took a dim view when Langley-based staff were sent out to work on their 'patch'. But Dawson had handled that, too, by telling Owens they'd be leaving once they'd shown the Dubai police how to use the explosive detectors they'd brought with them. That, he estimated, would take them three or four days to accomplish. Owens had grumbled at this delay, but had agreed to relay everything Dawson had told him back to CIA Headquarters.

'Leave Dick guarding the room, but go get John, will you?' O'Hagan instructed, as they climbed out of the police car. 'We'll go through what happened and make sure we've got all our beans in a row.'

As the three of them headed towards Dubai Creek, he began. 'Right. What happened at Al-Ramool, John?'

'It went as exactly as planned. Holden let me in, I terminated him in the study and wiped the hard drive on his PC. I grabbed all his disks and anything else I could find, trashed the place and left.'

'You took precautions?'

Petrucci nodded. 'Yes. I wore my Arab stuff, and sunglasses. I took a taxi both ways but not door-to-door. Nobody followed me in either direction, and nobody took any notice of me at the building itself.'

O'Hagan shook his head. 'Nobody you were aware of, John, but actually somebody did. The British SIS had a man watching, and he would certainly have seen you. Whether he noticed you is a different question.'

'I saw nobody,' Petrucci repeated, 'and I was checking constantly.'

'He was probably sitting in a café or a car, or maybe even in a building across the street, but I don't think it matters. The authorities won't be looking for a CIA officer working with their own police force, and certainly not one who was lying in his hotel room suffering from food poisoning.'

'So you reckon we're fireproof?'

'Unless something remarkable happens, yes,' O'Hagan replied. 'Hussein is going to be busy sorting out the crime scene, and he won't have much time to deal with us for a couple of days. Tomorrow's Saturday, and I doubt if anything will happen over the weekend, but I'll call him and suggest we start checking the hotels on Sunday. One of us is going to have to become an expert on those explosive detectors by then, so I'll brief Dick. Now, the CIA guy here suggested we should just pack our bags and head off back to Langley, because Holden's dead.'

'Maybe we shouldn't have whacked him so quickly,' Dawson said. 'If we'd done an interview with him today, we could have taken him out next week.'

O'Hagan shook his head. 'No. Holden was an amateur and a loose cannon. He'd already met John and me, and I couldn't risk him reacting when he saw us again. Hussein's quite a sharp cookie, and if he suspected Holden knew us, the shit would really hit the fan. Getting rid of him was the safest option.'

He pursed his lips and glanced around them. 'Right, the other matter is fairly minor. When we went over to Al-Ramool, Ed and I met a senior British SIS officer called Michael Watkinson. He's based locally and Hussein seemed to know him well. I don't think he's likely to be a problem, but the man with him possibly might be.

'His name's Paul Richter and he works for some kind of deniable outfit attached to the SIS, but he wouldn't be specific, and wouldn't show any ID either. None of that's real important, but what worries me is that he'd opened the door of Holden's apartment and been inside. In fact, he was still inside when we arrived with Hussein, which shows he's not afraid to break the rules. I don't know why he's out here, but he has the definite look of a trouble-shooter about him. If he gets too close to us, we may have to arrange for him to have an accident.'

British Embassy, Dubai

'Don't either of you two have a home to go to?' Watkinson asked, opening the door of Chris Halls's office and peering inside. It was late evening, and Richter hadn't emerged in over three hours, except to go to the loo and collect mugs of coffee.

Richter glanced up. 'I do have a hotel room and a bed with my name on it, but Chris here thinks she's getting close to cracking this, so I plan on staying around for a while.'

'No problem. But to avoid ruining her concentration, can you come to my office? There are a couple of things we need to discuss.'

When they got there, Watkinson sat down behind his desk. 'I've been talking to George Blakeney about Holden. He's very embarrassed because it happened on his watch.'

'He shouldn't be. He was supposed to be watching the building and following Holden if he left the premises. He wasn't there as a bodyguard and, as far as I'm aware, there was no known threat to Holden.'

'Agreed. I asked him to give me a description of everyone he remembers entering or leaving the building, and he's come up with a few, but nothing detailed enough to start a search. Almost all the visitors he can recall were Arabs – or at least they were dressed like Arabs – and he has no recollection of anyone looking out of place.'

'I'd be surprised if he had. Whoever did this knew exactly what they were doing. They went there prepared to wipe the hard drive beyond recovery, which requires specialist software that the murderer must have taken with him.'

'I thought you could just delete everything on a disk using a DOS command?'

'You can but it's pointless, because anyone with any serious knowledge of computers can recover it quite easily. Deleting a file simply stops it being accessible, but the data is still physically on the disk. Wiping the drive only makes sense if it's permanent, and that needs special software. It's even possible to recover data after a format, if you've got the right tools.'

'How's she doing?'

'Pretty well. She's discovered that there *is* a hidden partition on the hard disk and she's trying to identify the program used to create it. It'll take her some time.'

'OK. The obvious question is who did this. Any ideas?'

'Actually,' Richter replied thoughtfully, 'I think the "why" is more important than the "who". Holden could have been assassinated by somebody on contract or even by a member of the terrorist organization he's been working for.'

'You're sure of that? You're certain he was part of whatever was going on out here, that he wasn't a genuine psychic?'

'Holden was no more psychic than my cat.'

'Have you got a cat?' Watkinson asked doubtfully.

'No, but that's not the point. Holden being involved with the terrorists is the only scenario that makes sense. There were exactly two possibilities here. First, Holden could have been genuine, and been seeing these visions, or whatever you like to call them, and was assassinated by the terrorists so that he couldn't warn anybody else. If that was the case we have three questions to answer. How was he getting his information – premonition, telepathy or some other equally unlikely method? Second, how did the terrorists get to know about him? As far as I'm aware, no details about Holden have been released outside the intelligence community. Finally, why did his killer wipe his hard drive?'

'Go on,' Watkinson said.

'Now, if on the other hand he was in league with them, all those questions have simple answers. He knew about the bomb attacks because the people who planted them told him exactly where and when they were going to explode. The terrorists knew about him because they'd recruited him as a conduit to the authorities. And they wiped his hard disk because they knew it stored information that would prove his contact with them.'

'You make a good case,' Watkinson said, 'but that still doesn't answer everything. Were the two attacks Holden described organized by the same people? And why on earth were they using him to leak details in the first place?'

'I've no idea, but they must have had a reason. And I do think both attacks were coordinated by the same group.'

'If you're right,' Watkinson said, 'that also suggests something of real concern.'

'I know. Whatever the aim of this campaign is, the final act is probably imminent. And that worries me too.'

Nad Al-Sheba Racecourse, Dubai

Saadi stopped the car about two hundred yards from the racecourse, switched off the engine and extinguished the lights. For a few minutes the three men sat there, letting their eyes adjust to the darkness. Under their white *gel-labbiyas*, each was dressed in black clothing: trousers, polo-neck jumpers and trainers.

'It's time,' Saadi said, finally.

Massood walked to the back of the car and opened the boot. Inside it were four large grey rucksacks. On top of them were two rolled-up rope ladders, each secured by cord. He handed the ladders to Bashar, then pulled out the rucksacks. All three men pulled off their *gellab-biyas* and placed them in the boot.

'Remember,' Saadi hissed, barely louder than a whisper. 'If possible, avoid contact with the guards. If you're spotted and have to take action, use a garrotte or knife. And don't forget to bring the body back here.'

As he locked the car, Massood and Bashar each shrugged on a rucksack and picked up a second one. Saadi took the two rope ladders and led the way down the road, keeping close to the boundary fence until they reached the spot he'd selected earlier.

The fence was about nine feet high, a simple chain-link structure supported by concrete posts. Saadi stopped beside one of these and, as he untied the cord securing one ladder, Massood scrambled up the fence. When Saadi tossed him the end of the ladder, he looped it over the top of the post, letting it dangle against the outside of the fence. Then he repeated the operation with the second ladder, on the inside.

Within minutes, all three men and their bags were inside the racecourse. They concealed the ladders in a hollow dip in the ground a few yards away. Each man pulled on a rucksack and then Massood and Bashar seized the straps of the fourth one, and they followed Saadi towards the Millennium Grandstand. Within seconds, all three figures had vanished into the gloom.

British Embassy, Dubai

'You said there were a couple of things we had to talk about,' Richter reminded Michael Watkinson. 'What was the other?'

'I had a call from Saeed Hussein. The forensic people went over the horsebox. They found no definite evidence of explosives, but there were traces of two different types of oil on the hay. One was definitely gun oil, but the second proved more difficult to identify. There were only very slight traces and, in their estimation, it was probably the kind you find on oiled paper of the sort used for wrapping military ordnance.'

Richter nodded. 'That makes sense. Modern explosives come in either plastic or oiled paper wrapping.

It's confirmation, I suppose, that our deduction was right, but we're no nearer finding the terrorists or discovering what their target is. But if they risked bringing weapons and explosives into Dubai, the target must be here.'

The knock on the door was quick and urgent. Before either Watkinson or Richter had time to respond, it opened and Chris Halls burst in.

'I've found it,' she said simply.

Nad Al-Sheba Racecourse, Dubai

Less than an hour after Saadi and his companions had vanished into the night, they reappeared, empty-handed. They climbed back over the perimeter fence, walked up the road to the parked Renault, stowed the ladders in the boot, and pulled the *gellabbiyas* back on over their clothes.

Saadi started the engine, and three minutes later the road was empty.

British Embassy, Dubai

'It *was* a hidden partition,' Chris Halls explained. 'He used a program called Steganos Safe.'

'Is it unusual?' Watkinson asked.

Halls shook her head. 'No, but Holden did his best to make it as difficult as possible to find. He renamed the program file and tucked it away deep inside the operating system in a hidden, read-only folder, which is why it took me so long to find it. Then I had to crack the password to get in, but I've got a couple of tools that helped me do that fairly quickly.'

'So what's inside it?' Richter asked.

'Not as much as I was hoping,' Halls replied. 'Let me show you.'

She led the way to her office, sat down and touched the space-bar to remove the screen-saver. They stood on either side of her as Halls double-clicked a new icon – a tiny representation of a safe – on the desktop.

A box popped up listing a single secure partition: drive Z. Halls clicked the 'open' link beside it and immediately a password prompt appeared. She typed rapidly, pressed 'OK' and a directory listing appeared on the screen. There were just three names in it – 'Damascus', 'Manama' and 'Dubai'.

'That looks promising,' Richter observed.

Halls double-clicked 'Damascus'.

'As I said, there's not that much in here, but it proves that Holden *was* being fed information.'

The screen display changed to show six filenames. The first five mini-icons represented images, and the final one a Microsoft Word document. Halls double-clicked the first image, and a photograph of the entrance to a *souk* filled the screen.

Watkinson looked closely. 'That's the Bab Al-Nasr end of the Al-Hamidieh *souk*.'

Halls nodded. 'Three of the other pictures show different views of the interior, including one of the roof.' She quickly flicked through them.

'And the last picture?'

'That,' Halls said, 'is Saadallah Assad.'

An image appeared of a handsome young Arab boy with a slightly arrogant expression, looking off to the left. It wasn't a portrait, so Richter guessed it had been taken surreptitiously with a small digital camera.

For a few moments the three of them stared at the photograph of the young man who, just days or hours later, had caused the deaths of nearly thirty innocent people.

'He could almost be an actor,' Halls observed. 'I bet he had no shortage of female admirers.'

There wasn't anything Richter or Watkinson felt like adding to that remark.

'The Word document,' Halls continued, while opening the file, 'is entitled "Damascus data".'

It contained three short paragraphs. The first gave Assad's name and a brief word-picture, and the second a very abbreviated history of the Society of Muslim Brothers. The third listed a date, the same day Assad had triggered his suicide bomb, and a single, chilling sentence: 'Gonna be a big one!', and a brief instruction: 'Don't tell them it's Damascus. Just describe the *souk* and leave it at that.'

'Well, that's certainly clear enough,' Watkinson said bitterly. 'Let's see the Manama files.'

Halls opened the second directory. The contents looked very similar to the first – four image files and a Word document. She double-clicked the first photograph to reveal a street with cars parked along each side.

'That could well be Al-Mutanabi Avenue,' Richter

remarked, 'but I was only there after the explosion, so I can't be sure.'

'It *is* Al-Mutanabi,' Halls confirmed, 'and the Word file makes that clear. The next two pictures are of the same road, apparently taken at about the same time, because the parked cars are identical in each. The last one is a street map of Manama.' The images appeared, one after the other. 'This Word file is also fairly short.'

There were just two paragraphs this time. The first described the bomb vehicle as an old American car that would be positioned by two men wearing traditional Arab dress, and confirmed that it would be left somewhere on Al-Mutanabi Avenue. The second paragraph instructed Holden to suggest that the location was Manama, but not to mention it by name, only by reference to a landmark. The last sentence read: 'Think of an extra piece of information – maybe the airport on Muharraq Island or the Al-Fateh Mosque – and give them that.'

'You were right, then,' Watkinson said grimly. 'Holden *was* a mouthpiece for this bunch of terrorists, but I *still* don't understand what their motive was. Why were they using him?'

'The obvious answer is to establish Holden's credibility as a psychic, though I have no idea why that should have been so important. But that theory falls rather flat since he's just been murdered, probably by these same people. We're obviously missing something here – some other factor.'

'Exactly,' Watkinson sighed. 'Right, Chris, let's see the "Dubai" files.'

Halls double-clicked on the 'Dubai' directory and

leant back in her chair. 'That,' she explained, 'is what I meant when I told you there's rather less here than I was hoping.'

The 'Dubai' directory was empty but for a single Word file.

Chapter Sixteen

Richter woke early, despite having finally left the embassy well after midnight. His evening had been considerably improved by the sight of Carole-Anne Jackson waiting for him in the lobby when he arrived at the hotel, an empty coffee cup and a pile of magazines in front of her. She'd hopped a flight out of Manama, but hadn't called Richter because she guessed he'd be busy.

The Word file retrieved from Holden's computer had contained two brief but alarming sentences: 'Dubai hotel, close to the water. Very big bomb, maybe nuke.' Halls had been thorough, so he felt confident there were no other files hidden in the 'Dubai' directory. Further wildcard searches of the entire hard drive for any mention of Dubai had come up with nothing useful.

The only thing they now knew for certain was that the next target *was* Dubai itself, and not some other city in the Gulf.

Not that the information helped particularly. Dubai was full of hotels, the vast majority of them on the coast, including the developments running from Jumeirah to Umm Suqeim and from Deira towards the Al-Mamzar Beach Park and Sharjah. And as Watkinson had pointed out, apart from the Gulf itself, 'the water' could also

mean the Dubai Creek, which added even more potential targets to the list.

It had been a frustratingly inconclusive end to a fairly
promising day.

Al-Khaleej Hotel, Dubai

The six detectors provided by the CIA were E-3500
units manufactured by Scintrex Trace. This model was
one of the latest, most advanced, and – at around thirty
thousand dollars each – most expensive units available,
designed to detect all threat compounds, including radioactive sources. The device itself looked something like a
hand-held vacuum cleaner, but with a probe instead of
a suction intake, and a digital display in front of the
handle.

It took Richard Wilson only minutes to master the
basics, and after an hour he felt ready to pass himself
off as an expert.

O'Hagan had handed him a small plastic container
with a snap-on lid. He opened this and extracted a
man's gold ring bearing a large and rather vulgar red
stone, and a package wrapped in aluminium foil. Inside
the latter was a piece of Semtex plastic explosive.

Wilson slid the ring onto the third finger of his left
hand. He was right-handed, and it had to be worn on
his non-dominant hand. The ring had been made to
O'Hagan's precise design by a jeweller in Ohio nearly a
year earlier. The mount carrying the stone was hinged
on one side, the hinge itself hidden within the tiny cup
that was revealed when the ring was opened, and also

sprung, so that any pressure on the stone would compress the space below it. The mount was virtually airtight until the stone was depressed, when the downward movement exposed three small holes in the sides. This meant that the ring acted like a tiny pump, pushing air out of the internal cavity every time pressure was applied to the stone.

Wilson removed a tiny piece of the Semtex and tucked it into the cavity, making sure that the stone still moved freely. He then took the E-3500 into the furthest corner of the bathroom and carried out a sweep, but the detector registered nothing. After twisting the ring round until the stone was on his palm side, he moved his left arm casually up and across the front of the detector, while pressing gently on the stone with his left thumb. Scanning again, the detector scored a hit this time, and Dawson smiled, because now everything was ready.

After packing the unit away in its case, he called Dawson's room using his CIA alias. 'It's Andy Franks, sir. I'm pretty much ready.'

'Right. I'll contact Inspector Hussein and see if we can get started tomorrow.'

Dawson rang off, took out the card Hussein had given him and rang the police officer's home number. His call was answered almost immediately.

'Good afternoon, Inspector, this is Grant Hutchings. We were wondering if we could start checking the first of the hotels tomorrow. I suggest we start with the biggest and most distinctive, like the Burj Al-Arab and the Jumeirah Beach. If I was a terrorist, those are the ones I'd go for.'

Hussein's reply was apologetic. 'This Sunday is not a

good day because of the World Cup race meeting this weekend. All the hotels are full, and we wouldn't wish to alarm any of our important guests. But most of them will be leaving once the racing has finished, so might I suggest Monday morning instead?'

Dawson wasn't in a position to push things, and was fully aware how heavily Dubai relied on its tourist industry. On a day like that, the local authorities certainly wouldn't want to see a bunch of armed Americans wandering about looking for explosives in their most prestigious hotels. He bowed to the inevitable.

'No, that's no problem, Inspector. Monday morning it is.'

'I'll have a car sent to your hotel at nine.'

'Better make it two cars, because there'll be the four of us, plus the explosive detectors and a bunch of other equipment as well.'

'That won't be a problem. Two cars at nine on Monday, then.' Dawson could hear the sound of pen on paper as Hussein made a note.

'We'd prefer to start in one of the hotels straight away, without a prior demonstration. The detectors are easy to use, so we can show your men how to operate them in a realistic environment.'

'Agreed. I'll contact both hotels and tell them to expect us on Monday.'

Dawson put down the phone, paused for a second, then picked it up to call Alex O'Hagan's room and give him the news.

After that, he lay down on his bed and for a few moments stared up at the ceiling. Two years of meticulous planning and scheming, and by Monday midday they would almost certainly have entered the final phase. Nothing could stop them now – the endgame was so close he could almost taste the money.

Crowne Plaza Hotel, Dubai

Richter waited until late that afternoon before he decided to call London, and walked outside the hotel to use his mobile. Local time in Dubai was four hours ahead of London, making it early afternoon there, and he briefed the duty officer because he guessed Simpson probably wouldn't be at Hammersmith over the weekend.

'The James Holden thing was a red herring, and he was actually working with the terrorists,' he began, then explained the situation to date.

'So what was the point?' the duty officer asked. 'Why were they using him to leak information?'

'We've no idea, but we do know that their next target is a hotel here in Dubai. What little we found on the cloned hard drive confirms that, and the fact that Holden's killer went to such lengths to destroy it suggests this information was genuine – not disinformation.'

But even as he spoke this last word, Richter suddenly thought he glimpsed something of the truth, or at least something that might make sense of the inconsistencies. He ended the call quickly and returned to the hotel.

'Carole, we need to talk,' he began.

She looked puzzled, but nodded, and followed him to a couple of chairs in the far corner of the lobby. Richter leant forward and began speaking in a low voice. Four minutes later he sat back and waited for Jackson's response.

'Yes,' she conceded, 'that makes a certain sense, but it's still pretty unbelievable. Two bomb attacks set up in two different countries, just for this? I hear what you say, but I'm not convinced.'

'I don't have any better ideas,' Richter said, 'so I'm going to have to try it out on Watkinson, and quickly, because the clock is running. You coming?'

'Damn right I am. I'll see you here in five.'

He ordered a taxi, then went back outside to call Watkinson's mobile. 'It's Richter. I just might have worked out what's going on. What time is the World Cup race starting?'

'This evening, in about four hours, in fact. Why?'

'I'll tell you when I see you. Can we meet at the embassy right now?'

'Thirty minutes?'

'I'll be there,' Richter said, then he called Hammersmith again. 'You'll need to kick Simpson awake and tell him I have to talk to him.'

'I'll need a good reason to disturb him on a Saturday afternoon.' The duty officer sounded distinctly unenthusiastic at the prospect of calling his boss.

'I've got a *very* good one,' Richter replied, and told him what he'd worked out.

British Embassy, Dubai

'It suddenly dawned on me that because Holden's killer wiped the hard disk, we assumed the information contained on it was genuine. Then I realized that the data probably *was* genuine, but our conclusions might be invalid because we've been looking at it from the wrong angle. This, in fact, could be exactly what we thought it wasn't – a deception operation – and we've been making far too many assumptions.'

Watkinson didn't look convinced. 'I think you need to explain that.'

'It's like the old Antony and Cleopatra story. Cleopatra is lying dead on the floor. Beside her is broken glass and some spilt liquid. Antony is standing over her, looking down. What happened?'

'Have we really got time for riddles?'

'It'll take ten seconds, so humour me.'

'OK. Cleopatra has drunk poison and died. She dropped the glass, and the liquid on the floor is the rest of the poison. Antony's just arrived and found her like that.'

'Carole?' Richter asked, turning to Jackson.

'I'd assume pretty much the same, I guess.'

'Exactly,' Richter said. 'If you ask a hundred people to explain the same riddle, almost all of them will say something like that, because they're all making assumptions that aren't supported by the evidence. And all of them would be wrong.'

'So what's the real answer?'

'It's easy when you don't assume *anything* and ask the right questions. Because I used the names Antony and Cleopatra, you assumed I meant the Roman general and the Queen of Egypt, but that's not actually what I said. I just gave you two names. If I tell you that Cleopatra is a goldfish and Antony's a cat, absolutely everything about the scene changes. Assumptions can be *really* dangerous.'

'That's just a word game,' Watkinson objected.

'No, it's a useful example of what I mean. Look what we've got here. A man claims to have visions of terrorist bombings. When the devices explode we realize his information is extraordinarily accurate, so when he predicts another bomb exploding in a Gulf hotel we believe him. But Arab terrorists never give warnings, because they always aim for the maximum damage and the highest possible number of casualties, so this leaking of information through a man claiming to be psychic is entirely new.'

'Maybe this group has a different agenda, and might not want to cause maximum casualties,' Watkinson pointed out.

'It *has* got a different agenda, I'm sure of that. I believe its target is a small but very important group of people in Dubai.'

The question was obvious. 'Who?'

'The royal House of Saud,' Richter replied, and Watkinson's jaw visibly dropped open.

Hammersmith, London

'This had better be good,' Simpson snapped, from the doorway of the room where the duty officer sat at a wide L-shaped desk facing a telephone console and a bank of television sets displaying the principal real-time news channels, their audio outputs muted. On the other section of the desk were three computer monitors.

'It's Richter, sir.' The duty officer stood up as the director entered, unshaven and wearing casual clothes. 'He thinks he's uncovered an Al-Qaeda plot to assassinate the Saudi Arabian royal family in Dubai.'

'For fuck's sake,' Simpson muttered. 'All he was supposed to be doing was interviewing a barmy Englishman. What's his evidence?'

'It's mainly circumstantial, but what he told me does seem to make sense.'

'It had better, for his sake. Tell me about it.'

British Embassy, Dubai

'That's a hell of a leap of logic,' Watkinson said. 'What are your reasons? And who is it down to?'

'The second question is easier to answer. It's probably Al-Qaeda, and I'll explain why I think so in a minute. As for the leaks, that's the real question, and until today I had no idea of the answer. But it's really simple and obvious when you ignore your assumptions and just look at the facts. Holden was the lynchpin of this entire scheme, and those two bombs were detonated for one reason only – to establish his credibility, so that we would listen to what he said. Nothing else. Those incidents just proved Holden could "see" the atrocities before they happened, so that when he announced that a device was going to be planted in a Gulf State hotel, we'd immediately believe him. We'd then concentrate all our resources on trying to find which hotel the terrorists had picked, and ignore the real target.'

'Which is?'

'The VIP viewing stand at the racecourse, during the Dubai World Cup. That's why I asked you when the race was being held.'

Watkinson shook his head. 'I'm not following this. You said the target was the House of Saud. Now you're telling me it's a stand at Nad Al-Sheba.'

'It's both,' Richter replied, with a trace of impatience. 'Julian Caxton told me how the World Cup meeting attracts all the royalty and nobility of the Arab world. I've no doubt they stay in the top hotels or local palaces, so trying to target them individually would be very difficult. But the one occasion when they'll all be together in a single location at a fixed time is during the World Cup. My guess is that the explosives smuggled here to Dubai inside Shaf's trailer are already hidden under the VIP stand and attached to a timing device. And this evening, when all the sheikhs and princes are cheering on their horses, there'll be a sodding great bang and the entire stand will disappear in a cloud of dust. Unless we do something to stop it.'

'But why the House of Saud? Osama bin Laden *is* a Saudi by birth.'

'Yes, but he's had no love for the ruling family since they took away his passport and did their best to humiliate and disown him. And, if I *am* right, this isn't exactly a new plan. Back in 1991 bin Laden was expelled from Saudi Arabia for plotting to replace the royals with an Islamic regime.'

'You know there are nearly six thousand members of the Saudi ruling family? They certainly won't all be at Nad Al-Sheba.'

'No, but enough senior members will be there to

make this operation feasible. And I'm pretty sure Al-Qaeda *is* behind this, just because of the callous nature of the operation. Around thirty people died in Damascus, and another six or eight in Manama. That's nearly forty deaths whose sole purpose was to establish the credentials of one man, James Holden. And then they killed another dozen at the stables in Saudi Arabia to hide the fact that a horse had been stolen. They could have achieved the same objective by imprisoning the staff somewhere out of sight. That ruthless disregard for human life is an Al-Qaeda trademark.'

'But surely a mass killing here would just mean bin Laden becoming even more reviled than he is already, and ensure he could never return to his homeland.'

'If the people of Saudi Arabia thought bin Laden had ordered the assassinations for his personal benefit, they might react like that. But if he claimed it was done for religious reasons, he might be welcomed home to Riyadh. Don't forget that the House of Saud is perceived by many Arabs to be corrupt, Westernized and blasphemous, and this bloodbath could lead to Al-Qaeda establishing a firm base in Saudi Arabia, and maybe bin Laden even assuming power as the new religious leader of the holiest land in all Islam. That's the real nightmare scenario, the thought of Al-Qaeda controlling the Saudi oilfields, with everything that implies.'

'Holy shit.'

'Beautifully put. Now, what do we do about it? Who do you have to call?'

PAYBACK

Nad Al-Sheba Racecourse, Dubai

Saadi had been right about the security: all bags were being carefully searched. The three men had no trouble, because they were carrying nothing but tickets. They arrived separately, three anonymous *gellabbiya*-wearing Arabs in a cosmopolitan crowd of racing enthusiasts, and only acknowledged each other once they were inside.

'We'll meet where we agreed in forty-five minutes exactly,' Saadi instructed. 'Meanwhile, do nothing to attract attention, just enjoy the racing and merge with the crowd. But do *not* be late.' Saadi looked closely at the two men who'd been his almost constant companions for the last week. 'Remember the importance of our mission. We will strike at the very heart of the sickness that infects the palaces of Riyadh. We are the cleansing wind of pure Islam that will rid the holy land of the corrupt and blasphemous House of Saud.'

The three men walked away, their paths diverging almost immediately.

British Embassy, Dubai

Richter's Enigma phone rang.

'Why is it that every time I send you off to do a simple job of investigation you end up trying to start World War Three?' Simpson demanded.

'Not my choice,' Richter replied, 'and I'm not trying to start anything here. I'm trying to stop it.'

'How certain are you?'

'Right now I'm not sure of anything, but what's been happening out here seems to make sense only in one context – an attempt to mislead us into looking for a terrorist bomb in the wrong place. While we're all poncing about looking for a pile of Semtex in some fancy hotel, the terrorists will be out at Nad Al-Sheba assassinating the senior Saudi royals as they sit watching their horses go by. And this does pretty much tie up with what Salah Khatid learned in Germany. It's a relatively small target, but with obvious economic consequences that would affect almost every nation on earth.'

'I've talked to the Intelligence Director,' Simpson said, 'and he thinks it's possible you're right. And if you are, there's a clear threat to the Saudi oilfields.'

'The ID always did like to hedge his bets,' Richter remarked.

'Don't be impertinent. What steps are you taking locally?'

'I'm at the embassy with the local Six man, and we're just about to contact the Dubai police and tell them what we think we know, or rather what we believe we suspect.'

Simpson's snort of disgust was clearly audible. 'And what will *they* do? Issue a parking ticket for the terrorists' van, or whatever else they're driving around in? Don't they have any paramilitary forces out there? Something like the SAS or GSG-9?'

'I don't know, to be honest.'

'Well, I suggest you find out, and quickly. In the meantime, tell the plods by all means, but this looks like your problem, and now I expect you to solve it. Use whatever local resources the Six office has got, starting with getting yourself a personal weapon. You say you've got the local Head of Station with you now?'

'Yes.'

'Right. Put him on.'

Richter passed the phone to Watkinson and watched with interest, not to mention a certain weary sense of inevitability. Several times Watkinson started to speak, but was cut off on each occasion, and he finally handed the back the phone without another word.

'Richter.'

'Right, you'll get whatever help the local Six people can give you, not that it'll do you much good because I don't think they've got much to offer. But you *have* to sort this out. The Saudi oilfields are far too important to the West for us to risk any chance of losing them.'

Suddenly his tone became less hectoring and more serious. 'This is the formal bit, so listen carefully. Your original tasking is now cancelled. You're hereby authorized to take any and all measures necessary to prevent any acts of terrorism from occurring in Dubai. Once I've finished this conversation, I'll be contacting Vauxhall Cross and the FCO to ensure that the Dubai Government is made fully aware of your presence, and to ensure that you get all the assistance they can provide. All this will be put in writing, with copies for you, so you'll have all the backing you need. When's this race taking place? When do you think the attempt will be made?'

Richter glanced at his watch. 'The World Cup starts in a little under ninety minutes.'

'Christ, that soon? Right, you'd better get on with it.'

'Forceful man, your boss,' Watkinson observed, as Richter ended the call.

'That's been said before, though usually a lot less politely. What did he tell you?'

'I'm to give you a personal weapon – which I tried to tell him I wasn't authorized to do, not that it made any difference – and between the pair of us, with or without the assistance of the authorities, we're to ensure that the Saudi royal family and everyone else at Nad Al-Sheba enjoys a peaceful and uninterrupted day at the races. He's talking about going straight to the top of the Dubai Government and shaking some very important trees. Can he really deliver?'

'You don't know Simpson. He's direct, persistent and very well connected. He'll do exactly what he said he'd do. I don't particularly like the man, but I do respect his abilities.' Richter glanced at his watch again. 'Look, we've got to get going, Michael, and right now. What weapons have you got here?'

'You *are* sure about this?' Watkinson looked troubled. 'If we go busting into Nad Al-Sheba with all guns blazing, we're going to cause a hell of a diplomatic incident.'

'Only if I'm wrong,' Richter said, standing up. 'And if I am, causing a diplomatic incident will be the least of my worries. Now, what weapons have you got?'

'Not many. Half a dozen Browning Hi-Power nine-millimetre pistols, each with two magazines, three privately owned hunting rifles and a couple of shotguns.'

'And?'

'And that's it. Remember this is one of Her Majesty's embassies, not the local branch of Kalashnikovs-R-Us.'

'Shit,' Richter said, 'I was hoping for an assault rifle

at least. We can forget about the shotguns, because confronting terrorists touting Kalashnikovs when all we've got is a couple of Purdeys is a really good way to commit suicide.'

Watkinson grinned. 'Purdeys they're not – just a couple of skeet guns.'

'Even worse. And I suppose the hunting rifles are bolt-action single-shot twenty-twos, because no gentleman would dream of going hunting with a high-velocity auto-loader?'

'Not quite. One is a single-shot twenty-two, while the other two are about thirty-thirty calibre deer rifles, with magazines. But they're all bolt-action – you're right.'

'Forget them, then,' Richter said. 'We'll have to take the pistols and hope we get close enough to use them. Bring four of them, all the magazines, and every round of nine-millimetre you can lay your hands on. You do have some ammunition, I hope?'

'Two or three boxes of fifty, I think. I'll go and get everything together.'

'You know I'm carrying a weapon,' Jackson remarked, after Watkinson had left the room. 'It's only a nine-millimetre Glock, but I am pretty good with it.'

Watkinson was back in less than five minutes, carrying a cardboard box which he placed on the table in front of Richter. 'I've got to make some calls,' he declared, and left again.

Richter took out a pair of shoulder rigs, each fitted with two magazine pouches on the webbing below the holster. He pulled one on, then picked up one of the Brownings and checked its action. It was an old pistol, but seemed perfectly serviceable. By the time Watkinson returned, they'd loaded eight magazines, and Richter had one Browning in his shoulder holster, the other in his jacket pocket. The other two were laid on the table ready for Watkinson, along with four magazines.

'You'll find one of your magazines is a bit lighter than the others, Michael. There were two full boxes of nine-millimetre, but only eight rounds in the third box, so the last magazine has got ten bullets in it, not fourteen.'

'But yours are fully charged?' Watkinson asked.

Richter nodded. 'I'm almost certainly better at this kind of thing than you are, or at least, I've definitely had a lot more practice. And the fact is that if any of us get down to our last magazine, we're going to be so deep in the shit it won't matter anyway.'

'You're probably right.' Watkinson pulled on the holster. 'Are you coming on this jaunt, Carole?'

'You bet.'

'Do you need a weapon?'

Jackson shook her head, and opened the left side of her jacket to reveal why.

'Right,' Watkinson said. 'I've called Inspector Hussein and briefed him. He doesn't believe any of it, naturally, but he'll be waiting for us out at Nad Al-Sheba.'

Nad Al-Sheba Racecourse, Dubai

Forty-five minutes after they'd separated, they met at the back of the Millennium Grandstand, right beside a small maintenance door. It had been locked when they'd entered Nad Al-Sheba the previous night, but they'd forced it and merely closed it when they left.

Bashar had already shed his *gellabbiya* to reveal a pair of white overalls. Half the trick in being a successful impostor is to be in the right place at the right time, and anyone noticing him would see an engineer already inside the racetrack, and would assume that his identification had been properly checked at the gate.

The door accessed a workshop and storeroom, but inside was another door that opened into the void directly beneath the stand – a cavernous space filled with struts and girders and cross-braces, the far end of it vanishing into the gloom. Cables and pipes shared this void with pieces of machinery whose function Saadi couldn't even guess at. Fluorescent lights were attached to the girders, but enough light leaked in from the outside to make turning them on unnecessary. The air inside was hot and still, and the vast space felt stuffy and claustrophobic.

They strode across to a pile of cardboard boxes and Saadi tossed them aside, revealing the bags they'd concealed there the previous night. He opened one, took out a Kalashnikov and handed it to Massood, who checked the magazine was fully loaded, then slammed it back into place. Saadi inspected the other two assault rifles, then picked up one of the other heavy bags and made his way across the void.

Each bag contained about fifteen kilograms of C4 plastic explosive, enough to demolish a very substantial building. Most structures have load-bearing walls or columns of reinforced concrete which support their entire weight, but explosive charges positioned so as to blow holes in the walls or cut through those columns could collapse a large edifice in seconds. And Saadi knew exactly how to do that, because he'd been trained in Afghanistan by experts.

The biggest problem about the stand was that it wasn't a conventional building. Like most structures housing multiple levels of tiered seating, it needed an immensely strong steel skeleton. When Saadi had looked round the void the previous night, he'd realized at once that they couldn't hope to demolish the entire building, only one end of it. But the explosion and partial collapse would kill many of his targets, and then he and Massood could move in and finish the job with their Kalashnikovs. It was a simple and effective plan, and Saadi didn't think that much could go wrong with it.

When their taxi stopped outside the racecourse, they saw Hussein already waiting for them. He was flanked by five uniformed Dubai police officers, each carrying a Heckler & Koch MP5 sub-machine-gun.

'Michael,' Hussein greeted Watkinson, his expression worried. 'Are you sure about this?'

'Frankly, I'm not, but it seems to make sense, given what we know already. And if we're right, we have to do something immediately. The race starts just in a few minutes.'

Richter stepped up beside the two men, Carole-Anne Jackson behind him.

'This is your idea?' Hussein asked, and Richter nodded. 'Why do you think the attempt will be made during the World Cup event?'

'Because it's the biggest and most expensive race of the meeting, the only one that you can almost guarantee will be watched by everyone. It's when all the stands and enclosures will be packed full, so that's logically when they'll detonate the bomb.'

As Richter said the word 'bomb', Hussein almost flinched. 'Should we clear the stands before the race starts?' the Arab asked.

'I don't think that would be a good idea. If the terrorists suspect we've guessed their plans, they might decide to detonate their weapon immediately, just to kill as many as possible. And trying to clear the stands quickly would probably cause a panic.'

'So that means we have to find this bomb and disarm it?'

'Exactly, and we need to start looking right now.' Richter paused briefly. 'Actually, it might be possible to just get the Saudi lot – the royal family, I mean – out of the stand for their own safety. Could you manage that without alarming everyone else?'

'I can certainly try,' Hussein agreed, and led four of his officers off to start a very limited evacuation of the Millennium Grandstand, while Richter, Jackson and Watkinson, accompanied by the one remaining policeman, made their way towards the rear of the structure.

'Do you think he'll be able to get them out in time?' Watkinson asked.

'Probably not,' Richter replied, checking that the police officer was out of earshot, 'but I wanted him out of the way. We don't need a whole mob of people crashing around underneath the stand looking for a bomb. If this is an Al-Qaeda operation, there's a possibility they won't be relying on a timing device in case something goes wrong with it. This has to be a vital operation for them – one that could change the whole future of the Middle East.'

'So there'll likely be a suicide bomber inside, with his hand on a relay?'

'That's my guess, and if a whole gang of us bash on in, he'll take one look and press the button. We need a bit of finesse here.'

Within fifteen minutes, they'd strapped explosive around the struts and girders, all held in place with adhesive tape. Each pack of C4 had a slim pencil detonator inserted, and these were all linked by wires to a black plastic box, plain apart from a push-button, a single switch and a warning light. Saadi walked around one last time to check that all the C4 was securely attached, that the detonators were inserted and the cables connected. Then he stepped back and went over to join his two colleagues.

'We're ready,' he said simply.

Massood handed him a Kalashnikov, which had a length of stout cord looped through a hole in the stock. Despite having already checked the weapon once, Saadi did so again because they could afford no mistakes.

The *gellabbiya* completely covers whatever is worn underneath it, but another advantage is that it also enables quite large objects to be concealed about the person. Saadi had no doubt that, when they left the stand, what he and Massood would be carrying would be completely invisible.

Each *gellabbiya* had an embroidered seam running down the front, from the neckline to the bottom hem, and inside this were strips of Velcro. One firm tug would rip the seam in two, turning the *gellabbiya* into a cloak with sleeves. More importantly, this action would allow its wearer unrestricted access to whatever was concealed underneath.

Saadi removed his *gellabbiya* and handed it to Bashar, then lifted up the Kalashnikov, dropped the cord over his head and allowed the weapon to hang, muzzle-down, in front of him. Walking would be a little difficult, with the assault rifle banging against his legs, but Saadi wasn't planning on walking very far. Massood mirrored his actions and within minutes both men were ready.

Saadi pulled a racing programme from his pocket, checked his watch and did a quick calculation. 'Detonate the device in exactly eighteen minutes from now,' he instructed, 'no sooner, and no later.'

Bashar looked at his own watch and nodded agreement. For a brief instant none of the three spoke or moved, then both Saadi and Massood stepped forward, one after the other, and embraced him.

'*Assalamu alaikum wa barakatuhu wa rahmatulahi*, Bashar,' Saadi murmured, his voice barely audible.

'*Walaikum assalam*, my friends,' Bashar replied equally quietly. '*Ma'assalama.*' Go in peace.

Richter and Watkinson arrived at the grandstand only about two minutes after Saadi and Massood had emerged from the maintenance area and vanished into the crowds.

'Where will the Saudi royals be?' Richter asked.

'At the far end, I imagine, in the Del Mar Lounge on the fourth floor.'

'We're running out of time – the race starts in about fifteen minutes. We'd better split up. Take the police officer and check the front for an access door to the void under the stand. Carole and I will check the back and meet you in, what, five minutes?' Watkinson nodded. 'If you do find a door, don't open it.'

It didn't take them long to discover that there were two doors in the rear of the stand, one at each end, bearing notices in English and Arabic.The English said 'No admittance – maintenance staff only', and Richter guessed that the Arabic script said pretty much the same thing.

As they reached the far end, Watkinson reappeared with the policeman, both panting slightly in the hot, humid and essentially motionless air. 'Nothing at the front.'

'There are two doors in the back wall which may lead into the space under the stand.' Richter glanced at his watch. 'You said the Saudis would be watching the race from this end, so my guess is that's where the bomb will be. And if it is, the one thing we definitely shouldn't do is kick down that door over there.' Richter gestured behind him. 'That would pretty much guarantee that anyone lurking inside will do the Guy Fawkes bit immediately.'

Unsurprisingly, the other door was locked, but they were in no mood to go looking for keys. Richter stood squarely in front of it, waited as the noise of the crowd in the stand above rose to a roar, then raised his right leg.

There's a technique to breaking down doors, and what you don't do is charge at it, hitting it with your shoulder. Do that and you'll just bounce off, at least the first few times, because the whole door will give slightly, dissipating the force of the blow. You need to kick it, hard and focused, and right beside the lock. That way, all the energy of the blow will be concentrated where the door is weakest – the lock itself. On most doors, about half the thickness of the wood is removed to accommodate the lock, severely degrading its structural integrity.

On the first attempt, Richter felt the door give slightly. As his second kick landed, the wood around the lock splintered and the door swung open, crashing back against the interior wall of the maintenance area beyond.

Richter and Watkinson moved forward cautiously, pulling the Brownings from their holsters as they stepped inside. Behind them, the policeman and Jackson followed.

The area was empty, apart from tools and equipment stored in racks and on benches. But at the rear was another door. Richter stepped across, turned the handle and pushed gently. It opened immediately and he glanced into the space beyond, before closing the door again.

'That leads to the void,' Richter explained, keeping his voice down. 'Michael, can you stay here with Carole and Hussein's man while I look around?'

Watkinson nodded and began speaking in rapid Arabic to the police constable.

Richter opened the door again, just wide enough for him to slip through the gap, and closed it behind him.

For a few moments he paused, letting his eyes become accustomed to the gloom and working out the layout. Vertical girders formed a virtual forest of steel, with struts and cross-braces extending like branches above his head. Cables and pipes ran in all directions, snaking across the floor and up the girders and interior walls of the massive structure. Equipment and machinery squatted on the floor, some silent, but mostly running. Richter guessed these were air-conditioning units because of the massive pipes emerging from them. The constant noise would be a definite help: there was no way anyone inside would hear him moving around, so all he had to do was keep out of sight.

Chambering a round in the Browning, but leaving the safety catch on, he stepped forward cautiously, conscious that somewhere in the echoing space around him one or more terrorists were probably waiting, armed and alert.

Richter moved with infinite care, checking the ground before he took each step to ensure he didn't trip over anything, but mainly concentrating on the view in front. Every few steps he paused to scan the surrounding girders for packs of explosive or wires.

He saw nothing significant until he almost reached the far end, and even then didn't see anyone, simply because Bashar was lying prostrate on the ground, hidden from view by some machinery, facing in the direction of Mecca and saying his last, silent prayers. What Richter saw instead was nothing more than a thin red lead that appeared to terminate in a grey-coloured object taped to one of the uprights.

He stopped dead, crouched down and scanned the

area carefully. Within a minute he'd spotted three more similar grey lumps. For a moment he didn't move, then took one cautious step forward before freezing into immobility again.

Directly below the first object he'd spotted, a man suddenly rose into view as if he'd just erupted from the ground. Though he was wearing an overall, Richter didn't think for a moment that he was an employee of the racecourse.

The human eye is particularly well adapted to detect movement – a hangover from the days when early man shared his world with cave bears and sabre-toothed cats – and so Richter remained precisely where he was. The man didn't so much as glance in his direction, but looked towards a door in the rear wall. Richter realized immediately that the terrorists had got inside that way.

Richter had the Browning in his hand, but didn't even consider firing it. The distance between them was at least thirty yards, far too great a distance for pistol shooting. With a rifle Richter could have dropped him in an instant, and would have done without a second thought. For a moment he regretted not asking Watkinson to bring along one of the deer rifles from the embassy, but it was too late for that now.

The man in overalls looked at his watch, then turned away slightly. As he did so, Richter quickly squatted down, below the man's line of sight. For a moment he just listened, alert to any sound that could indicate that he'd been spotted.

He risked a quick glance around the side of the air-conditioning unit in front of him. The man in overalls hadn't moved, so Richter did. Still in a crouch, he turned and looked back towards the workshop where he'd come in, checking for any obstructions in his path. Then, still half-bent, he retraced his steps, moving more quickly the further away he got.

At the door to the workshop he looked back, but there was no sign of pursuit, no indication that he'd been detected. Richter opened the internal door and slipped into the maintenance area.

Jackson and Watkinson were standing beside a bench on one side of the workshop, the police officer on the opposite side, both men covering the door with their weapons. As Richter appeared, Watkinson lowered his pistol and flicked on the safety catch.

'There's at least one Arab, or someone dressed like one, at the far end of the stand, and I saw enough explosive to bring down a big chunk of the building. I didn't see a timer, so I guess the man himself is the trigger.' Richter noticed Watkinson glancing at his watch. 'How long have we got?'

'None, practically. The race will be starting in about four minutes.'

'Right. I can't take this guy by myself, because I can't get close enough to be certain of hitting him with my first shot. And if I miss, he's not going to bother shooting back – he'll just fire the bomb.'

'So you need a distraction to ensure he looks the other way?'

Richter nodded. 'Yes. In fact, I need two things. You'll have to distract his attention – just going into the other maintenance area and opening the inside door should do that. Second, I need a better weapon.' He glanced over at the policeman.

'That might be difficult,' Watkinson replied, keeping his voice low. 'You've got no legal standing here. Taking a Dubai police officer's MP5 isn't going to help your situation.'

For a brief moment Richter just stared at him, then crossed over to the police officer.

As if choreographed, Carole-Anne Jackson moved over to the internal door. When she got there, she bent forward as if to pick something off the ground, her skirt riding high up her thighs. The police officer's eyes widened in a mix of lust and disbelief as he watched her, and at that instant Richter moved.

He smashed his fist into the man's stomach, just above his belt. The officer gasped and folded forward. Richter stepped back and brought the side of his hand down in a short jab to the back of his neck. The man collapsed to the floor, unconscious.

'Nicely done, Carole.' Richter reached down, rolled the constable on to his back and relieved him of his Heckler & Koch.

'Right,' he said. 'Let's sort this bastard out.'

Watkinson stared across the workshop, his eyes flicking between Richter, Jackson and the unconscious policeman. 'Jesus Christ. Tact and diplomacy aren't exactly your middle names, are they?'

'We don't have time to fuck about. We've got less than five minutes to stop these Arabs blowing this whole place straight to hell. A cop with a headache doesn't matter. Now, you and Carole get round to the other door as quickly as you can. Call Hussein immediately and tell him there is a bomb, so he must get the Saudis out. By the time you reach the door, I should be close enough to take this guy. Just go into the workshop and make a bit of noise, bash something with a hammer, then push the interior door open. I'll take care of it from there.'

Watkinson hurried across to the outside door, Jackson following. Richter crossed to the other one, opened it and slipped back into the void, the MP5 slung over his shoulder, cocked and ready to fire, the bolt closed.

Bashar checked his watch again. He had less than three minutes to wait before he depressed the button on the firing box. In less than two hundred seconds, the corrupt House of Saud would effectively cease to exist. And that same instant would be the culmination of his life's ambition, when he would, in one glorious instant, leave his imperfect corporeal form behind and be immediately reborn in the divine presence of Allah.

The Prophet Muhammad and the *chouriyat* beckoned him. He reached down to pick up the small black box, holding it with a sense almost of wonderment. It seemed bizarre that a battery, a few ounces of plastic and a handful of electronic components could achieve so much within a single instant. With one movement of his finger he would change history, cleanse the holy land of Saudi Arabia, and ensure himself a place in paradise for all eternity. He truly was the instrument of Allah.

Richter retraced his steps through the darkness as quickly as he could. He had to be in position before Watkinson started his diversion in the workshop. It helped that this time he knew exactly where he was going. He also knew that the Arab should be in much the same place as before, preparing to detonate the charges.

Less than a minute later, Richter was again crouching behind the roaring air-conditioner. His target was plainly visible, standing amid a group of girders with packs of explosive attached. But what grabbed Richter's attention now was what the man was holding.

It was a small black box, perhaps the size of two packs of cigarettes which, in any other context, would have looked entirely innocent. But Richter knew it was the detonator. And the fact that the terrorist was now holding it clearly meant he was ready to press the button.

Richter guessed he had seconds at best to take the Arab down.

There was a sudden roar above Bashar's head as the spectators in the stand started yelling and shouting enthusiastically, and he instinctively looked up. That meant the World Cup race had just started, so only a minute to go. He lifted the box to chest-height and flicked the switch. Instantly the red light glowed, indicating everything was ready. All he had to do now was press the button.

'*Allahu Akbar*,' he murmured, and at that moment he heard a loud bang from somewhere nearby. It took him a moment to realize it had come from the workshop. Probably someone collecting a piece of equipment, Bashar guessed, then he smiled. Whoever it was had picked the wrong moment, as he would very soon find out.

But then the connecting door swung open, crashing back on its hinges.

Bashar reacted immediately. Ducking down, he put the box on the ground and stood up again, the Kalashnikov in his hands pointing straight at the workshop doorway.

The moment Bashar dropped out of sight, Richter ran forward, closing the distance between them. He'd covered less than five yards when the Arab stood up again, the assault rifle pointing away from him towards the sounds he had just heard.

Richter didn't hesitate. In one fluid movement he brought the Heckler & Koch up to eye-level and squeezed the trigger.

The light was poor, Bashar was about twenty-five yards away, and Richter had never fired that particular weapon before, which explained why the first two shots of his three-round burst missed completely. But the third bullet hit home, smashing into the stock of the Kalashnikov. It splintered the wood, knocking the assault rifle to one side, and then passed clean through Bashar's right forearm, kicking him backwards.

The big Arab howled with pain and shock, dropped the damaged weapon and clutched at his wounded arm. He stood upright for only moments, before dropping down out of sight, and Richter guessed that he was still going to try to detonate the explosives. And there wasn't a thing he could do to stop him, because the ground between them was littered with heavy machinery. As long as the terrorist stayed low, he was invisible and invulnerable.

Richter started to run, leaping over pipes and dodging around the humming and roaring equipment, his entire attention concentrated on finding a position from which he could kill the man he'd just wounded. But, even as he began to move he realized that nothing short of a miracle would prevent the terrorist from triggering the bomb.

Bashar was not the most intelligent of people, but he was a slow and reliable worker, within his limitations. This was why Saadi had selected him to detonate the explosives, rather than position him somewhere outside the stand with an assault rifle.

For a second or two, Bashar squatted on his haunches, trying to comprehend what had just happened. He'd heard a noise from the workshop but the shots had come from his left, from within the void, which meant there were at least two opponents after him. He assumed they were the Dubai police.

He dragged his eyes away from his shattered right arm, blood pumping from the wound, and looked at the Kalashnikov lying on the ground beside him. The stock was ruined, the wood splintered and its rear section severed, but because the AK47 has a pistol grip it could still be fired. And beyond the assault rifle lay the plastic box, the light still glowing, so he knew he could complete his task. He glanced at his watch. He had less than thirty seconds before the time Saadi had told him to fire the explosives.

To his left, even over the noise of the machinery around him, he could hear the sound of running footsteps.

Bashar reached down with his left hand and picked up the Kalashnikov by the pistol grip. It was awkward to handle: the heavy weapon was designed to be fired two-handed, and its natural balance had now been destroyed. Gritting his teeth with the pain, he aimed in the direction where he'd heard the footsteps, raised his arm slightly and pulled the trigger, sending a long burst of 7.62 millimetre bullets screaming across the top of the machinery beside him and deep into the void.

Richter saw the Kalashnikov the moment Bashar raised it, and immediately threw himself flat on the ground, rolling to one side and into the cover provided by a solid chunk of machinery. He had hoped his bullet might have wrecked the assault rifle, but that clearly hadn't happened. But at least the terrorist hadn't pressed the button to fire the explosives. Yet.

Bashar hadn't expected his shots to hit any of his attackers, but he guessed that they would now approach him more slowly and cautiously. He dropped the Kalashnikov and scrambled across towards the black plastic box.

His right arm was a throbbing, bloody mess, but all he needed to do was press the button, and that he could manage in an instant. He reached out. His finger was less than six inches away when he was suddenly aware of movement to his right.

He glanced up. Subconsciously he'd been expecting to see a Dubai police officer, but the figure in front of him was a woman. Not only that, but a woman wearing

Western-style civilian clothes. The sight was so unexpected that he paused, stopping the movement of his left hand, and stared up at her. Then he registered two other things: she was smiling slightly, and the black object she was pointing at him was a pistol.

For the briefest instant, time seemed to stand still and then, with a sudden grunt of rage, Bashar lunged for the box.

Chapter Seventeen

Saturday
Nad Al-Sheba Racecourse, Dubai

A hundred yards from the stand, Saadi took his eyes off the track, where the horses competing in the World Cup race were thundering towards him, and glanced down at his watch. Less than ten seconds to go. He turned away and began pushing through the crowd towards the stand, his left hand in the pocket of his *gellabbiya* supporting the Kalashnikov so that he could walk more easily.

He needed to be sufficiently far away from the blast that he wouldn't get hit by flying debris, but close enough to have only a short distance to run before he could start using his assault rifle. He stopped about sixty yards from the stand, and waited. Twenty yards to his right, Massood also stood ready. Behind them, the roar of the crowd grew in intensity as the horses raced towards the finish line. As the second hand of his watch swept round, the two men braced themselves.

The moment Bashar's fusillade ceased, Richter started moving. He glanced over the air-conditioner, then ran towards his target, taking advantage of every scrap of

cover. He stopped about fifteen feet short of his objective and took in the scene before him.

Carole-Anne Jackson was standing a few feet inside
the void, the workshop door open, her legs apart, both
arms outstretched in front of her, aiming her Glock
straight at the man on the floor. The terrorist seemed to
be frozen in place but, even as Richter stepped forward,
he suddenly shouted and lunged. Jackson didn't hesitate for a moment, squeezing the trigger three times in
quick succession, just as Richter fired the MP5 on full
auto.

Caught in the crossfire, Bashar never stood a chance.
Jackson's first two nine-millimetre bullets smashed into
the right side of his chest, tumbling him sideways. The
Glock's muzzle had lifted with each shot, and her third
bullet missed the target. But that didn't make any difference. Richter's five-round burst caught the Arab in
the head and back as he fell sideways, away from the
plastic box, and he was dead even before he stopped
moving.

Jackson stood still, her pistol still pointing at the
motionless and untidy heap of flesh and bone that until
two seconds earlier had been a living human being, but
she was looking everywhere except at the body.

'Any more of these bastards in here, you reckon?'
she called out, her voice steady.

'No,' Richter replied, trotting forward to confirm that
Bashar was as dead as he looked. 'He was the trigger-
man, just in here to press the button. Three people
arrived in Dubai with Shaf, so there'll be a couple of
shooters outside, ready to finish the job, but there was
only a single *shahid*.'

As Richter bent over the fallen man, Jackson lowered her pistol until it pointed at the ground. Then she spun round as she heard a faint noise behind and slightly to her left, bringing the pistol up again. Simultaneously, Richter stepped away from Bashar's body and brought the MP5 to bear.

Saadi waited expectantly, then tensed as, over the roar of the crowd, he heard several sharp but muted bangs. They were difficult to hear clearly, but to Saadi – who had considerable experience in the field – the noises sounded remarkably like sub-machine-gun fire. And that, he guessed immediately, meant something had gone wrong.

He glanced over at Massood, who was eyeing him with a peculiar intensity, then moved across to join him.

'Something's wrong,' Massood said softly, confirming what Saadi was thinking.

'I know.' Saadi looked again at his watch. 'He should have triggered the weapon by now. The police or security guards must have discovered him.'

'He had his weapon. He could have killed his attackers.'

'He could, but I doubt it. If he was still able, he would have fired the charges by now. I think he's been captured or killed.'

'Can't we launch our attack immediately?'

Saadi looked at him, then pointed at the stand towering above them. 'Even if we both fired our weapons, the most we'd achieve would be to break a few windows.

No, whatever happens we *must* trigger that device. That's the only sure way of completing our mission. You wait here and prepare yourself. I will go inside and fire the charges. I will not be coming out again. *In'shallah.'*

'*Ma'assalama*, Saadi,' Massood murmured, as his companion strode away.

Michael Watkinson stood framed in the workshop doorway, his Browning aimed in Richter's direction. The moment he was certain the situation was under control, he applied the safety catch, slipped the weapon back into his holster and approached them.

Jackson was less than happy with his technique. 'You need some serious retraining in close-combat tactics, Mr Watkinson. You *never* stand silhouetted in a doorway when there might be bad guys the other side of it. That's just an invitation to get yourself blown away.'

'Sorry. This isn't really my scene. What happened here?'

'We stopped him,' Richter said simply, as Watkinson stepped forward to stare at the dead man lying on the ground.

'You killed him?'

'Damn right we did,' Jackson replied. 'You don't fuck around with people like this. You get the chance, you take them down.'

'If you'd taken him alive, we could have questioned—'

'No way,' Richter snapped. 'Carole's quite right. If

we hadn't shot this bastard, right now we'd just be a couple of red smears on the side of a hole about twenty feet deep.'

'So what now?' Watkinson asked.

'The other bad guys are probably still waiting for the stand to collapse, then they'll move in and mop up any of their targets who managed to survive.'

'Do you want me to get Hussein's cops to try to find them?'

'That's probably not too bright an idea. They'll already know something's wrong because the explosives haven't gone off, so now they'll be particularly alert. If they see anyone they don't like the look of heading towards them, they'll probably pull out their weapons and start firing at anything that moves. We don't want that. I think we need to use a bit of finesse.'

'Which means?' Jackson demanded.

'You and I stay in here as a reception committee, because we're the best with the weapons. Michael, you go outside and take a look around. Watch out for anyone who doesn't seem too interested in the racing, or is staring at the stand or his watch. If you find Hussein, suggest he does the same, but discreetly. We don't want a crowd of cops rushing about.'

'And if I do spot someone?'

'Just keep him in view, without letting him know you're watching. There are thousands of people milling about out there, so staying out of sight shouldn't be too difficult. Just call my mobile if you spot anyone.'

'You think they'll come back in here?'

'They'll still want to detonate their IED because that's

their principal weapon. So, yes, I think one of them will be heading this way.'

With the big race over, crowds of people had started streaming past the stand, the overhead floodlights illuminating the scene almost as clearly as day, and Saadi had no difficulty blending in with them. As he turned the corner, the workshop door opened and a figure emerged. Saadi slowed slightly and watched as the man glanced round before making his way along the side of the stand towards the front.

Saadi hesitated for a moment, calculating the odds. The man had emerged from the same door that he and his companions had used. Some of the people who had attacked Bashar were probably still inside the void, at that end of the stand, so it made sense to him to approach from the opposite end.

'OK,' Carole-Anne said. 'While Watkinson's acting as look-out, what do *we* do?'

'We take care of this,' Richter said, picking up the black plastic box. The red light still glowed, indicating it was switched on.

Jackson looked at the object in his hand. 'Which is the trigger?' she asked. 'The switch or the button?'

'The button,' Richter said. 'I think.'

'You *think*?' Jackson raised her eyebrows. 'You want to have another guess? Because if you do, I'm right out of here.'

Richter shook his head. 'It's almost certainly the button – the switch will just turn on the firing circuit – but it doesn't matter because I'm not planning on touching either.'

He put the box back on the ground, leant the MP5 against a girder, and reached up. He seized a detonator and pulled it out of the plastic, then repeated the process with all the others, carefully laying each detonator, with its attached wires, on the ground, well away from the explosive charges. He then took a Kamasa folding tool from a leather holster on his belt, opened it up so that it formed a pair of pliers and picked up one of the wires, close to the detonator itself.

'You really want to do that?' Jackson asked, as he placed the jaws of the tool around the wire.

'This was a suicide bomb,' Richter said, 'so there'd be no point in incorporating counter-measures in it. That box is just a switch. All it's intended to do is send a current to the detonators, no more, no less. And if I'm wrong, all that'll happen is one of the detonators will fire, and they're too far away from the explosives to be a problem.'

He closed the jaws of the pliers and snipped through the wires. Nothing happened, and inside a minute he'd detached all the detonators. He tossed them to the back of the void and replaced each cable, securing it by thrusting the doubled-over end into the plastic explosive.

'Is that safe?' Jackson asked doubtfully.

'I know explosives,' Richter assured her. 'It's safe.'

Once he'd attached the last wire he bent down, picked up the box again and placed it on one of the nearby pieces of machinery. He looked at what he'd done and nodded in satisfaction: even a careful inspection would suggest that the explosives were still primed for detonation.

Richter picked up the Heckler & Koch. 'Now we wait,' he said.

Saadi walked briskly – or as briskly as the dangling Kalashnikov would allow – to the door at the end of the stand and looked at the shattered lock as he drew his pistol. Clearly the entrance had already been used, a deduction immediately confirmed by the sight of a Dubai police officer lying unconscious on the floor just inside.

This puzzled Saadi, and he wondered for a moment if he should kill the man as a precaution, but then he shrugged and walked to the rear of the workshop. He pulled apart the Velcro seam on his *gellabbiya* and dropped the garment on the floor, revealing the same all-black outfit he'd worn the previous night. He stuck the pistol into the waistband of his trousers, removed the Kalashnikov from around his neck, opened the rear door and stepped through.

Richter had insisted that Carole-Anne Jackson go back inside the workshop. Primarily, he wanted her out of the firing line but her skill with a weapon meant that she could provide vital support when the terrorists eventually arrived. She might also, he pointed out, be the first to meet them if they decided to come in through that workshop, though Richter guessed they'd follow the same route he'd taken.

He crouched down behind an air-conditioning unit, the MP5 – its magazine fully charged again – at the ready beside him. He was looking intently down the length of the void, alert for any sign of movement but, despite his vigilance, the black-clad Arab got to within twenty yards of his position before he saw him.

Saadi stopped beside a roaring machine and looked carefully around him. What he saw didn't immediately make sense. He could see no sign of the Dubai police or security officers he'd been expecting – in fact, he couldn't see anybody at all. But the explosive charges he'd prepared were visible, as were the wires linking the detonators to the firing box. And he could also see the box itself, the power light glowing.

At first, it looked as if Bashar had simply walked away, leaving the device ready to be detonated, but Saadi knew that couldn't have happened. Like the other *jihadis* selected for this vital mission, Bashar was dedicated and totally committed. He would never abandon his place of duty.

That meant Bashar had been captured or was lying dead somewhere nearby. Perhaps, Saadi suddenly thought, the man he'd seen emerging was some kind of undercover agent who'd killed Bashar and gone for help in dismantling the bomb. That simple explanation covered the facts as he now saw them, but alternatively there might be groups of armed men waiting in the gloom, ready to shoot him down the moment he approached.

But Saadi had no option: he had to try, had to make

the attempt. He took a firm hold of the pistol grip of the Kalashnikov, looked carefully all around him, and began inching his way forward, heading for the firing box, its red light like a beacon, drawing him in.

Richter watched the other man's careful approach. His target was obviously very alert, head and eyes in constant motion, the Kalashnikov swinging in an arc to cover the maximum area in front of him. Richter knew that as soon as he stood up, as he would have to for a clear shot, he'd be seen immediately and dragged into a fire-fight. Better to wait until his quarry got closer, when he would reach the firing box and see what was left of Bashar.

Saadi stopped moving as he reached the edge of the relatively open area where they'd prepared the charges. Huddled on one side was a dark, unmoving shape, a Kalashnikov with half its stock missing lying close by, and Saadi knew without doubt that Bashar had not run, had not left his post. He'd been cut down before he could complete his mission.

No matter. The wires were still in place, the firing box just an arm's length away. It would be the work of a moment to both avenge Bashar and topple the House of Saud.

With a muttered prayer, and almost without conscious thought, Saadi leant the Kalashnikov against a pillar and reached out for the box. He quickly checked that the wires were securely attached, looked up at the explosive charges taped to the girders, and rested his finger on the button.

He bowed his head and mouthed *'B'ism-Illah-ir-Rachmani-ir-Rachim'*, then took a last look around him. He glanced down at the plastic box, called out *'Abdu-baha'* in a voice that was almost a shout, closed his eyes and pressed the button.

Nothing happened for a couple of seconds, then a quiet voice from directly behind him said 'Bang'. Just as Saadi started to turn, a huge weight seemed to crash into the top of his skull and blackness supervened.

Richter checked the unconscious man in front of him, removed the Browning pistol from his waistband and put it into his own pocket. Then he stepped across to where Saadi had placed the Kalashnikov, picked it up and moved it well out of the way.

Carole-Anne Jackson watched him. She'd emerged from the workshop as soon as Saadi had shouted out, but by the time she stepped into the darkness, the Arab was already unconscious, the iron bar Richter had found ensuring instant and prolonged oblivion.

He went back to his victim and checked the Arab's pulse.

'Will he live?' Jackson asked.

'Maybe, but I don't much care either way. Right, that's two down, one to go.'

To one side of the Millennium Grandstand, Massood watched and waited. He didn't know how long it would take Saadi to trigger the bomb, but he was already worried. Above him he could see the unmistakable signs of a controlled evacuation. Uniformed police officers and racecourse officials were clearly visible, leading people away from the windows. As long as Saadi could detonate the explosives within two or three minutes, they might still achieve their objective, but if he delayed any longer, their principal targets would almost certainly escape.

Again he checked his watch, then made a decision. He would have to act independently. He moved away, heading for a point behind and to one side of the Millennium Grandstand, where anyone leaving the building would have to pass.

'Right,' Richter said. 'I'll sort out this bastard, then we'll wrap this up.'

He pulled down one of the wires still connecting the firing box and the plastic explosive, heaved Saadi on to his front and lashed his wrists together. Then he tied the unconscious man's legs to a thick steel pipe so that, even if he woke up, he wasn't going anywhere. He removed the magazine from each of the Kalashnikovs, emptied the shells into his pocket and cleared the breeches on both weapons. He took off his light jacket, slung the MP5 with its stock folded over his right shoulder, then pulled the jacket back on. The small submachine gun created a bulge in the fabric, but no part of it was actually visible.

'Right,' he said. 'Let's go outside and finish this.'

*

Unnoticed by Massood, Michael Watkinson stood beside a group of people in Western dress about seventy yards away and watched him. The lone Arab met most of the criteria Richter had told him to watch out for: the frequent glances at his watch and his constant study of the grandstand, and he was walking in a peculiar, stiff-legged way that suggested he had something concealed under his *gellabbiya*. Watkinson pulled out his mobile and pressed a speed-dial code.

Richter's phone was on vibrate and silent, and immediately he felt the tremor in his pocket he pulled it out.

'I've spotted one character who doesn't look like he belongs,' Watkinson said, and then described the man.

'That could be contestant number three,' Richter said. 'Where is he now?'

'Hanging around at the rear of the stand.'

'He's probably guessed their bomb isn't going to blow, so he's going to gun down the Saudis as they leave. Contact Hussein and tell him to stop the evacuation. We've disarmed the bomb, so now they're safer inside the stand than out of it.'

'What about this man?'

'Don't worry. Carole and I will take care of him.'

Massood glanced around, alert for trouble, but saw nobody who caused him any concern. Anyone wanting to leave the Millennium Grandstand would have to pass within fifty yards of where he was standing. At that range, with a fully loaded Kalashnikov and two spare magazines, he could do a *lot* of damage.

'We're going to do what?' Jackson demanded, as Richter ended the call.

'We'll go outside, find this Arab and take him down.'

'I don't think your Mr Watkinson is all that sharp at this kind of thing. Are you sure he's identified the right man?'

'No, but he's the best lead we've got. The racecourse is full of people, so we can't go charging out there waving assault rifles. You've reloaded your pistol?'

Jackson stared at him. 'Basic handgun one oh one. Of course I've reloaded it. What do you think I am – some kind of fucking amateur?'

'Just checking.' Richter smiled apologetically.

Inspector Hussein wasn't having an easy time. Simply getting inside the Millennium Grandstand was tricky, because the staff, used to local police officers waving their identity cards as a way to avoid the inconvenience and expense of buying tickets, initially refused him admittance. Not having time to argue, he overcame that hurdle by simply drawing his pistol and marching straight past, followed by his group of armed officers.

All the members of the Saudi royal family at the meeting were watching the racing from the Del Mar Lounge, which had been reserved for their personal use. Hussein again found his way barred, but this time by a group of bodyguards, and he had to wait until a palace official was found before he could explain his mission.

His ID was checked thoroughly before the official would take him seriously. The most senior members of the royal family were informed first, but that didn't make much difference. Within seconds, it seemed, everyone in the lounge knew that there was a bomb in the building and all they wanted was to get out. Immediately.

Hussein's armed officers ensured that the evacuation was relatively orderly, and he'd just managed to get most of them heading towards the exits when he received Watkinson's call telling him to stop what he was doing. He did his best, and most of the Saudis responded positively, retracing their steps and resuming their seats, but one small group, led by some minor princes, absolutely refused to do anything but leave the building.

And there was nothing Hussein could do to stop them.

Richter opened the external door and looked out. The area beyond was now full of people, which was both a help and a hindrance. It meant their quarry was less likely to see them coming, but would also make it more difficult to spot him.

'We're a couple,' Richter decided, 'so walk beside me on my right. That should help shield the MP5 from view.' Jackson linked her arm in his as they joined the edge of a moving throng. 'Watkinson described this guy as about six feet tall, heavy black beard, white *gellabbiya*, red and white *kaffiyeh*, somewhere in front of us. He's probably wearing a Semtex waistcoat, so we don't just walk up and tap him on the shoulder.'

'What do we do, then?'

'We play it by ear. It depends on where he is and what he's doing when we see him.'

To their left, a group of young Arabs emerged noisily around the corner of the Millennium Grandstand and began heading in roughly the same direction as Richter and Jackson.

Massood was getting concerned. Nobody resembling any member of the Saudi royal family had yet appeared. There were people surging all around him, and he still believed nobody had realized his intentions, but eventually someone was bound to wonder why he kept pacing up and down in the same spot.

And then, as he turned back again to look towards the grandstand, his face creased into a smile. It wasn't quite the group he had been hoping for, but he recognized a number of the younger Saudi princes heading his way. Obviously the exodus from the stand was just beginning, so he had only seconds to wait. But then his face darkened, because nobody else was following them.

Suddenly Massood realized they'd failed. The authorities must have killed Bashar and Saadi, and disarmed the bomb. He was all that was left. He was the sole remaining *jihadi*, and upon his shoulders now rested all the responsibility of this vital Al-Qaeda operation. He had no options left. He made his decision.

He watched the loose band of young Saudi princes get closer, his whole attention focused on them. For Massood, the other people around him had ceased to exist. His left hand crept up to the neckline of his *gellabbiya*. His finger and thumb closed on the material of the Velcro seam. Just a few more yards and then he would act. A futile gesture, perhaps, but at the very least he would be avenging his fallen comrades.

And then the leading Saudi was directly in front of him, a bare twenty yards away. *Now*, Massood thought, and pulled his arm down and to the left, ripping the seam apart to reveal the Kalashnikov assault rifle hanging on its cord.

With a great bellow of *'Allahu Akbar'*, he seized the pistol grip with his right hand and swung up the barrel to point at the approaching group, his left hand grasping the fore-end to steady his aim.

'Oh, shit,' Richter muttered, breaking into a run. 'There he is.'

About eighty yards away from them, a man in a white *gellabbiya* was levelling a weapon at a group of young Arabs directly in front of him. With a clear line of sight, Richter would have opened fire with the MP5 from where he stood, but behind the gunman were throngs of racing enthusiasts, and the risk of hitting one or more of them at that range was too great.

So Richter ran. He pulled his jacket open and grabbed the MP5, swinging it up into the firing position, but he was still too far away, and far too late.

To his right, Carole-Anne Jackson was also running,

simultaneously widening the distance between them to
ensure she had a clear shot, the Glock in her right hand.
But she, like Richter, had no chance of preventing what
was about to happen.

Massood took a moment to check his target, then
squeezed the trigger of his assault rifle. His ability with
the weapon was immediately apparent. Untrained troops
tend to hold the trigger down, which means that almost
every round except the first three or four will go high
and miss the target as the barrel lifts.

Massood had been trained to use the weapon the
same way all elite troops are instructed – the so-called
'double-tap': two shots; correct aim; then two more
shots.

His first two bullets took the leading prince squarely
in the chest, then Massood shifted his aim slightly, to
seek out another target. The terror in his next victim's
face was palpable, and Massood exulted in that, taking
a couple of steps forward. The front of the prince's
gellabbiya suddenly bloomed red and he tumbled backwards. His companions had turned and begun to run,
but nobody can outrun a bullet.

Another two rounds screamed through the air, seeking out Massood's third target. Then two more, and yet
another young man slumped forwards, shot in the back,
his blood staining the ground all around him.

Massood's face wore a smile of triumph. This was
what he had hoped to do, to help rid Saudi Arabia of
the corruption that infested it. He had eyes only for the
terrified young men fleeing in front of him, choosing

each target and dispatching him with the callous efficiency of an executioner.

Richter stopped, swung up the MP5 and took careful aim. There were still far too many people behind the terrorist, but he couldn't afford to wait any longer. With every second another innocent victim died. Collateral damage was a risk he was going to have to accept.

A few yards over to his right, Carole-Anne Jackson had obviously reached the same conclusion. At that moment she raised her Glock, took aim and squeezed the trigger.

Massood was shifting his weapon again when he suddenly became aware of the sound of two shots off to his left. A woman seemed to be aiming at him with some kind of a pistol. He hadn't been hit, though he knew the end was near: sooner or later the police would arrive and then he would die. But that was of no consequence to him as he quickly chose his next victim.

But before he could squeeze the trigger, something slammed into his left side and he staggered backwards. He looked down to see a sudden flare of blood erupting from a tiny hole in his black shirt, just below his shoulder. But his left arm was undamaged, and he still had work to do. He ignored the pain spreading across his body and again took aim at one of the running figures.

And then another sudden stab of pain, and another, and another, and Massood fell sideways, crashing to the ground. Surely it couldn't just be the woman, not with that pathetic little pop-gun. He raised his head and looked up. A tall man with fair hair and blue eyes was running towards him, a sub-machine-gun clutched in his hand.

Massood's strength seemed to be ebbing, his vision clouding, and now there was a roaring in his ears. With the last of his strength he pulled the Kalashnikov across his body, aiming it at the approaching man.

His right forefinger was taking up the pressure on the trigger when a shadow fell across him and he looked up to see the last sight he would ever see. There was a woman standing over him – and, just like Bashar in the dark emptiness under the grandstand, his immediate reaction was one of fury. How dare a woman have the temerity to interfere with the work of men, or obstruct his holy mission?

And then he didn't think anything else at all, as Carole-Anne Jackson blasted two nine-millimetre rounds through his head.

Chapter Eighteen

Saturday
Nad Al-Sheba Racecourse, Dubai

There were already two ambulances on standby at the racecourse, there to minister to jockeys who became separated from their mounts rather than the victims of gunshot wounds. Half a dozen others appeared within minutes.

The tally of dead and wounded was depressing, but it could have been a lot worse. Four young Saudi princes were dead, the Kalashnikov rounds fired at such close range having done horrendous damage to their bodies, and three others had been wounded, but they would probably live.

Two terrorists were dead, and nobody seemed particularly bothered about that. The third was unconscious, though it wasn't clear if he'd ever come round. Nobody was worried about him, either.

But three innocent bystanders had been hit by stray bullets, fired by either Richter or Jackson. Although they were in no danger from their wounds, the fact that they'd been shot at all looked like being the biggest problem of the afternoon.

'I'm going to have to kick this up a level or two,' Watkinson warned, 'and it's possible you'll face charges here in Dubai. They take a very dim view of people carrying firearms, and an even dimmer view of innocent civilians getting wounded.'

'Oh, magic,' Jackson muttered. 'I've just remembered what I really like about Arabs – absolutely fucking nothing.'

'I think it's called gratitude,' Richter said, his voice low and angry. 'If we'd just sat around back at the hotel and left them to it, they'd be looking at a fucking great hole in the ground where the Millennium Grandstand used to be, and wondering how to explain to the people of Saudi Arabia that most of their royal family would be coming back home in boxes. Sodding ingrates. I'm going to call Simpson.'

He called Hammersmith on his Enigma phone. 'I need to give you a SITREP,' he explained. 'We've got a few problems over here.' Quickly he outlined what had happened.

'You're sure there aren't any more of them waiting in the wings clutching Kalashnikovs or packs of Semtex?'

'No, I'm not sure, but I doubt it. Three men travelled out to Dubai with the horse, and we've got two dead terrorists here and one with a really bad headache. Unless some others came by a different route, I reckon that's it. And if there are any others, why haven't they popped out by now, guns blazing?'

'Right,' Simpson sounded pleased, 'a shame some of the local civilian population got mildly ventilated, but overall it's a good result, and it does close the loop on what Khatid reported. Anything else?'

'Yes. According to the local Six officer, we're quite likely to find ourselves in court on firearms charges.

Carole-Anne Jackson is authorized to carry a weapon here in the Gulf, so she's fire-proof from that point of view, but I've been toting a couple of Browning Hi-Powers all day and I also borrowed an MP5 from a local cop. And both of us fired a whole bunch of shells at the last bad guy, only some of which hit him.'

Simpson was silent for a moment. 'I know the way you operate, Richter. When you said "borrowed", can I assume that the police officer didn't have too much say in the matter?'

'Not a lot, no.'

'He is alive, though? I mean, you didn't kill the poor sod just to take his gun off him?'

'Of course not. He's just got a bit of a headache.'

'So the short version is that you were using an unlicensed firearm and a trio of local Dubai residents got wounded when you two took these terrorists down. Which of you shot these civilians?'

'We don't really know. Jackson fired three times, but thinks she only hit the terrorist once. I fired six rounds from the MP5, and I reckon three of those got him. So at least one of the injured civilians is down to me, but it could have been all of them.'

'Understood. Right, it shouldn't be too much of a problem.'

Richter ended the call and looked at Watkinson. 'One of the few good things about working for Richard Simpson is that he always does what he says he'll do.'

'And he's going to sort it out?'

Richter nodded. 'He'll sort it out.'

Inspector Saeed Hussein appeared beside them, flanked

by three police officers, one of whom conspicuously *wasn't* armed with a Heckler & Koch MP5.

'Here,' Richter said. He unslung the weapon, removed the magazine and ejected the loaded round from the breech. He passed the sub-machine-gun and magazine to the officer, who took them in a somewhat shamefaced manner.

'We owe you our thanks,' Hussein began. 'If you hadn't guessed what was happening, this could have been a total disaster.'

'I'm glad we could help stop it,' Richter said. 'So what now?'

Hussein looked slightly embarrassed. 'I'm afraid I must ask both of you not to leave Dubai until further notice. My superiors have issued specific instructions to me, and there may be certain legal repercussions as a result of the events of this afternoon.'

'I think, Inspector,' Watkinson said, 'that your superiors may be getting a call quite soon that should clarify the situation.'

British Embassy, Dubai

An hour later they were back in the British Embassy at Al-Seef Road, where Richter handed back the two Browning pistols, and the silenced Hi-Power that he'd taken off the terrorist. 'Call it a souvenir, Michael,' he said.

'What are you going to do now?' Watkinson asked.

'Neither of us can leave Dubai, at least for a while, so

I guess we'll just take in some of the sights. If you need me, you've got my mobile number. Whatever happens, I'm going to stay out here for a few days and take it easy. I think Simpson owes me that much.'

Nad Al-Sheba Racecourse, Dubai

The last casualty on the list of priorities for the ambulance crews was the sole surviving terrorist, who still lay unconscious under the grandstand.

Inspector Hussein led two of his men into the void, accompanied by a police photographer who'd been summoned to take pictures of the explosive charges before they were removed. Only after that had been completed did he allow the paramedics and mortuary staff into the building to remove the unconscious Saadi and the remains of Bashar.

He'd already received detailed instructions from an angry superior officer about the disposal of the bodies of the two dead terrorists. Both would be taken out into the desert that same evening, where a digger was already en route, and would be dumped without ceremony at the bottom of a substantial hole, into which would also be slung the carcasses of two large pigs. The pit would then be filled in and left unmarked.

In the meantime, the unconscious man was to be taken to the Al-Wasl Hospital on Oud Metha Road in Bur Dubai for emergency treatment. If he survived his injury, special plans had also been made for him.

PAYBACK

Al-Khaleej Hotel, Dubai

Responding to a call for 'Grant Hutchings', Dawson took the lift down to the lobby, where Hussein was waiting for him, a smile on his face.

'I have some good news for us both, Agent Hutchings. Have you heard what happened this evening at the Nad Al-Sheba racecourse?' When the American shook his head, he continued. 'Let me buy you a drink and I'll explain.'

The inspector outlined the events that had taken place. 'We were very lucky that the Englishman, Richter, worked out what was happening,' he said, and went on to describe how James Holden had featured in the scenario.

Edward Dawson's expression remained composed as he listened, but his brain was reeling from the almost unbelievable story he was hearing. An Arab terrorist group planning an attack right here in Dubai? And that blond-haired English bastard had somehow worked out the real reason behind the incidents they'd orchestrated in Syria and Bahrain. In fact, he'd made the right deduction, but he hadn't made the right connection.

'What happened to the terrorists?' Dawson asked. He was very aware that, if they'd survived and were questioned – most Arab countries used interrogators who were *very* good at extracting information – they would know nothing at all about either the Damascus *shahid* or the Manama car-bomb. That would blow Richter's theory right out of the water, and could lead to more investigations as the authorities tried to work out exactly

JAMES BARRINGTON

who Holden *had* been working with. But if the terrorists hadn't survived, their lack of knowledge would have died with them.

'Two of them were killed,' Hussein replied. 'The third is still unconscious, but he'll survive – for a while at least. Once he's fit to travel, he'll be taken to Saudi Arabia for trial, since his target was the Saudi royal family. The proceedings won't take long.'

That sounded convenient. From what Dawson knew of Saudi justice, the surviving terrorist's fate would be predictable and his punishment swift and brutal.

'Were there any other casualties?'

'Unfortunately, yes. The last terrorist opened fire at close range with an assault rifle. Four Saudi princes were killed and three injured. Richter then shot and killed the terrorist, but three bystanders were also injured.'

Dawson nodded. It sounded as if Richter was both resourceful and competent, and he wondered if O'Hagan would suggest taking him out. On the other hand, they were now only about thirty-six hours away from achieving their objective, and it probably made sense not to do anything that might draw attention to them.

'So, Agent Hutchings, now we know the real target was the House of Saud, we can relax. There never was a threat to a hotel here in Dubai. That part of Holden's story was just intended to divert our attention. My superiors have specifically asked me to thank you for your time and trouble, but now that the threat has been neutralized, we no longer feel your presence here is necessary.'

Dawson sat in silence for a few seconds, his mind working overtime. This was a sting in the tail he hadn't anticipated. They *had* to get themselves into the Burj Al-Arab on Monday.

He cracked his face into a smile. 'That's excellent news, Inspector. It'll be good to get back home again, but we can't leave Dubai just yet. You may remember that we had a problem with the Gulfstream on our way out here?' Hussein nodded. 'Well, the aircraft still needs to be checked out thoroughly, so we won't be able to leave until Tuesday at the earliest. And we still need to show your officers how to use the explosive detectors, so why don't we go ahead with the demonstrations on Monday as we'd planned? It'll only take a couple of hours.'

For a moment Hussein didn't respond, then nodded. 'I'd forgotten that we'd arranged that. I'll check with my superiors, but I don't think there'll be a problem.'

Crowne Plaza Hotel, Dubai

They lay side-by-side in the double bed in Richter's suite, their nakedness covered by a thin sheet, the air-conditioning humming softly in the background.

'What do you want to do for what's left of the evening?' he asked.

'Not a lot,' Carole-Anne replied. 'This has been, by any standards, a very full day. Between us we've prevented a bunch of the Saudi royals from being vaporized, shot two terrorists and been threatened with legal action for accidentally shooting a handful of bystanders. Absolutely anything else we do will *have* to be an anticlimax.'

'Dinner in bed, then?'

'No,' she said firmly, scooping up the hotel guide book from the bedside cabinet. 'Let's hit one of the restaurants here. Al-Dana? Or what about Sakura? Do you like Japanese food?'

Richter shook his head. 'No. I prefer whatever I eat to have at least stopped moving before it reaches my plate. Al-Dana or the Western Steakhouse will do for me. I could eat a steak,' he added hopefully. 'And what about tomorrow?'

'More of the same, with any luck. We can take a cab and drive around, do some sightseeing, I suppose. Have you had a chance to see the Burj Al-Arab yet?'

'Only in pictures,' he sighed. 'OK, I wouldn't mind doing the tourist bit for a while. It'll make a change from being shot at.'

'That's a deal,' Jackson said. 'Now get dressed, take me downstairs and feed me.'

Al-Khaleej Hotel, Dubai

The moment Hussein stepped into his police car, Dawson crossed to the reception desk, picked up the house phone and called O'Hagan's room.

'Bring the others and meet me in the coffee shop,' he ordered. Then he walked outside, pulled out his mobile and punched in a number.

'Roy,' he said, when the pilot answered, 'it's Agent

Hutchings. I'm calling about that fault on the Gulf-stream we discussed earlier. I've told Inspector Hussein we can't leave Dubai until Tuesday morning at the earliest. Is that forecast still correct?'

Sutter immediately grasped the hidden message being relayed to him. 'Yes. I can't do anything tomorrow, obviously, and I'll have to run some more checks on Monday, but if I don't hit any other problems the bird should be ready to fly by Tuesday.'

'Good,' Dawson replied. 'Just keep me informed.'

A few minutes later, in the coffee shop, Dawson outlined what Hussein had told him.

'So Holden was actually working for this bunch of Arab terrorists,' O'Hagan said with a smile. 'That's certainly news to me.'

'Me, too,' Dawson said. 'Anyway, the Dubai cops don't think there's now a credible threat to any local hotel, so we won't have to carry out the checks we planned. We'll just do a demonstration of the detectors, then head for home. The cars will be here at nine on Monday morning.'

Chapter Nineteen

Monday
Al-Khaleej Hotel, Dubai

Two Dubai police cars drew up outside the hotel, the inspector seated in the leading vehicle. The four Americans were waiting for him in the lobby, several bags piled beside them.

'Now I see why you needed two cars,' Hussein remarked. 'Are these detectors very big?'

'No,' Dawson replied, 'they're hand-held units, but the other bags contain batteries, chargers, calibration equipment, test gear and spares. It's a real comprehensive outfit.'

'I hope you don't mind,' Hussein said, turning in his seat as they drove away, 'but I have to make a small detour on the way to Jumeirah Beach. It's not very far out of our way – just down Shaikh Zayed Road.'

'No problem, Inspector,' Dawson assured him. 'As you said on Saturday, the pressure's off us now.'

Crowne Plaza Hotel, Dubai

Ten minutes later, both cars stopped outside the Crowne Plaza. Hussein went inside and headed for the reception desk to ask for Paul Richter.

The receptionist nodded. 'Who shall I say is calling?'

Hussein produced his identification. 'Ask Mr Richter to come down. I need to speak to him.'

After a couple of minutes, the doors of one of the lifts opened and Richter emerged, with Carole-Anne Jackson beside him. They strode across and shook Hussein's hand.

'What can we do for you, Inspector?' Richter asked.

Hussein smiled. 'It's more what I can do for you, Mr Richter. I'm pleased to say that no action will be taken over what happened at Nad Al-Sheba, so you're free to leave whenever you want, with the grateful thanks of our government.'

'Thank you,' Richter said as he escorted Hussein back towards the main doors. 'And thanks for coming here to tell us. I'm going to be staying for a few days longer. We're planning on doing some sightseeing, and perhaps a little shopping.'

'Unfortunately you've missed the annual Shopping Festival, but I'm sure you can still find some bargains.'

'I'm sure *I* can,' Jackson said with a smile.

As they watched the Arab police officer walk over to his car, a man's face peered out at them from the rear seat. Richter recognized Grant Hutchings, and there was another shadowy figure behind him. Hutchings nodded briefly in his direction.

Jackson opened her mouth to say something, but at that moment Richter's mobile rang.

'You're off the hook, Richter. Any time now someone will tell you you're free to go.'

'He's just left,' Richter said instantly, recognizing Simpson's waspish tones.

'Good. What time's the next flight to Heathrow?'

'As far as I'm concerned, some time on Saturday afternoon.'

There was a short pause as Simpson digested this. 'Are you asking for a holiday?'

'Yes,' Richter said. 'In fact, I'm telling you now that I'm taking the rest of the week off.'

'Right, I'll tell admin to knock it off your annual leave entitlement. No, hang on a minute. You did a pretty good job out there. I'll put you down for liaison and debriefing for the rest of the week.'

'Thanks a lot.'

'We'll pick up the tab for the hotel and any meals until Saturday, but the drinks will be down to you. Fair enough?'

Simpson's sudden generosity was somewhat unexpected, but Richter was grateful. 'Yes, thanks.'

Jumeirah Beach Hotel, Dubai

Like the iconic Burj Al-Arab, the Jumeirah Beach Hotel has become something of a symbol of Dubai. Designed to mirror the shape of a breaking wave, it's built on the coast next to the Wild Wadi Water Park, some thirty kilometres outside the city.

When the vehicles stopped, Dawson saw two other police cars already there. Hussein noticed his glance. 'I selected eight experienced English-speaking officers to train with this equipment.'

In the hotel itself, Richard Wilson – in the persona of CIA Agent Andy Franks – began his briefing to the assembled men. He opened one of the custom-designed carrying cases and extracted the unit. The officers stared at it with interest as Wilson described its operation.

'Because of the environment in here' – he gestured at the spacious foyer – 'and in most very modern buildings, you'll normally do atmospheric sampling.'

He reached into his pocket, extracted a small plastic bottle containing a grey lump and passed it to Dawson, then stepped back a few feet.

'That's a very small piece of Semtex,' Wilson explained. 'If you could open the bottle for a few seconds, then close it again, I can demonstrate just how sensitive this unit is.'

'How long does it take to register?' Hussein asked.

'About thirty seconds after activation,' Wilson replied. 'You saw my colleague open the bottle. That will have released a few microscopic particles of explosive and some vapour into the air, which is in constant motion because of the air-conditioning system. Most detectors aren't sensitive enough to work in those circumstances, but this unit definitely is.' He held up the E-3500; its digital display showed a positive result.

Wilson then fielded some questions about technique before Hussein glanced at his watch. 'We should move on to the Burj,' he said. 'The manager's expecting us.'

Five minutes later the police cars stopped outside easily the most recognizable hotel in the world.

Crowne Plaza Hotel, Dubai

Richter was sitting in the lobby studying a tourist map of Dubai. Carole-Anne Jackson was pointing out areas worthy of a visit, when she suddenly broke off.

'I know what I meant to ask you, Paul. When Hussein dropped by, there were two men in the back of his police car, and one of them seemed to know you. Who was he?'

'Oh, him,' Richter snorted. 'I met him just once, when we went to interview Holden. He pitched up with Hussein after we reported the murder. He's from your Company.'

'He's an Agency man?'

'Yes. His name's Grant Hutchings, and the other man was Roger Middleton. Hutchings and I had a bit of an exchange. I didn't like his attitude, and he didn't seem too keen on me either.'

'No,' Jackson said emphatically.

'What do you mean, "no"?' Richter demanded.

'I mean that wasn't Grant Hutchings.'

'What?'

'Which bit of that sentence didn't you understand, Paul? I said the man in that car wasn't Grant Hutchings.'

'Are you sure?'

'Of course I'm sure. I slept with him, for God's sake ... though it was a long time ago,' she added defensively.

'The CIA's a big organization. Maybe you have two agents with the same name?'

'I seriously doubt it. If he's out here, that means he's

in the Operations Directorate, like me, which cuts down on the numbers.'

Richter was suddenly aware of an overwhelming feeling of unease. 'Why would somebody want to impersonate a CIA officer in Dubai?'

'I have no clue,' Jackson said, 'but I think we need to look into this. Do you have Hussein's telephone number?'

Richter shook his head. 'No, but Watkinson does. I'll give him a call.' He rang the British Embassy.

'Ask him to find out what the CIA agents are doing,' Jackson hissed, as he waited to be connected. 'Don't tell him I think Hutchings is an impostor, just in case I *am* wrong. I don't want to look like a total klutz.'

'Right,' Richter said. 'Morning, Michael. Paul Richter. I'm just calling to let you know we've been given permission to leave Dubai . . . I've also got a question for you. When we went over to Holden's apartment, we met a couple of Agency guys with Hussein. Have you any idea what they're doing over here?'

'Why?'

'Just idle curiosity. They're a long way from home.'

'They were sent out in response to Holden's claim about a bomb being placed in a waterfront hotel. According to Hussein, they've brought out explosive detectors to help the Dubai authorities. But now we know that threat was just a diversion, I presume they'll be heading home.'

'Could you call Hussein and ask him something? I kind of got off on the wrong foot with Hutchings, so if these guys are still around I'd like to meet somewhere and make amends.'

'I'll call him right now.'

Richter turned to Carole-Anne Jackson. 'Apparently they came out here to help locate the hotel bomb Holden predicted, and he thinks they'll soon be heading back to the States.'

Jackson shrugged, looking uncertain. 'Maybe I *was* mistaken,' she said thoughtfully. Then, more confidently, 'No, I wasn't. That man definitely wasn't the Grant Hutchings I once knew.'

'Give me a moment. I'll call John Westwood.'

'You know him?'

'Yes,' Richter said. 'You haven't slept with him as well?' he asked suspiciously.

'I haven't slept with everyone in the CIA, and as far as I know John Westwood is a happily married man. I've worked for him in the past, is all. And,' she added, 'you do know it's the middle of the night over there?'

'Yes, but I know John well. If it's important, he won't mind being woken up.'

'OK, but keep my name out of it,' Jackson said. 'I'll probably have to go before a board of inquiry over that Nad Al-Sheba business when I get back to Langley, so the last thing I want is to piss off the guy who might be heading it.'

Burj Al-Arab Hotel, Dubai

'It's a big bastard, isn't it?' Dawson muttered, shading his eyes as he looked up at the huge white belly of the hotel building. The vast expanse of fabric vanished above them, curving into invisibility as it approached the very top of the structure.

Rising over three hundred metres above the Arabian Gulf, it's the tallest, and certainly the most architecturally adventurous, hotel in the world. The man-made island on which the Burj Al-Arab stands is three hundred metres offshore, and is linked to Jumeirah Beach by a causeway. But it isn't the island, or the causeway, or even the sheer height of the hotel that stuns the visitor: it's the shape.

The Burj Al-Arab looks like a huge billowing sail attached to a single mast, the apparent 'wind' inflating the sail from somewhere offshore. The effect is dramatic enough in daylight, but at night, when the front of the hotel is bathed in ever-changing colours by banks of massive theatre projectors, it's simply stunning.

O'Hagan followed Dawson's gaze. 'Yup, it's big. Let's get to it.'

Inspector Hussein's mobile rang as he led them towards the hotel entrance, and he stopped to answer it, moving slightly aside. Less than a minute later he closed the phone and, with a smile of apology, continued inside.

The Americans looked around as they emerged through the revolving doors. The interior was like nothing they'd ever seen before. In front of them a massive triangular water feature – a virtual pyramid of illuminated and precisely directed dancing water jets – extended up to the next level, escalators flanking it on either side. The decoration and colours were simply amazing, the atrium a riot of blue and white and gold, curving balconies ascending towards the roof. The aura of luxury was almost palpable.

The manager, who introduced himself as Salim Barzani, looked distinctly unhappy with the group assembled in the foyer – if one could use such a mundane word to describe the enormously opulent atrium, nearly two hundred metres high, in which they were standing. Hussein quickly explained that they were on a training exercise, and that there was no danger of any sort to the establishment.

'Very well. If you need anything, ask a member of my staff to come and find me.' With a final dismissive wave, Barzani stalked away.

Hussein turned to the Americans. 'Where do you wish to start, Agent Franks?'

'First, we need to look at the characteristics of a building with an atrium.' For several minutes he discussed air flow, air changes, temperature and humidity, then explained that, in order to undertake a proper check, samples would need to be taken at several different levels – at the top and bottom of the atrium, but also on one or two intermediate floors. 'I'd like to suggest, Inspector, that your officers should operate the detectors themselves.'

'I agree,' Hussein said, and instructed his men to open the cases.

Wilson approached each officer in turn, checking that they knew how the units worked. None of the policemen noticed the large and rather vulgar ring he wore on his left hand.

Thirty-eight seconds later, one of the officers reported a hit, and within a minute all the E-3500 units were similarly registering positive for the presence of explosives.

Crowne Plaza Hotel, Dubai

Richter ended his call to Westwood's home in Haywood, Virginia.

'John actually knows about the mission,' he confirmed, because he attended one of the briefings at Langley. It's a four-man team. Grant Hutchings is the senior agent. The others agents are Baxter, Franks and Middleton.'

Jackson shook her head. 'I don't recognize any of the other names.'

'He told me that Hutchings has worked out of Langley for most of his career, but he's also done tours in Vietnam, France and Germany.'

'When I knew him, he'd just finished an overseas tour, but I can't remember exactly where.'

Richter's mobile rang.

'It's Watkinson. I've just talked to Inspector Hussein and he confirms that the CIA officers will be here for a couple of days. At the moment they're with the inspector, instructing his officers in the use of explosive detectors. If you want to meet them, they're staying at the Al-Khaleej.'

'Got that, Michael. Sorry to have bothered you.'

'Everything seems to check out,' Richter said. 'According to Watkinson, they're training the local cops in the use of explosive detectors.'

'In other words, doing exactly what they're supposed to. So I must be wrong – is that what you're saying?'

Richter shook his head. 'Absolutely not. If you *are* right and Hutchings *is* an impostor, that means the others must be as well. If we take that as a fact, you'd expect them to act just like the real CIA agents right up to the moment when they take whatever action they've got planned.'

'Which is what?'

'I have absolutely no idea,' Richter admitted. 'But right now they're surrounded by armed police officers who'll be watching their every move, so I don't really see *what* they could do that those cops wouldn't be able to stop immediately.'

Burj Al-Arab Hotel, Dubai

Inspector Hussein had turned pale. All six detectors were now showing positive readings, and he knew that for sure because he'd checked each one twice.

'Could this be a mistake?' he asked. 'They aren't still detecting particles from the Semtex you used in the Jumeirah Beach?'

Wilson shook his head. 'No. Very few particles were released. If only one detector had registered a hit, I'd say it meant traces on our clothing, perhaps. But for all six to show positive? That's something totally different.'

'I must speak to the manager immediately,' Hussein decided.

Two minutes later he was back, with Salim Barzani a couple of paces behind him. 'You told me there was no threat to my hotel,' the manager said angrily.

Hussein was defensive. 'That was what we believed. We should now—'

'Inspector,' Wilson interrupted firmly, 'the analysis comes later. Our first priority must be to locate these explosives.' He turned to Barzani. 'What's security like here?'

'Very stringent, which is why I question the results you claim to have found. We already have explosive detectors installed in all external doors. So how could some terrorist have managed to get explosives inside?'

'You don't search the guests' luggage or anything like that?'

'Certainly not.' Barzani looked shocked. 'This is the best hotel in the world. The kind of people who stay here would never tolerate that kind of treatment, no matter what the circumstances.'

'Right,' Wilson said. 'The thing about explosives is that they all emit particles and vapours, but there are ways you can beat any detector. If I was trying to smuggle in some C4, I'd pack it in plastic sheeting and then tape the open ends shut. Then I'd wash the outside thoroughly, dry it and wrap it in more plastic, and wash that. I'd do that four or five times over, and at the end of it I'd be pretty sure there'd be no detectable emissions. Just to be certain, I'd pack it in three or four airtight storage bags, washing each one after I'd sealed it. Then I'd put the entire package in a big suitcase with soft clothes all around it to help absorb anything that managed to slip through. Wool and cotton are best. Once I'd done all that, I'd almost guarantee being able to take that case through any explosive detector yet made.'

'If what you say is true,' Barzani asked, 'then how did your hand-held units detect something here?'

'Simple,' Wilson said. 'When the case came through your portal detectors, the explosive was probably wrapped up the way I described it. Since then, whoever was carrying it has opened the package. That means somewhere up there' – he gestured – 'is a room with a bomb in it.'

'Suite,' the manager corrected him. 'We only have suites here.'

'Whatever. What we have to do now is find it.' He paused for a few seconds, looking up into the atrium, big enough to hold the Statue of Liberty. 'We'll start at the top and work our way down. Inspector, can you get your men to bring in the rest of our equipment?'

As Hussein turned away and started issuing orders, Wilson led the three Americans over to the bank of elevators.

The final phase of their long-planned operation was just about to begin.

Crowne Plaza Hotel, Dubai

Richter and Carole-Anne Jackson were waiting for a taxi to take them on their sightseeing trip when his Enigma mobile rang.

'Get to a secure location,' Simpson snapped.

Richter gestured to Jackson and then walked outside. 'Right, I'm outside the building. What's the problem?'

'There's been a hike in the overall alert state. We've just gone from Bikini Black to Black Special.'

'I'm in Dubai, Simpson. Couldn't you have told me

that when I got back? It doesn't really affect me over here, does it?'

'It might not, but the instructions from Vauxhall Cross were most specific. *All* British security personnel are to be informed. That obviously includes GCHQ, The Box, JIC staff, the intelligence sections of the armed forces, the CTC, and absolutely everyone else wearing any kind of an intelligence or counter-intelligence hat. It also includes you. Now, do you want to know the reason for this blanket coverage?'

'The question had crossed my mind.'

'You're going to like this, just not very much. This morning the people at Six took a call, strictly off the record, from your old sparring-partner Viktor Bykov.'

'Bykov? What the hell did he want?'

'He wanted, as quietly as possible, to alert us that the Russian military machine is down one nuke. Specifically, a few days ago two men, possibly Americans, persuaded somebody at a Russian ZATO to deliver them a suitcase nuclear weapon.'

'Oh, shit.'

'That sums it up nicely.'

'Why do the Russians think they were American?'

'They had US passports in the names of "Edwin Johnson" and "Richard Hughes". The FSB got photocopies from a hotel they were staying in.'

'What size weapon are we talking about?' Richter asked. 'And how the hell did they get it out of Russia?'

'It's a biggie, with a predicted yield of one kiloton, which is why we're all hopping about like freshly fucked ferrets. They apparently carried it overland by lorry and train down to Sochi, loaded it into an air ambulance and

flew out of Russia and south over Turkey. The aircraf
landed at Cairo, and there the weapon and the two mer
vanished. Present whereabouts unknown, but Egypt's
not a million miles from where you are, so keep your
eyes open.'

Richter was already making mental connections and
constructing a hypothesis – a hypothesis that answered
some of the questions that had been nagging at him. The
possibility that the CIA agents were impostors, James
Holden's 'premonitions' and his subsequent murder, the
Damascus and Manama bombings and the present activ
ity of the 'CIA team'. If you mixed them together in the
right way, you got a very definite wrong answer.

If he was right, there was absolutely no time to waste
'I'll ring you back,' he said. He immediately phoned
the British Embassy. 'This is a Military Flash call,' he
snapped as soon as the receptionist answered. 'Get me
Michael Watkinson.'

In seconds the Englishman was on the line. 'Watkin
son. Who is this?'

'Richter. Look, I don't have time to explain all this
right now, but call Inspector Hussein immediately. Tel
him not to let those CIA agents take anything inside any
buildings. There's a real possibility they're impostors
and they're trying to plant a bomb.'

'Paul, I can't just ... That's ridiculous. They're CIA
agents, for God's sake.'

'How do you know? Have you checked their identi
fication?'

'No, but I'm sure Hussein has.'

'I've no doubt they showed him something, bu

whether he did a proper check is quite another matter. He was expecting a team of CIA agents, and four men turned up just when and where they were supposed to. My guess is that any checks he did would have been cursory at best. Anyway, just tell him what I said.'

'What's your source for this?'

'You'll hear some time today, but do it, and do it now. If I'm wrong, you can shoot me later. And find out where the CIA men are. I've got to call London.'

'OK, I'll blame you if it all goes wrong. Just get back to me as soon as you can.'

Richter rang Hammersmith. Simpson was back on the line within seconds. 'Somewhat abrupt there, Richter. What's going on?'

'Right now, I don't know, but one or two peculiar things have happened out here.' He quickly explained some of the apparent anomalies.

'That's very thin, Richter,' Simpson replied. 'You're going to look a complete idiot if that CIA guy's identification is confirmed.'

'I'll risk it, and I've looked like a complete idiot plenty of times before. But there are a couple of things you can check for me.' Richter explained what he wanted, then rang off.

As he turned back to the hotel, Carole-Anne Jackson walked over, mobile in hand. 'You've heard about the missing Russian nuke?' she asked.

Richter nodded. 'It puts a different slant on Grant Hutchings and his merry men, doesn't it?'

'You think the two Americans who stole the weapon could be part of the CIA team?'

'It's possible. I've got my section checking a couple of things that could confirm it. It shouldn't take them long to find the answers.'

Burj Al-Arab Hotel, Dubai

Richard Wilson stood on the twenty-fifth floor and looked around. To say the building was luxurious was a bit of an understatement. It had cost an absolute fortune to build and furnish, and you needed exceedingly deep pockets to stay there. The smallest suite occupied nearly one hundred and seventy square metres, while the massive Royal Suites, outside one of which Wilson was standing at that moment, covered almost eight hundred and were provided with their own private lifts and cinemas. The last house Wilson had owned back in the States would have fitted three times over inside just one of them.

Behind him, Hussein watched as four of his men stacked the Americans' cases in the corridor. Hovering beside the inspector, Salim Barzani looked decidedly worried. Wilson thought he probably spent a lot of his time looking worried, but at this moment he definitely had something to be concerned about. Behind the manager, three hotel staff stood waiting beside the concierge desk – at the Burj Al-Arab, the guests check in inside their suites, so each floor has its own permanently manned concierge desk, designed in the shape of a golden shell as an extension of the aquatic theme predominating throughout the hotel.

'Grant, you take one detector and start at the other
nd,' Wilson instructed.

Hussein motioned to his officers to keep out of the
vay, as the Americans took the units out of their cases
nd moved apart. They turned on the detectors and
headed slowly towards the door of the suite. There they
topped and, after a murmured conversation, turned off
he units.

'We weren't expecting this,' Wilson announced. 'We
guessed that the bomb would be in a suite lower down.
was going to eliminate the upper floors first, but both
he detectors are showing similar readings. There are
aint traces of explosive here in the corridor, which might
imply be due to the hotel's air conditioning, but we've
definitely got strong hits right beside this door.'

'So you think the bomb is somewhere inside this
suite?' Hussein asked.

'Possibly, though the readings aren't definite. Who's
n there now?'

Hussein turned to Barzani, who shook his head.
Nobody.'

'Who was the last occupant?'

'I won't disclose his name until you're certain there
really is a bomb in there, but I can tell you that this
suite was occupied by an important Arab businessman
until yesterday evening.'

'Has the suite been cleaned since he left?'

Barzani shook his head. 'We've no bookings for
another few days, so it's just been inspected but not yet
properly cleaned.'

'Do you have a pass-key?'

Barzani nodded and stepped forward.

'Allow me,' O'Hagan said, and took it from him 'We're the experts at this, so we'd better go in first. Stay out here until we've either found something or con firmed there isn't anything to worry about.'

As O'Hagan unlocked the door, Dawson and Petrucc picked up the biggest of the cases and two of the smalle ones and carried them to the door.

'What's in those?' Hussein asked.

'The big case holds a portable x-ray device,' Wilson said. 'If there is a bomb in this suite, we'll need to scan it before we can disarm it.'

'Of course,' Hussein murmured, then jumped slightly as his mobile phone rang.

'Ready?' Wilson asked. He and O'Hagan entered first, holding the E-3500 detectors out in front of them.

Behind them, Hussein's eyes widened as he listened to what the caller was saying.

At the door, Petrucci glanced back at the inspector Their eyes met and in that instant the American realized that someone, somewhere, had at last made the right connection.

Hussein dropped the phone and reached inside his jacket, but Petrucci was much faster. He'd already lev elled his pistol before Hussein managed to draw his weapon. 'Don't move!' he yelled.

Hussein ignored him. 'Stop!' he yelled. 'Stop them!'

The four police officers looked confused – the shouted order making no sense. But the pistol in the American's hand was something else, something they could immedi ately relate to. Two of them pulled out weapons, but heir speed was also their undoing. Although they moved fast, they didn't move fast enough.

Dawson grabbed his pistol and both the Americans immediately opened fire. Four shots – so close together that they sounded like only two – echoed off the walls, and the two constables fell backwards, their weapons tumbling from their hands.

'Don't move,' Petrucci yelled again, adjusting his aim to cover Hussein and his two remaining officers. Dawson's weapon reinforced the threat while behind Petrucci, O'Hagan and Wilson reappeared with guns drawn.

Hussein stood as if frozen, his right hand still inside his jacket. The two remaining constables gaped incredulously, their horrified glances alternating between their dead companions and the four Americans, with no idea what was happening, or why. The manager, Barzani, thrust his hands into the air and stood quivering with fear.

'That's a good idea,' Petrucci said. 'You lot' – he gestured to the remaining police officers – 'drop your pistols on the floor and put your hands up. We don't need any of you here any longer,' he added, when they'd obeyed his order, 'so go away. But Hussein stays with us.'

With a terrified nod, Barzani turned and scurried off, the remaining police officers and the hotel staff following him. They were almost walking backwards, their eyes still fixed on the Americans.

Once they'd gone, Petrucci gestured for Hussein to come closer. 'We need you alive, Inspector, at least for the moment. If you do exactly what we tell you, you

might still walk away from this. Now, who calle
you?'

'Who are you people?' Hussein demanded.

Petrucci jabbed the barrel of his pistol sharply int
the Arab's stomach, and he bent forward, retchin
painfully.

'I'll ask you again. Who called you?'

'Michael Watkinson,' Hussein replied after a few se
onds, his voice rasping painfully. 'After Richter calle
him.'

'That bastard,' O'Hagan snarled from the doorwa
of the suite. 'I knew he was trouble right from the star
But there's nothing he can do to stop us now. We're i
the clear.'

British Embassy, Dubai

Sitting at his desk in the embassy, Michael Watkinso
was first puzzled, then alarmed. Richter had to b
wrong. He just couldn't see how the four CIA officer
who he knew had arrived in Dubai on board a Stat
Department aircraft, could possibly have been inter
cepted or suborned. But Richter's deduction about th
intentions of the Arab terrorists at Nad Al-Sheba ha
been uncannily accurate, so he couldn't simply ignor
what he said.

When he had rung Hussein to pass on Richter's mess
age, he had learned that they were currently at the Bu
Al-Arab. But when he warned that the Americans coul
be trying to plant a bomb, Hussein hadn't responde

Then Watkinson had heard a dull thud followed by loud shouting, followed by at least two gunshots.

He'd waited for Hussein to continue speaking, hoping that his warning had been in time, but slowly realization began to dawn. He held the phone close to his ear, straining to hear anything further, but all he could detect were mumbles of conversation, too indistinct to make out. Then somebody closed Hussein's mobile, ending the call, and there was only silence.

Watkinson stared at the handset for a few moments, then phoned Richter.

Crowne Plaza Hotel, Dubai

When the taxi arrived, Richter told the driver to wait. The sightseeing trip they had planned obviously wasn't going to happen, but having a car at their disposal seemed a good idea. The vehicle was sitting outside the hotel, engine running, while Richter waited for a phone call to confirm his suspicions.

The moment his mobile rang, Richter snatched it. 'Michael?'

'Wrong – it's Simpson. I've got a couple of answers for you. In the same order as you asked the questions, they are "no" and "yes – Cairo".'

'Right,' Richter replied. 'No and yes. Thanks for that. It looks like we've got major problems at this end.'

'Anything we can do to help?'

'I don't think so at the moment. I'll call you as soon as I know what's going on.'

Carole-Anne Jackson looked at him questioningly 'And "no" and "yes" mean what, exactly?'

'It means you were right. Simpson contacted Langley with two questions. I asked if the CIA employed more than one man named Grant Hutchings – the answer was no – and if the CIA team's Gulfstream diverted to Egypt. It did, to Cairo, so I think it's fairly clear what happened.'

For a moment Jackson was silent, then she looked at Richter. 'If I were a terrorist,' she said slowly, 'I'd be trying to hit a building that was unmistakably a symbol of Dubai. I'll bet they're targeting the Burj Al-Arab.'

'Makes sense,' Richter agreed. 'Let's get out of here.'

As their taxi pulled away, heading towards Al-Jumeirah Road, Richter's mobile rang again. This time it *was* Watkinson.

'They're at the Burj Al-Arab,' he announced, his voice angry. 'I passed Hussein your message, but I think the bad guys got the drop on him.'

'Shit,' Richter said. 'That's what I was afraid of. Thanks, Michael. We're on our way out there right now. You'd better brief the consul and get him moving. I know this may look like the beginning of something, but actually I think it's the end of a long, clever and very carefully planned operation.'

'What do you think these bastards want?'

'My guess,' Richter replied, 'is money. Lots and lots and lots of money. This is going to make the Great Train Robbery look like a couple of kids knocking over the sweet shop on the corner.'

Chapter Twenty

The Americans were busy. Wilson and Dawson were running through the operations to get the nuclear weapon ready. Petrucci was preparing a charge of plastic explosive, taken from one of the cases which had been wrapped, Hussein noticed with sick realization, in exactly the way Wilson had described minutes earlier. O'Hagan was checking the entire suite to ensure there were no other entrances they hadn't secured.

Hussein was lashed to an upright chair, on the suite's upper level, watching the four Americans with shocked and helpless disbelief. He'd seen the ID carried by Hutchings when they'd arrived in Dubai aboard an aircraft the CIA had told him to expect, yet they had to be impostors. There must have been a substitution, somehow and somewhere.

Not that there was anything he could do about it, because he could barely move. His hands and feet were already numb, but even if by some miracle he managed to free himself, there was no way he could overpower four armed men. They would kill him instantly, the same way they'd shot down his men outside.

The man Hussein had known as 'Roger Middleton' – Alex O'Hagan – stepped across and stood in front of him.

'Inspector Hussein, let me explain a few things to you. That device over there is a tactical nuclear weapon. It has a yield of about one kiloton, meaning one thousand tons of TNT, and we'll detonate it, right here in this suite, unless your government agrees to our demands. If that happens, this hotel will cease to exist. The Jumeirah Beach Hotel and many other nearby buildings will also be destroyed or badly damaged. I don't know the exact blast radius, but I can assure you the explosion will be devastating. Dubai will be finished as a financial centre, wiped out as a tourist attraction, and contaminated by radiation for years to come. Do you understand what I'm saying?'

Hussein nodded dumbly. He understood only too well the relative fragility of Dubai, a small strip of desert relying on tourism and high levels of outside investment. The moment confidence in the place was lost, the smart money would leave. All of the country's most ambitious projects would fail, leaving Dubai in the doldrums.

'Now,' O'Hagan continued, 'our demands are simple enough. We don't personally care whether anyone knows what's happening or not, but we're quite sure your government will want to keep this incident as secret as possible. So no police cars, no fire appliances, no helicopters. Do you understand?'

Again Hussein nodded.

'Make sure you do, because in a few minutes you'll be relaying everything we've said to the most senior police officer you know. We'll provide you with the serial number of the nuclear weapon, together with details of the location from which it was obtained. That will allow your security people to verify that the weapon is exactly what we say it is.

'You'll make it clear to them that we aren't suicide bombers, but we've all risked our lives to get this far, and if we're captured we can expect execution, so we're quite prepared to end this operation here. That means if we're attacked, we'll explode the device.

'We'll be setting this weapon to detonate on a four-hour timer. Then we'll leave here by car – one of those Rolls-Royces outside will do – and drive to the airport where our Gulfstream jet will be fully fuelled and ready to go. Only when we're clear of your airspace will we transmit the abort code enabling you to deactivate the weapon. If any attempt is made to intercept us on the way to the airport, or if our aircraft is targeted either before or after it gets airborne, we won't transmit the code, and the weapon will explode. Is that absolutely clear?'

Hussein couldn't trust himself to speak, so he just nodded again. This was, he knew, all his fault and, whatever happened in the immediate future, his head was almost certainly going to roll. If only he'd taken the time to check the Americans' identity documents properly when they arrived . . . He forced his mind back to the present.

'The last thing we want is fairly predictable. We need a payment of three billion American dollars in the form of easily negotiable and untraceable assets. Gold, silver and platinum bullion, and diamonds would do, plus cash in American dollars, Euros, pounds Sterling and Japanese yen only, bearer bonds and other financial instruments. Because of the aircraft's weight limitations, we'll accept no more than five per cent as bullion, and another five per cent as cash.'

He paused to ensure what he was saying was being understood by the bemused-looking police officer. When Hussein nodded, O'Hagan continued.

'This sum must be delivered to our aircraft within twenty-four hours – that's by twelve noon tomorrow. We'll leave the Burj Al-Arab when we've received confirmation from our associates that the total sum is on the plane. We have scanners on board that can detect forged banknotes, and assay equipment to check the bullion. For every attempt to provide forged currency or any kind of counterfeit asset, the sum demanded will increase by one hundred million dollars. If the ransom isn't delivered by the deadline, a penalty of one hundred million dollars will be added for every hour that it's delayed. OK, is there anything you don't understand?'

'No,' Hussein replied, finally finding his voice.

'Now we want you to explain everything I've told you to a senior police officer. And please don't say anything stupid,' he added.

'And I'll know if you do,' Petrucci warned him from across the room, in fluent Arabic, and Hussein realized then that he had no options left.

Jumeirah Beach Hotel, Dubai

Richter told the taxi driver to stop, and he and Jackson climbed out of the vehicle. For a few moments they stood looking at the huge offshore hotel.

'It's big, all right,' Jackson remarked.

'You've seen it before, obviously.'

'A couple of times, but I've never actually been inside. So what the hell do we do now?'

'I don't know,' Richter admitted. 'It all looks peaceful enough over there, but if Watkinson's right, that's deceptive.'

'You're sure this is extortion?'

'Yes. If it was a terrorist attack, they'd just have positioned the bomb somewhere and triggered it. And the perpetrators don't fit the profile. They're American, for starters, highly prepared and well organized, and this operation has been planned for a long time. Just finding out where those suitcase nukes were stored must have taken them months. I mean, the West only heard about the weapons a few years ago, and until now the Russians have never officially admitted they even existed. Then they had to work out some way of getting themselves into the CIS and stealing one. If they'd just intended to blow up something, they could have fabricated an IED in a couple of days. And why choose Dubai? It's not exactly a hotbed of Muslim extremism. It's a tolerant and cosmopolitan city that welcomes all races and religions. But Dubai has one thing that probably attracted them more than anything else.'

'Money,' Jackson said.

Richter nodded. 'Exactly. The city is enormously wealthy, and I'm certain that this is all about money. Let's get out of this heat. I'll buy you a drink.'

They were sitting in one of the lounges offering a view of the Burj Al-Arab when Watkinson called.

'They've made contact,' he said, 'and we need to talk Where are you?'

'The Jumeirah Beach Hotel. And you?'

'I'm in a car heading out of Dubai City, so I should be with you in about ten minutes.'

A quarter of an hour later Watkinson sat down and joined them. He took a sip of iced orange juice and put the glass down on the table. 'You were right,' he said, keeping his voice low. 'It *is* extortion, but in a whole new league. The Americans are using Inspector Hussein as their mouthpiece. They're holed up in one of the Royal Suites in the Burj Al-Arab with a tactical-yield nuclear weapon, and they're going to detonate it unless the Dubai government gives them three billion dollars within the next twenty-four hours.'

Burj Al-Arab Hotel, Dubai

The Americans were happy with the way things were going so far. Hussein had relayed all their demands to his chief superintendent at the Old Fort, who – after a brief period of flat disbelief that ended when he checked the situation with a near-hysterical Salim Barzani on a second line – had agreed to tell the Dubai government.

O'Hagan had ordered a two-watch system, with himself and Petrucci taking the first shift while Wilson and Dawson slept. At six that evening, they would change over, and again at midnight. Nothing was likely to happen before mid-morning the following day, but they hadn't come this far to fall at the last hurdle. They'd be better prepared to handle any eventuality if at least two of them were fully rested.

Jumeirah Beach Hotel, Dubai

Richter took a thoughtful sip of his Coke. 'Apart from the money, that's more or less what I expected. The Gulfstream carrying the CIA agents diverted to Cairo with a technical fault. That was where the air ambulance carrying the stolen Russian nuclear weapon landed, and so two plus two was pretty much bound to equal four. How do you think the Dubai government will react, Michael?'

'I'm not sure, to be honest. Nothing like this has ever arisen before, but my guess is they'll agree because the alternative is too horrific to contemplate. The sum demanded may be enormous, but it's probably less than the Burj Al-Arab alone would cost to rebuild. And by Dubai's standards it's pretty much small change. The Burj Dubai development alone will cost about six billion dollars before it's finished, and recent building projects around the city amount to three hundred billion. When you contrast the ransom demand with the long-term consequences for Dubai as a whole if they detonate the weapon, it's utterly insignificant.'

'So they'll just roll over and play dead?' Jackson demanded.

'If you want to put it like that, yes,' Watkinson said, 'and I don't blame them, either. There's no sign that these four men are bluffing. They supplied details of the

nuclear weapon, and about half an hour ago Vauxhall
Cross has confirmed that the serial number checks out.
They've already killed two police officers in the Burj Al-
Arab who—'

'They've killed a lot more than that,' Richter interrupted. 'I've only just made the connection. I was wrong
about Holden's premonitions diverting attention away
from Nad Al-Sheba. He was nothing to do with those
Arabs – it was much simpler than that. All those people
in Syria and Bahrain died for one reason only – so that
a team of alleged CIA officers could get a suitcase into
a high-security hotel without anyone stopping them to
see what was inside it. The last thing anyone would
think of checking would be a case carried by CIA agents
who were in the UAE at the request of the government,
and even escorted by Dubai police officers. Hell, the
Burj Al-Arab's own staff probably carried the weapon
into the hotel for them! It was a brilliant scheme.'

'And the reason they stole the nuke is obvious, too,'
Jackson observed. 'They couldn't hope to get enough
conventional high explosive into the hotel to make their
threat viable. The worst-case scenario would have been
the destruction of a couple of suites or maybe one whole
floor, and the Dubai authorities might have been prepared to risk that level of damage. To make it work they
needed something powerful enough to destroy the whole
building.'

'Exactly,' Richter agreed. 'The question is what do *we*
do now?'

'I don't think there's anything we can do, unless
you'd like to make a contribution towards the ransom,'

Watkinson said. 'I've already signalled Vauxhall Cross requesting instructions, but they'll probably just tell me to keep a watching brief. The consul will no doubt tell the Dubai government that we'll provide all the help and assistance possible, but in reality there's sod-all we can do. This is *their* problem, and they're going to have to solve it.'

'I've got two questions,' Richter said thoughtfully. 'First, is there any way of hitting the suite they're occupying before the ransom payment's made? It's a hypothetical question.'

'The answer is not easily, and it would be *very* ill-advised. The Americans have let Hussein see everything they've done so far. They've mounted explosive charges on the doors and there are no other ways into the suite. They're armed with pistols but they know they're facing the death penalty if they're captured, so if it comes to a fire-fight, they'll just trigger the nuke.'

'OK. The second question is what happens after they leave the suite. These guys are stuck in the hotel with the weapon at the moment, but how are they going to keep the threat believable once they get the money and walk?'

'They'll set the weapon on a four-hour timer before they leave the building. The delay will allow them to transmit the abort code once they're well clear of UAE airspace.'

'That's interesting.'

'Why?'

'Well, if they're telling the truth, which I wouldn't put any money on, that means there *is* an abort code. What's interesting is that most nuclear weapons don't have one. They usually rely on an external signal and an explosive charge to blow up the warhead once it's been launched, but before it actually hits the target.'

'But this weapon was specially designed by the KGB for terrorist use,' Watkinson replied. 'It was intended to be concealed and then blown up on a timer, so a code to stop the detonation does make sense.'

Burj Al-Arab Hotel, Dubai

Since Hussein had relayed the Americans' demands to his superiors, the telephones in the suite they occupied had remained silent. But in the middle of the afternoon one began ringing, and O'Hagan got up to answer it. Or, to be exact, he picked up the cordless handset, took it across to Hussein, pressed the 'answer' button and held it to his ear.

The voice at the other end spoke Arabic, with only a brief message to convey and one question to ask.

'They've agreed to your demands,' Hussein translated, 'and are hoping that everything will be completed no later than ten tomorrow morning. They would like to deliver the heavier items like bullion and cash this afternoon and I said that wouldn't be a problem. The financial instruments will take longer to prepare.'

'Good. I thought they'd see sense.' O'Hagan replaced the handset, picked up his mobile and called Roy Sutter's cellphone.

'We have a go,' he explained. 'Get to the plane within the hour, and expect to stay there until we finally leave, so take along everything you're going to need. The first consignment should arrive this afternoon, and it'll be the heavy stuff, so check the weight distribution and make sure it goes in the right place. We should be with you by late morning tomorrow.'

'We're on our way,' Sutter replied.

'Now, I'm sure we're dealing with honest and upright citizens here,' O'Hagan announced to the other three men, with a slight smirk, 'but we don't relax. I don't see how they can get to us, and the weapon is still the ace card, but we stay alert.'

Jumeirah Beach Hotel, Dubai

Watkinson received another call just as Richter and Jackson were deciding what to do about lunch. He left the lounge to answer it, and came back a few minutes later. 'The government's imposed a total news blackout. They intend to pay the ransom, then forget it happened, and make absolutely sure nothing like it can ever happen again.'

'So we just walk away and forget about it?' Jackson asked.

'Spot on,' he said with a sigh. 'Those are my direct orders. Her Majesty's Government's representatives are instructed to support and assist the local authorities in whatever way they may be requested, but are to take absolutely no action unless and until specifically directed. If you contact Langley, Carole, I think you'll find the Company will tell you pretty much the same.'

Richter said nothing, just gazed out of the window towards the Burj Al-Arab.

'And maybe you'd better talk to your secret squirrel outfit, Paul.'

'Yes, I will. I've got a couple of calls to make first.'

Something about the tone of his voice caused Watkinson to stare at him. 'You're not planning any kind of freelance operation, I hope? That would be a *really* bad idea.'

'Me?' Richter raised an eyebrow. 'Perish the thought. But what about the practicalities? Can the government raise the ransom in time?'

'That won't be a problem. They'll just draw the bullion and gemstones from their own safety deposits. The cash, bearer bonds and other stuff they'll borrow from the principal banks. They'll probably have it in place by mid-morning and, with any luck, this whole thing could be over by lunchtime tomorrow.'

Dubai International Airport

Dubai Airport has two terminals, with a third approaching completion. The biggest and busiest is Sheikh Rashid Terminal, also known as Concourse One, which handles most of the commercial traffic. Terminal Two caters mainly for regional, charter and executive flights, and the Gulfstream was parked on a small hardstanding adjacent to it.

When Sutter and Haig arrived, they were escorted straight out to the aircraft; clearly instructions had been given to ensure they weren't delayed. Haig started the Honeywell APU to haul down the cabin temperature, then stowed away their drinks and food, while Sutter rang O'Hagan's mobile to let him know they were in place.

And then there was nothing they could do but wait.

Jumeirah Beach Hotel, Dubai

Once they'd finished lunch, Jackson contacted the British Embassy in Manama using her cellphone, but there were no messages or instructions for her from Langley.

Richter's call to Hammersmith was short and inconclusive. His section had received no tasking from anyone involved in the situation in Dubai so, as far as Richard Simpson was concerned, there was nothing for Richter to do.

'I don't like this any more than you do,' Simpson complained, 'and if I had my way I wouldn't even talk to these bastards. I'd empty the building, call up a couple of helicopter gunships and strafe the top floors of the hotel. No warning, no negotiation. With any luck, that would kill everybody inside the suite and not give them time to detonate the weapon. All it would need would be a touch of paint and a few new carpets.' Clearly, Richter realized, Simpson had never seen the interior decor and furnishings of the Burj Al-Arab. 'And even if the weapon did blow, I'd still have three big ones left in the kitty to rebuild it. But it isn't my hotel, and it isn't my problem. Or yours, either. Let the Dubai authorities sort this out themselves. This isn't a good time for any kind of cowboy action from you.'

'Oddly enough, the local Six rep told me very much the same thing.'

'So you shouldn't have any trouble understanding the message, should you? Just watch what happens tomorrow, and keep me informed.'

'Anything new from your people?' Jackson asked him as he finished the call.

Richter shook his head. 'Pretty much the same as the message we got from Watkinson. They're probably right, of course, but it really goes against the grain to let these bastards walk away with three billion dollars.'

'But there really isn't any alternative, is there? Neither of us has any official standing here in Dubai, and even if we had, what *could* we do? The government has already agreed to pay them, so we'd get no help from the police or anyone else. There are four armed terrorists sitting in an inaccessible suite at the top of the tallest hotel in Dubai, and guarding a primed tactical nuclear weapon. How the hell could we even get inside the building, far less do anything to take these guys down? Our best plan is to just do what everyone's telling us, which is to walk away, pretend nothing's happening, and enjoy the rest of our time here.' Jackson paused and eyed Richter closely. 'But you're not going to do that, are you? I can read it in your eyes.'

Richter grinned. 'I don't know,' he replied. 'You're quite right. There *is* nothing we can do, but something about this still niggles me.'

'You mean apart from the three billion dollars' ransom?'

'Yes. I can't put my finger on it, but I have the distinct feeling that there's another component, some other dimension that we're missing.'

'I don't agree. To me, this just looks like a really big extortion job.'

'Maybe.' Richter still didn't sound even slightly convinced. He reached for his coffee cup, then stopped and again stared through the window towards the elegantly stunning white offshore hotel. 'Christ,' he muttered. 'Could that be it?'

'What?'

'Listen, we still don't know who these people really are, do we?'

Jackson shook her head. 'We know they're American, or at least able to pass as Americans, but that's all. We'll probably never know their identities, unless one of them does something stupid when he spends his share of the ransom and gets picked up that way. At least we know what they want.'

'Are you quite sure about that?' Richter asked. 'Are you certain it's just the money?'

'What else could it be?'

Richter didn't answer directly, but instead changed tack. 'Has anything ever struck you as familiar about Dubai? Anything that reminds you of another city?'

Jackson gave him a puzzled stare. 'I'm not that good at guessing games, Paul, so why don't you just tell me what's on your mind?

'I'm thinking about the commercial centre, around Shaikh Zayed Road.'

'And that means what, exactly?'

'Maybe nothing, maybe everything. Excuse me, I'm going to make a phone call.'

'Who are you calling?'

'A man I know in Moscow,' Richter replied, as h
walked away.

Dubai International Airport

Sutter and Haig had been waiting in the Gulfstream fo
nearly an hour when a small convoy arrived, two polic
cars flanking a large armoured van.

Haig opened the cabin door as the vehicles came t
a halt beside the aircraft. Alert for any tricks, the tw
Americans watched from opposite ends of the cabin a
four men carried a *lot* of steel boxes up the steps int
the aircraft.

The moment the delivery was finished, Haig secure
the Gulfstream's outside door. None of the boxes wa
locked, and in minutes they were all open. Sutter did
rapid count, checking the listed weight and purity o
the bars of gold, silver and platinum they contained
then called O'Hagan again.

'Seems like we're in business,' he declared. 'I recko
we've got around one-fifty mil in bullion here. We'll d
random sampling now, and I'll only call you again i
we hit a problem.'

Jumeirah Beach Hotel, Dubai

Getting through to Moscow wasn't easy, even using th
number Richter obtained from Hammersmith. He kep
getting either an engaged signal, which was at leas
encouraging because it implied that there *was* a phon

t the other end, or complete silence. But he persevered
nd eventually his call was answered.

'Viktor?' he began. 'It's Paul Richter.'

'I don't . . . Ah, yes, Paul. I had a feeling you might
ecide to call me. How can I help you?'

'This line isn't secure, General, so I must be circum-
pect. We understand that you lost something recently,
 piece of military hardware. Do you recall the inci-
ent?'

'Yes, of course. We immediately advised all interested
arties, and I have every confidence that the missing
quipment will be recovered soon.'

'Actually, I think it's already been found in Dubai.'

'Dubai?' There was a pause. 'I didn't know that. I will
ave to confer with our diplomats in the Emirates.'

'They probably won't know anything about it yet,
ecause the device is being used as part of a negotiation.
Ve're trying hard to ensure that nothing happens that
night embarrass either the Dubai government – or the
quipment's manufacturer.'

'You mean it's not in your hands?'

'Far from it. That's why I've got some questions. First,
oes it incorporate a timer?'

'Yes,' Bykov replied. 'Those devices all had timing
ircuits incorporated so they could be positioned and
hen activated later.'

'My second question concerns the abort code. We are
ed to believe that once the timer was set the device
ouldn't be deactivated without a special code. Is that
orrect?'

'Yes. Each device had a unique abort code. Is that all
ou need to know?'

'Just one other matter, General.' Richter asked a fina question, and Bykov replied immediately.

'No, never. It was always kept separately. In fact, have it here in my office.'

This was better than Richter had hoped. 'Can you le me have it?' he asked.

'No, I'm afraid not,' Bykov said. 'For obvious rea sons, it's classified.' He paused. 'If it's important, I car try to obtain permission to release it to you. Would tha be satisfactory?'

'Yes, General, as long as it doesn't take you too long We're on a deadline out here, and need that informatior by tomorrow morning.'

'I see.' Again Bykov paused. 'Did you have any trouble getting through to me today?' he asked, in ar apparent non sequitur, then chuckled. 'The Moscow telephone system is perhaps not as efficient as it coulc be. Let me give you the number of my personal mobile.

Richter took a small notebook and pen from his jacke pocket.

'The number is seven three four, eight six nine, two six five eight,' Bykov continued, 'and obviously you have to prefix it with the Moscow dialling code. Please read it back to me so I know you've copied it correctly.

'Seven three four, eight six nine, two six five eight.'

'Yes, that's correct. I'll try to get clearance to disclose the other information to you, but I'm not especially hopeful that it will be granted in time. May I wish you good luck, and don't forget to try my number.'

Before Richter went back into the hotel, he rang several other numbers on his mobile, but in every case all he got was the 'number unobtainable' tone.

Dubai International Airport

The next delivery of boxes held cash. Sutter and Haig had already stowed the bullion safely, taking careful account of the aircraft's centre of gravity, and they'd worked out where the money should go. It was going to be a really tight fit in the cabin on the way out of Emirates airspace, but Sutter doubted if anyone would complain.

Taking samples at random, Haig had finished his checks on the bullion, and each bar had been exactly as its accompanying documentation had described. It certainly looked as if the Dubai authorities were playing it straight, but Sutter didn't trust anyone, and neither did Haig, so they then started checking the bank notes as well.

Dubai

'Michael,' Richter began when Watkinson answered, 'we need to talk urgently. I've just discovered something that must be relayed to the Dubai government immediately. Carole and I are on our way to the embassy now, and this isn't something I can talk about over the phone.' Their taxi was speeding along Al-Jumeirah Road.

'For Christ's sake, Paul, weren't our orders clear enough? I thought you understood that we'd be taking no part in this affair.'

'I did, and I do, but what I've found out may mean

the Dubai government has to handle the situation com
pletely differently. Look, let me explain it to you, and to
the consul as well, if you like, and then you can decide
what to do about it. But I'll tell you this for nothing,
Michael, if you *don't* tell the Dubai authorities what I've
found out, then sometime tomorrow relations between
Britain and the UAE will plummet to an all-time low.'

Chapter Twenty-One

'Who are these people?' George Arthur Graham demanded somewhat testily of his subordinate as the four of them sat down around a table.

Watkinson had taken Richter at his word, and had requested that the consul attend the meeting, though it had been clear from the start that Her Britannic Majesty's Consul General to Dubai and the Northern Emirates had not been particularly keen on talking to either of them, or even having them inside the building.

'These people,' Richter snapped, 'are sitting in this room with you, so the least you can do is exercise a little common courtesy and talk to us directly, instead of acting like we're a couple of dog turds you've just spotted on your carpet.'

The consul – his initials may have spelt 'gag', but there was no humour in the man – reacted as if somebody had just punched him in the stomach. Richter guessed that few people ever dared address him in such a manner.

'Who we are isn't particularly important,' Richter continued. 'It's what we've got to tell you that matters. But, since you've asked, this is Carole-Anne Jackson of the CIA who's currently on secondment to the Manama office of the SIS.'

411

Jackson smiled sweetly at Graham, who still seemed to be struggling to find words.

'My name's Paul Richter, and I work for an outfit called the Foreign Operations Executive. It's loosely associated with the SIS in London, and if you've never heard of FOE, that's because nobody thinks you've ever had a *need* to know about it.'

Watkinson interjected, the oil not entirely smoothing the troubled waters. 'Richter here is the officer who deduced what was happening at Nad Al-Sheba on Saturday, sir. Miss Jackson was also involved.'

'I don't care who you are or what outfit you work for,' Graham snarled. 'You will accord proper respect to senior diplomats, particularly when invited into the embassy itself.'

'Respect cuts both ways,' Richter replied, equally sharply, 'and if you keep feeding me this line of crap I'll walk straight out of here.'

'Pardon me for interrupting this high-level pissing contest,' Carole-Anne Jackson said sweetly, 'but this isn't actually achieving anything except to provide an impressive display of testosterone. We're running short of time now, so why don't you all *shut the fuck up*, and let's discuss what we've found out?'

The three men stared at her with varying expressions of shock. Unexpectedly, it was Graham who recovered first. 'Very well. I accept we got off to a bad start. What is this information you've obtained?'

'First, let me do a quick recap,' Richter said. 'Four terrorists have smuggled a nuclear weapon into the Burj Al-Arab and will detonate it unless the Dubai government pays them three billion dollars. Once they've got it, they'll climb into their Gulfstream and head off into the wide blue yonder. While making their getaway, they'll set the nuclear device to explode on a timer, and then radio the abort code to the Dubai government so that the bomb can then be disarmed. Is that a fair summary?' Watkinson and Graham both nodded.

'Now, I asked Carole this same question, but she didn't know what the hell I was talking about. Does the area around Shaikh Zayed Road remind you of anywhere else? And, before you answer that, let me ask you another – why did the terrorists pick the Burj Al-Arab?'

'The answer to your second question's easy,' Watkinson replied. 'Because the Burj is Dubai's best-known landmark, and it's instantly recognizable worldwide.'

Richter nodded encouragement. 'But why did they pick *that* particular building if all they wanted to do was threaten the government? Why not pick somewhere with a much larger population density? Take the worst-case scenario: if that weapon detonates, the Burj Al-Arab will be destroyed. It would be a spectacular bang, of course, but the loss of life would be fairly insignificant, precisely because of the hotel's offshore location. But if they'd chosen somewhere like the Crowne Plaza – which would have been no more difficult tactically – the potential death toll would have been enormous, and that would have provided a much greater lever to threaten the government. So why the Burj?'

Neither man replied, but Richter didn't seem surprised.

'Let me take it from the beginning. You're right, the Burj is as much a symbol of this city as the Houses of

Parliament are for London, or the Eiffel Tower for Paris. Or the Twin Towers used to be for New York. I mentioned Shaikh Zayed Road, because many people think that district resembles Manhattan.'

'I can see where you're going with this, but it's preposterous,' Watkinson said. 'You're trying to equate Dubai with New York but there's no real similarity at all.'

'You're wrong, Michael,' Richter said quietly. 'Both cities are symbols of their countries, and both are major financial centres – or, at least, that's what Dubai is trying to become. Both have – or had in the case of New York – iconic buildings that immediately identify them.'

'So what are you suggesting?' George Graham sounded puzzled.

'I'm suggesting that the huge ransom demand is only the secondary reason for this attack, but that's what everyone's become focused on. As a result, they're not seeing the bigger picture. They haven't recognized the real reason why there's now a suitcase nuke sitting primed and ready at the top of the Burj Al-Arab.'

'And that reason is what?' Graham persisted.

'This attack has almost nothing to do with money, and everything to do with revenge. These four Americans haven't the slightest intention of transmitting the abort code for their weapon. They intend to take the money and run, leaving the bomb still ticking, and laughing at the stupid Arabs for believing them. And when it detonates, the Burj Al-Arab will come crashing down just the way the Twin Towers did in New York. They've picked Dubai and the Burj for the same reason that Osama bin Laden picked New York and the World

Trade Center – because they're outstanding symbols of those cities. They intend to visit upon Dubai the same sort of devastation and catastrophe that a handful of Arab terrorists managed to achieve in Manhattan. Revenge for 9/11 – that's the *real* reason for all this, and that's what nobody here in the government of Dubai has worked out yet.'

'And what about the ransom?' Watkinson asked. 'If you're right and this is a revenge attack, why didn't they just detonate the bomb as soon as they got it into place?'

'The ransom is payment for the job,' Richter replied. 'This has been a long and complex operation, and these four guys intend to be well rewarded for their efforts.'

'This is all very interesting, Mr Richter,' Graham interrupted, 'but it's mere speculation. You haven't talked to these terrorists, so you can't be certain of what you're saying. The Dubai government is satisfied that this is just a case of extortion and that, once the ransom demand has been met, the incident will end peacefully. And I agree with them.'

'You're wrong, and so's the Dubai government, and I can prove it.'

'How?' Watkinson demanded anxiously.

'You really believe the terrorists will transmit the abort code once they're clear of Emirates' airspace?' Richter asked, and the two men nodded. 'Well, I know that they won't, for one very simple reason.'

'What's that?'

'Because they haven't got the fucking abort code, that's why.'

Dubai International Airport

They'd opened thirty cash boxes in all and run five hundred notes of various currencies through the forgery detector, and every one had proved genuine.

That suggested the Dubai authorities were going to comply with O'Hagan's demands, and so there should be no problems the following morning, when the financial instruments were due to be delivered.

The two men would stay on board the Gulfstream that night, with the cabin door locked and surrounded by cash and bullion, and they both thought they'd sleep perfectly well. With any luck, Sutter thought, as he phoned O'Hagan's mobile to confirm the authenticity of the money, they'd be on their way out of the UAE in less than eighteen hours.

British Embassy, Dubai

A long silence followed Richter's words, finally broken by Michael Watkinson. 'How do you know that?' he demanded.

'I know because I've got the right contacts and I know what questions to ask. I called an officer named Viktor Bykov who's number three in the hierarchy of the GRU, the Russian military intelligence organization. He knew all about the suitcase bomb. In fact, he was responsible for releasing details of the theft to the West. He told me that the abort code was *never* stored with the weapon. It was always kept in a sealed envelope, along with the maintenance and other documentation. All the Americans took from Zarechnyy was the nuke, and I know that because Bykov had everything else sitting on his desk at the Aquarium.'

'Aquarium?' George Graham queried. 'I don't—'

'It's a slang term for GRU headquarters,' Jackson told him. 'It's a building at the Khodinka airfield in Moscow.'

'The Americans,' Richter repeated, 'have *only* got the weapon. They haven't got the abort code, so there's no way they can transmit it to the Dubai government. If they do set the timer, it's because they intend that weapon to detonate.'

'But they might only pretend to set the timer running,' Graham suggested, with a hint of desperation.

'In that case, why bother with getting a genuine nuke at all? They could have just knocked up a convincing fake and used that instead. No, I'm certain the weapon is real, and unless somebody does something pretty damn quickly it's going to explode. And I don't want to even think about the consequences of a group of American terrorists detonating a Russian nuclear weapon in Dubai.'

'I'm still not convinced,' Graham said, stubbornly.

'That's your decision, but if you won't do anything, I'll just shove the whole thing to my boss back in London. He's extremely persuasive, and I've no doubt he'll be kicking any number of aristocratic arses in the FCO before the afternoon's over just to get things moving. If he does, you'll probably be first in the queue down at the job centre next week. Why not tell the Dubai government what we suspect? Just tell them that we have received information suggesting the terrorists don't have the weapon's abort code and leave it at that. If they do nothing, it's their problem, but at least you'll have told them. That way you'll have done all you can.'

Crowne Plaza Hotel, Dubai

'What do you think they'll do?' Jackson asked Richter as they re-entered their hotel.

'I don't know. If Watkinson does check with Bykov through Vauxhall Cross, he'll be able to confirm what I've said, but that only makes the situation worse, not better. Until I stuck my oar in, the Dubai government was probably resigned to paying the money and saving the Burj. Now, whether they deliver the rest of the funds or dig their heels in and refuse, there's a good chance there'll be a hell of a bang down at Jumeirah Beach tomorrow. Right now, I can only see one way of stopping this.'

'How?'

'Play along with the terrorists: give them the ransom and let them leave the hotel. Then get a team into the suite to disarm the weapon, and stop the terrorists at the airport, or wherever, and retrieve the loot.'

Jackson smiled gently. 'It sounds easy the way you say it,' she said, 'but there are a couple of problems with that scenario.'

'I know, but it's the only way I can see this business ending without that nuke going off. Every other approach is likely to involve a fire-fight at the Burj, and the possibility that the terrorists will go ahead and trigger the weapon.'

They sat down at an empty table and placed their order for drinks.

'I do have one ace up my sleeve that nobody knows about,' Richter revealed. 'When I talked to Viktor Bykov, he—'

'Oh, yes, I meant to ask you about him,' Jackson interrupted, 'but the atmosphere back at the embassy didn't seem conducive to a discussion about your precise relationship with a high-ranking officer in the GRU.'

Richter grinned. 'Honestly, it's not as bad as it sounds. I first ran into him in France a while ago, during a covert op. He survived, but his boss didn't, and I think he felt grateful to me, despite the fact that we managed to completely foul up the Russian plan. Since then, I've worked with him in Russia, on a separate operation, and we've enjoyed what you might call cautiously friendly relations.

'Anyway, he refused to tell me the abort code for the stolen weapon because it's classified. He said he'd try to get it declassified, but wasn't very hopeful of doing that quickly enough. But he insisted on giving me his mobile phone number, so that I could contact him immediately. In fact, he made me write it down.'

Richter pulled out his notebook to show Jackson what he'd written – 734 869 2658.

'So, you've got his mobile number. So what?'

'Look at it again, Carole. Bykov reminded me that I had to prefix it with the Moscow dialling code.'

'Hang on a minute. If it's a mobile, you never prefix

it with an area code. All you put in front is the country code, and for Russia that's a seven.'

'Exactly, and the moment he said that, I guessed he was actually telling me something else. And Russian telephone numbers are seven digits long, not ten. The area code adds another three numbers – like zero-nine-five for Moscow – making ten in all, but all ten-digit Russian numbers begin with a zero, not a seven.'

'Unless he was knocking off the leading zero and adding the Russian country code. That's a seven. That would work.'

Richter shook his head. 'No. Bykov insisted I had to add the Moscow dialling code. And I tried dialling that number, with and without the country code for Russia and the area code for Moscow. Every time it came back as number unobtainable. That' – Richter pointed at the page of his notebook – 'isn't a telephone number in Russia, or anywhere else. I think what Bykov gave me is actually the abort code for the weapon now sitting in the Burj Al-Arab Hotel.'

'Are you sure?' Jackson sounded far from certain.

'No, I'm not. At least, I'm not convinced enough to give the number to Graham. I'd be prepared to input it into the weapon myself, but I wouldn't ask anyone else to try it, just in case I'm completely wrong.'

Chapter Twenty-Two

The police arrived at the Crowne Plaza at nine, and within fifteen minutes Richter and Jackson were sitting in the back of a Dubai police car – a white Mercedes saloon with dark green doors sign-written in Arabic – and driving to Al-Etihad Street.

At the headquarters, they were ushered into a comfortable interview room. The door soon opened to admit a very tall thin Arab with a heavy black beard, wearing the uniform of a senior police officer. He introduced himself as Chief Inspector Hafez Ghul and, like almost every other resident of Dubai that Richter had met so far, spoke perfect English.

'Thank you for agreeing to meet us here,' Ghul began. 'I've been in contact with the government division organizing the ransom payment, and they've decided to delay delivery of the final tranche to allow us time to review the situation. Despite this, the last instalment of the ransom will be delivered to the aircraft within three hours, so we've very little time left. Now, why are you so certain the terrorists don't have the abort code for the weapon?'

Richter quickly recounted his conversation with Viktor Bykov.

'You're sure this Russian intelligence officer has no reason to try and mislead you?'

'No. In fact, absolutely the reverse,' Richter replied firmly. 'If that bomb detonates, experts would probably be able to establish that it was of Russian origin, and that's the last thing the government of the CIS would want. If Bykov could have told me the abort code without compromising his position, I'm sure he would have done so.'

For the moment, he decided not to mention Bykov's 'mobile phone number'.

'So these terrorists are lying about something. It's even possible that they don't have a nuclear device in the hotel at all, but that seems the least likely scenario, as they've supplied the serial number of the weapon to us and Inspector Hussein has actually seen it. If they *do* genuinely have the weapon, then either they've no intention of setting the timer, and their threat is a bluff, or they *will* set it and reduce the Burj Al-Arab to rubble.' Ghul glanced at his watch and looked back at Richter. 'So we must consider our options quickly. What would you recommend?'

'It's my belief that these Americans want revenge for the 9/11 attack on New York as much as they want the ransom money, so I'm certain that they *do* have the weapon and they *will* set the timer. And as that's the worst-case scenario, we might just as well work on that.

'I think there are only two options. Either we attack them while they're still holed up in the Burj, or we get into the suite immediately they've gone. Once they've left the building, they no longer have access to the nuclear weapon and they can easily be stopped by the police. There might be an exchange of fire, but there are only four of them armed with handguns, so the outcome shouldn't be in any doubt. The aircraft can also be disabled – just have a sniper shoot out the tyres.'

The others nodded reluctant agreement with his summary.

'Right, those are the options, but there are problems with both of them. Assaulting the suite would be difficult and dangerous. Dubai isn't equipped for this kind of situation. Countries faced with serious terrorist threats tend to keep highly trained paramilitary forces on standby, but not here. If we could call on the SAS, an assault might be worth considering, but even then it would prove very difficult. The suite is situated near the very top of the hotel. They've booby-trapped the doors, and the only other way in is through the windows. Try abseiling down from the helicopter landing pad, and that would become immediately obvious.

'If you went in through the doors, you'd probably lose the first wave of your troops to the explosive charges, and then the terrorists would fight back. They seem pretty professional, so you'd lose even more men in the fire-fight that would follow. And remember, they've got nothing left to lose. They know that if they're captured, they're sure to be executed, so there's no reason why they wouldn't detonate the bomb. That's the worst option, by far. The second is to wait until they've actually left the hotel. The downside is that by then the weapon will have been armed. You've been told that they'll set the timer for a period of four hours?'

'Yes,' Ghul nodded. 'They said that would allow them time to get well clear of the area before transmitting the abort code.'

'Well, my guess is that they'll set it for a much shorter time than that. All they need do is get airborne because once they're off the runway, the sooner the bomb goes off the better for them. In the subsequent chaos and confusion, the last thing anyone will be thinking about is keeping track of their aircraft. I reckon they'll set the fuse for two hours, tops.'

'So, what's your recommendation?'

'Make the payment, then let the terrorists get away from the hotel, but take them out somewhere between there and the airport.'

Ghul paused for a few moments before he spoke. 'I'll convey your recommendation to my superiors, though I can't guarantee their agreement. There only seems one other matter to consider – how do we defuse the weapon if we don't have the abort code?'

Richter leant forward. 'I may be able to help with that.'

Burj Al-Arab Hotel, Dubai

They were waiting only for the financial instruments – the bearer bonds and so on – to arrive, and then they could leave. A negotiator had confirmed, through Hussein, that delivery of these might occur later than they'd hoped, but still within the timescale specified.

As far as O'Hagan could see, they would be on their way out of the hotel no later than noon.

olice headquarters, Dubai

. little before eleven, Hafez Ghul returned to the inter-
iew room and sat down heavily. He didn't look happy.

'I'm sorry to say that my government doesn't believe
ne terrorists intend to detonate the bomb. The minister
ninks they're only interested in the ransom and, as long
s it's paid, that will be the end of the matter.'

'They're wrong,' Richter said flatly.

'I agree,' Ghul replied. 'What you've said makes too
nuch sense to be ignored.'

'Is there anything you can do to change their mind?'

'No.' Ghul shook his head. 'You have to understand
ur Arab mentality. The decision has been made, and
nat decision will now stand, no matter what further
vidence anyone can produce.'

'But what about the abort code?' Richter demanded
n frustration. 'You told them that the terrorists couldn't
ossibly know it?'

'Of course, but one of the government intelligence
dvisers believes you're wrong, and that they *do* have
ne code. He's certain that the number you were given
s just a piece of disinformation. He's obtained further
etails about the theft of the weapon. Apparently an
dministrator was involved who had access to some of
ne documentation and so could have supplied the abort
ode to the Americans.'

'Yes, but how—?'

'I'm sorry, Mr Richter. That was what the government
vanted to hear, and that's what they did hear, whether
: was the plain unvarnished truth or a complete fiction.

They've also instructed me to tell you that under n⟨
circumstances are you to take any further part in thi⟨
operation.'

'Message received. So what can we do now?'

'Apart from putting as much distance as we ca⟨
between ourselves and Jumeirah Beach in the nex⟨
ninety minutes, obviously?' Carole-Anne Jackson inter⟨
jected.

'Exactly.' Ghul favoured her with a smile, but he wa⟨
clearly uncomfortable about having a woman in th⟨
room, especially one Richter appeared to regard as a⟨
equal. 'Despite my instructions, I still believe you'r⟨
right. But what *can* we do?'

Richter thought for a few seconds. 'So the Duba⟨
government's going to follow the terrorists' demands t⟨
the letter? They're not going to try to delay them on th⟨
way?'

'No,' Ghul said, 'but they're also not clearing th⟨
roads for them.'

'Good,' Richter said. 'Once you know they've left⟨
could you arrange a convenient accident somewhere⟨
Something to delay them slightly?'

'That should be easy. We have enough accidents her⟨
as it is.'

'And can you get me a helicopter – an arme⟨
helicopter?'

'Possibly.' Ghul paused to think. 'There's a Jet Range⟨
at the International Airport, and a Bell 212 down a⟨
Minhad Air Force Base, just a few kilometres south⟨
west of here. They're not normally armed, but the 21⟨
could be. We've a couple of miniguns stored at Minhad.'

'Excellent,' Richter said. 'Have a minigun mounte⟨

n the Bell 212, and get it here as quickly as possible. If that's going to be difficult, just organize the Jet Ranger, and I'll have to forget about the weapon.'

'You have a plan?' Jackson asked, as the police officer left the room.

'Of a sort, I suppose. The chopper can take me to the landing pad at the top of the Burj. From there, I can get into the suite and disarm the nuke once the bad guys have left. Then I'll fly the Bell over to the airport and stop the Gulfstream.'

'Jesus. I always thought a man with a plan was a dangerous thing. Just a few grey areas there, don't you think? Like how are you going to get into the suite? And that's just for starters.'

'I've got a few ideas,' Richter said, 'but you're right – it's not going to be easy.'

Ghul returned moments later. 'We're in luck,' he announced. 'One of the miniguns was already mounted in the Bell, and the ammunition drum is being fitted right now. They'll call me as soon as it's ready for take-off.'

'Excellent. Two other things. Can you arrange for the helicopter to bring some plastic explosive and short-fuse detonators and a complete climbing kit? I'd prefer a Mitchell Climbing System or a Double Bungie Rope Walker but if they can't find either of those, an ordinary abseiling kit will do.'

'You're going to get inside from the helicopter pad? Do you have any idea how high that is?'

'About two hundred and fifty metres, I reckon,' Richter replied.

'Heights don't bother you?' Ghul asked.

'No. Falling scares the shit out of me, but heights don't bother me at all.'

Dubai International Airport

Just after eleven-thirty a grey Mercedes drove onto the hardstanding and stopped beside the Gulfstream. In most respects, the aircraft was ready for take-off, after a final refuelling carried out first thing that morning to replenish the fuel used by the APU. The only thing left was the balance of the ransom, and Sutter guessed that was in the Mercedes.

Twenty minutes later, Haig had examined enough of the bearer bonds and letters of credit to satisfy himself that they were genuine. Sutter called O'Hagan's number on his mobile.

'That's everything,' he said. 'Over to you.'

Burj Al-Arab Hotel, Dubai

O'Hagan closed his phone. 'We've got it,' he announced. 'Let's get out of here.'

Petrucci walked across to Hussein, who was still lashed to the chair. The police officer welcomed the news implied by O'Hagan's remark. At last his ordeal was nearly over.

'I'm going to call the lobby,' Petrucci explained. 'Tell them we'll be down in a few minutes and to have a car ready. Warn them that we've placed explosives on the doors, so if anyone attempts to enter the suite in the next three hours, the charges will explode. They must wait until we transmit the abort code for the weapon, and then we'll tell them how to get in.'

Petrucci called the lobby, and Hussein carefully passed on the message to the staff waiting anxiously below.

'Very good,' Petrucci said, ending the call. He picked up a bag and moved away.

Standing right beside the nuclear weapon, O'Hagan input numbers into a keypad, then closed the lid of the box that contained the device. The other two men picked up their bags and checked their pistols.

O'Hagan glanced around the suite to ensure they'd left nothing of importance, then walked across to Hussein. He pulled a length of tape from a roll and fastened it across the police officer's mouth to silence him.

'It's been a pleasure doing business here in Dubai, Inspector,' he said. 'We're leaving now, but before we go I'd like to tell you a little story.

'In 2001, none of us here even knew each other. We were all ex-military or ex-Agency, and were living and working in New York. It was hot in the summer and cold in the winter, but it's a great city for the most part. All that changed on the eleventh of September that year when a bunch of Arab fanatics steered a couple of hijacked aircraft into the World Trade Center buildings. Nearly three thousand innocent people died in that attack, but what's more important is that the four of us on this mission and the two pilots waiting at the airport lost close family members who happened to be inside those two buildings. When the dust finally settled, three of us had lost wives, two brothers, and I'd lost both my sons as well. My whole family destroyed in just a few seconds. And all because a bunch of *fucking Arab lunatic* decided to declare war on America.'

He paused as if to calm himself, and then continued 'This, you see, is the first real counter-attack. Forge Afghanistan – that was just a knee-jerk reaction by bunch of politicians. And Iraq was nothing to do with Al-Qaeda – that whole operation was just so Uncle San could get his hands on Saddam's oilfields, nothing else But this little party? This is the real thing. When we're done, the Burj Al-Arab will be a pile of radioactive rubbl sitting at the end of a melted causeway. You knock ou towers down, and we'll knock yours down, and Duba will be finished for ever. An eye for an eye, all that kin of thing. As a good Muslim, you should understand that.

Hussein's eyes were wide and desperate, his hea shaking from side to side.

O'Hagan smiled at him. 'Your government believe we've set the timer for four hours, but I actually set i for sixty minutes. And they think we'll transmit th abort code, but we won't, because we have no clue wha the code is, or even if there is one. Now we've activate the weapon, there's nothing anyone can do to stop i exploding. In about fifty-five minutes you'll find out i Allah really is waiting for you. My guess is that he isn' but I'm just a crude infidel, so what do I know? O'Hagan smiled briefly and turned away.

Petrucci had positioned a wad of plastic explosive o one of the double doors, and thrust into it was a spring loaded wire, hanging down from a battery-powere delayed-action detonator.

O'Hagan flicked a switch on the detonator, looped th

nd of the wire over the other door's handle, and pulled
e door closed behind him. Ten seconds later the charge
as automatically armed, and would explode the
oment the wire was pulled more than a couple of mil-
metres out of the detonator by, for example, somebody
oening the suite door.

plice headquarters, Dubai

've just heard from the Burj Al-Arab,' Ghul announced,
turning to the interview room. 'The Americans are
out to leave the hotel.'

'Any news about that helicopter?'

'Yes. It should be here in less than ten minutes.'

urj Al-Arab Hotel, Dubai

'Hagan stepped out of the elevator and looked round.
he lobby was virtually empty, with only a handful of
anagement staff, including Salim Barzani, waiting
ere.

Without a word, the four Americans walked out of
e hotel. A white Rolls-Royce Silver Seraph limousine
ood waiting outside, engine running, rear doors open.
hey were about thirty kilometres from the airport,
most home and dry.

The car pulled away in virtual silence, heading along
e causeway leading to the mainland.

'I could get used to this,' Petrucci remarked, sinking
ack in the leather seat.

'There's no reason why you shouldn't,' O'Hagan
replied, 'but we're not through with this yet, so sta
sharp.'

Al-Etihad Street, Dubai

The Bell landed on the tarmac outside police head
quarters, as Ghul, Richter and Jackson stood watching
The pilot signalled them to approach, and they crosse
the road towards the aircraft.

The minigun was mounted inside the rear cabin, be
side the open doorway. They climbed inside, sat dow
and put on seatbelts and headsets. Immediately, th
noise of the two Pratt and Whitney turbine engine
dropped to a more bearable level.

Moments later, the helicopter lifted off and swun
round to port, climbing rapidly as the pilot started th
transit to Jumeirah Beach.

Dubai

The Seraph was accelerating steadily along Al-Jumeira
Road when the driver saw brake lights in front of hi
and slowed down.

'What's wrong?' O'Hagan growled.

'An accident, sir. It happens all the time. People driv
too fast along this road, even though we've got a lot c
slow-moving trucks because of the building work.'

The Rolls-Royce stopped completely, and they peere
through the windscreen. A cement lorry had pulled ou

overtake another vehicle of the same type, and some-
ow the two trucks had collided. In fact, they seemed
have become virtually welded together, completely
locking the road. Two men in bright blue overalls, obvi-
usly the drivers, were standing beside the vehicles yell-
g at each other. It was clearly going to take some time
clear the road.

'That's all we needed,' Wilson muttered darkly.

'I don't like this,' O'Hagan said. 'This could be delib-
rate, to delay us.' He glanced at the traffic behind
em. 'I don't care how you do it, but get us out of
ere.'

'But there's nowhere to go, sir.' The driver gestured
t the chaos.

O'Hagan pulled out his pistol and waved it in front
f the man's face. 'Find a way,' he snapped, 'or I'll shoot
ou and drive the fucking car myself.'

Ten minutes later, the Rolls-Royce was edging along
side street just to the south of Al-Jumeirah Road. It was
till caught in a queue of traffic, because other drivers
ad had exactly the same idea, but at least it was moving.

O'Hagan was pleased. If the accident back there
ad been an attempt to stop them reaching the airport,
had failed. They would get there a little later than
lanned, but that was all.

urj Al-Arab Hotel, Dubai

he hotel looked almost as impressive from the air as it
id from the ground, but none of them had any interest
n its aesthetic appeal. They were staring down at the

helipad on the twenty-eighth floor, which looked abou
the same size – and just about as fragile – as a dinne
plate.

Even when the Bell touched down on it, the helipa
still seemed tiny. Two men were waiting by the step:
Ghul having used his mobile to warn the hotel the
would be landing.

'Chief Inspector Ghul? My name's Salim Barzani, an
I'm the manager. I was told no action was to be take
until after the Americans had left Dubai.'

'I've been given new orders,' Ghul said. 'We must g
into the suite as soon as possible. How many entrance
does it have?'

'You can't use any of the doors,' Barzani said firmly
'They're wired with explosives. We must wait until w
receive instructions from the Americans on how to ope
them.'

'We can't,' Richter said. 'We just don't have time. Th
suite's three floors below us – right?' Barzani noddec
'OK. I'll get ready.'

'Have you done this before? Climbing and abseiling
I mean?' Jackson asked uncertainly.

'Only a little,' Richter admitted, 'but I know th
technique.'

'You're mad,' she said, as the two of them heade
back to the Bell.

'Probably, but right now we're pretty much out c
options. Here, give me a hand putting on this gear.'

'What is it?' Jackson asked, looking at the harnesses

'It's called a Mitchell Climbing System. The problen
with abseiling is that it's very good at descents, bu

limbing back up the rope is a bitch. With one of these,
can come up as fast as I go down.'

Richter pulled out his notebook and put it in his
ouser pocket. He then buckled on the two harnesses
nd ran the long ascender cord through the rollers on
ie chest plate, leaving the cord and its two attachments
the Stiff Step at the lower end, and the Ultrascender
t the other – dangling free in front of him.

'Barzani's just told me there are two maintenance cra-
les you can use,' Ghul said, walking over to the heli-
opter, 'but they're both down at the base of the tower.'

For a moment Richter looked interested, then shook
is head. 'They'll take too long to get up here. I'll have
) use the rope. Secure it to the staircase supports on
ie lower level.'

Ghul took one end of the rope and tied it round a
iick steel stanchion supporting the staircase, jerking it
everal times to make sure it was secure.

Richter ran the rope through the other bearing on the
hest plate and tossed the free end over the edge of
ie roof. He stepped across to the parapet and looked
own. The artificial island on which the Burj Al-Arab
tood was a mind-numbing seven hundred feet below
im. But if he slipped, he wouldn't fall straight to the
round: the curved front elevation of the building would
iean he'd slide down it for most of the way, but he'd
till be just as dead at the end of it.

'I'm getting too old for this kind of thing,' he mut-
ered, and moved back to where Jackson was standing.
f this all goes wrong, you've got the number, right?'

'One in my bag, and another in my pocket,' Carole-

Anne confirmed. 'And all you're going to do now
look through the window?'

'Yes. If I can see how they've rigged the explosive
maybe we can work out how to get inside witho
getting our heads blown off.'

Jackson rummaged in her handbag and gave him
small pair of binoculars. Richter inspected all the equi
ment once more, he climbed up onto the parapet ar
sat down facing inwards. The most difficult phase
the operation, he had realized as soon as the helicopt
had landed, was going to be getting over the parapet
both ways.

'This isn't going to be very elegant, but it will l
quick.'

He lay flat on his back, checked that the two Ultra
cenders were firmly attached, his hands gripping ther
his feet firmly lodged in the Stiff Steps, and rolled sid
ways, out over the edge. For the briefest of instants l
was in free-fall, then the climbing rope snapped taut
the Ultrascenders not moving a fraction of an inch on tl
rope – and he jerked to a halt, instantly slamming in
the side of the building.

The impact knocked the breath from his body, and f
a few seconds he hung there helplessly. He looked up
see Jackson and Ghul staring down at him, nodded wi
a confidence he honestly didn't feel, and took one bri
look down. This wasn't the most sensible of moves as
reminded him forcefully that his life now depended c
a hundred metres of eleven-millimetre climbing rope,
handful of straps and a few mechanical gizmos simil.
to those he'd last used in the Lake District more than fi\
years earlier.

He took a deep breath, unhitched the upper Ultrascender, lowered his body a cautious foot, then re-
attached it. He unclipped the lower one, straightened
his leg and then clamped that Ultrascender back on the
rope. He'd never been particularly proficient in the use
of this climbing system, but it was virtually foolproof.
He tried to relax – not easy when dangling from a half-
inch rope seven hundred feet above the ground – and
concentrated on getting down.

Chapter Twenty-Three

Tuesday
Dubai

The delay on the Al-Jumeirah Road had cost them tim
but O'Hagan wasn't concerned. The traffic was movi
– if slowly – and he calculated they'd reach the airpo
within half an hour.

He called Sutter and quickly explained the situatio
'Everything clear at your end?'

'Ready and waiting. We'll get the first available o
bound slot. Just call when you get to the airport.'

Burj Al-Arab Hotel, Dubai

The moment O'Hagan had left the suite, Hussein tri
to struggle out of his bonds, but after fifteen minute
effort all he'd done was to open up cuts on his wris
and ankles. He knew he wasn't going to be able to fr
himself, but still he tried, because he had no oth
option.

He was also trying to move the chair around so th
it faced Mecca. In the last minutes before the weap
detonated he was determined to recite his prayers. F
thought he could probably tip the chair forward as we
but he was saving that manoeuvre until the end.

Suddenly a shadow caught his eye – a movement
here no movement should be – and he snapped his
ead round to see clearly. Impossibly, the figure of a
an was stationary outside one of the suite windows.

For an instant, Hussein thought he must be halluci-
ating, then he saw the rope and the harnesses. The man
eld both hands in front of his face, and Hussein realized
e was studying the interior of the suite through a small
air of binoculars.

With a sudden surge of hope, the inspector thought
rescue operation must have been mounted.

Then he remembered the American's final words, and
alized his only hope of survival was if they could get
m out of the building in time. Whatever happened,
d whatever anyone did, the Burj Al-Arab was doomed.

ough small, the binoculars were powerful. Richter
d immediately spotted Hussein but ignored him, his
le concern being the doors, and how the Americans
d booby-trapped them.

But he couldn't see enough. The doors were visible,
ut he couldn't see the handles – the obvious place to
cure an explosive charge – because of the furniture.

Hanging there any longer would be a waste of time.
hat he had to do was get inside. He began the climb
ck up to the roof.

Dubai

The driver was doing well now. Once they'd cleared t
chaotic traffic around Al-Jumeirah Road, he'd work
his way successfully through the side streets and no
they were well into Mankhool, heading for the Clo
Tower Roundabout. Once they reached it, the airpc
would almost be in sight.

O'Hagan reckoned they'd reach the Gulfstrea
within ten minutes, and be airborne ten minutes aft
that. And then absolutely nothing could stop them.

Burj Al-Arab Hotel, Dubai

The manufacturers of the Mitchell Climbing Syste
claim that an experienced user is able to climb either u
or down a particular distance at approximately the sar
speed. By the time Richter hauled himself over the ed;
of the parapet, he was perfectly prepared to agree wi
them.

Ghul extended a hand as soon as Richter's head a
peared, and seconds later he was leaning safely again
the parapet's interior wall.

'I couldn't see the door handles,' Richter reporte
'but we must assume they've attached charges. It loo
like I'm going to have to go in through a window.'

'I'll get the plastic explosive.'

'We haven't got time for that. I'd have to low
myself down, attach the charge, climb up here, wa

r it to blow, and then go down yet again. There's a
uicker way.'

'The minigun,' Jackson suggested.

'Got it in one,' Richter said. 'You're good with weapons,
arole. Get airborne in the Bell and punch a few rounds
rough the window. Just make sure you aim carefully,
·cause our friend Hussein's inside, trussed up like a
rkey.'

'No problem.' She turned towards the staircase.

'I'd better go with her,' Ghul murmured, 'in case the
lot has problems taking orders from a woman.' He held
it a plastic bottle. 'Here. You'd better have some of this.'

'Thanks.' Richter took it. He was already sweating
·ofusely in the blazing sunshine, and needed to keep
⊃ his fluid intake. He'd drained about half the water
hen he heard the Bell start up. As it lifted off the
elipad, the pilot swung the helicopter in a tight turn,
lowing its right side to face the hotel.

Richter leant over the parapet to watch, and seconds
ter heard the sudden spurt of sound as Jackson fired
.e minigun. Below him, glass shattered, and he quickly
positioned the rope to hang directly over the damaged
indow.

By the time the Bell had settled back on the helipad,
ichter was over the parapet and on his way down.

ubai International Airport

he car was stopped at the entrance by two police
fficers. As soon as they'd confirmed that the passengers

were from the Burj Al-Arab, they were directed onto
service road leading to the hardstanding on which th
Gulfstream was parked.

A couple of minutes later, the four Americans wer
strapping themselves into the leather seats, surrounde
by boxes and bags containing more money than th
Gross Domestic Product of about sixty of the world
poorest countries. In the cockpit, Sutter and Haig ha
started to run through the pre-start checklist.

Burj Al-Arab Hotel, Dubai

Richter was getting much better at it. This time it too
him only about ninety seconds to lower himself dow
to the level of the shattered window. Even so, h
remained supremely conscious of the yawning dro
below him.

Jackson had been as accurate as Richter expecte
and the toughened glass had offered little resistance t
the 7.62-millimetre rounds that had punched through i

The hole was too small for Richter to get through, s
he took a firm grip on the Ultrascenders, removed h
feet from the Stiff Steps and kicked himself powerfull
away from the front of the building. He swung ou
wards about eight feet, then back towards the windov
hitting it with both feet outstretched. Glass shattere
but the hole was still too small. So he swung out agair
the strain on his arms growing intolerable, and ye
again.

The fourth time he hit the ruined window, h
momentum carried him right inside the room. Th

mbing rope started to jerk him backwards, but he
stantly released both the Ultrascenders and went
ashing and rolling onto the sumptuous carpet of the
oyal Suite.

ubai International Airport

ith a whine, the port-side engine began to spool up,
en it settled into a muted roar. Two minutes later,
utter started the starboard engine. After-start checks
ok them just under a minute and, as soon as they were
ompleted, he requested taxi clearance.

It was unfortunate that two commercial aircraft had
quested the same just moments before, and even before
at there were already three aircraft heading for the
inway threshold. So, as the Gulfstream turned off the
ardstanding, it was number six for take-off from run-
ay 12 Right.

But even with that amount of traffic ahead of them,
ey still confidently expected to be in the air within ten
inutes.

urj Al-Arab Hotel, Dubai

ussein stared at Richter with pleading eyes as he
orinted past, but at that moment the Englishman was
oncerned with one thing only – the suitcase nuclear
eapon.

For a few seconds he simply stared at the aluminium
ase sitting on the table with its lid closed. He could

detect no anti-tamper devices on it, but perhaps Husse⟨ might have seen something.

Richter strode across to the bound police officer a⟨ ripped the tape off his mouth. Hussein howled in pai⟨

'Did you see those Americans put explosive in t⟨ box? Or attach anything to it?'

'No. They just set the timer, closed the lid and walk⟨ out. Please untie me now.'

'Later.' Richter ran across and checked all round t⟨ box again, trusting what Hussein had said, but wanti⟨ to be certain. Taking a deep breath, which he kne⟨ made no difference at all, he unclipped the two catch⟨ lifted the lid and peered inside.

The interior looked remarkably innocuous. In a fab⟨ pocket was a set of keys. On the underside of the ⟨ were instructions in multiple languages. He scann⟨ quickly to the end of the English section, where he re⟨ the words 'Abort code':

The *abort code* must be entered a minimum of *five (5)* minutes prior to programmed detonation. *Entry of the abort code after this time will be ineffective.*

That seemed to amount to the only available info⟨ mation. To complicate matters, there were two keypa⟨ with numeric displays located either side of the weap⟨ itself, not one as he'd expected. On the far right w⟨ a single gated switch, and two glowing red and gre⟨ lights. In the centre were two unmarked amber warni⟨ lights. Richter guessed these might be circuit-testi⟨ lamps, but he hadn't time to read the instructions ne⟨

them, because he'd just seen the twin countdown
ners.

The two digital displays showed different infor-
ation. The right-hand one indicated a time, but it was
viously not local so he disregarded it. The one on the
t was counting down in seconds, and as Richter looked,
e counter passed '400'. Five minutes equalled 300 sec-
ds. He had around a minute and a half left to enter
e abort code.

Richter wasn't a religious man but, as he pulled the
tebook out of his pocket, he muttered a silent prayer
at Bykov had given him the right number.

He opened the book, glanced at the figures, then
ck at the counter. '378', '377', '376'. He punched the
n digits onto the left-hand keypad, making absolutely
re that he was pressing the correct button each time.

Then he looked at the digital display. '354', '353',
52'. 'Oh, shit,' he muttered. Had he used the wrong
ypad, or did you have to do it twice? Or were the
mbers actually wrong? He moved his hand across
the other keypad and entered the same ten-digit
quence.

He looked back at the display. The numbers were
ll counting down. Then at the other panel, the one
at showed the time. That had now cleared, and a
essage in Cyrillic script was displayed. Richter trans-
ted it aloud: 'Abort code accepted. You have fifteen
conds to confirm.' As he looked, the figure '15' in the
essage changed to '14', and then '13'.

Again he entered the ten-digit sequence, as quickly
he could while still ensuring he got it right.

This time, when he checked the digital displays, the

Cyrillic message in the right-hand one simply state 'Detonation aborted. You may now switch off the mec anism.' In the left-hand display the numbers had final stopped. The timer read '307'.

Richter reached for the gated switch, then withdre his hand. He was suddenly aware that the numbe displayed on the weapon might prove useful. He al realized there was very little time left to stop the Ame icans. He took the keys from the inner pouch, closed t lid, clicked the catches home and locked both of them

He ran over to the staircase and down to the doub doors. As he'd guessed, there was a plastic explosi charge taped to the handle. It was a common enou type of detonator: delayed action – usually ten to thir seconds – until switch-on, then activated by any kind pressure applied to the wire attached to it. The easie way to disable it was to cut the wire. The problem w that if the cutters slipped, Richter himself and a lar part of his surroundings would be immediately vap ized.

He studied the tape securing the plastic explosi to the handle. That seemed the safer option. Rich took out his Kamasa multi-tool and selected a kni blade. Holding the explosive firmly in his left hand, carefully cut through each piece of tape, then mov the plastic explosive to ease the pressure on the wi Once it was completely slack, he pulled out the deton tor and tossed it to one side, then dropped the explosi on the floor.

Richter flung open the doors to find Ghul and Jac son waiting outside. A nervous-looking Barzani stoo beside them.

'It's disarmed,' Richter announced. 'Now we've got
stop that aircraft.'

'I'll call the airport,' Ghul said.

'We need more positive action than that. I'll take the
hopper.' Then he pointed towards the upper level of
the suite. 'Hussein's still tied to a chair up there.'

Before Ghul could respond, Richter strode past him
towards the lift and pressed the button. Jackson slid
into the elevator beside him just as the doors started to
close. Less than a minute later they were back on the
roof, heading for the staircase leading to the helipad.

The pilot was still in his seat, presumably waiting
for further orders from someone, the engines running
though the rotors were braked. Jackson glanced at Richter and caught his almost imperceptible nod. While he
climbed into the rear cabin, she wrenched open the cockpit door and slid into the co-pilot's seat.

The pilot looked somewhat startled, and even more
so when Jackson pulled on a headset and instructed
him, in crisp and precise Arabic, to take off.

'You can't order me around,' he began, but his voice
died away as she produced her Glock 17 and aimed it
directly at him.

'Think again, or you'll find yourself meeting Muhammad way sooner than you ever expected,' she said.
'Now get this bird in the air.'

Chief Inspector Ghul arrived on the roof just as the
Bell lifted off. For a moment or two he watched it
heading east, back towards Dubai City and the airport
beyond, then reached into his pocket for his mobile
phone.

Dubai International Airport

'November Two Six, Dubai Ground. Execute a one hundred and eighty degree turn and return to your stand.'

'What the hell?' Haig exclaimed. The Gulfstream was just about to enter the runway.

'What is it?' O'Hagan called out.

'They've ordered us back to the hardstanding.'

O'Hagan unbuckled his seat belt and strode forward. 'Is the runway clear?'

'Hell, yes. We were the next aircraft in line.'

'Right, fuck them. Probably somebody in their government's got cold feet – or a sudden attack of stupidity. Just go.'

Sutter eased the throttles forward, turned the Gulfstream onto the runway, then pushed them fully forwards. The aircraft immediately began accelerating.

As the Gulfstream crossed the piano keys, the Bell 21 swept over the airfield boundary, already flying close to its maximum speed of one hundred and thirty knots.

'I must get clearance,' the pilot shouted. 'This is an active commercial airfield. I can't fly over it.'

'You won't be flying over it, just going as far as the runway. And trust me, you won't be getting into any trouble. Well, maybe not,' she added, *sotto voce*, peering ahead for any sign of the Gulfstream.

And then she spotted it. 'Paul, it's on the runway, and already rolling. You want to forget this and whistl

p some fighters? There are Mirages stationed at Al-
Dhafra. They should be able to catch it easily.'

'Not if I can help it. Tell laughing boy in the driving
eat to get us down to ground level and intercept that
ucking Gulfstream. We need to be on the aircraft's left
o I can bring this minigun to bear.'

Richter heard a babble of Arabic in his headphone,
hen the Bell dived forward. He braced himself against
he side of the open doorway and looked ahead.

The G450 was approaching take-off speed just as the
elicopter drew alongside, some fifty metres clear, on
he left side of the runway. Richter didn't hesitate. As the
Gulfstream accelerated, he pointed the minigun straight
t it, aimed for the centre of mass and squeezed the
rigger.

The General Electric M134 minigun fires six thousand
ounds a minute in its normal configuration, an almost
ontinuous stream of bullets pouring out of the six rotat-
ng barrels.

Richter's aim was initially a little off, the first bullets
assing over and beyond the Gulfstream, but he immedi-
tely corrected. The stream of 7.62-millimetre ammunition
ipped through the thin and relatively delicate skin of
he passenger cabin, moving down and forwards, tearing
ragged line through the metal that almost bisected the
ircraft.

n the cabin, the four Americans stared in horrified dis-
elief as the bullets howled through the fuselage, oblit-
rating everything they hit. O'Hagan tore off his seat belt

and rushed over to one of the port-side windows to look out. The Bell 212 was flying parallel, only yards away. In the open cabin door, an ugly black weapon was pointing directly at him. O'Hagan instantly recognized the minigun – and then the face of the man behind it.

'That fucking Richter,' he screamed, as the jet began to break up around him.

In the cockpit, Sutter and Haig became aware of an increase in noise and vibration, but couldn't immediately identify the cause. Haig called out 'V2 – rotate, and Sutter eased back on the control column. Just as he did so, the stream of bullets from the minigun reached the cockpit, killing both men instantly.

The minigun fell silent as the last shell was fired, but Richter had done more than enough. The Gulfstream was going nowhere now. The nose slowly lifted, then the weakened fuselage crumpled behind it, the aircraft seeming almost to fold backwards. It lurched sideways, one wingtip hitting the ground, and then cartwheeled, spraying debris, bodies and boxes of money and bullion and gemstones as it left the runway. The tanks had been full and, even before the wreckage came to rest, a spray of fuel from a ruptured line caught fire and turned the tumbling aircraft into an inferno.

'May Allah forgive me,' the pilot murmured, as he watched the pyre with horrified eyes. Fire engines and ambulances appeared as if from nowhere, converging on the blazing wreckage.

'You stopped them,' Jackson observed, her voice sounding husky on the intercom.

'I guess I did,' Richter replied. 'Let's get back to the Burj straight away. I have a feeling this is not a good place for us to be right now.'

Burj Al-Arab Hotel, Dubai

Richter and Jackson took the elevator from the roof down to the Royal Suite. Its lobby was a scene of noisy chaos, a crowd of Arabs in *gellabbiyas* and *kaffiyehs*, others in suits, milling around with uniformed police officers. All of them seemed to be talking at once, either to each other or into mobile phones, or both at the same time.

They scanned the crowd for Hafez Ghul. He was difficult to miss, being one of the tallest men in the room. But it still took a few seconds to spot him standing at the back, being loudly harangued by a couple of Arabs in traditional garb. By then the rest of the people in the room had fallen almost completely silent, their eyes fixed on Richter and Jackson, the atmosphere definitely unfriendly if not downright hostile.

Ghul crossed straight over and spoke quietly to Richter. 'There are some very senior members of the government and police force here, and what they would like to do more than anything else at the moment is arrest both of you.'

'Why?'

'Because they still believe the terrorists would have kept their side of the bargain and told them the abort code. Because they'd hoped to keep this entire episode quiet, and now that's impossible because of the carnage you've caused at the airport. Pictures of that burning aircraft will appear on news broadcasts around the world within hours, and it will cause untold damage to Dubai's image. And, finally, because you were specifically instructed to take no action over this.'

'Right. Come with me,' Richter said grimly. He marched up the staircase and strode across to the weapon, most of the Arabs reluctantly following him. He fished around in his pocket for the keys and undid both locks, then snapped up the catches, but didn't lift the lid. 'If you could please translate, Chief Inspector,' he suggested, but Ghul shook his head.

'I think everyone here speaks sufficient English.'

'Let me explain what happened,' Richter began. 'The terrorists told you that they'd set the timer for long enough to allow somebody to enter this suite and disarm the weapon. And they said they'd radio the abort code to you once they were airborne. Correct?'

'Yes,' snapped an Arab with a long grey beard. The deference with which the other men in the room looked at him suggested he was the most senior official present. 'The timer was set for four hours, but your stupid and ill-considered actions have now stopped us obtaining the code. We're evacuating this area before the four-hour deadline, and now we'll certainly see the Burj totally destroyed.'

Richter glanced at Ghul. 'I tried to tell them,' he shrugged, 'but they wouldn't believe me.'

'You don't need to evacuate the area, and the Burj Al-Arab is perfectly safe,' Richter insisted loudly. 'I've already disarmed the bomb.'

'You can't have,' another man said angrily. 'The only people with the abort code were the terrorists, and now they're all dead. You're lying simply to save your-self.'

Richter completely ignored the interruption and con-inued. 'This is the bomb,' he explained. 'When I open he lid you'll see two small screens inside. One of them displays a message in Russian, and the other shows the number of seconds before the explosion was due to take place. Four hours is fourteen thousand four hundred seconds, correct?' After a moment to do the calculation, several heads nodded.

Richter glanced at his watch. 'The four Americans left his hotel about eighty minutes ago – some five thou-sand seconds. So, if they'd been truthful and the bomb was still active, the timer should show around two and a half hours, or nine thousand five hundred seconds, remaining before detonation.'

He paused and beckoned them closer. 'So let me show you what they actually set it for,' Richter said, and lifted the lid.

Chapter Twenty-Four

Friday
Dira Square, Riyadh

Expecting a large turnout, the police had cleared th
square of vehicles early that morning. They now rope
off an oblong area right in front of the Qasr-al-Adl, th
Palace of Justice, in which they laid out a blue plasti
sheet some five metres square.

Shortly before the time appointed for midday prayer:
a white van arrived and parked outside the Emirate Pa
ace. Four men emerged from it and within about half a
hour had set up a professional-quality video camera,
satellite uplink dish on the roof of the van itself an
a low-power transmitter that would send a continuou
broadcast to a receiver inside the palace.

By the time the *mu'addin* proclaimed the *adhan*, every
thing was in place. The square almost emptied as peopl
departed to perform their ritual cleansing before th
jumu'ah, leaving behind just a handful of curious Wes
erners and non-Muslims, but it quickly filled again onc
the obligations of religion had been fulfilled.

The crowd parted as two cars and another white va
approached, the latter driven by a police officer. Th
broadcast crew in the square instantly swung the cam
era round to record their progress. As the van move
through the crowd, an Arab stepped forward, shoutin

mething, and banged his fist on the side panel. Then
nother did the same, and within seconds everyone
ho could reach the vehicle was either hitting or kick-
g it.

The van halted and the crowd fell suddenly silent.
ne rear doors were opened and two officers dragged
it a swarthy Arab wearing a stained white *gellabbiya*.
e was resisting desperately but, with his elbows pinned behind his back and his wrists tied, it was an
nequal struggle.

Most people who arrive in police vehicles at Dira
quare on a Friday are clearly drugged and usually
indfolded, but the instructions issued from on high
id specified that this man was to receive no such
ercy.

The moment the crowd caught sight of him, the
elling started again. The officers marched their pris-
ner, barefoot and still struggling, to the centre of the
astic sheet, where they forced him down on to his
nees, and positioned themselves on either side to stop
m rising.

An official from the Interior Ministry stepped for-
ard, waited until the crowd had fallen almost silent,
id then extracted a sheet of paper from his pocket. In
loud, clear voice he apologized that, despite prolonged
uestioning, they had still not discovered what the man's
ame was, then read out the offences committed.

Immediately the crowd began shouting again as a
ll, strongly built figure stepped forward, followed by
police officer carrying a long sword with a curved
ade. Normally the executioner will approach the con-
emned man from behind, jab him in the back with the

end of the blade to make him raise his head, and the
decapitate him with a single blow. But on this occasion
the executioner had received special instructions.

He stepped in front of the man once called Saad
bowed to the crowd, then turned back to the police off
cer and accepted the sword. He ostentatiously tested the
sharpness of the blade with his thumb, then swung th
weapon a few times, the scimitar hissing through the ai
as the crowd roared approval. Then he turned back
the kneeling man, placed the tip of the sword under h
chin, and forced him to look up, into the eyes of the ma
about to kill him.

For a few seconds the two men stared at each othe
the condemned criminal and his executioner. Then th
tall Arab handed the sword back to the police office
moved behind his victim and nodded to the other polic
men who stood waiting there. One of them positioned
low stool under Saadi's chest, forcing the bound ma
down onto it, then ran a rope around his torso to hol
him there. A ripple of unease ran through the crow
this practice was not usual.

Another officer placed a short plank on Saadi's bac
under his bound wrists, so that his hands and forearm
were resting on the wood. The executioner bent to chec
that it was positioned to his satisfaction, then accepted
knife with a long, sharp blade from another officer, an
again walked forward to face the camera and the crow
The people shouted again, with renewed bloodlust, divir
ing the man's intentions. He paused to let Saadi see th
knife clearly, then sliced through the cords securing th
prisoner's wrists.

The executioner nodded to the police officers standin

n either side of the bound man. They looped lengths of
ord around Saadi's forearms, a few inches above the
wrists and pulled them tight into rudimentary tourni-
quets to ensure that he wouldn't pass out from loss of
blood. Then they forced his arms down firmly against
the wood. With the efficiency of a butcher dismembering
carcass, the executioner sliced though Saadi's left wrist
nd tossed the severed hand onto the plastic sheet. The
rowd roared again, shouts of *'Allahu Akbar'* – God is
great – echoing from the buildings around the square.
he executioner cleaned the blade of the knife on the
ack of Saadi's *gellabbiya*, then proceeded to sever his
ight hand.

An officer repositioned the plank, and the procedure was repeated on each of Saadi's legs. The double-
amputation took longer, but within ten minutes both
evered feet were also lying on the plastic sheet right in
ront of the condemned man.

By now, Saadi was hoarse from screaming, the incred-
ble pain from his mutilated limbs worse than anything
e could ever have anticipated. But his yells were easily
drowned out by the roars of approval from the crowd.

Only then did the executioner stride around to the
ront of the sheet again and retrieve the long sword
rom the police officer. Again the tall Arab stared down
t his victim with a smile of satisfaction. Everything had
been done precisely as his instructions had specified.
That just left the finale.

He turned the sword over in his hand so that the
harpened edge of the blade faced upwards, then slid it
underneath Saadi's throat and pulled it up and backwards. The blade cut deep into the bound man's throat,

severing his windpipe and producing a new gush of blood. Just as the executioner had anticipated – he'd been allowed to practice the manoeuvre on two condemned men of no importance three days earlier – Saadi's head jerked back. With one swift movement, the executioner lifted the scimitar high above his head, turned the blade again, and brought it slicing downwards, severing the Arab's neck with a single blow.

Saadi's head flew off, followed by a huge spurt of bright arterial blood. The head bounced three times before rolling to a stop at the very edge of the plastic sheet. Two men in the crowd leant forward, then hawked and spat directly at it, while behind them the roar of the people in the square rose higher and higher – 'Allah Akbar, Allahu Akbar'.

Chapter Twenty-Five

'I'll see you around, I guess,' Carole-Anne Jackson said, picking up her new Gucci weekend case. Stuffed full of brand-new clothes, it was the evidence of her finding enough spare time to enjoy a little retail therapy. They were sitting over a coffee in the food court on the first floor of the International Airport, and the check-in desk for Jackson's flight back to Manama had just opened.

'You've got my numbers in London, so whenever you feel like taking a look around the old country, just give me a call. I can't promise you this kind of luxury' – Richter waved his hand in a vague gesture that implicitly encompassed the whole of Dubai – 'but we could still have ourselves a good time.'

It had been a very busy week. The Dubai government had settled Richter's bill at the Crowne Plaza and moved the pair of them, free of charge, into the second Royal Suite at the Burj Al-Arab. Then government officials had wined and dined them at every opportunity, whisking them by Rolls-Royce from restaurant to reception to restaurant to hotel. It had been an exhausting gastronomic feast, and Richter was delighted it was finally over. All he was really looking forward to now was beans on toast and a cup of instant coffee.

In between engagements, he and Michael Watkinso had helped government officials prepare a statemen explaining that the unfortunate crash at the airport ha been caused by a mechanical failure that had tragicall resulted in the deaths of all those on board the Gul stream. The government also sent an official message c condolence to the CIA.

Richter had already briefed John Westwood, using th secure facilities at the British Embassy, to ensure tha Langley knew what had really happened. He guesse that the four real CIA agents had probably been burie somewhere in the desert near Cairo, and their bodie might never be found. He also suggested that Westwoo should contact the Gulfstream Corporation and explai exactly why their almost-new thirty-five-million-dolla executive jet had burst into flames on take-off.

The suitcase nuclear weapon had been removed fror the Burj Al-Arab, and delivered to the local CIA officer for transfer to Langley for specialist examination.

The good news for the Dubai authorities was tha they had recovered all of the bullion and gems from th wreckage of the Gulfstream, and most of the cash toc because it was locked inside steel boxes and had sur vived the fireball with only slight charring. The majorit of the financial instruments had been incinerated, whic meant they couldn't be exercised, so that was entirel satisfactory. Those documents that had survived woul probably be destroyed anyway.

It had been, by any standards, a good result.

They stood up, and Jackson walked away towards th stairs that led to the ground floor and the check-in desk Richter watched her retreating figure, wondering if the

ould ever meet again, waved as she turned back to
ok at him at the top of the staircase, then sat down
gain. He still had over an hour to wait before he could
heck in for his own flight.

eventy minutes later, Richter retrieved his passport
om the unsmiling female Immigration Officer sitting at
er desk wearing traditional garb. He walked the short
istance to the final security checkpoint, slid his briefcase
nto the conveyor belt and strode through the portal
canner. Two minutes later, he stepped into the depar-
ure hall, which was something of a revelation.

It was enormous. It looked to Richter as if it was
robably about a quarter of a mile from end to end, a
ong and wide two-storey building lined with both an
xtraordinary variety of shops and the numerous depar-
ure gates. Futuristic light fittings decorated the ceiling
igh above, and huge palm trees marched in a double
ow down the ground floor. It made every other airport
e'd ever visited look positively shabby and boring.

As he stared around him, he noticed a group of Arabs
n traditional dress standing watching him. They had an
ndefinable look that suggested they were government
mployees, or at least some kind of officials, and Richter
ssumed they'd come to see him safely off their patch.

And they had, but there was a little more to it than
hat.

'Mr Richter, the government of Dubai wishes once
gain to offer you its heartfelt thanks for helping us
esolve our recent difficulties,' the spokesman began.

'That's my job,' Richter said simply.

461

'I know, but we are very grateful to you. Now, we'
aware that your salary is paid by your government.'

'That's true, such as it is.'

'Quite,' the Arab nodded. 'We're also aware that offe
ing you any kind of financial reward for your servi
here in Dubai would be wholly inappropriate. But v
did wonder if you'd like to buy a ticket in one of o
prize draws? Perhaps for the Ford car? We can arran,
its delivery and registration in the United Kingdom,
any other country, at no charge.'

'Thanks, but I'm not a gambler,' Richter said, shaki
his head, 'and I don't really like Fords.'

'But the odds in this draw are very good,' the Ar
insisted, 'and the car is quite special – you might call
a limited edition.' He pointed down the hall to a raise
plinth perhaps thirty yards away on which a brand ne
Ford GT was displayed.

Richter stared at it with a kind of longing. The origin
version, the GT40, was arguably the greatest sports-raci
car of all time, built for one purpose only – to win t
Le Mans 24 Hour race and defeat Ferrari, a task it h
achieved with consummate ease on several occasior
The current model, built to the most exacting standar
and in extremely small numbers, shared that impeccab
pedigree. It was low, sleek, beautiful, expensive, inde
cribably quick and hopelessly impractical, and Richt
would have just loved to own it, but he reluctantly shoo
his head. 'I'm sorry, but I don't gamble,' he repeated.

'At these odds, there's very little gambling involvec

'OK,' Richter demanded, 'how many tickets are the
in this raffle? A thousand, two thousand?'

'Usually there are a thousand, but we've amende

e rules slightly. In this draw there are only ten tickets,'
e man smiled, 'and we've decided to offer you a dis-
ount on the price as well. Normally our vehicle raffle
ckets are priced at about five hundred dirhams, but
e've reduced the price of these to just one American
ollar each. You can of course buy all ten tickets, if you
ish. So are you still certain you don't want to try your
uck?'

Richter looked again at the Ford GT, back at the
rab's smiling face, and without the slightest hesitation
ulled out his wallet. He selected a ten-pound note and
anded it over. For a moment, the Arab looked con-
used – he'd been expecting dollars.

Richter filled in his contact details, took a last linger-
ig look at his new ten-dollar Ford, tucked the raffle
ckets into his wallet, and finally headed for his depar-
ure gate. He glanced back to see the Arab still holding
e ten-pound note.

'Thanks very much indeed,' he called out. 'You can
eep the change.'